Jordan Land

Jordan Land

Will Armstrong

iUniverse, Inc.
New York   Bloomington

iUniverse books may be ordered through booksellers or by contacting:

iUniverse
1663 Liberty Drive
Bloomington, IN 47403
www.iuniverse.com
1-800-Authors (1-800-288-4677)

Because of the dynamic nature of the Internet, any Web addresses or links contained in this book may have changed since publication and may no longer be valid. The views expressed in this work are solely those of the author and do not necessarily reflect the views of the publisher, and the publisher hereby disclaims any responsibility for them.

ISBN: 978-1-4401-5177-4 (sc)
ISBN: 978-1-4401-5178-1 (ebook)

Printed in the United States of America

iUniverse rev. date: 07/31/2009

Contents

▼

My thanks to Ann Ewing and Maureen Brister for once again undertaking the onerous task of proof reading, also to Brenda Hoyle and Margaret Rhind for their support and assistance and to my friend Bill Clinkenbeard for his advice and encouragement when required. Finally, my sincere thanks to Linda and Nigel who tied up all the loose ends and also liaised so successfully with iUniverse.

Also by Will Armstrong

Jordan Luck

CHAPTER I

▼

The rattlesnake woke suddenly. Something had disturbed it. Vibrations, and they were getting closer. Raising its head questingly, the snake searched the surrounding terrain, forked tongue flickering. Sensing that the vibrations were closing fast now, it withdrew carefully beneath a convenient bush and waited there, coiled, silent and deadly.

Angling down the long slope, the red roan gelding blew through his nostrils as he headed towards the few small pools of scummy liquid, all that was left of Mustang Springs ponds. His rider swayed easily to the movement, mind busy with the implications of the scene before him. Mustang Springs was dry!

The horse trampled past the bush and the diamond back rattler sounded a warning. Startled, the giant roan reared and spun away, snorting angrily. At the same moment the snake struck ... and missed.

Controlling his raging mount with one hand, John Jordan drew the slim throwing knife in a blur of continuous movement. The 'Arkansas Toothpick' flashed in the sun and pinned the rattler's wedge-shaped head to the ground.

Holding the snorting gelding on a tight rein, John waited until the snake's thrashing death throes had subsided. Dismounting, he retrieved the gleaming weapon, wiping the blade carefully, before returning it to the riveted leather scabbard lying snugly between his shoulder blades.

A lean, powerfully built, blond six-footer, there was an aura of menace about John Jordan. Taken by Comanches at the age of eight, he had spent the next ten years as their captive, gradually becoming more and more Indian in

his ways. Given the name Yellow Panther he had been accepted as the great
Ten Bears' adopted son, blood brother to many warriors, and eventually as a
'dog soldier' (a hunter) known and respected by all the tribe. His escape, and
subsequent return to his family, was now part of East Texas frontier lore.

A loner, possessing unparalleled skills as a horse tamer, John Jordan was
to all intents and purposes a white Comanche.

Now, he led his mount towards one of the small pools and watched as
the gelding sucked greedily at the brown liquid.

Big Red was a moody unpredictable equine giant, who lived only for one
person; John's brother, Hardy Jordan. As a two year old he had been beaten
and tortured by Comancheros in an attempt to break his spirit. Rescued by
Hardy, Red had become a one man horse. The only other person he would
tolerate on his back was John, and that was a tenuous partnership at best;
one which could be broken at any moment. Only the young rider's superb
understanding of horses kept it going. Deep down Red was an outlaw, with
a sullen smouldering temperament. As John's father, Jim Jordan had said
grudgingly, 'He can outrun and outstay any horse I've ever seen. But,' he had
added warningly, 'deep down he's a killer, and don't ever forget it.

Well, John grimaced wryly, looks like we're in big trouble Red. Pa ain't
gonna like this one bit. Best thing we can do is push on and take a look at
the Pecos. Swinging into the saddle he reined the giant gelding round and
headed west. On the ground the first ants moved unerringly towards the
dead snake.

'Miz Wallace.' The little coloured maid bobbed nervously in the doorway.

'Yes?' Her young mistress looked up from the book she was reading.

'Mistuh Wallace, he says to tell you he aimin' to take young Mastuh James out
ridin' less'n you got any other plans.'

Sara-Jane shook her head. 'No Amelia, tell Mister Wallace that'll be fine.'

Sara-Jane Wallace smiled contentedly as she returned to her novel. Clay was
a good husband and father. Damn! I'd almost forgotten. It's time to nurse little
Mary. She pulled hard on the ornamental bell-rope beside her chair.

Silence … then a sickening jolt, followed by a crashing sound just behind her.
What … ?

'Sara-Jane!'

She stared into her father's angry sweat-streaked face.

'What in tarnation are you haulin' on old Dusty's line like that for?
You're supposed to drive round rocks, not over 'em! You darned near busted
a wheel, 'sides makin' enough noise to stampede the stock! An' the Lord only

knows what Ma'll find when she opens up the wagon come evenin'. What's got into you gal?'

'I'm sorry Pa,' Sara-Jane said meekly. 'Guess I was daydreamin'.'

'Daydreamin'!' Jim Jordan wiped his brow with the back of his hand, and rolled his eyes heavenwards. ''Case you've forgotten, this here's a trail drive an' I aim to get us to Arizona in one piece come hell or high water. Now,' he dismounted, frowning heavily as he did so, 'hold up while I take a look at the wagon. Last thing we want is for you to go bustin' wheels along the way.' He paused, suddenly alert. 'Come to think of it, just how much drivin' you done since we left the Circle J?'

'Pa ...' Sara-Jane gulped nervously, 'It don't seem to make no difference how hard I try. I just can't seem to get the hang of it. Then Ma gets all fired up an' says I ain't tryin'.' Her voice trembled. 'Horses an' me don't get along. Not like Ellie-May,' she finished tearfully.

Her father's weather-beaten face tightened into bleak lines as he looked up at her. 'Now you listen to me gal, an' listen good.' There was a sudden harshness in his tone. 'This here's your job, an' the sooner you get a handle on it the better. You got a team there that'll take you to Arizona if you let 'em alone. All you got to do is look out for rocks an' holes along the way. So your mother's tetchy? What's new? Anyways, she's got a lot on her mind. An' if Ellie-May, or any o' the crew mess up they'll answer to me. Same as you are right now!'

Sara-Jane's face flamed and she gritted her teeth. Pa was usually so quiet and easygoing that you forgot about the violent temper he had spent years learning to control. Because of this, family members felt it all the more keenly when he bawled them out.

'Pa ... I'm real sorry, it won't happen again.'

Her father surveyed his attractive younger daughter and his anger subsided slowly. Damn it, she's only sixteen when you get right down to it, he thought wryly. Don't seem all that long ago since I used to pick her up and dandle her on m'knee. Still, this here's Injun country an' you don't get no second chances. You're either quick or you're dead. 'Course, if Ma had been as tough as she usually is, Sara-Jane would've got a whole lot more practice in by now. Guess it means I got to take a hand.

Sighing heavily, he put a foot in the stirrup and swung stiffly into the saddle. Bob, his Cleveland saddle horse, waited patiently until his rider settled himself. 'A'right; no harm done, an' I reckon you're allowed one mistake. Good thing I happened along when I did. Now,' he raised his hand and signalled to the other two wagons, halted back along the trail, 'let's roll.'

Sara-Jane shook out the lines and the team moved off placidly, the chuck wagon rumbling into motion behind them.

Jim Jordan pushed his hat back and mopped his brow with the back of a leathery hand. Damn it, old Paint an' Dusty could make it to Arizona on their own. All Sara-Jane has to do is hold onto the lines and let 'em follow the trail.

Wonder what she was thinkin' 'bout anyways? Clay Wallace most likely. She's real set on him. He frowned, thinking about the young Easterner. An' in spite o' what he agreed wi' Ma, I reckon he feels the same way.

The rancher watched the neat accommodation wagon approaching, its team of high-spirited Clevelands fretting at their bits and being deftly controlled by Miguel Jerez, the small stout Mexican he had hired before the drive began. Old Miguel maybe ain't much to look at, but he sure can handle a team.

Swappin' the buckboard for that dougherty wagon was real good business. Means Ma an' the gals ain't got to sleep in the open, an' that's somethin'. His tanned face crinkled with amusement. 'Course it means her an' me ain't sharin' blankets for the first time in years, but what the hell, I ain't no randy young rooster!

The outfit rolled past and he waved to the two flaxen-haired little girls sitting beside his wife. They waved back tentatively, smiling shyly as they did so. Mary-Lou Jordan signed to her husband to pull alongside. He eased Bob close to the open window, one eye on the rolling wheels.

'What happened?' Ma queried tersely.

Jim Jordan grimaced. 'Sara-Jane. Daydreamin' she said! Lucky I come along when I did, else the team would've been all tangled up. As it is there ain't no harm done, less'n some o' your gear's come adrift in the chuck wagon, an she's had a lesson she ain't likely to forget in a hurry. Hi gals; how're you likin' the trip?'

'Howdy Mister Jordan. It's nice, ain't it, Miz Jordan?'

Ma's expression thawed perceptibly. She had a soft spot for the two little girls, Sarah and Mary Johnson, who had seen their parents killed by raiding Indians. Abducted by these same Indians, the girls had been rescued by Hardy Jordan. With no known relatives, and pressurised by her son, Ma had reluctantly agreed to give them a home.

Now they were heading west, along with the rest of the Jordan family, to start a new life in Arizona at the giant Flying W ranch.

'It surely is, Sarah. Let's hope you think the Flyin' W's just as nice.'

'If Mister Bull's there it will be,' eight year old Sarah said confidently. Mary, aged six, nodded in emphatic agreement. Since their rescue, the girls idolised the Jordans' middle son. The strange thing was that the giant bounty hunter and gunfighter, christened Hardy, but known to everyone as Bull, felt the same way about them.

Ma's cold blue eyes narrowed and she looked thoughtfully at her husband. 'You have words with Sara- Jane?'

Jim nodded. 'Sure did. Still an' all, she's only a kid. Got to give her time to grow up.'

Mary-Lou snorted derisively. 'Shucks, I weren't much older than her when I married you. Then Lance an' Hardy come along. What wi' them an' the homestead there weren't no time for this growin' up nonsense. You just had to get on wi' things as best you could. Trouble wi' Sara-Jane is she ain't got no stomach for ranch life. It's got so I'd ruther drive m'self than let her mess things up.'

Pa frowned. 'Ain't sure that's a good idea,' he said dubiously. 'Seems to me she needs to keep at it if she's ever goin' to handle that team.'

Ma bristled. 'Jim Jordan, I'll thank you to leave me to sort out m'daughter my own way!'

Her husband raised a placating hand. 'A'right!' he said hastily. 'Only, ... you ain't gettin' any younger, an' you're handlin' the cookin' as well. Don't go blamin' me if things get tough!'

'I ain't likely to,' Mary-Lou said tartly. 'Reckon I've allus managed to hoe m'own row up till now!'

Yeah, Jim Jordan thought sourly as he shot a sidelong glance at his stocky, grey-haired wife; an' made the rest o' us suffer at the same time! Still an' all, cain't say I blame you, seein' as how you found your folks lyin' dead in the dust after the Injuns had finished wi' them. An' your mother had been raped too. 'Taint no wonder that you just froze up. Growin' up wi' that on your mind musta been hell. Then I come along. For a while it looked as though you was loosenin' up; then John was took by the Comanches. Nigh on ten years we never saw hide nor hair of him. Seemed like that was it. An' when he did come back he was more like an Injun than the Comanches themselves. No wonder you found it hard to take. Let's just hope the new start'll make a difference.

He angled Bob away from the rolling wheels and turned to wait for the huge, gaily painted Studebaker wagon, hauled easily by the six big horses. The tall figure seated on the bench seat lifted a hand in greeting. Now there is a real outfit. Ben Turner's a freighter, right down to his boot-heels. Musta been hell for him, losin' his wife an' son wi' that fever. Let's hope this move'll give him a fresh start, same as the rest of us.

'What happened?' Turner pointed ahead with his whip.

The grey-haired rancher shrugged. 'Nothin' much. Sara-Jane wasn't thinkin' straight. She damned near turned the chuck wagon over.'

Ben grinned and his normally grave features lit up. He's a different fella when he smiles, Pa reflected.

'Well, she's young. She'll learn.'

Jim Jordan frowned. 'She'd better. Trail drivin's a rough school, an' if you make a mistake it can be your last. How about your outfit?'

'Everything's fine. Duke there,' he indicated the powerful off fore leader, 'come near castin' a shoe yesterday, but I tightened it last night.'

'Alright.' The rancher raised a hand in acknowledgement. 'Guess I'd best head back to the herd an' start pushin' that drag again. See you.' He nudged Bob with his heels and cantered off back along the trail.

Ben eased the team into motion and settled himself comfortably. Jim Jordan's a good man. He don't go tearin' up the sod an' raisin' hell generally, like some trail bosses, but he gets there just the same. An' he still puts in a full day alongside young fellas like Lance and Jake. Yeah; he nodded his head sagely, he's alright.

Back along the trail Pa drew aside to let the approaching remuda come through. Led by Dance, the Cleveland Bay stallion, the horse herd drifted past, a slim rider on a deep-chested blue roan cantering watchfully behind. Among the prevailing browns and bays he caught a glimpse of a golden palomino, flaxen mane and tail streaming proudly.

Pa grinned as his elder daughter halted her mount beside him. 'See you're workin' your string like a real top hand. Reckoned I saw Goldie in the remuda.'

Ellie-May smiled tightly. Tall, blue-eyed and blonde, with a figure most women would have killed for, her twin passions were horses and guns.

She's just like Ma, he thought soberly. Never loosens up. Ain't forgot that bust-up 'tween them 'bout her wearin' Levis! Man that was something. Still, she was right. She's as good as any man when it comes to ranch work.

'Everything alright up ahead?'

Her father nodded. 'Everything's fine.' I ain't gonna tell you Sara-Jane come near turnin' the chuck wagon over. You're like a coupla cats, allus clawin' at each other. 'I'll head on back an' take over the drag. That'll let young Rafe up here wi' you again.'

'Rafe's got the makin's', Ellie-May said tersely. ''Course he's young; but he's learnin'. She heeled the roan into its stride. 'Better get movin' 'fore that remuda runs up onto the wagons.'

Watching her canter off, Jim Jordan scratched his stubbled jaw pensively. Dunno how Rafe puts up wi' her. 'Course he was desperate for a job. Reckon he'd have taken anything. Still, cain't be easy, takin' orders from a sassy female like Ellie-May. His ears caught the bawling of cattle on the move. She's right about one thing though, he's got the makin's o' a real good cowhand.

The distant skyline was suddenly alive with tossing horned heads as the herd topped the trail crest and started down the long slope. Pride surged through the grizzled rancher. Hell, I ain't done so bad. Them Durham/ Longhorn crosses is right good stock. An' you won't find better horseflesh in the whole South-West than there is in that remuda. Pity Dave Wilson cashed in his chips an' left Ma the Flyin' W. We was doin' alright at the old Circle J. Mebbe it was only a two-bit outfit, but we bred good stuff an' everybody knew that.

I ain't cut out to be no cattle king. Spread the size o' the Flyin' W is too rich for my blood. Not Bull though. The rancher grinned as he thought of his powerful, ambitious second son. Him an' Ma got it all figured out. Could be they're right. Mebbe I ain't up to it. I dunno.

He eyed the tall figure of his eldest son, riding point on the far side of the approaching herd. Lance now, he ain't got no interest in ranchin'. Army's his life. He's only here 'cause they wanted somebody to check out what the Injuns are up to. Pity he had that run-in wi' Jud Moore 'fore we left though. He reckons he's over it, but killin' a man, even a fella like Jud, can come back to haunt you.

The nearside point man swung away from the herd and headed directly towards him. Now there's a fella to ride the river with. Jake's the best segundo I ever had, even if he is half Comanche. His expression hardened perceptibly. An' as long as I'm around he'll be part o' the family. Don't matter a damn what Ma thinks. Hadn't been for the Larsens we wouldn't have got John back. Old Sven died for this family, an' his son stays wi' us as long as he wants to.

Jake Larsen reined his pony to a halt. A powerfully built twenty year old, with the fair colouring of his Swedish father, Jake would have passed as white anywhere. Only his deep-set dark eyes gave a clue to his part-Indian ancestry.

'Trail clear?'

Jim Jordan nodded. He sure don't waste words. Never says Boss, Mister Jordan, or even Jim. That's his mother's blood. Comanches got pride. She was kin to Ten Bears an' Jake ain't never gonna forget that.

With a start he realised the young half-breed was looking at him curiously. 'Yeah. Should hit the Leon 'bout noon. One good thing, rivers are low right now.' Them eyes o' his seem to bore right through you. 'How about the herd?'

'Herd's fine.' Jake grinned. 'Young Rafe thinks he's a real cowhand now, workin' the drag an' all.'

The rancher chuckled. 'He'll learn. Eatin' dust ain't no fun when you got to do it every day. Anyways, I'd better let him get back to the remuda, else I'll have Ellie-May to reckon with. Mike an' Andy makin' out alright?'

'Yeah. They're a coupla good old boys, an' they know cows.' He kneed his pony into its stride. 'See you at the river.'

Jim Jordan waited for a moment, watching the young segundo loping up the side of the herd, then he swung Bob into the dust of the drag.

The small figure, busily pushing the stragglers on, eyed the rancher warily as he ranged up alongside.

'Howdy, Rafe. Seems like you're right busy.' With practised skill Jim eased a recalcitrant cow into its stride. 'Thanks for coverin'. Reckon you can head on up to the remuda now. Take it easy passin' the herd. Don't want to go startin' a stampede.'

'Right, Mister Jordan. Uh ... be glad to take a turn any time.' I sure was lucky to get hired by the boss. He's a real fine guy.

'Sure son.' Jim chuckled wryly. ' Guess it ain't all that easy workin' wi' Ellie-May. Still an' all, you're doin' right well. You'll be a top hand some day.'

Rafe Allen's thin anxious face lit up. 'Gee, thanks Boss ... I mean Mister Jordan!' He lifted his pony into a canter. 'On m'way now.'

The rancher's mouth twitched. He's like a young pup. Give him a bit o' praise an' he's happy. Hell, he's only sixteen. All the same, he is doin' right well. An' he's a mannerly youngster. Reckon his folks did a real fine job there.

Carefully, alert to the sounds round him, he chivvied a truculent Durham bull that seemed determined to turn back. Reluctantly, the rumbling giant gave way and headed after the herd. Jim Jordan lifted his gaze to the horizon and nodded contentedly. Everything was fine.

CHAPTER 2

▼

The bunkhouse had a comfortable 'lived in' appearance and, compared with some of the flea-pits Joe Masterson had endured, it was a palace.

Leaning back in his battered chair, the red-haired foreman eyed the other members of the Flying W crew, as they relaxed after a hard day on the range. *Helluva late to be brandin' but there ain't no help for it. Everything was way behind 'fore we come.* He flexed his right knee and grunted with the pain.

'Ah, compadre.' The stocky Mexican seated opposite looked at him in mock solicitude. 'You are getting past it, no? It is all this worry.' Manuel Ortega shook his head sorrowfully. 'You will become old before your time. Amigos,' he appealed to the other hands scattered around the room, 'is it not so? When I see that calf kick you I say to myself, Joe, he is slowing up.'

There was a chorus of assent from the others. 'The hell wi' you all,' Joe rose stiffly. 'That calf was damn near a yearlin' an' you know it. Reckon I'll go see old Tex. Might be he'll let me have some o' that special liniment he's allus braggin' about.' To the accompaniment of ironic laughter he limped through the doorway.

'Joe's doin' alright.' Chester Jones, ex-cavalry sergeant, and one of the two negro hands in the crew, looked up from the riata he was braiding. 'This ain't a bad outfit to ride for. Good boss, good foreman, pay's alright an' the grub ain't bad. Nah,' he bent again to his task, 'things could be a whole heap worse.'

'Amigos,' Manuel smiled indulgently. 'Joe and I, we are compadres. We have been together a long time. I was a brush vaquero before I sign up with

Shanghai Pearce. That is where I meet Joe. But he is the serious one, and sometimes I like to, how you say, josh him a little. A man should be able to laugh at himself once in a while. Is that not so Anders?' he appealed to the blond giant in the corner, busily honing a wicked looking knife to razor sharpness.

There was a rumble of agreement from Anders Lindstrom. He paused for a moment, whetstone in hand. 'By damn you are right there. Me, I laugh when I fight. It is a good feeling'

'Yeah.' Sam Alderson, stretched out on his bunk, winked at his brother Mike, idly leafing through a mail order catalogue. Short, grey-haired, and identical twins, the Aldersons, at forty, were, apart from Tex Morton the cook, the oldest members of the Flying W crew. 'Well now, it might be fun for you, but fellas that get into a fight wi' you either end up on the floor, or runnin' for the door. Either way it don't seem much like fun to me.'

The Dane paused in his task and waved a huge hand negligently. 'It is not my fault that there are so few big men like myself.'

'There's the boss.' Jeff Short grinned from his position at the other end of the riata. 'He's taller than you, an' he'd likely weigh out 'bout the same. Try him.'

'Ah yes.' Lindstrom's face lit up. 'The other day he come in when I am making a set of shoes. I ask him to be my striker; he is keen to learn about everything. So he take off his shirt and work damn hard as striker. Man, what muscles,' he went on dreamily. 'To fight him, that would be something.'

Chester Jones scowled in mock anger at his partner. 'Ah swear Jeff, you're worse than he is, encouragin' him like that. It's fellas like you get us black folks a bad name! Times Ah wonder how you ever made sergeant wi' the old 11th. 'Case you've forgotten, me an' you was a mite low when the boss offered us a job. Now we's earnin' good money an' eatin' reg'lar, an' Ah aim to keep it that way.'

Grinning to himself Joe made his way gingerly across the yard, the bantering voices fading behind him. They're comin' on fine. Work hard an' kid around, like a good outfit should. They got pride in the Flyin' W now.

All 'cept him. The foreman scowled as he eyed the lanky cowhand turning a limping black pony into the corral. Jem Anson, you are one lucky hombre. Should have had your neck stretched by rights; you and that no-good Dave Sands. You nigh bled this spread white wi' your thievin'. Beats me how Dave Wilson didn't cotton on to it. Somethin' mighty strange there. Ain't no man in his right senses would've made Sands foreman. He was a mean one.

Didn't faze the boss none though when he found out what'd been happenin'. Run Sands right off the spread he did. Told the sonofabitch he'd be dead meat if he ever showed up on the Flyin' W again. Cain't figger why he didn't do the same wi' this fella. Maybe it was 'cause Jem spilled the beans 'bout everything; I dunno. 'Course he's workin' for his chuck an' nothin' more. Ain't much of a life but … better than a rope necktie!

Joe paused beside the corral, waiting as Anson slid the last gate pole into place.

'What happened to your bronc?'

Anson turned quickly, tension in every movement. 'Struck hisself comin' down that slope back o' the ranch.' He gestured to the hill rising behind the Flying W buildings. 'Just bruisin' I guess. Anyways, I'll get Tex to take a look at 'im come mornin'. He's good wi' broncs.' He turned away abruptly.

Frowning, Joe watched the rangy figure bow-legging towards the bunkhouse. Maybe I am a mite hard on him. Ah, what the hell. Jem knew the score when he throwed in wi' Sands. Best go see 'bout this knee.

He paused at the cook-shack door. 'Tex! You there?'

'Sure, where else would I be? Only a dang fool like me would waste time cookin' for this outfit.'

The foreman eased carefully through the doorway.

A piece of grubby paper in one gnarled hand, the fiesty old cook was peering into a tall cupboard and muttering to himself. 'Need more potatoes an' beans. Onions as well. Nothin' like a onion for givin' stew a bit o' taste. Coffee's gettin' low … oh howdy Joe. What in hell you been doin' wi' your leg?'

'Got kicked by a calf,' Joe said succinctly. He shifted uneasily, aware of the pain in his knee. 'Like to try that liniment o' yours.'

'Yeah, sure.' The grizzled oldtimer scrabbled at the back of a shelf and emerged triumphantly with a heavy glass bottle, the label already yellow with age. 'Knew she was there somewheres.' He scowled shortsightedly at the faded writing. 'Apply three times daily … rub well in. A'right, drop your pants an' let's have a look at this here knee.'

Joe complied gingerly. The knee was red and swollen.

'Mm …' Tex peered at it shortsightedly. 'Sure don't look good an' that's a fact. Reckon I'd better get some o' this on right quick.'

The old cook shook the bottle vigorously. 'Damnation … it's been a helluva time since I last used this stuff.' He struggled with the recalcitrant cork. 'There she is.' It came free with an audible pop, and the old-timer poured some of the thick yellow liquid into a cupped leathery palm. 'Hang on to this here,' he passed the bottle to the foreman, 'an' lemme at that knee.'

'Hold it!' Joe looked searchingly at the bottle. 'This here's horse liniment!'

'What in hell you beefin' about?' Tex was rubbing strongly now. 'You an' a horse both got knees ain't cha? Works for one it'll work for the other.

Seems t'me cowhands is gettin' a sight too fancy nowadays.' His voice became reminiscent. 'Now I remember last time I used this stuff. It was a coupla years back. That big grey the boss rides; Kiowa. He banged his knees when the boys was breakin' 'im.' The old cook straightened up with a grunt. 'There, that should do it.'

'Hell!' Joe gritted his teeth as he hauled up his Levis. 'Damned knee feels like it's on fire.'

'Doin' good.' Morton washed and dried his hands deliberately. 'Allus said, 'less medicine's hurtin' it ain't doin' no good. Now, where in hell did I put that there list?'

Mary-Lou Jordan filled the empty plate with savoury smelling stew and returned it to her eldest son. She indicated the golden crusted pile, fresh from the Dutch oven. 'Biscuits there if you want 'em.'

'Thanks, Ma.'

His mother watched closely as he made his way across to where Ben Turner was sitting. The teamster nodded an invitation and Lance hunkered down beside him. *Somethin' bad's eatin' at that boy.*

'You reckon a stove-up old cowhand could mebbe get somethin' to eat round here?'

Turning sharply, Ma found her husband, eyes twinkling, regarding her quizzically.

Tight lipped, Mary-Lou took the proffered plate. 'I swear Jim Jordan, you never change. Cain't you be serious once in a while?'

Pa grinned as he helped himself to a couple of biscuits. 'Reckon there's enough serious folks around without me addin' to 'em.' Grunting with the effort, he eased down and settled his back comfortably against the chuck wagon wheel.

'Lance you mean?' Plate in hand, Mary-Lou lowered herself to sit beside him.

'Wasn't thinkin' o' nobody special,' Pa mumbled evasively. *Damn it! Me an' my big mouth. She's as sharp as a razor.*

They ate in silence, then ... 'Pa; that night at the Rockin' H, when Jud Moore an' Cliff Henderson was killed. Just what did happen?'

'Ma!' The sudden rasp in Jim Jordan's voice made his wife look at him in surprise. His normally pleasant features were set in harsh lines. 'Just leave it, will you? What's done's done. It don't do no good rakin' up the past. Sheriff Lane said it was an open an' shut case. Reckon that's good enough for me.

Right now I just want to enjoy this here stew. Then I'll have me a smoke 'fore I saddle up for m'night herdin' stint. Don't seem too much to ask.' He glanced sideways at his inwardly seething wife. 'Believe me, it's for the best.'

Silence, tangible and bitter, hung between them.

CHAPTER 3

The Pecos was low. John Jordan dismounted and walked Red down to the crossing, waiting patiently while the roan drank. The big horse rolled the brackish water in his mouth, disliking the unpleasant taste.

'I don't blame you,' John grinned as Red flicked his ears inquiringly. 'But it's better than nothin'.' He took a long look at Horsehead Crossing. Won't be no trouble here. River's low and the banks ain't steep. Small herd like ours will go across easy. Grazing on the far side is good, plenty of gramma and bluejoint.

Red nipped at his sleeve. 'Alright,' John swung up into the saddle. 'We'll head back.' He eased the big horse round and up the slope. Pa ain't going to like this. Wish I had better news.

John swayed easily to the rhythm of Red's longstriding gait. The Pecos was far behind them now, and with luck they would make Mustang Springs again before nightfall.

Red snorted and pricked his ears. From ahead, beyond a turn in the trail, came the neigh of a panic-stricken horse, an incoherent shout, and the shrill scream of a … ? The hair on the back of John's neck lifted, he knew that scream … a cougar!

A riderless horse careered around the bend in the trail. Blood streaked its flanks and discoloured the empty saddle. A long-eared pack mule appeared next, bucking frantically as it tried to shed its load. Red shied to one side and John urged the roan forward round the bend, the big .45 held firmly in his right hand.

He took in the situation at a glance. The bearded man on his knees scrabbling for the dropped rifle, and, crouching beyond him, the snarling cougar. As John watched, the giant cat sprang. Desperately, rifle held across his chest, the man strove to hold it off, but the weight of the cougar toppled him backwards into the dust of the trail.

The .45 crashed twice in quick succession and the snarling cat collapsed across its intended victim. Ears laid back and teeth bared, Red pawed at the ground.

'Easy now.' Cautiously, John dismounted and walked towards the groaning man now struggling to free himself from the weight of the cougar. Stooping, the young rancher rolled the dead cat clear and helped the bearded figure to sit up.

'Thanks.' Deep-set blue eyes peered at him from below bushy brows. 'I think my leg's broke. Thought I was gone that time for sure.'

'Mm.' John's hands explored the injured limb.

The bearded man sucked in his breath and winced.

'You could be right.' The young rancher rose lithely to his feet and drew his long Bowie knife. 'Let me cut a couple of branches to hold it straight. How about the rest of you?'

The big man flexed his right shoulder gingerly. 'Fell on it when the cat dropped on me from that big rock. Don't think there's anythin' busted, but,' he looked at the blood soaked sleeve, 'm'arm's clawed up pretty bad.'

'Right,' John finished splinting the leg. 'Let's have a look at that arm.' He slit the torn sleeve and eyed the deep gashes running from the shoulder right down to the forearm.

'You got any whiskey?'

'Bottle in my saddlebags ... hell, my horse ain't here.' He made to get up and fell back groaning.

'Lie still.' John rose to his feet and reached for the dropped reins. Vaulting into the saddle he swung Red round and took off back down the trail.

The mule hadn't gone far. It was grazing peacefully by the side of the trail, about half a mile on and looked at them incuriously as they raced past. A mile further on they found the stranger's horse. It snorted nervously as they approached.

'Whoa boy … easy now.' Gently, John eased Red forward. The linebacked dun whinneyed and stood still. Dismounting, the young rancher walked towards it.

Talking softly, he stroked its neck while he checked the saddlebags. Yes, there was the bottle of whiskey. The dun flinched as he examined the deep gashes where the cougar's claws had found their mark. Blood from the wounds dappled its flanks.

Carefully John eased the dun up beside Red. For once the roan behaved well, allowing him to swing into the saddle and lead the other horse.

They found the mule still grazing quietly. John tied its lead rope to the dun's bridle and got back into the saddle. The mule protested halfheartedly and then fell into line.

The bearded stranger was lying where John had left him. His eyes opened as they approached.

'Thanks mister. Thought I'd lost Dan and old Pete for sure.'

'Lie still.' John wiped the arm clean and sloshed whiskey onto the gashes.

'Hell and damnation … that rotgut sure stings. Oh, m'name's Mace, Jeb Mace. Thanks for shootin' that cat off me. I'm beholden' to you.'

'Jordan … John Jordan.' Delving in his saddlebags he came up with a clean bandanna, which he wrapped tightly round Mace's lacerated arm.

The bearded man scowled. 'You belong these parts?'

John shook his head. 'No, I am scouting for my folks. They are bringing a trail herd through here. Now hush up till I get a travois fixed up. Got to get you to Fort Concho.'

'Ain't goin' to no fort!' There was an undercurrent of fear in Mace's voice.

'You have no choice.' John wasn't prepared to argue. 'There is no water round here.'

'Son, there's good water not more'n a dozen miles from here. You get me there an' I'll be fine.'

John paused in the act of shaping a long branch into a travois pole. 'You are sure about this water. Folks told me this stretch from the Concho to the Pecos was dry, and yet you say there is good water round here?'

Jeb grinned. 'Yeah, found it m'self. You just get me on that there travois an' I'll show you.'

John grunted and bent to his task.

★ ★ ★ ★

Four hours later they topped a long mesquite-covered rise. Below them the ground fell away steeply to a small brush-choked ravine. Further back larger trees bulked starkly.

'You see it son?'

John nodded.

'Right, head down that way an' you'll find a trail that leads through the scrub. Go slow, 'cause there ain't much room. You'll come out in a grass clearing, an' that's where the water is. Let's go now.'

John eased Red down the slope, the dun and the mule close on either side. The trail was narrow, as Mace had said. Pushing the mule ahead he lengthened the lead rope on the dun. They wound their way through the underbrush and came suddenly into a small grass clearing, no more than an acre in size. A red cliff ran along one side. Backed against it was a rough lean-to shack, and close beside it a spring from which water bubbled.

'That's it, mister.' There was a note of pride in Jeb Mace's voice. 'The best hideout in Texas. That there's m'shack across by the spring. You take a right good look at that water. That spring comes up and runs right along the base o' the cliff for about ten yards 'fore it disappears again. Figger there must be an underground river round here somewhere. Now, if you can help me into the shack an' gimme them packs off that mule, maybe I can fix us a bite o' chuck.'

John paused frowning. 'You're aimin' to stay here?'

'Sure son. Till my leg heals anyway. I was on my way out when that cougar jumped me. Now, if you get me them packs I'll be obliged.'

Unsaddling completed, John watched Red drink at the spring. Finished, the big roan turned away and began grazing.

Big Red cropped busily at the dew-laden grass and swished his tail at the unwelcome attentions of early morning flies.

Watching, John Jordan grinned to himself as he thought how the big horse had become accustomed to another rider. It wasn't that his temperament had changed in any way. Where other people were concerned, he was just the same moody outlaw with the killer streak, that Bull had bought from the Comancheros years ago. Somebody, somewhere, had beaten and tortured Red until he hated all human beings. Only Bull, and to a lesser extent himself, were accepted as riders, and he, John's mouth twisted wryly, very much on sufferance. It was only his own skill with horses, his ability to virtually talk to them that had been instrumental in this happening.

'Sure wish you'd stay for a spell.' Mace had come out of the lean-to behind him.

'No.' John was firm. 'I must get back and tell my folks that Mustang Springs is dry.'

'Pity.' There was a note of suppressed excitement in Mace's voice. 'Guess I'm just gonna have to keep you here!'

John turned quickly and found himself looking into the muzzle of a .45.

'Sure hate to do this.' There was a wildness in the bearded man's eyes. 'Now, unbuckle your gunbelt and toss it on the ground in front of you.'

'You seem to have forgotten something,' John unbuckled the gunbelt and dropped it in front of him. 'I saved your life remember.'

'I know that.' Mace's voice rose and Red raised his head and looked at the man curiously. 'I'd have killed you last night when you were sleepin' but I couldn't bring m'self to do it. Now I got no choice. Cain't run till this leg's healed, an I ain't riskin' you tellin' folks 'bout this place.'

'I give you my word I will not tell anyone.' With mounting excitement John saw that Red had stopped grazing and was moving up behind Mace.

'Cain't trust you. Cain't trust anyone. The gold's mine. Gonna keep it all.' He was shouting now.

'Keep it then.' John raised his hands placatingly. If only he could reach the hidden knife in the neck sheath. Red was very close.

'Cain't take the chance,' Mace was shouting again, the .45 centred and steadied. 'Got to kill you … '

Every muscle stretched, John dived sideways, his hand flashing to the hidden knife. There was the crash of a shot and everything went black.

'Shouldn't have done that, son. Got to admire your guts though.' Jeb Mace limped forward and looked at the trickle of blood from John's head.

'Hell, I only creased him!' He straightened and became aware of the looming shadow of the horse.

'Get away you …', with a backhanded swing he struck the roan across the muzzle with his gun.

Screaming with fury Red lunged forward. Long yellow teeth clamped on Mace's arm and, losing his balance, he fell under the plunging horse. Red reared and struck at the screaming man, reared and struck again. He pounded the broken bleeding thing lying in the dust until it was silent, and only then did he draw off snorting, blood streaking his forelegs.

Silence fell in the clearing.

CHAPTER 4

▼

'That's quite a story Clay,' Bull Jordan grinned at the slim figure sitting opposite. 'An' Dunc never guessed?'

'That it was all for his benefit?' Clay Wallace shook his head. 'No, and that's maybe just as well. That foreman of his, Jud Moore; now there is one bad man. I wouldn't like to be around if he found out.'

The big man nodded sombrely. 'Yeah, I know what you mean. I've known some hard men that were hellraisers, but they weren't bad clean through like Jud. An' he's fast with a gun, don't ever forget it.'

Clay grimaced. 'I'm not likely to. Your brother Lance doesn't seem too worried about him though.'

'Lance?' Bull paused for a moment deep in thought. 'Waal, 'fore he bust up with Pa, Lance raised considerable hell in that neck o' the woods. Seemed like whenever there was trouble he was mixed up in it. Me, I think it was just a wild streak, but I reckon we'll never know. Anyways, Pa an' him had it out, then he cut loose an' left. Hung out around El Paso for a coupla years.' He frowned. 'Never talks 'bout that time. Next thing we knew he was headin' off to the war. Went right through it. Don't know what happened, but he was a different guy when he come back. Quieter, but harder an' I reckon a whole lot more dangerous. He was plannin' to join the Rangers, but them 'carpetbaggers' down in Austin put paid to that idea. They wasn't havin' no good old southern boys patrollin' the country. At least, not for a while yet. So he 'listed in the Fourth Cavalry, Mackenzie's bunch. Signed on for a four year stint. Come to think o' it,' he added reflectively, 'that hitch'll be up next year. Wonder what he's aimin' to do then?'

'Has he always been based at Fort Concho?'

Bull shook his head. 'When he first joined up he did spells at Fort Clark an' Fort Davis down in the Big Bend. Then, 'bout a year ago he come to Fort Concho. Wasn't there all that long when he made sergeant. Now that was a surprise. Never figgered Lance would cotton to that kind o' responsibility.'

'Tell you one thing, they think a lot o' him down at Fort Concho. Last time I come through there I said somethin' 'bout him. Hell, he's m'brother, reckon I can say what I like. Anyways, this young trooper, he ups an' tells me I don't know nothin' 'bout my own brother!' He shook his head wonderingly. 'First time in years anybody talked to me like that.'

'What happened?' Clay looked at him curiously.

'Nothin'. Figgered mebbe I had it comin'. Don't worry about Lance. I ain't never seen him draw, but I reckon he's faster than Jud.'

'Mm.' Clay looked up. 'How long do you reckon it'll take your folks to get here with the herd?'

'Waal,' Bull ran a hand through his hair. 'Let's say a month to Horsehead Crossing on the Pecos. Then maybe another month to get here. Say ten weeks at the outside. 'Course they could be quicker than that. It's only a small herd. Depends on the kind o' crew Pa's managed to get together.'

'Don't know how he made out on that one, but he was working on it when I left. Now, what about that beef contract you were talking about? Have you been to Camp Crittenden yet?'

Bull shook his head. 'Nah. Anyways,' he added defensively, 'they're still buildin'.'

'All the more reason for making our move now. I suggest we ride over there tomorrow and make our pitch.'

The big man's brows drew down in a frown, then his face cleared. He laughed and threw up his hands. 'Alright, I reckon I had that comin'. I've been so tied up here that I ain't been thinkin' straight.'

'And while we're at it,' Clay was pushing hard now, 'I think we should talk to the stage company about those remount contracts. The ranch needs an income from somewhere.'

Bull nodded. 'That's true. Till we run a trail herd up north we got to keep the place goin' somehow.'

Clay yawned and stretched. 'Think I'll get a breath of night air before I turn in.'

'Sure. Reckon I'll sit awhile m'self. Got things on my mind. '

It was dark outside. Clay Wallace leaned on the porch rail and listened to the night noises. Light showed dimly through the bunkhouse windows, and there was a sudden burst of laughter from inside. Down in the corral, a splutter of hooves and an angry squeal indicated that the use of the water trough was being disputed. The smell of sagebrush invaded his nostrils and he inhaled deeply. Clay Wallace, you're a long way from Atlanta. Who would have thought you'd end up out here on the frontier partnering an ex-bounty hunter? Not a man to cross, he mused sombrely. Six feet four, if he's an inch. Weight … two hundred pounds; maybe a little more. I would hate to go up against him in a fight. Hard, ambitious, and a touch arrogant. A good friend and a bad enemy. Another cattle king in the making.

Clay's thoughts turned to his wealthy, class-conscious parents. Their only child's been quite a disappointment to them. I could have been well on my way to being chairman by now. Chairman of Wallace, Baker and Vincent; Accountants, Real Estate and Property Developers. What a mouthful! That's what Father wanted; a son to succeed him. Not me though. At least, not until I've proved I can make it on my own. Now that I've given up gambling I'll have to think of something. This accountancy work with the Jordans could be the beginning. Especially as it gives me an excuse to see Sara-Jane. Alright, so I've finally admitted that she attracts me, what's wrong with that. Marriage now, that could cause problems. Not for me; I reckon Sara- Jane would make a great wife, but I couldn't see Mother accepting a rancher's daughter. And there's no other way I'm going to get Sara-Jane. If Miz Jordan catches me fooling with her younger daughter, I'm dead! Especially after that agreement I made with her. He shivered suddenly; and if she doesn't kill me that man in there will!

Behind him the door opened and closed quietly. The darkness deepened suddenly as the giant figure of Bull Jordan loomed at his shoulder.

'Still here?'

'Yes; been doing a lot of thinking. Trying to figure out where I'm going in life.'

The big cattleman shrugged. 'Too deep for me. Play it as it comes I say. Right now I got a good hand an' I aim to take the pot.' The bunkhouse lights went out suddenly. 'Boys are hittin' the sack early. Don't blame 'em. Big day's brandin' ahead o' us tomorrow. Reckon I'll do the same. You comin'?'

'Mm … ' the ex-gambler took a deep breath. 'I'd like your advice on something.'

'Shoot.'

Carefully, Clay outlined his agreement with Ma. 'That was before I met Sara-Jane. Now I find I'm attracted to her, and I think she feels the same way about me.'

There was a long intimidating silence, then Bull spoke. 'Guess I don't allus see eye to eye wi' the rest o' the family,' he began reflectively. 'Don't mean I ain't got feelin's for them though. Sara-Jane's a good kid. A mite high-spirited mebbe, but she's alright.' His tone sharpened. 'You right serious 'bout her?'

Clay hesitated fractionally. The night seemed suddenly menacing. 'I … yes I am.'

'You don't seem too sure,' Bull said grimly. 'I'd hate to think this was just a passin' fancy. Eastern folks got different ideas from us, an' I wouldn't want to see Sara-Jane gettin' hurt. I take it you ain't got no gal back east?' he queried suddenly.

'No … no … nothing like that!' Well, it's true, he thought defensively. There's Blanche Vincent, and I know both families kept pushing us together. Strengthen the company, Father said. But there was never anything between us.

'Alright, you asked for m'advice an' I'll give it you straight. Speak to Ma … an' Pa as well. Tell 'em how you feel. It's up to them then.'

'Mm … ' Clay said doubtfully.

'You ain't happy 'bout the deal? Reckon it's the best you'll get. Just one more thing, 'fore I turn in.' There was a sudden edge to his voice. 'Mebbe Sara-Jane is only a rancher's daughter from a two-bit spread in east Texas, but she's just as much a lady as them high-toned gals you grew up with. You step outa line with her just once an' I'll kill you! That is;' he chuckled grimly, 'if Ma don't get to you first! 'Night now.' The door closed behind him.

Clay Wallace, ex-accountant, property developer and one-time gambler, laughed shakily to himself. Clay old son, it's make or break time. You can go home and live high on the hog; or you can stay here and tough it out. The choice is yours. Quietly, he made his way indoors.

Out on the range coyotes wailed mournfully. Darkness enveloped the Flying W.

CHAPTER 5

▼

The remuda milled uncertainly, the circle patrolled by Ellie-May and Rafe Allen. Dance, the big Cleveland stud, slowed to a walk, then stopped and began grazing. Ellie-May relaxed thankfully, at least he was easy to handle, not like some stallions, forever wanting to fight or break loose.

Below her, Lance was easing the last of the cattle into the river. In midstream, their mounts belly deep in water, Mike Glenwood and her father urged the herd across. On the opposite bank she could see Andy Boone and Jake swinging the leaders onto the bedground for the night.

Four days, she thought tiredly, four days we've been pushin' the stock hard, an' we're only just crossin' the Brazos. Looking back, she saw the chuck wagon cresting the rise. Ma ain't been wastin' any time. Don't know how she does it. Me, I feel as though I could sleep for a week already.

Rafe waved and pointed. Turning, she saw her father signalling to start the remuda across. Damn, I should have been watchin'.

Kneeing the palomino she started to push the horses, Dance in the lead, down the bank and into the river. The big stallion's placid temperament was a godsend as he splashed his way across, the rest of the remuda trotting quietly behind him.

Ma Jordan eased the chuck wagon down the slope as the last of the remuda scrambled up the opposite bank. Tiredly, she set the brake and watched her husband ploughing across the river towards her. Lord, it's been a long day. Now I got to start cookin'. Guess I'm gettin' too old for this. Jim was right, though I hate to admit it. Reckon Sara-Jane'll just have take on the drivin' full-time.

'You all set to cross?' Jim Jordan looked hard at his wife. Signs of strain were showing on Ma's face.

'Yeah. Don't look too bad to me.'

'Nah. River's low. If you follow me everything should be fine. How you feelin'?'

'Tired,' Ma admitted.

'Reckon you oughta let Sara-Jane take on the drivin' full time. '

'Yeah.' Mary-Lou clutched at her tattered dignity. 'Been thinkin' that m'self, only ... you know how it is. She ain't never been much good with horses.'

'She'll never get a better chance to learn.' Jim Jordan said grimly. He rode past the chuck wagon to where Miguel Jerez had halted the Clevelands.

'Everythin' alright Miguel?'

'Si senor, everything is fine. The team ... they are the best.'

'Yeah, they're pretty good.'

'The river, ... it is not too deep?'

'Nah ... should be alright. I'll lead the way an' you just follow the chuck wagon.'

'Si. Senor, it is not my business, but it is a long day for Senora Jordan. This is not good.'

'Yeah,' Jim rubbed his chin. 'Been thinkin' on that m'self. Reckon it's time I did something 'bout it.' He raised his voice. 'Sara-Jane!'

'Yeah Pa.' His younger daughter peered out of the accommodation wagon.

'Startin' tomorrow you're drivin' full-time.'

He looked at Sara-Jane's startled face. 'Yeah, I know you don't like horses, but your ma has enough to do wi' the cookin' an' she's needin' a break.'

Driving! Sara-Jane gritted her teeth. 'Alright Pa, reckon I should have tried harder before.'

Her father shook his head. 'It ain't your fault. I'm supposed to be runnin' this drive an' I should have made you get a handle on the job when we started out.'

He looked at the two small faces regarding him gravely from the coach window. 'Sarah ... Mary, you all set for the crossin'?'

'Yes, Mister Jordan.' Sarah Johnson spoke with all the confidence of her eight years. 'It's not too deep is it? Mary don't like when it's deep, Ain't that so Mary?' Six year old Mary nodded as she stared round-eyed at the big horse snuffling at the open window.

'He won't hurt you,' Jim assured her. 'An' no, it ain't too deep.' He eased the Cleveland on towards the big Studebaker wagon which was just pulling up. The wheelers settled into their backing straps as Ben Turner set the brake.

'You alright Ben?' He looked consideringly at the serious young man on the high wagon seat.

Ben Turner smiled. 'Sure Mister Jordan. Nuthin' to worry about. Only got a three thousand pound load an' this team could haul that forever.'

Jim Jordan grinned as he looked at the big horses. 'Guess you're right at that. Now, I'll lead across, same as we did at the Navasota. Ma'll go first, then Miguel an' your outfit last. Give'm plenty o' room an' we shouldn't have no trouble.'

He reined the Cleveland round and cantered back to the head of the line.

The big horse splashed into the Brazos as Jim turned in his saddle and beckoned Ma on.

On the bed ground the herd and the remuda grazed contentedly.

CHAPTER 6

▼

Red snuffled at the prone figure. John Jordan groaned and his eyes flickered open. The big horse drew back snorting, ears flattened and eyes rolling. John groaned again and tried to sit up. Pain lanced along the side of his head. His fingers touched the spot and came away wet. Blood! ... he felt the shallow furrow grooved by the bullet. I was lucky he thought shakily.

Gingerly John turned his head. The broken trampled body caught his eye, then the wild-eyed blood-stained roan. He drew in his breath sharply. Red, I always thought you would do this some day. Thing is, are you still primed to kill?

Only one way to find out. Shakily he climbed to his feet and staggered towards the spring, watched carefully by Red. Dropping on his knees John drank deeply, then bathed the side of his head. The shock of the cold water and the increased pain made him dizzy; he remained kneeling for a further moment waiting for it to clear.

Rising, he stood for a moment thinking. Then he walked towards the giant roan, speaking softly as he did so. Red pawed the ground and neighed shrilly. Still talking quietly, John continued to move towards him. Slowly the fire died out of Red's eyes and his ears came forward. Gently the man placed a hand on the big horse's shoulder. Beneath his touch he felt the tense muscles relax.

Satisfied, John stood for a moment stroking the glossy neck, then turned and walked towards the lean-to. Behind him Red dropped his head and started to graze.

It was dark in the lean-to. The smell of stale food and unwashed bedding came sharply to his nostrils. Dimly, in a corner, he saw what he was seeking; a shovel. Picking it up he went outside. Selecting a spot under the trees he started to dig. Dizziness continued to attack him and he had to pause from time to time.

Eventually the shallow grave was ready. John made another trip to the lean-to and returned with a pair of grimy blankets. Folding one of them he laid it in the bottom of the hole. Then, watched closely by a snorting Red, he dragged Mace's mangled body across to the graveside.

Ten years of living with the Comanches had hardened John Jordan to most things, but the destruction caused by the gelding's pounding hooves sickened even him. Gently, he eased the body into the open grave and carefully folded the second blanket over it.

Sombrely, he paused for a moment. Jeb Mace, our trails crossed for a short time only. You tried to kill me, but I would hate to die as you did. Wish I knew why you did it. Anyway, I hope you rest easy. Head bowed, he muttered a few words in Comanche, then, picking up the shovel proceeded to cover the blanketed corpse. Tamping the soil down, he replaced the sods he had cut earlier. Satisfied, the young rancher made his way back to the lean-to.

The dead man's jacket hung from a peg on the wall. John took it down and explored the pockets. Some coins, a clasp knife and a plug of tobacco. About to put it back on the peg he felt something through the material. Carefully slitting the lining he drew out three pieces of paper.

Unfolding the first one he found himself staring at a fair likeness of Jeb Mace, a younger Jeb Mace, without the beard. Not for the first time John blessed the fact that, following his return from the Comanches, his father had laboured long and hard to teach him to read and write. In this he had been aided by Jake Larsen.

Old Sven Larsen had been an educated man who had drifted west looking for adventure. Respected by the Comanches as a man of learning, his marriage to a relative of Ten Bears had strengthened his standing in the tribe. The birth of Jake had brought home to him the problems his son would face because of his mixed parentage. There and then he had decided to educate the boy to the best of his ability. His son had proved an apt pupil, and in turn had fired young Jordan with the same ambition.

Now he stared at the caption under the picture.

$1000 REWARD

A reward of $1000 is offered for information leading to the arrest of Sergeant Daniel Curtis Henry, Trooper Jackson Willis, and Trooper Hiram Oxbow, on a charge of murder and robbery. A further reward of $500 will be paid for information leading to the recovery of $20,000 in gold, stolen by the aforementioned Sergeant Henry, Troopers Willis and Oxbow. Any persons having information relevant to the above crime should contact their nearest army post, or failing that, their local law enforcement officer.

Philip J. Kearny
General
U.S. Army

The other papers were two yellowing newspaper cuttings. One was an account by a correspondent of the Tucson Times, regarding the disappearance of a consignment of gold during 1863.

The gold, to be used to pay the garrison at Fort Sumner and also to finance the Apache reservation at Bosque Redondo, was being delivered by an army escort. The money, all in fifty dollar gold pieces, and the entire escort, a lieutenant, a sergeant and six troopers of the 5th U.S. Cavalry, had disappeared without trace. The report hinted that foul play was not being ruled out.

John opened the second cutting, dated a month later. It stated that the disappearance of the gold and the escort was now partially solved. A scouting troop of cavalry had stumbled across the bodies of the lieutenant and four troopers. From all indications it appeared they had been shot in the back. There was no sign of the gold, or the escorts' mounts. Investigations were continuing, and a reward of $1000 had been offered for information leading to the arrest of Sergeant Henry, and Troopers Willis and Oxbow.

Folding the papers carefully, John thought for a moment. The saddlebags on the mule! His eyes roamed the interior of the lean-to. There was a pile of clothing in the corner. Beneath it he found the two big saddlebags.

Unbuckling one of them, he delved into it. His hand clutched heavy discs of metal. Carrying the bags to the door he poured the coins onto the ground.

Octagonal Californian gold pieces gleamed dully in the sunlight. Breathing deeply, John started to count. Ten minutes later he sat back on his heels and stared at the pile. Three hundred and twenty gold coins. Sixteen thousand dollars! His mind tried to fill in the blanks in the story. Were Willis and Oxbow dead, or were they, even now, close on Henry's trail? He shrugged; dead most likely. Judging from his own experience, Henry wouldn't have let a couple more dead troopers stand in his way. Possibly he had spent some of the intervening years in Mexico. Maybe he had even hoped to get a boat and make his way east, where he could lose himself in one of the big cities. And if it hadn't been for an old tom cougar he might have done just that. Instead, he lay wrapped in a couple of tattered army blankets, in a shallow grave in West Texas, while the gold glittered in the sun.

John's mouth twisted sardonically as he gathered up the coins. No wonder the Indians laughed at the white man's greed for gold.

He touched his wound gently. His head still ached but the raw groove had crusted over. Well, maybe that was for the best. Delving into his saddlebags, he hauled out a clean bandanna and tied it in a narrow bandage round his head.

Got to get back and tell Pa that there's no water between the fort and the Pecos. Sure is a pity about the spring. If only there had been a dam … a dam! He walked out into the small grassy clearing and looked about him carefully. The two horses and the mule switched their tails and continued to graze.

It could be done. On three sides the clearing sloped upwards from the spring. Under the sandstone cliff water bubbled to the surface, ran a few yards and disappeared back into the ground.

Grabbing the shovel he hurried towards the sinkhole. Yes, he was right. All it needed was a stone the right shape and some sods to plug the crevices. Feverishly he set to work.

Ten minutes later, wet and muddy, he stood back satisfied. Already the pent-up water was beginning to swirl against the base of the cliff. Soon it would start to spread across the clearing. Before it found an outlet he reckoned it would be five feet deep at the cliff base. If only the plug held until they got here with the herd.

Cautiously, he caught up Red and saddled him. The big horse rolled his eyes and sidled nervously, but that was all. Carefully John transferred the gold to his own saddlebags.

Swinging into the saddle, he drove the dun and the mule ahead of him along the narrow trail and out into the open ground beyond. Reckon we'll need to widen that trail before we bring the herd through. He turned north and headed for the fort. In the clearing the swirling water rose steadily against the cliff base.

CHAPTER 7

▼

The tents were pitched in precise rows, just as he had stipulated. The smell of sawdust and raw lumber wafted pleasantly through the open window, while the bustle of construction was everywhere. Yes, Camp Crittenden was taking shape. Colonel Calhoun smiled contentedly.

A tall, spare fifty-five year old, Calhoun knew that there would be no further promotion for him. There were too many young hotshots from the war chasing too few posts.

So be it then, he was content with what he had. This task, the construction and establishing of a new frontier post was something which gave full rein to his organizing ability. With luck it would see him through the next five years, when he would retire and go back to Vermont, where he originally hailed from.

Now he stood at the window of his small office and watched his plans taking shape. His eyes narrowed at the sight of two riders jogging through the lines of tents, escorted by one of the patrolling troopers, then he nodded approvingly.

Captain McLean was a good second-in-command. A seasoned Indian fighter, he had waited to see what line his colonel would take. However, although Calhoun was essentially an administration man he was nobody's fool. The first thing he had done was to take McLean aside and tell him that he would always be prepared to listen to the captain's advice. This had established a bond between them, a bond that had become even stronger over the past months.

It had been McLean's suggestion to have the perimeter of the camp site patrolled by mounted troopers; a suggestion which the colonel had acted on immediately. And it had paid dividends. Incoming travellers were stopped at the perimeter and their business ascertained. The risk of theft, particularly of stores lying in the open, had been virtually eliminated.

He turned away from the window as the riders pulled up outside. There was a subdued murmur of voices and then a knock on his door.

Calhoun seated himself at his desk.

'Come in.'

His orderly entered from the outer office.

'Two gentlemen to see you Colonel.' Trooper Davidson was precise in everything he did. He'd made it up to sergeant during the war and still entertained ambitions to get his rank back. The post of orderly was a beginning.

'Did they say who they were?'

'Yes sir.' Davidson consulted the piece of paper in his hand. 'A Mister Hardy Jordan, he's a rancher, and a Mister Clay Wallace, he's an accountant.'

'Mm.' Calhoun frowned. 'This Jordan ... is he local?'

'Yes sir,' again the paper was consulted. ''Pears he owns the Flying W ranch. It covers most of the land to the southeast of the post. Seems he's only come here recent like.'

'Alright, send them in. Thanks Davidson.'

'Sir!' Trooper Davidson saluted and did a smart about-turn.

I'll have to promote him, the colonel thought wryly, otherwise he'll wear me out with his eternal spit and polish.

In his opinion the two men who came through the door could not have been more dissimilar. The giant, powerfully built range man and the slim, neat accountant made a strange combination.

'Gentlemen.' He rose and extended his hand. 'A pleasure to meet you both.' Calhoun belonged to the old school who believed that politeness didn't cost anything.

They shook hands and he motioned them to be seated. 'Now, what can I do for you?'

'Waal, Colonel,' Bull settled himself comfortably, 'm'name's Jordan, Hardy Jordan an' this here is Clay Wallace. I've just taken over the Flyin' W south o' here, an' I was wonderin' if you were in the market for beef?'

The colonel shot him an interested glance. 'I certainly am Mister Jordan. We brought some beef cattle with us, but we've been running through them fairly quickly. Construction work makes for hungry men. In addition, I'm supposed to open talks with Cochise and that means more beef. The idea is to establish an agency here. Whether that will work or not I don't know, but I've got to try.'

He paused for a moment. 'Before we go any further I'd like you to meet my second-in-command, Captain McLean. McLean has been on the frontier for a number of years and has a better grasp of local conditions than myself.' He laughed as he saw the look exchanged by the two men. 'Surprised at my admission? Gentlemen, I'm under no illusions. I'm an administrator pure and simple. I can set up a post and make it a going concern with the best. But when it comes to Indians I'm a babe-in-arms compared to men like McLean. Excuse me a moment.'

He rose and opened the door.

'Davidson!'

'Sir!'

'Could you find Captain McLean and ask him to report to my office. I'd like him to meet these two gentlemen.'

'Yes sir!' There was a clatter as Davidson departed hurriedly on his mission. The colonel seated himself again.

'Forgive me asking, Mister Wallace.' He looked directly at Clay. 'But where do you fit into all this?'

Clay grinned. 'That's a fair question. I'm employed by Mister Jordan as his accountant. Also, I hope to set up my accountancy firm in the territory.'

There was a knock at the door.

'Come in.'

The man who stepped into the office looked every inch the typical cavalry officer. Fit, athletic and intelligent, at twenty-seven Norman McLean was that rare breed, a West Point graduate who had made the jump to successful Indian fighter. Throughout the war he had been stationed out west, and the experience he amassed during campaigns against the Comanches, Sioux and Apaches was probably without equal.

Liked by his brother-officers and idolised by his men, McLean was overdue for promotion, but the postwar log-jam had prevented it. The only thing that stood in his way was his own intolerance of bureaucracy. However, in Colonel Calhoun he had found the perfect role model. Calhoun disliked paperwork just as much as the young red-haired captain, but he was smart enough to keep his dislike to himself. And, slowly but surely he was converting his protege. Norman McLean was finding that learning was a two-way process. He passed his know-how on the Apaches and local conditions to the colonel, who in turn, taught him how to outwit the faceless men in Washington.

Now, the young captain snapped off a salute and looked inquiringly at his commanding officer.

'At ease. Norman, I want you to meet Mister Jordan, a local rancher, and Mister Wallace, his accountant. Gentlemen, this is Captain McLean, my deputy.'

'Well I'm damned,' Bull glanced sideways to see Clay grinning at the captain.

'Norman McLean! I'd know that red hair anywhere.'

'Clay … Clay Wallace, well I'll be … it was the moustache that fooled me. How many years is it?'

Clay shook his head. 'Too many.'

'I take it you gentlemen know each other.' There was an interrogative note in Calhoun's voice.

'Oh, sorry sir, you too Mister Jordan. Yes, Clay and I grew up together. We were classmates at school. Then we lost track of each other. My father wanted me to manage the family plantation, but we didn't see eye to eye about slavery, so that was that. However, I managed to get accepted for West Point. When I graduated I drew the frontier. Then the war came and we were all asked to choose. I chose the North.' He paused and looked away. 'When my father found out he disowned me. I've never been back.' There was a long silence then he looked at Clay. 'What about yourself?'

'Not so different from your story, but I don't think I'm ready to tell it just yet. Good to see you anyway.'

The colonel coughed. 'Right gentlemen, can we get down to business? Norman, Mister Jordan here has beef for sale. I'd like your views on the subject.'

'Well sir,' McLean leaned back in his chair. 'We do need a supplier for the camp, and of course there's the matter of the agency. If we succeed in setting it up then we'll also need supplies for the Indians.'

'Just what I thought.' Calhoun rested his elbows on the desk and frowned thoughtfully. He looked at Bull. 'How soon could you supply us, Mister Jordan?'

Bull grinned. 'Two, three days I can have whatever you want here. Oh, 'nother thing. We've been clearin' our stock out o' the brush an' we got about fifty young bulls I want to get shot of. Don't want to chance cuttin' them. Allus the risk o' infection, an' I don't want them in a trail herd. Cause nuthin' but trouble. Let you have them cheap. Anyways, we won't always be dealin' in Longhorn beef. My folks are headin' this way from Texas with some Durham breedin' bulls, so we'll be upgradin' our stock.'

Calhoun looked inquiringly at his second-in -command.

'Sounds alright to me sir. I've eaten buffalo bulls and they were real tasty.'

The colonel nodded. 'Agree on a price and draw up a contract. Then we can sign it. That should keep the gentlemen in Washington happy. Anything else?'

Mc Lean frowned. 'There's the matter of remounts,' he said diffidently. 'Once we start patrolling we can expect casualties, both men and horses.'

'Damn, you're right. What about it Mister Jordan?'

'We got some good saddle stock back at the ranch. Be happy to have you look them over any time. Then we're bringin' in a Cleveland stallion and twenty Cleveland and Morgan mares. In time we plan to upgrade our horseherd as well.'

'Clevelands eh ... and Morgans?' The colonel nodded approvingly. 'Mister Jordan, you're a man with an eye to the future. I'll be interested to see how your plans work out.' He turned to Clay. 'You too Mister Wallace. This won't always be the frontier. Civilisation will catch up with us one day and when it does it'll be the man who thought ahead who'll be successful. I wish you both luck. Now, if you care to go with Captain McLean, you can work out a price for the beef and then we can have a contract drawn up.'

He rose and the others did likewise. 'Goodbye gentlemen.' They shook hands. 'It's been a pleasure doing business with you. I hope to see you again soon.'

McLean escorted them to their horses.

'I'll drop by in two or three days with the contract. Then we can look at your stock and agree on a price. Clay,' he looked directly at Wallace, 'it's been good to see you again. Hope you make it with your own business.'

'So McLean an' yourself go back a ways,' Bull commented as they jogged through the camp.

'Yes. We were classmates just like he said. His family owned a big plantation down Georgia way. Lots of slaves too, and that was something Norman couldn't stomach. Him and his father fought like wildcats over it. Old Judge McLean is as stubborn as a Missouri mule and Norman takes after him. Still, I never thought the old man would disown his son.' He sighed deeply. 'The war has a lot to answer for.'

'Reckon we all got a lot to answer for,' Bull said darkly. 'Don't hold with slavery m'self. Man's got a right to be free.'

'Maybe you're right,' Clay admitted, 'but what about the Comanches, the Apaches and all the other tribes? They were here before us. You could say this is their land!'

'Damn you Clay!' Twisting angrily in his saddle Bull saw the twinkle in his companion's eyes and subsided, grinning shamefacedly. 'Alright, you got me hogtied on that one. Don't know what the answer is. Reckon if they were to leave me alone I'd do the same. Anyways, let's leave it at that. The main thing is we got a beef an' remount contract now.'

'Mm.' Clay nodded, thankful that the argument was over. 'Still of a mind to go to Tucson?'

'Sure. Quicker we have a word with the stageline the better. Anyways, we got enough horses to supply them an' the army.' Swaying easily in their saddles they headed north.

The buckskin gelding was no cowpony but he was learning fast. He angled in beside the Durham bull and gently eased the lumbering giant back into the herd. Lance Jordan grinned and patted his mount's neck. Damned if I don't think you got the makin's. Sure must be a change from cavalry work.

Across the small herd he watched Jake Larsen turning a recalcitrant cow, who shook her head threateningly before wheeling away. He waved and the young half-breed waved back. Jake's good, he thought. Pa was right to make him segundo. Some day he'll make a real fine cattleman.

Looking back he saw his father covering the drag, his bandanna pulled up to mask his nose and mouth against the pervasive dust. Beats me how the old man does it. He's fifty-two now an' he can still rope an' ride with the best. Sharp too; he pulled me outa that mess at the Rockin' H. Memories crowded in on the tall sergeant. Why is Jud's killin' needlin' me like this? Hell, I've killed men before an' they didn't trouble me near as much. 'Course other times it was wished on me; gunnies wantin' to try their luck, or the war, where it was kill or be killed. Never made up m'mind to kill a guy cold-bloodedly before. Ah, what the hell. His mouth twisted sardonically; Jud Moore was a killer, he deserved to die.

Lord, I'm tired. Still, we're beginnin' to move like a trail outfit now. The rivers bein' low like that helped. Didn't have no trouble with the wagons either.

The remuda, big Dance in the lead, was closing up on the herd. Beyond them he could see Sara-Jane, a look of grim determination on her face, clutching the lines of the chuck wagon team. Lance grinned. If only she'd learn to leave old Dusty and Paint alone they'd drive themselves.

Movement caught his eye and he looked again across the herd. Jake Larsen was pointing. Some three hundred yards ahead a small party of Indians was drifting across the trail. The big sergeant felt the familiar tension in his stomach. It never changes he thought wryly as he drew the field glasses from one of his saddlebags. Comanches, six o' them. 'Bout a dozen loose horses as well. Looks like they been on a raid.

Five of the party closed up round their prizes and cantered on stolidly. The sixth brave, mounted on a flashy pinto, halted and waited a hundred yards off the trail. As Lance lowered the field glasses he was conscious of Jake waving Andy Boone up into point position. Turning to look back he saw his father swinging round the end of the herd to take Andy's post. Yeah, that was fine, the drag could look after itself for the time being.

Slowly, Jake began to angle out towards the waiting Indian. Gently, Lance eased the Spencer carbine out of its boot. Don't know what Jake has in mind, but if that Comanche makes a wrong move he's dead.

The big sergeant watched closely as Jake signed to the brave that he wanted to talk. The distance between them closed and he could tell that words were being exchanged. The tense moments lengthened, then the Comanche wheeled his pony and took off after the others. Watching keenly, Jake waited for another moment, before wheeling his mount and trotting back to the herd.

He spoke briefly to Andy, who nodded and fell back to take up his original position at swing, exchanging words with Jim Jordan as he did so. Lance saw his father angle across the rear of the herd and move up beside Glenwood. They talked briefly and then the Cleveland was moving again up his side of the herd.

'Howdy Pa. What in tarnation was all that about?'

Jim Jordan grinned at his eldest son. 'Lance, if there's such a thing as a lucky break that was it. That there was a Comanche raidin' party on their way back from a raid down into the Bend. The young buck that waited behind was Lone Horse. Seems like him, Jake an' John, hunted together one time. He was curious 'bout the herd an' where we were goin'. Jake told him we were John's folks bound for Arizona.'

'What about the raidin' party?'

'Headin' up north with them horses. 'Pears old Black Kettle's settin' up camp on the Washita. Looks like they're gettin' ready to winter there.'

'Jake's a handy guy to have around ain't he?'

His father nodded. 'Yeah. Now I got to go tell Ma an' the others. Maybe it'll make her a mite more friendly to Jake.' He wheeled the Cleveland and paused. 'Oughta make the Leon tomorrow night. Good water an' grazin' there. Bet you wish you'd stayed wi' the cavalry!' His laughter floated back as he headed for the wagons.

CHAPTER 8

▼

John Jordan touched the bloodstained bandage round his head and grimaced. The bullet graze along the side of his head had taken more out of him than he had expected. That, and the fact that he was determined to make the stage station at the head of the Concho River by nightfall, had made it a long tiring day in the saddle. He'd allowed himself a midday break at Mustang Springs, during which time he had bathed his head and then attempted to wash the blood off Red's forelegs.

That had been a mistake. Triggered probably by the scent of fresh blood from John's wound, Red had attacked. Only the fact that John had the big horse tied to a convenient branch had enabled the young rancher to roll clear.

It had taken a good half-hour, and all the wiles of his Comanche horse know-how, before he finally got the raging gelding quietened down.

The young rider frowned worriedly. Somehow, killing Mace had triggered those memories of torture by the Comancheros that had lain locked in Red's brain. It was going to be a long time before he forgot, and probably only when he was reunited with Bull.

The evening shadows lengthened as they breasted the slope. Alongside the trail Spanish dagger and giant cactus were beginning to take on weird shapes in the gathering dusk. John grinned as he remembered how Sara-Jane hated the twilight. As far as his youngest sister was concerned every waving bush was a potential Indian.

Not like Ellie-May, he thought approvingly. She listened and learned. Any Comanche lore passed on to her was absorbed, to be acted upon when needed.

From the crest of the rise he could see well down the valley. There! In the distance, a pinpoint of light glimmered faintly, marking the stagecoach way station. He spoke softly to Red. 'Not much further now.' The giant roan pricked his ears and lengthened his stride.

Jed Lomax, black bearded lead hand, raised his head and listened intently. 'Rider comin'.' He put aside the harness strap he had been working on and reached for his rifle. 'Tell Amos.' He jerked his head in the direction of the main station building. Henry Grant, a tall saturnine Missourian, nodded and slipped out of the harness room.

Carefully, Jed peered through the gathering dusk. He could just see the loom of a horse and rider.

His voice lifted in a shout. 'Alright stranger, identify yourself.'

'John Jordan.' The voice was clipped and without any drawl. 'Scoutin' for the Circle J trail outfit. I came through here some four days back. Like to put up for the night.'

'What's happenin'?'

Jed turned to find the burly figure of Amos McQueen, station boss, at his elbow. 'Rider headin' east.' Jed informed him tersely. 'Says his name's Jordan an' he's trail scout for an outfit called the Circle J. Wants to put up for the night.'

Amos thought for a moment. 'Alright, open the gate.'

John dismounted wearily. The long day had taken its toll. 'Thanks. Got anywhere I can stable Red on his own.'

Amos Mc Queen looked at him curiously. 'Is that necessary? Surely he ain't gonna cause that much of a ruckus with other horses?'

'He's a mankiller.' John said succinctly. 'Killed a man yesterday. He belongs to m'brother Hardy and he's a one man horse. He just puts up with me and no more. I wouldn't want any of your fellas gettin' hurt, so if you got a place for him on his own I'd be obliged.'

'Mm ... a mankiller eh?' Red snorted and Amos stepped back hastily.

'Alright, we got a blacksmith's shop back o' the main building. Useta keep an old freight wagon there, but the company called it in a coupla weeks ago. There's a stall at one end. Use it when we're shoein' horses. Bed'm down in it. You want somethin' to eat? Got some beef an' beans, an' there's a pot o' coffee on the stove.'

'Sounds good to me,' John grinned. 'Soon as I get Red bedded down I'll be there.'

Jed watched the young rancher lead Red towards the lean-to.

'You believe that horse is a killer?'

Amos shrugged. 'Dunno, an' I ain't aimin' to find out. That goes for the rest of you,' he added warningly. 'Pass the word.'

Henry Grant grinned dourly. 'You can tell them Mex roustabouts but I don't think it'll make much difference. They all reckon there ain't no horse they cain't tame.'

'You tell 'em just the same.' Amos turned on his heel and stalked away.

John secured Red to a wall-mounted ring at the far end of the lean-to. Then he removed the two heavy saddlebags and placed them in the manger. The saddle he hung on a peg behind the stall. A pile of gramma hay lay in the corner and he dumped an armful in front of Red.

Closing the lean-to door he made his way across to the main building.

'All fixed?' Amos looked up as the young rancher entered the room.

'Yeah.' John looked about him. It was a cheerless room, with narrow slits instead of windows and lit by a handful of flickering candles. A cooking stove stood against the end wall, while a series of crude bunks had been built down either side of the room. Rough tables and chairs covered the central floor area. At one of the tables a group of Mexican roustabouts talked quietly amongst themselves.

McQueen gestured to a cast-iron pot bubbling on the stove. 'Beef an' beans there. Pot o' coffee on the side. Get yourself a plate and dig in.'

The food was hot and spicy. John could feel his strength returning. Amos caught his eye and grinned.

'Good chuck?'

John nodded.

The station boss indicated a thickset Mexican busy at the stove. 'Vincente there handles the kitchen chores. Best cook on the line.'

The young rancher finished eating and rinsed his dishes in the washtub. He yawned widely.

Pick yourself a bunk.' McQueen waved his hand. 'Spares down that side. We keep 'em ready in case the stage has to stay overnight.'

'Thanks.' John threw his blanket roll onto one of the bunks. Hanging his hat on a wall peg he tugged off his boots.

'This outfit you're scoutin' for, the Circle J, they're headin' into some mighty tough territory.'

'Yeah.' John settled himself in the bunk. 'Bound for Arizona.'

Amos eyed him closely. 'Lot o' Apache trouble out there.'

'Mm, ... you get much trouble with Comanches here?'

McQueen shook his head. 'Nuthin' since we opened up. 'Course, now the war's over the Army's been bearin' down kinda heavy.'

'When's the next stage due in?'

'Early mornin'.'

'Reckon I'll get some sleep then.' John turned on his side.

Amos looked at the youngster. Quiet fella, he thought, don't give nobody any trouble. Aloud he said, 'Who's doin' guard duty tonight?'

Jed rose to his feet. 'Me an' Hernando are takin' the first stint. Henry an' Raphael the second.' He crossed to the gun rack and drew out two rifles, one of which he tossed to Hernando, a middle-aged grey-haired Mexican who had risen from the table. Together they made their way outside into the velvety darkness.

The first grey light of dawn was just beginning to show. John came awake like a wolf and lay still, every sense alert. A horse snorted nervously in the brush corral. Silently the young rancher slipped out of the bunk.

Buckling on his gunbelt, he padded across to where McQueen lay on his back, snoring noisily. Gently shaking the sleeping man he clamped a hand over Amos's mouth. Signing for silence, John bent and whispered in his ear. The foreman nodded and swung quietly out of the bunk. Together they eased the main door open a fraction. John slid through it and vanished. The door closed gently behind him and Amos set about wakening the others.

Cautiously John rounded the end of the main building. His foot touched something soft and he looked down. Henry Grant lay face down in the dust. He had been stabbed and then scalped. John's mouth set grimly as he worked his way cautiously along the end wall to where he could see the corral. The light was spreading now. A body sprawled loosely by the brush fence, while beyond that a shadowy figure struggled to open the corral gate.

The .45 in John's hand crashed once and the struggling figure at the gate toppled sideways and lay spread-eagled in the dust. John threw himself flat as a volley of rifle fire erupted from the narrow windows. Hoofbeats receded rapidly and the gunfire echoes died away.

'Jordan!' McQueen's voice rose in a shout, 'You alright?'

'Yeah.' John lay still, eyes probing the grey dawn. 'Hold your fire. I'll look around. Reckon they've gone though.'

He rose and made his way to the corral gate. The intruder lay where he had fallen. John turned the body over. Well, well, if it ain't Yellow Dog. Long way off his home range. He noted the two fresh scalps dangling from the Comanche's belt. Reckon he lost out after all.

Carefully he checked the front of the station. The tracks of three unshod ponies showed plainly. Looks like it was just three of them chancin' their luck.

Rising to his feet he hailed the main cabin.

'McQueen!'

'Yo!'

'All clear now. Just three young bucks. Thought they could pick up some horses. I got one an' the other two hightailed it. Henry and Raphael are both dead though.'

'Hell,' Amos led the rush through the door. 'Both dead? This the fella did it?' He indicated the dead Comanche.

'Yellow Dog? Yeah, he's one of Tosawi's boys.'

'Tosawi?'

'Yeah. Sorry, you'd call him Silver Knife.'

McQueen frowned. 'How come you know this Yellow Dog? Seems mighty queer to me.'

John shrugged. 'Comanches took me when I was eight years old. I was with them until I was eighteen. Me and Yellow Dog grew up together. He's about a couple o' years younger than me. Just a wild kid. He was always in trouble.'

'Waal, he sure as hell won't trouble nobody now. Shame 'bout Henry an' Raphael though. They were good men.'

'Yeah.' Jed Lomax was in an ugly mood. 'Henry was my sidekick. Now I got to bury him. Don't seem right somehow. Anyways,' he drew the long Bowie knife, 'I reckon I got a right to this fella's scalp.'

The .45 materialised as if by magic in John's hand. 'Put that knife up or I'll blow your head off! There'll be no more scalpin' round here. I'll bury him as he is.'

There was a moment's shocked silence, then Lomax slid the long knife back into its sheath. He looked sullenly at John. 'How come you're such an' Injun lover? Shoulda thought you'd want to see them all dead. '

John holstered his gun. 'Injuns are folks, just like us. There's good an' there's bad. I've seen both kinds. Yellow Dog here; he was wild an' reckless. Guess he was always goin' to wind up like this. Mebbe we'd all have ended up like him if we hadn't been lucky. Now,' he lifted the dead Indian and slung him over his shoulder, 'just hand me a shovel an' I'll bury him up there on the ridge outa your way.'

☆   ☆   ☆   ☆

Shovel in hand John Jordan looked down at the body lying in the shallow grave. Sleep well my brother, you died as you would have wished, fighting the 'white eyes'. I do not ask your forgiveness, you were a Comanche warrior and you knew the risks. At least you pass to the other side whole. To those in the station below you are just a wild Indian. They never knew you as I did. Goodbye my friend, rest in peace. He sprinkled earth on the body and began to fill in the grave.

'You're welcome to stay an' have breakfast with us.' Amos watched John tighten the cinch and position the heavy saddlebags. 'Least we can do. You saved the horses this mornin', mebbe us too.'

Jed Lomax scowled. 'Speak for yourself. Any man who draws a gun 'cause of a dead Comanche ain't no friend o' mine!'

John shook his head. 'Thanks Amos, but I got a long ride if I'm goin' to make the fort tonight. Just one thing.' His right hand flicked over his shoulder, something flashed in the morning sun, and the slim throwing knife quivered in the corral post thirty feet away. Walking over, John jerked the blade free and slipped it into the neck sheath. He turned and surveyed the silent onlookers coldly.

'I'll be comin' through this way again soon an' I'll take it personal if that grave's been touched! Adios now.'

Easing into the saddle, he guided Red through the gate and down towards the river. The two men watched silently as John let the big horse drink deeply before swinging up onto the trail and heading east. To the west a distant dust plume signalled the inbound stage.

Amos McQueen let out his breath in an explosive whistle. 'Whooeeh! Jed boy, some day that tongue o' yours'll get you killed. That young fella is chain lightnin' with a gun or a knife an' don't you ever forget it. '

Jed flushed angrily. 'Don't reckon he's all that special m'self.'

'Then you got rocks for brains!' Amos said caustically. 'Anyways, we got better things to do than stand here gabbin'. The stage'll be here soon. Let's get the team ready.'

CHAPTER 9

▼

The sign was plain. A sizeable herd of horses had crossed the dry sandy wash recently. Bull knelt and ran his hand over one of the hoofprints. 'An hour's start mebbe, not much more. Five riders an' about fifty head o' loose stock. You see it like that Joe?'

The foreman nodded. 'Yeah, the boys are checkin' the horse herd now but I reckon you're close. Five riders at least, two each side an' one workin' the drag. 'Course, there could be another fella up front but the herd's blottin' out his tracks. Comancheros or rustlers I guess. Them saddle horses are shod.'

Bull rubbed his chin reflectively. 'Could be you're right, though there's just a chance it's Injuns ridin' shod saddle stock they've picked up somewhere.'

'How do you know all this?' Clay Wallace looked at Masterson curiously. 'All I can see is a lot of hoofprints in the sand.'

'Look there,' Bull rose to his feet and pointed. 'There's two horses runnin' wide on each side o' the herd. The prints are deeper 'cause they're carryin' weight an' you can see the marks o' the shoes. Comin' up behind is another set o' deep prints which ain't been stamped on. An' we know the herd ain't shod. There you have it.'

'What about the time?'

The big man shrugged. 'The sand in them hoofprints is dry and a touch warm. Where it ain't been kicked up it's still feels cold. Sun ain't had time to burn off the coldness, so I reckon an hour to an hour an' a half's 'bout right.'

He stared into the distance. 'My guess is they're headin' for the Border. We got to move fast. Joe, I'll take Jeff, Chester, an' Clay with me. Time Clay got a feel for this kinda work. Yeah, I know what you're thinkin' Joe but it ain't on. This is my hand an' I'll play it my way. I intend puttin' down a marker for anybody that thinks he can tangle wi' the Flyin' W.'

Joe nodded thoughtfully. 'Yeah, might save us a deal o' trouble later on. Right, I'll get the boys workin' on them remounts. You all take care now, you hear.'

He wheeled his pony and cantered off.

Bull looked questioningly at the other three. 'Reckon I should have givin' you all a chance to speak 'fore now. Alright, anybody got anythin' to say?'

Jeff and Chester exchanged glances. 'Don't see much to talk about.' Chester looked sideways at his partner. 'We ride for the outfit, we fight for the outfit.'

Clay Wallace nodded. 'That says it for me too.'

'Alright.' Bull swung up onto the big grey. 'Let's ride. Quicker we catch up wi' them, the quicker we get this thing over.' He squinted into the sun. 'Reckon we could be up with them by midday.'

Silently, each busy with his thoughts, the four riders crossed the draw and headed south.

Dave Sands twisted in his saddle and stared nervously round him. Not for the first time he cursed his stupidity in getting involved with Sanchez. Broke, after being run off the Flying W, he had drifted south to see if the Comancheros would stake him. Unfortunately his arrival had coincided with the news of the gunfight at the Flying W. He had been coldly informed by Sanchez that, unless he could supply the horses as they had originally agreed, he was of no further use to them. Sands was well aware what that meant. Nobody could watch their back forever and he knew too much to be allowed to ride away.

Reluctantly, he had agreed to lead the raid. Now here he was heading south with fifty head of prime saddle stock. Maybe we'll be lucky after all. Sure don't want to tangle wi' that Jordan fella again.

Bull scowled as he looked at the tracks. 'We're gainin' but not fast enough. Anybody got any ideas?'

'Waal,' Chester said hesitantly, 'mah guess is they're goin' to head for Evalde. Most o' the Comancheros hang out down that way. He pointed up ahead, 'see them small hills there? They run in a line 'bout ten miles due south. Folks headin' for Evalde generally go down the right hand side o' them, there's some ponds down that side hold water most o' the year. So, if we was to go hard down the left hand side we might just get ahead o' this bunch.'

'Right,' Bull kneed the grey into his stride, 'let's go.'

The horse herd drank greedily at the small pond. Sands looked back down their trail. Still nothing.

'Senor,' the scar-faced Comanchero grinned as he brought his pony alongside, 'You worry too much. There is no pursuit.'

'Maybe, but I don't trust Jordan, he's mean.'

'Ah … ,' the Mexican shrugged his shoulders expressively, 'he is only another rancher. So he got lucky once. It will not happen again.'

'Hope you're right,' Sands said tersely. 'Let's get them horses gathered up. Time we was movin' on.'

They were almost there now and the horses were blowing hard. Strung out, Bull in the lead on the big grey, they swept around the base of the last hill and pulled up. Nothing moved. The long valley was empty.

'Waal,' Bull looked closely at the ground, 'it's been used as a trail before, but there ain't nothin' been through here recent.'

Chester swallowed nervously. 'Still think Ah'm right, Boss.'

Bull nodded. 'I think you are too. Right,' he swept the area with a considering eye. 'You an' Jeff fort up in them rocks over there. Me, I'll hole up in that clump o' mesquite on this side. Clay,' he turned to Wallace, 'take the mounts back into them cottonwoods an' hold 'em there. Bring 'em up when you see me signal like this.' He waved his hat.

'Now,' he turned to Jeff and Chester, 'I want three saddles empty with the first three shots. Then it's open season on the others.'

Clay Wallace's face whitened. 'That's murder!'

'Mister!' Bull's voice was like ice. 'When I want your opinion I'll ask for it. Till then, get them horses under cover an' watch for my signal. Rustlin's a hangin' offence an' these fellas know the score.'

Wordlessly Clay picked up the reins and headed for the trees.

Jeff finished loading his Winchester and looked sideways at Bull. 'You were a bit hard on him, Boss,' he said mildly.

The big man scowled fiercely. 'Maybe I was, but this ain't no picnic. We make a mistake here an' we're buzzard bait. I know, I know … ,' he raised his hand as he saw the look on Jeff's face. 'He's a good guy, but he ain't used to our ways yet. He'll learn!' He'd better, he thought harshly.

The horse herd streamed through the pass and out into the long valley. By now Sands was beginning to believe they had got clear away. The grass was lush and the pace slowed as the horses snatched mouthfuls.

Bull settled himself and watched them approach. The distance shrank rapidly. Two hundred yards, one fifty, a hundred. Hell, that's Sands! Aiming coldly, he fired. The pony stumbled and the bullet meant for the ex-foreman's heart took him high in the shoulder.

'Damn!' Bull swore disgustedly and dropped the following rider with a clean shot. Beyond him Jeff and Chester had already emptied two saddles and were concentrating on the fifth rider who was fleeing back up the valley.

Gritting his teeth against the pain, Dave Sands spurred his pony and raced for the opening beyond the cottonwoods.

Jaw set, Clay sighted carefully and squeezed the trigger.

The sound of the shot caught Bull unawares and he wheeled quickly, just in time to see Sands topple tiredly out of the saddle. A wisp of smoke drifted away from the cottonwoods.

Bull waved his hat and Clay brought the horses out of the trees at the gallop. He raced them up to the rancher as Jeff and Chester dashed across to join them.

'Well now,' Bull vaulted into the saddle and looked carefully at Clay. 'That was Sands you dropped, wasn't it?' The gambler nodded wordlessly. 'Seems like I misjudged you.' He looked at the other two and grinned. 'Fellas, you're right handy with them Winchesters. Reckon that drag rider ain't gonna stop runnin' till he hits Mexico City! Alright, let's round up the herd. We'll load them fellas onto their mounts and take them in as well.'

It was night when they reached the ranch. Lights glimmered in the bunkhouse and the stable.

'Run the herd into the horse pasture,' Bull ordered. 'We'll check 'em over in the mornin'. I'll take them saddle mounts an' the bodies down to the barn.' Lord, he thought, I'm tired. Don't reckon I'll sleep much tonight though. Killin' men don't get no easier, no matter how often you do it.

'Evenin' Boss.' Joe crossed from the stable. 'You got the horses back then?' The swinging lantern cast weird shadows and the foreman glimpsed the long bundles lashed across the saddles. He held the light higher.

'What the … !'

'Save it, Joe.' Bull climbed down stiffly and stretched his aching muscles. 'The boys are all fine. This is what's left o' them rustlers, all bar one fella that's most likely still runnin'. Now gimme a hand wi' them bodies. We'll put 'em in the wagon overnight, an' take 'em in to Sheriff Dawson in the mornin'.'

Gritting his teeth Joe threw back the cover on the nearest body. 'Hell, this here's Sands!'

'Yeah.' Bull brushed past him with a bundle over his shoulder and lowered it carefully into the wagon. 'Seems like he didn't take the advice I gave him.'

They worked silently together, until all four bodies were laid out in the wagon and covered with a tarpaulin. Then Joe paused and rolled a cigarette. He tossed the sack of Bull Durham to his boss and lit up.

'Alright, what happened?'

Tersely, Bull outlined the day's events.

Joe whistled sharply. 'Whooeeh … them two black fellas are real salty ain't they?'

Bull nodded. 'You got to remember they was cavalry sergeants. If you make sergeant in any cavalry outfit you're good, but a black sergeant has to be twice as good. '

'What about Clay?' The foreman looked at him shrewdly.

The big man finished rolling a cigarette and stood for a moment deep in thought. 'Reckon I misjudged him. When the chips were down he did alright. This is a hard country Joe. You don't get but one lesson, so you make the most of it. Now, let's get the rigs off them horses an' we'll call it a night.'

Together the four filed into the cook shack and collected their cups, plates and eating irons. Old Tex scowled as he ladled out giant helpings of beef stew. 'You fellas think I'm runnin' a hotel round here?'

'Sorry 'bout this Tex.' Bull grinned at the feisty oldtimer. 'We'll try an' not let it happen again.'

'Shucks, I ain't complainin'. Them horse thieves got to be cleaned out. Just don't like to see good chuck spoilt. Biscuits an' a fresh pot o' coffee there. Dig in.'

Bull and Clay crossed the yard and headed towards the ranchhouse, the lantern in the rancher's hand throwing long wavering shadows ahead of them.

Inside, Bull lit the big table lamp, then blew out the lantern and hung it in the kitchen. He came back yawning widely.

'Reckon I'll get me some shuteye. You got any sense you'll do the same.'

'Don't feel like sleepin',' Clay muttered morosely.

'Clay!' There was an edge to Bull Jordan's voice. 'Now, you listen to me an' you listen good. Them fellas knew the score. I'll do the same thing tomorrow if I have to. This ain't back east, where everything is all nice an' legal. This here's Apache country. Man makes a mistake out here it's liable to be his last. Some day things'll be different, but that'll be a while yet. I know you feel bad about Sands. Don't. He'd been dead a long time, only he didn't know it. Now, I'm for bed. It's been a long day.' He paused in the doorway; 'Oh, and in case you're wonderin', I won't sleep any too good tonight either!' The door closed behind him.

CHAPTER 10

▼

Sheriff Dawson mopped his brow and peered into the wagon. 'You fellas at the Flyin' W into some new kind o' freightin'? 'Pears to me every time you bring this wagon to town it's full o' dead bodies!' He glowered at Bull and Clay sitting on the wagon seat, but the twinkle in his eye belied the scowl. 'An' what the hell you doin' with them Diamond D broncs?' He pointed to the four horses tied to the rear of the wagon.

'Sheriff,' Bull climbed down and faced the frowning lawman. 'I'm right sorry if we're givin' you any trouble. Them fellas run off fifty head o' my horses yesterday. Me, Clay here,' he gestured towards Wallace still holding the lines, 'an' a couple o' the boys, took out after 'em. Caught up wi' them down in the Saddle Hills. Five all told. T'other one got away.' He flipped the cover back. 'These hombres didn't.'

The sheriff's eyes bulged. 'Hell, that's Sands!'

'Yeah, I warned him to stay off Flyin' W range. Seems like he didn't hear too good.'

'An' them Diamond D horses?'

'That's what they was ridin'. Reckon they stole 'em. I would have returned 'em but Joe tells me old Donovan's a mean cuss. I wouldn't want to be caught herdin' his stolen horses across his ranch. He's liable to shoot first an' then ask questions!'

The sheriff nodded and grinned. 'Yeah, I reckon old Jack would at that. Same goes for that gal o' his. Naw, you did the right thing. Now, if you just drop them bodies off at Hen Wills's place, an' leave them horses at the livery

stable, that'll be fine. 'Fore you leave town gimme a statement just to keep
everything right.'

'Sheriff,' Bull paused and turned back from the wagon. 'Just one thing. I
didn't ask them fellas to give up. Clay here reckons I should've.'

Clay Wallace flushed with embarrassment and bit his lip. Sheriff Dawson
looked at the young Easterner sharply before he spoke.

'Mister Wallace, this here's mighty rough country. Lemme give you the
law as we play it. Next to bushwhackin' there ain't no worse crime out here
than stealin' a man's horse. A man afoot in this territory's dead unless he's
helluva lucky. If you'd brought them fellas in alive they'd have been hung.
That's the law. Now you just saved the territory all that expense. Mebbe some
day when things are a mite more civilised we'll see things different. Till then,
that's the way she lays.' He paused and rubbed his chin. 'You happy with
that?'

Clay nodded. 'Thanks sheriff, I reckon I've got some apologising to do.'

'Not to me you ain't.' Bull climbed onto the seat beside him. 'In your
boots reckon I'd have done the same. Anyways, let's roll. We got things to do.
Be seein' you sheriff.'

Dawson watched the wagon rumble off down the street. *That's a queer
mixture, an' they spark some too.* Shrugging his shoulders he turned on his
heel and entered the office.

'That's quite a story.' Captain McMillan leaned back in his chair and
studied the young man sitting in front of him. 'In fact, if it wasn't for the
evidence,' he indicated the saddlebags and papers on his desk, 'I'd have
difficulty in believing it. And that's all there was?' He looked sharply at John
again as he spoke.

'Yes Captain.' *I know what you're thinking and I cain't help you.* 'Sixteen
thousand dollars in gold, a wanted notice an' some newspaper reports.
Nothing else.'

'Mm,' the captain rubbed his chin reflectively. 'That's four thousand
dollars unaccounted for.' He paused. 'What do you think?'

John felt a slow anger beginning to build inside him. He controlled it
with an effort. 'Well, he'd been on the run for nigh on five years. Part of that
time at least he'd have Willis and Oxbow along with him. Then, I reckon
they must have holed up for a fair spell in Mexico. Three ex-cavalry troopers
wouldn't find it easy to hide on this side of the border. Not with them wanted
notices posted up. So they were likely down south. They'd need food, liquor
and fresh horses. Likely wimmen and gamblin' took a part of it. Anyway,

that's all guesswork. I don't know and to tell the truth I don't much care. I found sixteen thousand dollars and I brought it in. Don't rightly see what more I could've done.'

Captain McMillan's face reddened as he frowned at the papers in front of him. Then he looked up and smiled. A grim, tight-lipped smile. 'Mister Jordan, I seem to have offended you. I'm truly sorry. Call it the working of a suspicious military mind. No, you were quite right in everything you did, and I suspect, in your summing up as well. Your brother, Sergeant Jordan, has the same ability to evaluate a situation. How is he anyway?'

'We passed on the trail.' John said shortly. The captain's probing questions still rankled. 'Right now I reckon he's findin' out that trail herdin' can be as tough as patrollin'.'

McMillan looked at the young rancher shrewdly. 'Mister Jordan, your brother is one of my most valued officers. I'd give a great deal to undo the unfortunate impression I seem to have created. All I ask is that you make a statement of the events as you have described them and sign it. Just for the record. Oh, and the reward of five hundred dollars for the recovery of the gold. That is yours and I'm authorised to pay it.'

John sat for a moment deep in thought. 'You got any widows and orphans on the post?'

Captain McMillan looked surprised. 'Yes we do, as a matter of fact. Patrols take casualties fairly regularly. It's one of the facts of frontier life that our masters in Washington seem to forget. But why … ?' he broke off, comprehension dawning on his face. 'You mean …?'

'Use it for them,' John said tersely. He stood up. 'I want no part of it.'

A visibly embarrassed captain rose hastily to his feet. 'Mister Jordan,' he said awkwardly, 'This is a very generous gesture on your part and I shall see that it is so entered in our records.' His innate Southern charm came to the fore and he extended his hand. 'No hard feelings I hope?'

The young rancher grinned ruefully and took the proffered hand. 'None at all. Reckon if I'd been sittin' in that chair, an' a fella had come in with part of a gold shipment I'd have been a mite suspicious m'self. Now, if you'll just let me take care of m'horse then I'll come back and make that statement you want.'

Mcmillan stood at the window and watched the giant roan jog down the street. Good-looking horse, he thought admiringly. Who'd think he killed a man two days ago? He turned back to his desk and shouted for Lieutenant Jackson.

✭   ✭   ✭   ✭

Jim Jordan shifted tiredly in the the saddle and drew the back of his hand across his brow. Lord but it's hot. Gettin' towards the end o' September an' things are still just as dry as they were back in the summer. Waal, there's one thing, we ain't had no trouble an' that's a blessin'. Nigh on three weeks we been on the trail now. Stock's got used to travellin' an' they ain't as ready to spook as your Longhorns. Them Durham bulls steady things down. Same with old Dance. He just lopes along at the head o' the remuda. Reckon if Ellie-May was to put a halter on him she could lead him all the way to Arizona. Cattle are in fair shape. Pity 'bout them two late calves last week though. Sure would have liked to have taken them with us, but it just weren't possible. Still, that homesteader was right glad to take them. Said them Durham crosses were just what he needed to improve his stock.

He looked ahead to where Lance and Jake were riding point. Lance has settled in right well. Allus said, once you've herded cows you never forget it. An' that buckskin, he's shapin' up to be a real good cowpony.

His gaze shifted to Jake. Now there's somebody who's made good. He's taken to trail drivin' like a duck to water. Make a damned good trail boss some day. Handled them Injuns well too. Even Ma's beginnin' to see that he's good.

Looking back, he saw Sara-Jane perched on the driver's seat of the chuck wagon. Jaw set, lines clutched in both hands, she had eyes for nothing but the trail ahead. Her father grinned. One thing's for sure, she'll never make a teamster. He swung his mount to one side and waited patiently as the remuda eased through, Ellie-May and Rafe controlling the herd neatly. There's one outfit that's buttoned up a treat, he thought admiringly. Horses in each mornin' ready, an' the ropes up for the corral 'fore we finish breakfast.

The chuck wagon rolled past. Sara-Jane shot him a quick glance. 'Hi Pa.' There was a tenseness in her voice.

'How you makin' out?' Her father tried to keep the enquiry casual.

'Alright I guess.' She sawed at the reins.

'Take it easy.' Her father groaned inwardly. 'Give 'em a mite more slack an' old Paint an' Dusty'll trail along after the remuda just fine.'

'Sure Pa.'

'Where's Ma?'

'Back with Miguel an' the girls.'

'See you then.' He cantered the cowpony up alongside the accommodation wagon admiring Jerez's style as he did so. The old Mexican could handle a team alright.

Ma and the two little girls peered out. 'Hi Ma, them gals givin' you any trouble?' The twinkle in his eye belied the question.

'Shucks.' Ma looked much more relaxed. 'They're good gals. I been readin' to them.' She paused and closed the book. 'When you reckon we'll make the Concho?'

'Tonight I think. Ain't no herd up ahead, so the bedground will be clear.'

'Think John'll be there?'

Jim Jordan frowned. 'Hard to say. He's had time to get back. I told him to stay at the fort, but he might come out to the bedground. It's about ten miles downstream from the fort.'

Three hours later, just as the sun was dipping behind the western hills, the herd leaders topped the rise leading down to the Concho River. The long sweep of the bedground spread out before them. As Jake and Lance turned the herd round on itself the cattle came to a gradual halt, before lowering their heads and starting to graze. Ellie-May and Rafe drifted the remuda on beyond them, then swung round in a similar manoeuvre. Behind them the three wagons rolled down the slope and pulled up in line. Sara-Jane set the brake with exaggerated care and climbed down tiredly. Grinning widely, her father materialised at her elbow. 'Well done gal! Just you go an' help Ma an' I'll see to the team.'

'Thanks Pa.' Sara-Jane threw him a grateful glance before disappearing round to the rear of the chuck wagon. Ma had already dropped the tail-gate to the full length of its supporting chains, and now, assisted by the girls, was fitting the two wooden posts, which did duty as legs, underneath. Sara-Jane lifted down the dutch oven, followed by the giant coffee pot. Reaching under the wagon she hauled some dry pieces of wood out of the 'caboose', and passed them to her mother. Expertly, Ma laid the fire and put a match to it. Then, setting up the fire irons and the pot hooks, she placed the dutch oven in position. Gradually the camp began to take shape.

Miguel Jerez led the Clevelands clear of the wagons before he released them to graze. He was feeding them a handful of mesquite beans when Ellie-May cantered up on her palomino.

'Howdy, Miguel. You got that pair eatin' out o' your hand I see.'

'Si senorita. Tell me, how is Pancho?'

'Your mule? Settled into the remuda right good. Him an' big Dance are real friendly. They're grazin' down by the river just now.'

'That is good. I worry about him sometimes.'

Ellie-May smiled and kneed the palomino into motion. 'Don't you worry 'bout Pancho. He can take care of himself.' She cantered towards the chuck wagon.

Leading two of the big draught horses, the other four ambling along behind, Ben Turner lifted a hand in salute as she passed. Goodlookin' gal, he thought wistfully. Reminds me o' Peg.

Miguel watched him talk to the big horses for a moment before he released them. The little Mexican knew Ben's story. 'Senor, the night, it is time for thoughts.'

'Howdy Miguel. Guess you're right. Still, ain't no use lookin' back. We'd better head on in for our chuck. Miz Jordan can be right fierce if you ain't there on time.'

'Si, that is so.' They laughed quietly together and walked towards the wagons.

'Ma, that smells right good.' Lance took the loaded plate of beef and beans from his mother. Sara-Jane poured him a cup of coffee from the big pot. 'Thanks, I could eat a steer m'self.'

'Shucks.' Ma loaded another plate and handed it to Rafe Allen. 'Way you fellas eat beef there won't be no herd left by the time we hit Arizona!' The corners of her mouth twitched at the laughter which followed her riposte. 'Who's got the first trick tonight?' she queried.

Jim Jordan took a swig of coffee. 'Jake and Mike are down there now. Ellie-May's wi' the remuda.'

'Right.' Ma relaxed against the worktable. 'I'll have somethin' ready for them when they come in.'

Filling a plate with food she lowered herself beside her husband. They ate quietly for a spell, then Ma spoke.

'Reckon we'll see John at the fort tomorrow?'

Jim Jordan chewed thoughtfully for a moment. 'Reckon so,' he said finally. 'That's where we agreed to meet, and he likes everythin' just so. Remember, he was lookin' for signs o' water on that dry section, so that would take some time. Sure hope there's some there though.'

In spite of the warm evening Ma shivered. 'Jim, what happens if there ain't no water?'

Her husband frowned. 'Then we drive right through,' he said grimly. ''Course it'll be rough on the stock but there ain't nuthin' we can do about that. If Mustang Springs is dry we're in trouble. We'll fill the waterbarrels tomorrow. If the worst comes to the worst I'll try to save Dance and the bulls.'

Across from them Lance got up and dumped his dishes in the wash bucket. Faintly on the breeze came the sound of Ellie-May singing as she circled the remuda. Suddenly her brother tensed.

'Rider comin' in,' he announced.

'You sure?' Jim Jordan rose quickly and picked up his Winchester.

'Yeah, heard a shoe clink against stone. He's comin' down the slope.'

'Hullo the camp.'

'Glory be, that's John.' Ma scrambled hastily to her feet.

The outline of horse and rider loomed out of the darkness.

'Howdy, boy. You made it then?'

'Yeah Pa. Got in to the fort three days ago.'

'What about Mustang Springs?' Jim Jordan could contain himself no longer.

'Pa,' John swung down off Red and turned to face his father. 'The Springs are dry.'

CHAPTER 11

▼

Jim Jordan's face whitened under its tan. 'That's it then,' he muttered grimly to himself.

'No it ain't, Pa.' John's clipped tones cut across his father's thoughts. 'I found water some ten, fifteen miles south o' the Springs. Reckon it'll see us through!'

Swiftly he outlined the events that had taken place since he last saw them. The attack by the cougar, and his subsequent rescue of the outlaw Henry, alias Mace. Then the trip to the hideout and the ex-sergeant's fanatical determination to keep him there at all costs. The killing of Henry, by Red. Finally, his discovery of the gold, the damming of the spring and the fight at the stage station.

Ma looked the big gelding standing quietly at the rim of the firelight. 'Allus knew that horse was a killer,' she muttered darkly.

'Ma, that ain't fair,' Jim Jordan protested. 'Red saved John's life.' He swung back to his son. 'You sure he ain't turned outlaw?' he queried anxiously. 'Bull sets a lot o' store by that cayuse.'

John paused for a moment. 'Pa, I just don't know. Before this happened him an' me were gettin' along fine. Now I ain't sure no more. Don't reckon we'll know till we get him back to Bull.'

He looked at Lance. 'Something else I got to tell you. Lootenant Jackson and a patrol are comin' with us as far as the spring. Jackson told me 'fore I saddled up this mornin'. Guess Captain McMillan wants to be sure I'm tellin' the truth,' he added bitterly.

Lance grinned. 'It ain't like that at all, John. McMillan's a straight up guy, he'll believe you. Only thing is, the Treasury boys come into this, it bein' their gold. You know what them fellas are like, they want everything signed an' sealed. Anyway, I got second trick wi' the herd tonight. See you in the mornin'.' He swung into his saddle and cantered off followed by Andy Boone.

The small cavalry patrol, complete with pack mule, waited patiently outside the fort. Faintly on the morning breeze came the bawl of cattle on the move, then the cambered top of the accommodation wagon appeared over the rise.

Lieutenant Jackson turned in his saddle and looked at the four troopers lined up beside him.

'All set then?' They nodded. 'Right, we'll swing in behind the horse herd and follow on there. Any of you see Sergeant Jordan, give me a call. Like to have a word with him.'

The accommodation wagon rolled past, the two Clevelands highstepping under Miguel's careful guidance. That's an old Army ambulance wagon. Wonder where they picked it up? Jackson waved to Sarah and Mary peering out of the windows. They waved back, smiling self-consciously.

Next came the chuck wagon with Sara-Jane on the driving seat, her gaze fixed on the wagon ahead. Good looking girl, he thought idly. Seems a shame she's got to do a teamster's job. Damn, this country sure is hard on women.

The lieutenant watched the Studebaker lumbering towards him, the six big horses hauling it easily. He remembered Ben Turner from his fort days. Good outfit. Hope he makes it where he's going.

Now the first of the cattle were drifting past and he signalled to Lance, who was riding point. The tall sergeant beckoned and Jackson cantered up beside him.

'Howdy lootenant,' Lance eased an inquisitive bull back into the herd. 'You fancy signin' on for the drive?'

Jackson laughed. 'No thanks. Think I'll stick to cavalry patrolling. Alright if we drop in behind the horse herd?'

'Sure. Just watch out for m'sister, Ellie-May. She can be right sharp at times.'

The lieutenant laughed and swung away as the remuda clattered past. Nice looking horseflesh, he thought approvingly. The Jordans know their job. Wonder why the sergeant warned me about his sister?

A slim rider on a stocky black cowpony cantered up the side of the horse herd and gave the waiting patrol a hard look. Jackson waved and the rider swung towards him.

'Howdy, I'm Lootenant Jackson. Alright if we drop in behind the remuda?'

'Sure, Lance told me that's what you aimed to do. Don't get too close else you'll push them broncs up into the cattle. Oh, I'm Ellie-May.'

The lieutenant's jaw dropped. 'You're Ellie-May!' he stammered, acutely aware of the smothered laughter from the troopers behind him.

'Yeah, that's right.' Ellie-May looked at him coldly. 'What's eatin' you? Ain't they got gals back east?'

Jackson flushed. 'Yes,' he replied shortly, 'but they don't wear Levis, or guns, and they don't ride straddle!'

'Yeah?' Ellie-May's tone was biting. 'I'd look real cute lopin' around the remuda side-saddle an' wearin' a dress! Now, I got work to do. Just don't get too close.' She kneed her mount into motion and cantered away.

Lieutenant Jackson felt his face burning. 'Right,' he barked, turning to the grinning troopers. 'You heard the lady. Move out, but don't get too close.'

The patrol swung onto the trail and settled in behind the remuda.

Joe Ogilvy bunched the loose horses ahead of him and turned them neatly up the slope. He eyed the small ranch headquarters appraisingly. Old Jack Donovan knew what he was doin' when he built the Diamond D. Place is like a fort. An' you got to come at it uphill across open ground. Three times, accordin' to my reckonin', he's stood off Apaches in there. 'Course them four old-timers he's got as a crew are as salty as he is. As for that gal o' his, she's got to be tough to live out here. Sure hope he's got them big dogs o' his tied up. He shivered. Wonder if it's true that he's trained 'em to hunt Apaches?

A man appeared from one of the buildings, followed by two huge Irish wolfhounds. Sighting the oncoming horses the dogs bayed in unison, a deep savage sound, like rolling thunder. As they surged forward the man shouted harshly and motioned them back. Reluctantly, their baying fell to a rumble and they slunk in behind him.

Ogilvy swore to himself. Hell, imagine gettin' caught afoot wi' that pair. You wouldn't last ten seconds!

He hazed the horses into the yard and, leaning over, closed the gate behind him.

'A'right, deppity.' Donovan's harsh voice cut across his thoughts. 'Quit gawpin' an' tell me where ye found my hawses? An' how come there's one missin'?'

In a territory noted for its hard men, fifty-four year old Jack Donovan was a legend. Somebody had once said that he was all whang leather, whipcord and rattlesnake juice, and the description had stuck.

It was rumoured that he had been 'most everywhere and done everything. Certainly he'd ridden with John Chisum and Shanghai Pierce, when they were opening up the great cattle trails. It was also known that he'd fought in the Mexican war of '48 and had scouted for General Wingate against the Navajos.

Looking down at the five foot nine, lean, bow-legged old cattleman, Ogilvy could well believe it. The man appeared to be indestructible.

'Uh … oh yeah. Waal, you'll have to take that up wi' that fella Jordan. That's your new neighbour at the Flyin' W. Seems a band o' Comancheros ridin' your horses, raided his horse herd. Got away wi' nigh on fifty head. Anyways, Jordan an' his boys took out after 'em an' got the horses back. Killed four o' the Comancheros.' He grinned. 'Reckon the other fella's still runnin'.'

'Hmph.' Donovan scowled. 'How come this fella Jordan didn't bring them hawses back himself?'

'Waal,' Joe said cautiously, 'he figgered if you caught him crossin' your land with your horses, you might just shoot first an' then ask questions.'

The rancher showed his teeth in a thin-lipped mirthless smile. 'Damned right I would! Tell you what deppity, light down an' have a cup o' coffee. Like to hear more about this new neighbour o' mine.'

Ogilvy looked dubiously at the giant dogs. They crouched, watching him intently and occasionally rumbling deep in their throats. 'You sure they're alright?'

'The dawgs? Hell yes! Still, if you ain't happy … g'wan.' He waved his arm and shouted at the wolfhounds. They got up and, still rumbling, stalked, stiff-legged, into the barn.

Joe dismounted cautiously and, tying his mount to the rail, followed Donovan into the ranch kitchen. He looked about him curiously. This was the first time he'd ever been inside the Diamond D ranchhouse.

The kitchen was comfortably furnished and neat. Everything about it, from the chequered cloth on the big deal table in the centre of the room, to the brightly covered cushions nestling in the two armchairs, showed a feminine touch. At the big stove a tall dark-haired young woman was stirring something in a pot. She turned and smiled pleasantly.

'Ann, this here's Deppity Ogilvy from Dorando. He's just brung in four o' them hawses that was rustled. Seems like we got our new neighbour to thank for gettin' them back. Thought mebbe you could rustle up a cup o' coffee. Like to hear more about this fella Jordan.'

Ann Donovan laughed. 'Sure Pa. Coffee and a piece of pie comin' right up. Take a seat, Mister Ogilvy.'

'Thanks.' Ogilvy removed his hat and sank gratefully into the big chair. He watched as she busied herself with the coffee pot.

Tall, with dark wavy hair and a superb figure, Ann Donovan was the subject of much interest and speculation by all the unattached males on the surrounding ranches. However, she seemed supremely indifferent to all their blandishments and perfectly content to continue running her father's house, as she had done since her mother's death seven years before. Privately, Ogilvy wondered how much of this was due to her feisty parent. Cain't say I'd care to come callin' if I knew he was around. An' them dogs! He shivered involuntarily.

'You alright?' He came to with a start to find his hostess regarding him curiously.

'Yeah.' He grinned shamefacedly. 'Just thinkin' 'bout them dogs. They scare me.'

'Shucks,' Jack Donovan gestured impatiently. 'Nuthin' wrong wi' them dawgs. Best guard dawgs in the whole dang territory.'

Placing coffee and pie on the table, Ann Donovan motioned to her father and the deputy to join her.

'A'right, deppity.' Donovan took a swig of his coffee and looked keenly at Ogilvy. 'This fella Jordan, how does he stack up?'

'Waal,' Joe thought for a moment. 'I reckon he's a hard man. Sure wouldn't like to go up against him. Twice he's brought that wagon o' his in wi' dead Comancheros stacked up in it like cordwood.' He paused and chewed on a mouthful of pie.

Donovan shrugged. 'You got enough men and rifles that ain't no big deal.'

Ogilvy's mouth tightened. 'You know that big Dane that rides for the Flyin' W?'

'Lindstrom? Sure. He's a good man.'

'Waal, Lindstrom was sidin' Jordan when five Comancheros rode in. One o' them was the Navajo Kid.'

'The Navajo Kid, hey.' Keen interest showed in Donovan's face. 'I hear he's fast.'

'Was,' the deputy corrected grimly. 'Accordin' to Lindstrom, the Kid drew on Jordan an' Jordan killed him. Lindstrom knifed the boss man, big scar-faced fella name o' Casner; Charlie Casner. He was old Sanchez's segundo. Come to think of it,' he added reflectively, 'I never knew Lindstrom was that good wi' a knife. Then Miz Jordan, that's Jordan's mother, she starts shootin' from the house. Wings another fella, an' the rest just give up.'

'Salty lady, hey.' The rancher rubbed his chin. 'Where does she fit in?'

'She's the new owner. 'Pears the Wilsons brought her up an' they left the Flyin' W to her. Now she's gone back to Texas an' her son's runnin' the outfit. 'Course she's comin' back wi' the rest o' the family an' a trail herd o' breedin' stock.' Ogilvy drained his cup and stood up. 'Thanks Miss Donovan, that was real nice, but I got to be ridin'.'

Ann Donovan smiled. 'Glad you enjoyed it.' She looked thoughtful. 'This Jordan, what's he like?'

The deputy grinned. 'Big fella, six feet three or four I guess. Weight mebbe two hundred pounds. Age, 'bout thirty I'd say.' His eyes twinkled. 'That answer your question?'

She coloured and laughed. 'Just curious.'

Her father rose from his chair. 'Don't hold wi' wimmen an' guns,' he said tetchily. 'Never know when they're gonna start blastin' an' they cain't shoot worth a damn.'

'Yeah?' Joe paused in the doorway. 'Don't think Jack Anderson an' his brother Clint would agree with you.'

'Hey.' There was a faraway look in Jack Donovan's eyes. 'I remember them. Dutch van Doren useta ride wi' them. Salty bunch,' he added thoughtfully.

'That's right. They were. Trouble was they tried to hold up Miz Jordan an' her two daughters. When the smoke cleared away van Doren was dead, an' both the Andersons was shot up bad. They're in the pen in Austin now.'

'What about Miz Jordan an' her daughters?' Ann Donovan queried anxiously.

'Not a scratch. Adios miss, an' thanks again.'

CHAPTER 12

▼

Big Red breasted the long slope, his ears pricked and the scent of water in his nostrils. John Jordan's eyes widened as he surveyed the scene in the small valley below. The pent-up water had backed up from the sandstone cliff, through the trees and was now spread across the valley.

Didn't expect it to be this big already, he thought as he drew rein. Saves us cuttin' a way in for the stock though. They can water out here.

'Well now,' Lieutenant Jackson drew his big cavalry mount to a halt. 'Who'd have thought it.' He motioned to the lone trooper alongside him. Together they rode their horses down to the edge of the pond and let them drink their fill. Behind them they could hear the bawling of the approaching herd. 'Reckon we can find the grave alright?'

'Guess so.' John dismounted and tied Red to a convenient tree. He unbuckled his gunbelt and hung it on the saddle horn. Then he pulled off his boots. The lieutenant looked at him with narrowed eyes. 'Are you going to wade in?' he demanded.

'Yeah.' John pulled his shirt over his head. 'I ain't takin' Red back in there. Might just be enough to turn him into an outlaw … a killer; all the memories.' He eased out of his Levis.

Jackson stared at the tall athletic body. Four long white scars running from the shoulder down the right arm caught his eye. 'How did you come by these?' he queried.

'Cougar.' John was rummaging in his saddlebags. He pulled out a Comanche breechclout and tied it round his waist. 'Thought he was dead and he wasn't. Good lesson to learn.' Knife in hand, he started into the shallow water.

'What happened?' The lieutenant urged his horse after the tall figure.

'Nothin' much.' John ploughed stolidly ahead. 'Managed to get my knife into him an' that was it.'

They had reached the edge of the trees. 'Go easy along here.' John splashed his way into the undergrowth. 'This trail's real narrow.' Jackson nodded and urged his reluctant mount forward.

Suddenly they were in the clearing. Jackson looked about him keenly. Yes, there was the lean-to just as young Jordan had described it.

John turned towards the trees higher up, and the lieutenant swung his horse after him. 'This is where I buried him,' John gestured up the slope. 'Looks like we got here just in time.' He splashed ahead.

Water was already within a couple of yards of the crude cross when they reached the grave. Dismounting, Jackson kept a tight hold of his already nervous mount.

Levering with his knife, John removed the layer of turf and then brushed away the soil covering the blanket wrapped corpse. Easing back the sheet he straightened up.

Jackson gagged involuntarily. His horse drew back snorting, the smell of death strong in its nostrils.

'Ain't pretty is it?' John said quietly. 'Now you see why I ain't goin' to bring Red in here.'

The lieutenant fought the rising bile in his throat. Three years of frontier fighting had hardened him, but the wreckage of a human being lying there was the worst he had ever seen. The man's body had been trampled to a pulp, though the face was relatively unmarked.

'Strange that his face is hardly touched,' he commented unfolding the reward notice.

John Jordan frowned. 'Yeah. Thought about that myself. Mebbe he tried to save his eyes, or mebbe he fell forward at the beginning. Guess we'll never know. Anyway, you satisfied?'

'Yes.' Jackson took a final look at the notice before folding it and returning it to his pocket. 'There's enough resemblance to satisfy me, and I'd say so at an inquiry. Cover him up and let's get out of here.'

The herd had spread out and begun to graze on the slopes of the valley, while the remuda jostled at the water's edge slaking their thirst. They lifted dripping muzzles for a moment, watching curiously as John and the mounted lieutenant splashed their way across the shallow sheet of water.

Jake Larsen waited until his friend had rubbed himself down with his shirt.

'Alright?'

John nodded. 'Sure, ' he said tersely.

Jake looked at him and shrugged. Turning in the saddle he waved to Andy and Mike. They wove their way through the cattle and paused, looking at him inquiringly.

'We'll cold camp here tonight. No fires, I ain't takin' no chances. Tell young Rafe I want to see him when he's got the remuda settled. Come first light we move out travellin' west. We still got thirty odd miles to go 'fore we hit the Pecos an' I aim to push the stock hard. Either o' you want to say anything?'

They shook their heads.

'Right. Let the stock drink as much as they want, then bed 'em down on the top o' the rise. John,' he twisted in his saddle, 'I reckon you an' me'll take the first trick tonight. That alright wi' you?'

'Sure.' John grinned to himself. This was a different Jake. Pa was right to make him segundo, he feels part of the family now. 'I was just wonderin' what the lootenant plans to do?'

'Well,' Jackson thought for a moment. 'Seems like I owe you something, so me and Jorgensen here will be happy to fit in with whatever Mister Larsen has in mind. If it's alright with him we'll take our turn night herding.'

Jake coughed to hide his embarrassment. It was the first time anyone had called him Mister Larsen! 'Why sure lootenant, an' I'm right obliged, we bein' shorthanded splittin' up like we did.'

He looked at the sun beginning to slant down towards the west. 'I'll take a swing round the herd. Reckon if we can get the stock bedded down the boys can have a bite o' that chuck Miz Jordan packed for us.' Swinging his mount round he cantered away.

Ellie-May was in a black mood. Since yesterday morning she had been riding escort on the wagons with Pa, Lance, and the three troopers, while Rafe Allen headed away south with her beloved remuda. 'It ain't fair,' she muttered rebelliously as she scowled at her father riding unconcernedly ahead. I was in charge o' the remuda an' it should have been me that went. Pa had no right to stop me just 'cause it's a cold camp.

Sensing she was being watched, Ellie-May turned quickly in the saddle and saw Sara-Jane smiling wickedly at her from the high seat of the chuck wagon. Damn, she raged furiously, now she'll needle me that I ain't good enough to do a man's job, an' I know I can. Just 'cause it means sleepin' in the open, Pa says no!

Her temper communicated itself to the palomino and the high-spirited animal jinked sideways nervously. Ellie-May got her emotions under control and, talking softly, soothed the edgy horse.

Jim Jordan heard the splutter of hooves and reined in frowning. He waited until his elder daughter came up alongside him.

'Ellie-May,' he began heavily, 'quit takin' your temper out on Goldie. He's purty near pure bred an' high strung as well. Sort o' horse you should be gentlin' all the time. Some day you could be in a mess o' trouble an' you'll need him to do what you want without spookin' on you.'

'Pa, I ain't …'

'You just hush up and listen to me Ellie-May!' His daughter subsided sullenly. When Pa spoke like that even Ma listened. 'You got an ugly temper an' you got it from me.' He saw the surprised look on Ellie-May's face and went on, 'I was just like you when I was young. Always gettin' fired up with my folks. Wouldn't listen to good advice. Now you got a chance to profit from my mistakes so listen good. That there trip to the spring that John found is goin' to be tough. The boys will be sleepin' rough an' eatin' cold chuck. They're gonna be pushin' the stock hard to catch up with us, but I reckon they'll have two nights at least on their own. I know you can do a man's job, but you'd have been the only woman along, an' Jake has enough to worry about without seein' that the boys mind their manners. Here it's different. You ain't the only woman, an' you sleep in the wagon. Means you ain't allus in their hair, an' they can cuss without lookin' over their shoulder all the time. Now do you understand?'

Ellie-May swallowed nervously. 'Yeah Pa, an' I'm real sorry for actin' up like I did.'

Her father grinned. 'Forget it. We all got to learn.' He leaned over and patted the palomino's neck. 'Just go easy with Goldie, it ain't his fault. Now, if you like, ease up an' side Miguel. I'll ride next to Sara-Jane an' keep her outa your hair.'

Ellie-May laughed. 'You don't miss much, Pa. ' She lifted Goldie into a canter and moved ahead.

Jim Jordan grinned to himself. Cain't afford to when you're raisin' a family. He nudged the big Cleveland up alongside the chuck wagon.

'Howdy, Pa.' Sara-Jane grinned at him from the driver's seat.

She's gettin' better, her father thought approvingly. At least she don't saw at the lines no more.

'Hi Sara-Jane. How's the team makin' out?'

'They seem alright. We got enough water in the barrels for tonight, tomorrow mornin' an' noon.'

'Yeah.' Jim Jordan rubbed his chin. 'Reckon we'll hit Horsehead Crossing by nightfall tomorrow. Once we're there we're alright. Don't know if Jake'll catch us up before then, but my guess is he'll bust a gut tryin'. Anyway, we're makin' pretty fair time, so he might just have his work cut out.'

'You like Jake, don't you, Pa?'

'Yeah.' Her father stared into the distance. 'We owe Jake an' his father a lot. Hadn't been for them we likely wouldn't have John now. Some day Jake will make a real good foreman, maybe even a rancher, an' I aim to be around when it happens.'

The cattle bawled fitfully. They were being hustled on by the riders and they didn't like it. Up front the lead herd bull drifted to the left round a clump of mesquite. The black cowpony lengthened its stride to cut him off and Jake's quirt cracked menacingly. Sullenly, the bull swung back into the herd.

The pace slackened as they breasted a long rise and the cattle snatched mouthfuls of mesquite beans. Thankfully, Jake mopped his brow and slowed his mount to a walk. That was close. Good thing the grazin's still damp an' they ain't been workin' up a thirst. If they was Longhorns they'd have been runnin' yet, he thought wryly.

Across the herd John waved and pointed. Waal, there's the Horsehead trail 'bout a mile ahead. Now we can let them settle down an' drift easy. He looked back and nodded approvingly when he saw that Rafe had the remuda bunched close behind. Good youngster that. Pity about Ellie-May though, she sure would have liked to be here. Grinning to himself, he remembered the look of fury on the tall girl's face, when Jim Jordan had told her flatly that she would be staying with the wagons.

A thought struck him. Turning in his saddle he beckoned to Andy Boone, riding swing behind him. The elderly rider ranged up alongside. 'Andy, you mind takin' my place for a spell while I drop back an' have a word wi' the lootenant.'

Andy Boone nodded. Over the past weeks he'd grown to like and respect Jake. There was something about the way the young half-breed went about his work, the calm way he accepted responsibility, that made the cowhand think back nostalgically to his own youth and what might have been. He watched as Jake swung round the rear of the herd towards Jackson who was keeping an eye on the drag.

'Lootenant, we're just about to strike the trail an' head west. Don't rightly know if the wagons are ahead of us, though it seems likely. You mind coverin' swing on this side while I check back for sign?'

'Why sure. What about the drag though?'

'It'll be fine till I get back. Ain't plannin' to be all that long.'

'Sure.' Don Jackson moved off up the side of the herd.

Behind him, Jake swung his pony to one side and watched the remuda stream past. He knew that Jim Jordan had taken a chance in splitting the outfit and sending the stock south to water at the spring. It was Comanche and Lipan country; they could have been jumped anywhere. But it had paid off. They were back on the trail without loss, and, with luck, would hit the Pecos tomorrow. A glow of pride spread through Jake as he turned onto the trail and headed east.

Two hundred yards on, the trail crossed a sandy draw and he found what he was looking for. The rutted wheeltracks of three wagons showed plainly in the sand. There was something else, and he looked more closely. Unshod ponies had crossed the draw after the passage of the wagons. The back of Jake's neck tingled as he swept the surrounding country with a practised eye. Headed southwest. Wonder how many? Is it just a small raidin' party, or is it a bunch o' young bucks painted up an' loaded for bear?

He came to a sudden decision. I'll trail them till I figger out how many an' where they're headin', then I'll cut an' head for the herd. He kneed his mount forward.

The trail led southwest for a mile, until it struck the broad swathe where the herd had passed. Jake cast about until he found the unshod hoofprints on the other side. They were angling west now and he nodded, satisfied. Four ponies, two mebbe carryin' double. Seen our tracks an' they're curious. Ragtag huntin' party I reckon. Mebbe they've tried their luck already an' lost mounts. They'll trail along just out o' sight, then hit us early mornin'. Horses'll be what they're after. Could cause us trouble, but I don't reckon they'll push it if we're ready. Time I was headin' back to warn the boys. Urging his mount into a gallop he headed after the herd.

CHAPTER 13

▼

The campfire glowed red in the dusk. Ma Jordan finished scouring the last dish with sand and passed it to her younger daughter. Wiping the tin container clean, Sara-Jane placed it with the others in the chuck box.

'Sure will be glad when we can use water for washin' again.'

'Yeah, I know.' Ma was tired and feeling low. 'Sometimes wish I'd never heard o' the Flyin' W!'

Sara-Jane looked at her mother anxiously. 'Ma, that ain't like you at all. Never heard you talk like this before. You sure you ain't sickenin' for somethin'?'

Ma shook her head as she raised the lid of the chuck box and secured it. 'I'm fine. Reckon somebody walked over my grave, that's all.' Her husband appeared round the end of the wagon. 'Pa, you reckon we'll make the Pecos tomorrow?'

Jim Jordan thought for a moment. 'Yeah, 'bout evenin' I guess. Goin to be a tight squeeze but I reckon we got just enough water in the barrels for the teams.'

'You reckon the boys are makin' out alright?'

Jim frowned. 'Jake'll be doin' fine,' he said pointedly. Ma bit her lip in vexation at her blunder. 'He's the best segundo I've seen yet. His plan was to start real early from the spring this mornin' an' push the stock hard while the grazin' was damp. Once it dries out an' he cuts our trail, then he'll have to go easy. Let them take their time. These ain't wild stock. The bulls are pure Durham, an' the cows are second crosses, so they cain't take drought like Longhorns. No,' he turned away, 'I ain't worried. Reckon they're cold campin' 'bout fourteen, fifteen miles back. Likely catch us 'round midday tomorrow.'

'Jim.'

Her husband turned back. 'Yeah?'

'I'm sorry for what I said just now. I didn't mean nuthin'.'

'Mary-Lou.' Ma stiffened. When Jim called her that he was about to say something serious. 'Jake's old man died for this family. Don't you ever forget that. An' Jake would do the same. Far as I'm concerned he's family!'

Frowning, he strode away.

His wife watched him disappear into the darkness. She sighed heavily and became aware of Sara-Jane standing silently by the wagon. 'Waal,' she demanded sharply, 'you heard what your pa said. You think I'm wrong too?'

'Ma,' Sara-Jane searched hesitantly for the right words. 'Jake's a good man. It ain't his fault he's half Comanche.' Her voice became stronger. 'Pa's right. He is family an' he's earned his place. I'm goin' to bed now, Ma. 'Pears to me you got some thinkin' to do. 'Night now.' She vanished into the darkness.

Left alone, Ma stood thinking deeply. Ain't often Jim takes a stand, so when he does I got to listen. He's right, Jake is family. Trouble is when I look at him I see … no! She shook her head determinedly. Hannah said I'd got to stop thinkin' like that. Somehow I got to treat Jake right. Tiredly she walked towards the accommodation wagon.

Dawn was still some way off. Big Red blew through his nostrils and pawed the ground. Rifle in hand John Jordan watched him closely. The giant gelding's unease had communicated itself to the other two horses. All three were now staring towards the south. A faint movement caught the young rancher's eye and he turned quickly. Jake was awake and watching intently.

'Injuns?'

John shrugged. 'Maybe. Could be the bunch you trailed yesterday. You reckoned they were short o' mounts. Means they could be gettin' ready to try for the remuda. Shake out the lootenant.'

Lieutenant Jackson came awake quickly. John explained what happening. 'Could be nothin' but I wouldn't bet on it. The three of us'll check it out.'

Jake was already in the saddle. 'I'll warn the boys. If it is a raid an' they get through us, then it'll be up to Andy an' the others.' He rode off quietly towards the herd.

The lieutenant and John swung into their saddles. 'Reckon if it is that bunch an' they're a huntin' party like Jake figgers, then they might not push a charge all the way. Let's hope not.'

They cantered slowly south waiting for Jake to catch up. John pointed ahead. 'If they come, it'll be across that grass there an' they'll be comin' fast. It's the way I'd come if I was goin' to hit the remuda.' He looked about appraisingly as Jake rode up.

'We'll wait here behind them cottonwoods. If they come we'll hit them from the flank. They'll be meanin' to cut a piece o' the remuda an' they won't be expectin' us here. That alright with you, Jake?'

Jake grinned. 'Sure.'

'Lootenant, you got any better ideas?'

Don Jackson laughed. 'I've been listening to your brother for the last three years, I might as well listen to you now. Go ahead, I'll back your play.'

John smiled. 'Right. Jake reckons two o' their mounts could be carryin' double. I want every pony down at the first pass. What sort o' long gun you got?'

'Spencer carbine. Repeater.'

'That's fine. Me an' Jake's got Winchesters. I hate killin' ponies but there ain't no other way.'

Jackson looked at him. 'What then?'

'We pull back an' wait. If they're just huntin', chances are they'll walk away. If not, we kill 'em. Jake, how are things your end?'

'I got the boys rousin' out the stock right now. At least if they get spooked they'll be runnin' the right way!'

John grinned. 'Jake, that's right good thinkin'.'

They drew their mounts into the cottonwoods and checked their rifles. Jackson's mouth felt dry. He swallowed nervously. Why do I always feel like this before a fight? Look at those two sitting there quietly. But then I guess they've seen it from both sides!

Time passed slowly. It was light now. Jackson focused on the distant dark line of mesquite. Must be nearly a mile, he thought idly. What makes those two so sure? Is it some sixth sense they've picked up from the Comanches?

John leaned forward. 'Here they come.'

Moving fast, four ponies emerged from the distant scrub. 'Lipans I reckon,' Jake grunted. 'Two o' their mounts carryin' double like I figgered.'

Jackson grinned. 'I'll take your word for it.' They waited tensely.

The Indians were halfway across the grassland. 'Now!' John urged Red into his stride.

The giant roan bulleted down the slope and across the grass, Jake's black gelding and the big cavalry horse strung out behind him. Diagonally they closed on the racing ponies. Jackson's scalp prickled as the high Comanche yell drifted back on the morning breeze.

Sighting carefully, John triggered the Winchester. The foremost pony, a rangy sorrel, turned a somersault and came down heavily, pinning his rider. Twisting in his saddle John shot again. A grey pony, carrying two Indians, slowed to a stop and fell sideways. The two Lipans forted up behind it. Sweating, John looked back. Jake had dropped one of the remaining ponies and Lieutenant Jackson the other.

Talking quietly he eased Red down to a canter and let the others catch up.

They came up fast and John let Red stretch himself again.

Together they reined in on the far side of the grass plain. 'Well,' Jackson's face was flushed. 'That was neat. What next?'

'We wait,' John said carefully, loading more rounds into the Winchester, 'until they make up their minds whether they want to hunt or fight.'

The tense moments dragged on. Flies buzzed in the early morning sun while the horses shook their heads and stamped impatiently.

There was movement behind the dead ponies. One of the Indians rose cautiously and looked towards them.

'Just testin' us,' Jake grunted. John nodded. They listened intently.

'What … ' Jackson began; John held up his hand for silence. Another Indian rose. Between them they rolled the dead sorrel over and helped its rider to his feet. The remaining three braves rose together.

Jake and John looked at each other and grinned.

'No singin' an' no chantin'.' Jake watched the defeated group head south, their injured comrade supported among them. 'Lipans for sure. Looks like we pulled it off.'

'What about the singing?' Jackson queried.

'Well now,' John watched the Lipans disappear into the distance. 'If they'd been singin' or chantin' a challenge then we'd a fight on our hands.'

'But surely we could have just ridden away and left them?'

Jake looked at him carefully. 'Lootenant, it ain't as easy as that. Injuns went about on foot for a long time before they had horses. These fellas,' he waved towards the horizon where the Lipans had just disappeared, 'are some o' the best foot runners you'll ever see. We cain't push the herd that fast an' they could have just hung on our flanks an' given us a mess o' trouble. As it is, I reckon they've had enough. Be thankful they wasn't Comanches or Kiowas. Anyway,' he added, neck reining the black gelding round, 'time we was movin' 'fore the boys start worryin'.' Swinging onto the trail they cantered after the herd.

Jim Jordan kneed the Cleveland in the belly and tightened the cinch again. The big horse grunted and nipped playfully at his sleeve. Grinning, the rancher swung up into the saddle. He patted the big horse affectionately. 'Bob, you just listen to me. You're gettin' kinda old for such foolishness.'

He looked at the wagons. Every team was hitched up and ready to roll. This is a good outfit, he thought. They know their job without bein' told. Wonder how Jake's makin' out?

Faintly downwind came the bawl of hard-driven, thirsty cattle. Glory be, Jake's caught up with us. Reckon the herd's got the scent of water. Might as well let them go through.

He cantered across to the waiting wagons. 'Folks, sounds like the herd is right close behind us. Reckon Jake'll be keen to get them to water so we'll let them go through.'

Everybody nodded. He turned to the assembled riders. 'Lance, you an' me'll drop into our places wi' the herd. Ellie-May, you take up wi' the remuda. Fellas,' he grinned at the three troopers, 'it ain't my business to tell you what to do, but I reckon that the lootenant'll be droppin' back to join up wi' you.'

They nodded in unison.

The remuda gathered at the water's edge, bickering amongst themselves as they drank. Beyond them the herd had spread out and were already grazing their way along the bedground. Lieutenant Jackson, Jim Jordan and Jake lounged in their saddles looking across the Pecos. To the west the sun was just beginning to drop behind the Guadalupe Mountains. From the wagons came the familiar sound and smell of the camp being set up for the night.

'Jake,' Jim glanced at the serious young man, 'That was a neat piece o' work this mornin'. 'Pears to me you did right well. You too lootenant. I'm beholden to you.'

Jackson laughed. 'I just made up the numbers. Jake and John did all the brainwork.'

The rancher looked at him shrewdly. 'Lootenant, don't you go sellin' yourself short. You could have been one o' them starchy fellas an' pulled rank. But you got brains an' you didn't.'

Jackson nodded, suddenly serious. 'Your son, Lance, straightened me out on that point a long time ago. I owe him a lot, including my life. Anyway,' he grinned again, 'I can always say I've heard the Comanche war whoop from the other side!'

Jim Jordan looked questioningly at Jake, who flushed. 'John an' me, we got all fired up, an' we was whoopin' an' hollerin' comin' down the slope.'

The rancher chuckled and slapped his thigh. 'Betcha them Lipans wondered what was comin' at 'em!' He turned to the young lieutenant. 'Suppose you an' your boys'll be headin' back now?'

'Yes. John showed me the body and it was Henry alright. So that closes the case. Don't suppose we'll ever know what happened to the other two. Most likely he killed them and buried the bodies.'

'Yeah.' Jim Jordan looked again at the river. 'Horsehead Crossing. Just over four weeks, we're makin' fair time. Now we got the stretch to El Paso. We'll head up the east bank o' the river here, an' cross above Pope's Camp. Been nice havin' you along lootenant. Don't know if we'll meet again but I sure hope things go right for you. Army needs fellas like you out here.'

Jackson laughed. 'It's been an experience. At least I can say I've ridden drag on a trail herd now!' Together, they walked their mounts towards the wagons.

CHAPTER 14

▼

The sun was just beginning to burn the early morning moisture off the sagebrush, but there was a cool breeze from the creek. Big Red, fresh after a night's rest, was setting a pace that he could keep up indefinitely. John Jordan swayed in the saddle, his eyes alert while he mulled over his father's final instructions.

'Tell Bull we'll be followin' the stage route from now on. We left 'bout the end o' August an' I reckon we'll be there by the end o' November. That means we'll be comin' through Apache Pass. Check out water an' grass on the way. An' you might mention to the stage stations that we're comin' through. It's just plain good manners to let them know. We'll be usin' up grazin' an' they got their teams to think about. The Southern Overland ain't John Butterfield. Money an' stock are tighter wi' them. Don't reckon you'll see another trail herd. Guess we must be the last this year. Still, we got water an' feed all the way to El Paso an' it ain't a big herd. So, less'n the Injuns are out, or rustlers jump us, we should be alright.' He had looked up at his youngest son. 'Guess I don't have to tell you that's 'Pache country out there an' we're kinda short-handed. If Bull can spare a couple o' riders an' you meet us somewhere along the trail I'd be right obliged. Take care now. Adios, see you sometime.'

He was right about the feed an' water, John mused as Red pounded ahead. This is the best stretch o' trail so far. If it's like this all the way to El Paso the outfit should make good time. Just hope they don't run into no trouble.

His thoughts turned to the stage stations already behind him. Emigrant Crossing, Pope's Camp and Delaware Springs. Pope's Camp. He must have been as stubborn as a Missouri mule. All that time an' money spent drillin' for water an' nothin' to show for it. Still, at least he left the Southern Overland a ready made way station.

Fording the Pecos could be tricky though. Reckon if it gets any higher the wagons'll be floatin'. Then they got a thirty mile drive to Delaware Springs with good grazin' along the way. Plenty o' water in the creek so they won't be puttin' no strain on the station.

All morning Guadalupe Peak had loomed up tantalisingly, yet still it seemed no closer. I swear, you'd think somebody was movin' it, John thought sourly. Good thing we got an early start from Delaware Springs.

Just after noon he stopped to water Red at Independence Spring. A deep pool of clear water fed by an underground source, the spring never failed. Swinging out of the saddle, John waited until the big roan had slaked his thirst, then he knelt down and drank quickly, alert all the time for danger. Rising, he tested his cinch, at the same time warding off Red's attempts to bite.

Damn you Red, don't you ever give up? Soon as we get to the ranch Bull can have you an' welcome. Me, I'll be glad to get back on old Paint.

Swinging into the saddle he headed west. Sure is a funny name for a way station: the Pinery. The crew at Delaware Springs reckoned it was on account o' the pine trees that grow up this way, but I ain't seen nothin' o' them so far.

The Pinery was sited in a gorge of the mountain, and the sun was just beginning to slide down into the west as he approached. Already he had revised his ideas about the way station. On both sides of the gorge pines grew thickly and he could see that the corral had been stoutly constructed of the same material.

Horses milled restlessly in the enclosure and the first neigh of welcome carried to him on the wind. Red pricked his ears and answered shrilly.

'Trail herd you say?' Bearded Jim Farwell lit his battered pipe and scowled thoughtfully. 'Late in the year ain't it?'

John shrugged. 'Ain't got much choice. The folks sold up an' they're movin' out to Arizona. Anyways, it's only a small herd. Breedin' stock mainly, and the remuda. Good stuff.'

'You had any trouble with the Injuns so far?'

'Nothin' to speak of.'

'Waal, that remuda's gonna be right temptin' for Cochise an' his boys. An' rustlers. Allus a good market for saddle stock.'

'Mm.' John frowned. 'How come the Apaches don't bother the stage all that much?'

'Hard to tell. It's been said that Cochise is still holdin' to that agreement he made with Tom Jeffords some years back. Dunno if you know Jeffords?' John shook his head. 'Big red-haired fella, Taglito, the Injuns call him, that bein' Apache for Redbeard. Anyways, in '62, or mebbe it was '63, Jeffords got the contract to carry the mail from Tucson to Fort Bowie up in Apache Pass. Reckon the army must have known what they were lettin' him in for, 'cause accordin' to the story it was a right profitable contract.'

'Waal, that there's the Apache stampin' ground. Jeffords never had a chance. They bushwhacked his boys until nobody would ride that mail run. Looked like Jeffords was out o' business.'

John looked at the bearded man. 'Then what happened?'

Farwell sucked on his pipe. 'The damnedest thing you ever heard of. Jeffords rode alone through the Chiricahua Mountains, right into Cochise's camp. When he got there he shucked off his gunbelt and handed it to one of the squaws. Next, he walked across to where Cochise was sittin' and sat down beside him. They sat and said nothin' for a spell, like Injuns do at them meetin's. Then Jeffords told Cochise he wanted a personal treaty with him so he could carry on his business.'

'An' Cochise agreed?'

'Yeah. Seems like he was so impressed wi' Jeffords' guts in ridin' in alone to see him that he felt he couldn't do nothin' else. Anyway, that was it. From then on Jeffords didn't have no trouble. His riders came an' went an' nobody bothered them. Talked to one o' them one time in Tucson. He said it was so peaceful ridin' that trail he damn near fell asleep!'

John grinned. 'Seems hard to believe.'

'Yeah, I know, but it's true just the same. Reckon some o' that goodwill rubbed off on the stage line 'cause we ain't had much trouble since we opened up again. Oh, we get the occasional attack but I reckon it's just young bucks testin' themselves.'

'What about Jeffords? He still around?'

'Sure. Story is that he visits regular with Cochise, though if he does he don't talk about it.'

'Waal,' John rose to his feet. 'Thanks for the chuck. An' the grain for Red. Reckon I'll be on my way. How far to the next station?'

'Cornudos de los Alamos? Long haul; sixty miles or thereabouts. That's a fair-sized outfit they got there. Good supply o' water too. 'Course there's water 'bout halfway, at Crow Springs, if you don't mind the taste o' sulphur. Anyway, nice meetin' you mister, an' we'll be right glad to help your folks any way we can, when they come through. Adios now.'

John raised his hand in salute and urged Red forward. Jim Farwell watched them dwindle in the distance. Sure is a young fella in an awful hurry. If it had been me I'd have stayed the night here. Shrugging, he turned back into the station.

CHAPTER 15

▼

Ben Turner brought the big horses to a halt and set the wagon brake. Climbing down, he stretched tiredly before walking down to the river's edge. Miguel and Sara-Jane pulled up behind the Studebaker and waited, the Clevelands champing impatiently at their bits.

The tall teamster looked worriedly at the muddy swirling water. Damn, there's been rain upstream. Ain't too bad right now, an' I reckon my team can muscle through, but I ain't so sure 'bout the others. Deep in thought, he walked back to the wagons.

Ma stuck her head out of the accommodation wagon. 'Waal Ben, what d'you think? Reckon it's safe?'

'Ma'am,' Ben's manners were something that Ma always admired. 'No river crossin' is ever entirely safe. I'll go first. The ford is well marked and unless one o' the team steps in a pothole everything should be fine. If I'm havin' trouble I'll bring two o' the team back and trace the other wagons in turn. 'Sides, mebbe it's not as deep as I think. Anyway, you wait here.'

'You take care now.' Ma had a soft spot for the tall quiet teamster. There was an underlying sadness about him that troubled her.

Ben smiled and his face lit up momentarily. Climbing back onto the driving seat he spoke quietly to the team. They moved forward as one, and the big wagon rolled down the slope towards the Pecos. At the edge of the river the leaders stopped, paddling for a moment and unsure.

The teamster spoke sharply. 'Gee Duke, Silver.' Sara-Jane flinched as the long whip cracked menacingly. Snorting nervously, their ears pricked, the team surged into their collars and took the strain. Slowly the water rose around them.

The others watched tensely as the freight wagon ploughed on into midstream. Miguel crossed himself and muttered under his breath. Steadily the big horses fought their way across. Once the wagon lurched and Ma clenched her hands until the knuckles showed white, but it was only a small pothole. Now they were in the shallows on the other side and Ben's voice rose, commanding and encouraging. Now they were climbing up the opposite bank. One last tremendous heave and they were on the grassland beyond. Water streamed from the underside of the wagon as it rolled to a stop. Ben stood up on the seat and waved. They were across!

The watchers waited anxiously as the tall teamster climbed down and begin to unhitch the big horses. Working methodically, Ben stripped the trace chains from the swing and wheel teams, then picketed them alongside the wagon.

'He's comin' back.' Ma said decisively. 'Thought he would.'

They watched as the distant figure hooked up the leaders' traces. Then he led them alongside the wagon and, clambering onto Duke's back, headed down the bank into the river.

'Right Miguel!' Ma was already climbing down from the accommodation wagon. 'Let's get that extra hitch laid out.'

'Si senora.' Miguel unhooked the spare hitch from the side of the wagon. Jim Jordan had insisted that each wagon carry a spare and Ma blessed him now for his forethought. Together they positioned the hitch in front of the Clevelands and stood ready as Ben forded the river with his leaders.

He slid down from Duke and backed the two big horses into position.

'Reckon you could have made it alright,' he said over his shoulder to Miguel as he fastened the lead team's doubletree to the end of the wagon tongue, 'but we won't take no chances. Too many folks been killed doin' that. Now you just give me a lift.' Miguel locked his hands to form a stirrup. Ben put his foot in them and swung neatly onto Duke's back.

'You an' the gals all set Miz Jordan?' Ma waved an acknowledgement. 'Right, let's roll.'

Sarah Johnston stared down at the swirling water. 'Will we have to swim, Miz Jordan?' she queried anxiously.

'Shucks no.' Ma felt the wagon lurch beneath them. Up front Miguel was talking in a quiet monotone, soothing the excitable Clevelands. 'Why d'you think Pa had all the wagon beds lined with canvas. No,' she added, taking a firm grip of the window strap, 'we'll be alright.'

Duke and Silver powered up the bank, the Clevelands prancing nervously behind them. Ben slid down quickly and unhitched the traces.

'Right Miguel,' he said incisively. 'I'll head back for Sara-Jane and the chuck wagon. I've a feeling the river's rising.'

He's good, Ma thought, surprised. How come I never noticed it before. Maybe he's at his best when things are tough. She climbed down and busied herself replacing the hitch on the side of the wagon.

Sara-Jane had the spare hitch unhooked and laid out when Ben cantered up.

'Good.' He swung the big horses round and jumped down. 'Let's make this quick. I think there's been a storm up in the hills.' His hands were moving deftly as he spoke, running out the traces and coupling up the extra hitch. Satisfied, he straightened up.

'Think you can make a stirrup like Miguel?' His deep-set brown eyes twinkled. Sara-Jane nodded and locked her hands. Once again Ben swung up and settled himself on Duke's back. He waited while Sara-Jane scrambled back onto the seat and picked up the lines. 'All set?' She raised her hand, a strained look on her face.

'Don't worry,' his voice came back strongly, 'them big fellas'll pull us through.' The four horses lunged forward as one and splashed into the river.

They were climbing the opposite bank when Ma heard the dull roar. Then she saw it. A four foot wall of water sweeping towards them, tree trunks and other debris being carried along with it.

She shouted frantically, but Ben and Sara-Jane were both totally locked in on their task and oblivious to everything else.

Desperately, she snatched up the shotgun and loaded two rounds. Miguel's eyes widened and he grabbed for the Clevelands' bridles. Ma pointed the gun at the sky and triggered both barrels.

The boom of the shotgun alerted Ben. He turned to see Ma waving and pointing upstream. A hundred yards away the floodwater was sweeping towards them.

The teamster dug in his heels and yelled, a long high-pitched yell that drove the big horses forward over the top of the bank and onto the grassland beyond, old Paint and Dusty struggling to keep pace with them. For a few heart-stopping seconds the floodwater sucked greedily at the chuck wagon, then they were clear and careering across the grass.

Drawing the snorting leaders to a trampling halt, Ben dismounted quickly. An ashen-faced Ma leaned shakily against the side of the accommodation wagon, the shotgun still cradled in her hands, while Miguel held on grimly to the plunging Clevelands.

There was the sound of someone retching, and the teamster turned to find Sara-Jane being violently sick beside the chuck wagon.

She straightened up and smiled wanly. 'I'll be alright now, it's just that it happened so suddenlike.'

'It usually does. Don't you worry. You did alright.' He turned as Ma came up. 'Thanks ma'am. That was right smart thinkin' with the shotgun. We'd never have made it if you hadn't warned us.'

Appreciation warmed Ma's eyes as she looked at him. 'You did alright yourself. Hadn't been for you we'd have been in the middle o' that river when the water hit us. Sara-Jane,' she turned to her daughter, 'you did right well. Seems like you'll make a teamster yet.'

'Ma, I was scared.'

'I was just as scared, gal. Thing is, scared or not we kept goin'. Sure hope that water drops 'fore the herd gets here.'

'Yeah,' Ben Turner nodded grimly. ' Reckon it's gonna be chancy gettin' them across if it don't.'

Ma Jordan was suddenly all business. 'Waal, the boys won't thank us if they make it across an' we ain't got any chuck ready for 'em. Let's get started.'

Three miles downstream, Jim Jordan eased the big Cleveland to a halt and watched the floodwater sweep past. Jake ranged up beside him.

He jerked his head at the river. 'Sure don't look good.'

The rancher nodded. 'That's a fact. Just hope the wagons made it alright. Still, 'nother three, four miles an' we'll be at the ford. Better tell Ellie-May to hold the remuda back an' give us room.'

Jake nodded and swung away down the side of the herd.

Just over two hours later the leaders topped the rise and angled down towards the ford. Jim sighed with relief as he saw the three wagons drawn up neatly on the opposite bank. Across the herd, Lance waved and pointed. His father waved back happily. Jake drifted up from his position at swing.

'Gonna cross now?' he queried.

Jim Jordan rubbed his chin. 'Guess so, less'n you got a better idea?'

Jake looked at the heavy clouds overhead and shook his head. 'Nah, weather could get worse. Reckon we'd better push on. 'Sides, Ellie-May an' Rafe'll be crowdin' us wi' the remuda. Let's go.'

Busy preparing the evening meal, Ma paused and watched anxiously as the leaders plunged into the river. It ain't a big herd, reckon they'll be alright, she comforted herself.

They were halfway across now and swimming strongly. On the upstream side of the herd, Lance's buckskin was striking out powerfully. That cavalry hoss sure has taken to cow work. Behind him, Andy Boone was keeping a watchful eye on the herd's progress, while downstream Jake and Mike Glenwood were working hard to hold the cattle in line. In the distance she saw her husband chivvying the stragglers into the water.

The tree was old and heavily water-logged. For years it had lain in the little hill creek, until this last big storm had flushed it out into the Pecos. Low in the water, it struck Andy's wiry cowpony squarely on the shoulder before the old cowhand was aware of it. Snared by a projecting snag one wildly lashing foreleg snapped under the impact, then horse and rider went under.

'Damn!' The big Cleveland thrashed the water as Jim Jordan urged him forward. Feverishly the rancher scanned the racing muddy torrent. There! The merest hint of a shadowy form. He clutched desperately and hauled Boone's limp body across his saddle while the big horse forged ahead.

They splashed through the shallows and up the bank. Ben and Miguel eased the rancher's burden down and laid it on the grass. Hurriedly Ma dropped to her knees. For a long moment she bent over the body, then she straightened up and rose shaking her head.

'He's dead,' she announced flatly.

'Dead! He cain't be!' Mike Glenwood pushed through the others and dropped beside his friend, face anguished. 'Me and Andy, we've come too far for that.'

'Mike,' Ma knelt and brushed the wet hair back from the dead man's forehead. The horseshoe shaped depression showed high on his temple. 'See that? Horse caught him when they were goin' down. Guess he was knocked cold, then he drowned. Never had a chance,' she added heavily.

Beyond them the last of the herd was spreading out across the bedground, while in midstream the remuda was being pushed hard by Ellie-May and Rafe.

Ben Turner bent and gently helped Mike Glenwood to his feet.

There was a wild look on the old cowhand's face. 'We were like brothers,' he said brokenly. 'Grew up together, farmed together, then we come west an' built that little spread down in the brasada together. Like brothers ... .' He turned away sobbing bitterly.

It was night now and there was a chill in the air. Grim-faced, Ma tightened the shroud round the corpse and sewed quickly, the long needle glinting in the lamp light. The sound of a spade striking stone came faintly to her ears. She paused and peered into the darkness.

A hurricane lantern threw wavering, elongated shadows against the background of the chuck wagon. It lit up the wild figure of Mike Glenwood as he laboured to complete the grave for his dead friend.

'Wouldn't let any of us help him.' Jim Jordan had come to stand beside his wife. 'Said it was the least he could do. Glad you talked him into havin' a shroud for Andy. I guess I've seen too many trail drive cowhands dumped in a grave with nothin'.'

'Don't seem right any other way.' Ma had recommenced her sewing. 'Always like to see them laid out decent. Help me turn him over, I'm nearly finished. There!' She straightened up and stood back. 'That's it. When you buryin' him?'

'First thing in the mornin'. We'll lay him out in Ben's wagon. Mike wants to sit with him for a spell an' it seemed only right.'

Dawn was grey, with a threat of rain in the air. The herd was still bedded down and only individual horses from the remuda were making their way down to the river to drink. Peering out from the accommodation wagon, Sara-Jane shivered as she watched the group round the open grave. The Johnson girls were still sleeping and Ma had asked her to keep an eye on them to make sure the youngsters stayed where they were.

Lance and Ben Turner lowered the body into the grave and stepped back. All the men, and Ellie-May, removed their hats. Faintly, on the morning breeze, Sara-Jane heard her father's voice lifted in prayer. Yes, she thought, Pa's good at that. Might be he's usually easy-going, but when the chips are down you can count on him. She watched her father step back and motion Mike Glenwood forward.

The old cowhand picked up a handful of soil and dropped it into the open grave. He turned away and she saw him being comforted by her mother.

Tears pricked her eyes as she watched Lance pick up the spade and commence filling in the grave. Beyond him Ben Turner was hitching his team to a giant boulder. Sara-Jane grimaced, she knew what the rock was for. Once it was in position over the grave nothing would be able to get at the body.

Lance finished tamping down the last of the soil. Straightening up, he signalled to Ben.

The six big horses trampled the turf as they took the strain and dug in. Slowly, very slowly, the huge boulder began to move. It slid across the grass in the wake of the team. Carefully, Ben wheeled them round and drew the boulder into position. It covered the raw earth completely and he grunted with satisfaction.

'Nothin's gonna get at him now.'

Spade in hand, Lance nodded. 'That was a right smart idea o' yours.'

Ben shrugged. 'Saw it done years ago, up north. Kept it in mind ever since. If we run the herd round the rock nobody'll ever know there's a grave there.'

Lance bent and unshackled the heavy towing chain. The team moved forward at Ben's command and the loose end of the chain eased out from under the boulder. Picking it up, Lance fell into step beside the tall teamster. Together they followed the team toward the big wagon.

'Mind givin' me a hand to hitch the team? Reckon Mister Jordan'll want to be movin' on right smart.'

'Sure. Though Pa won't want to crowd Mike. The old man's got a feelin' for somethin' like this. Where you want this chain?'

'Stow it in the toolbox, then hold up the wagon tongue till I get the pole straps buckled.'

Together they went quietly about their task, the big horses positioning themselves intelligently to the soft-spoken commands.

'Sure is a good team you got here. Best I've seen I reckon.'

Ben nodded. Sadness showed for a moment on his face. 'Seems like they're all I got left now. I treat them just like family.'

The big sergeant nodded. 'Yeah, know what you mean. I feel the same way 'bout Buck.'

He hooked on the last trace and unkinked a twisted line. Then, straightening up he looked squarely at Ben. 'It ain't my business but it must've been hell for you losin' your wife an' the boy like that.'

The teamster nodded sadly. 'Yeah. Even now it still hurts. But, like your pa said when we first met, life don't stop an' I got to get used to that. Mebbe startin' over again in Arizona'll help. Here comes your pa now. Reckon he's set to roll.'

Jim Jordan cantered up on a wiry grey cowpony. He had picked himself a good string and he worked them carefully in turn. The pony was short-bodied and deep-chested, with more than a hint of Morgan blood. He danced sideways as the rancher drew rein.

'Easy Smoke, easy boy.' The pony quietened down and stood still, ears flicking nervously.

'All set, Ben?'

'Sure, just say the word.'

'Alright, lead out. We'll give you an hour's start then we'll hit the trail wi' the herd an' the remuda. We're well up on time an' we ain't got any big rivers to worry about till we get to Messila.'

Lance looked at his father. 'How's Mike takin' it?'

Jim shook his head. 'Bad. They were real close them two. More like brothers than partners. It'll be a long time 'fore he gets over it. Mebbe Arizona'll help; I dunno.'

Frowning, he eased Smoke round. 'We got thirty miles to Delaware Creek. That'll take us a coupla days. Them's breedin' stock an' it ain't my intention to run 'em hard. See you tonight, Ben. Lance, you ride point with Jake as usual. Me an' Mike'll take swing an' young Rafe can ride drag. Ellie-May'll have to handle the remuda on her own.'

He tapped the pony with his heels and cantered off.

Ben settled himself on the wagon seat and eased off the brake. 'Your father's a good man,' he observed quietly.

'Pa? Yeah, sure is. You wouldn't think him an' me useta fight all the time. Wish I could have that time over again. '

The teamster smiled. 'Seems like I ain't the only one with regrets.' He spoke quietly to the team and the trace chains tightened. 'See you tonight.'

Lance watched the accommodation wagon roll past, Miguel holding the Clevelands on a tight rein. Sarah and Mary waved from the windows. He waved back, then turned to watch Sara-Jane, her face set and determined, easing the chuck wagon in behind. Cain't be easy for her, he thought, but she's stuck at it. Reckon she might make a teamster yet.

Ellie-May cantered up leading his mount, a tall powerful blue roan, already saddled.

'There you are Lance. You'll be wantin' me to cut up your meat next!'

'Thanks.' Lance grinned. In spite of her barbed tongue he and Ellie-May hit it off pretty well. 'Reckon I'm gettin' old!'

Testing the cinch, he eased himself gingerly into the saddle. The roan liked to pitch first thing in the morning. True to form, the pony got his head down and went at it, but there was no real vice in his efforts and he soon gave up.

Lance settled himself in the saddle as Jake came up.

'We're gonna mill the herd round that boulder then we'll head out. I'll push them round if you'll turn 'em.'

Ten minutes later it was done, and Lance sent the roan cantering up the side of the herd to his position at point.

Swinging the remuda in behind the herd Ellie-May took a last long look back at the campsite.

The bedground round the great boulder had been churned up by the milling cattle. All that remained were the ashes of the campfire and the boulder itself, crouched like a huge beast of prey over the grave.

Ellie-May shivered involuntarily. Then she turned away and rode after the remuda.

CHAPTER 16

▼

The heat from the open forge was stifling. Half-buried among the red hot embers, the iron tire glowed dully. Carefully, using special, long-handled, U-shaped tongs, Anders Lindstrom moved the metal circle round and nodded to Bull. Rivulets of sweat streaming down his face, the big rancher pumped vigorously on the handle of the bellows, set in the side of the forge. He slowed as Anders raised a warning hand.

'Not too much, by golly. You make her too hot an' the iron she turns brittle. Then she breaks when we put water on her.'

'Sorry Anders.' Bull mopped his face with a sweat soaked rag. 'You got to remember I'm new to this.'

'Maybe.' Both men were stripped to the waist and the Dane's muscles rippled as, tongs in hand, he moved the tire still further round in the glowing heart of the forge. 'You learn quick though. Some fellas, they never learn.'

Stepping back, Anders motioned to Bull to continue pumping. Grinning, he watched the big man's shoulder muscles rippling with the effort.

'Boss, some day you an' me, we got to wrestle. I think you give me a helluva fight!'

Bull laughed. 'Anders, damned if I know what to make of you. Ain't you got enough work as it is?'

The Dane's answering laugh rumbled deep in his throat. 'Man's always got to have time for some fun.'

A shadow fell across the open doorway and Joe Masterson stepped into the building. He drew in his breath sharply as the heat from the forge struck his face.

'Whoo-eeh! I thought it was warm work brandin' them yearlin's but it weren't nothin' like this.'

Lindstrom grinned. 'Joe, you come at the right time. Me an' the boss here, we're just gettin' ready to carry this tire out to the pit an' drop her on the wheel. Grab them two hammers,' he indicated two long-handled, heavy hammers, leaning against the wall, 'an' come with us.'

'Now, Boss,' he clamped the U-shaped tongs neatly on opposite sides of the shimmering circle, 'do just like I told you. Lift the tire real slow, then turn it straight up so we can walk through the door with it.'

Gingerly, Bull followed Anders as the Dane backed through the doorway, the glowing iron ring suspended vertically between them. Quickly, they made their way to a shallow, circular pit, five feet in diameter, and encircled with curved stone slabs, dug in the ground just outside. Resting on the slabs was a wagon wheel, minus its tire, and secured by a short iron post set in the center of the pit.

'How come this wheel threw its tire?' Bull panted, as they cautiously revolved the fiery metal circle into a horizontal position and lowered it carefully onto the wheel. The smell of burning wood rose like incense, as the glowing ring burned its way into position.

'It was the last one by golly. I did the others 'bout a year ago.' Deftly the big Dane fitted the tongs about five feet apart on the tire and bore down on them. 'Now,' he nodded to Bull and Joe, 'you tap her down.'

Working from opposite sides they hammered the tire down onto the wheel rim. Anders freed the tongs and darted round the pit. 'Again now, on the other side, quickly!'

Once more they drove the tire down until it was flush with the rim and fitted snugly all round. Raising a cautionary hand the blacksmith motioned them to stop. Grabbing the hammer from Joe, he tapped his way round the circumference of the wheel and finally straightened up, grunting with satisfaction.

'That is a damn fine job. Some day you two make good blacksmiths, but not yet!'

Joe laughed. 'Anders, if you wasn't so big an' ugly I'd tell you what I think, but I don't hanker to have my ribs busted!'

The big Dane chuckled as he picked up a bucket of water. 'Maybe you should get Boss here to fight me.' Working quickly round the wheel he poured the water carefully onto the tire. Steam rose from the cooling metal.

Bull stepped back and grinned. 'Anders, I got enough troubles right now, without gettin' stove up tanglin' wi' you. Anyways, I see Clay on his way down from the house, an' he's got somebody with him.'

'Couple of big men, aren't they?' Norman McLean eyed the group round the wheel appraisingly as he and Clay crossed the yard.

'Yes; don't know who I'd put my money on if they locked horns. Bull's maybe an inch or so taller than Anders, probably out reach him as well, but I'd say Anders is the heavier. One thing's certain. If they're on your side you don't have to worry about the opposition!'

McLean laughed. 'That's for sure.' They stopped at the group. 'Good day, Mister Jordan, seems like you can turn your hand to most things. Didn't know you were into the wheelwright trade though.'

'Shucks,' Bull finished tucking in his shirt-tails. 'I'm only the hired hand at this job. Anders is the brains.'

The giant Dane reddened with pleasure. 'Boss, you an' Joe learn real fast. Some day you be as good as me.'

'Alright, Captain McLean, what can I do for you? Oh, this here's m'foreman Joe Masterson. Him an' Clay sit in on any deals.'

'Fine.' The two men shook hands. 'I've brought that contract for the beef and I thought we could look at your stock and agree on a price. Then maybe we can go into the question of the remounts?'

'Sure, why not? What about them 'stags' Joe? How many we got?'

'Forty-eight all told. I got Manuel an' Jeff holdin' 'em down on the flats, along Saddle Creek. Then we got fifty good mounts, four year olds, in the horse pasture. Mike an' Sam have just started breakin' them.'

Bull nodded. 'Waal now, seems like we're all set up for you, Captain. What d'you want to see first?'

McLean laughed. 'Let's look at the horses. Beef is beef as far as I'm concerned.'

They stood in a quiet group by the corral and watched critically as the Aldersons saddled a rangy bay.

'They're good, aren't they?' McLean jerked his head towards the corral.

Bull nodded as he watched Sam swing cautiously into the saddle and settle himself. Mike let go the head rope and ducked through the corral rails.

Leaning forward, Sam eased the blinder up off the horse's eyes. For a second the bay stood motionless blinking in the sudden light, then he exploded into action. Head down, legs braced like steel springs, he bucked his way across the dusty corral, Sam sticking like glue to his back and talking quietly all the time.

At the last moment his mount wheeled away from the fence and took off at a dead run round the corral.

Bull grinned. 'He'll be alright now. That's just high spirits. See how he wheeled away from the fence? Your real outlaw would've tried to scrape Sam off against it.' He turned as Mike joined them. 'Howdy, Mike. This here's Captain McLean. He's lookin' for remounts. Reckon we can supply 'em?'

'Sure.' Mike watched the circling horse slow to a canter then to a walk. 'This is a good bunch. Me an' Sam won't have no trouble gentlin' 'em.'

Sam Alderson halted the sweat-streaked bay opposite them, and, swinging down, tied the horse to the corral fence, talking quietly all the while. Then he bent and slipped through the rails.

'Howdy, Boss. We'll let him feel the saddle for a spell. He's alright.'

'Howdy, Sam. This here's Captain McLean. He's in the market for remounts.'

'Waal,' Sam hitched his worn Levis a shade higher, 'He won't find none better round here. This bunch would fetch top price anywhere.'

McLean laughed. 'Your boys are good salesmen, Mister Jordan. Don't reckon I've got much choice other than buy your stock after that build-up. Besides, I like the way you operate. Too often the remounts we get are half broken and they do more damage to the recruits than the Apaches! If all the mounts you've got for sale are as good as that bay, I'll give you forty dollars a head.'

'Forty dollars?' Bull kept his voice carefully non-committal. 'Seems fair.' Forty dollars! he exulted inwardly. That was top price. 'How many would you want?'

McLean thought for a moment. 'Let's say a score to start with. Then, once we get an idea of the replacement rate, we can place a running contract. That suit you?'

Bull calculated quickly. Eight hundred dollars, with the promise of more to follow. 'What about the 'stags'?'

'These scrub bulls? I'll be straight with you. You won't find much demand for them round here. Three dollars a head. After all, you're not having to drive them to the railheads up north.'

'That's true. An' after that? What price you offerin' if we start supplyin' steers to you regular like?'

'Well,' McLean frowned with concentration, 'If they're as good as the ones I saw when I was riding in, I'll give you six dollars a head on delivery.'

'Captain, you just got yourself a deal!' the big rancher grinned widely. 'Why don't you stay overnight an' meet the boys? We got a good outfit.

Couple o' ex-cavalry sergeants among them, an' you're gonna be dealin' with 'em when they make deliveries. How about it?'

McLean nodded. This man Jordan is going places. Already he's got his crew involved in decisions. I can see that he's aiming to build an empire. Wonder where Clay fits into all this?

'Be glad to. Like to swap some more yarns with Clay anyway.'

Sam Alderson took another hitch at his Levis as he watched the four men making their way to the ranch house. 'You heard the man, Mike. Twenty horses now an' more later. Let's get at it.'

His brother groaned theatrically and rolled his eyes. 'Don't know if my old bones can stand it!'

Sam chuckled. 'Wouldn't shout too loud 'bout that if I were you. From what the boss was tellin' Joe, his young brother is a top hand when it comes to workin' horses. An' he's got a sidekick, fella name o' Larsen, who's just about as good.'

They walked towards the corral.

'How come this young Jordan's such a hotshot wi' horses?' Mike slipped through the corral rails and patted the bay's neck. The horse pricked its ears and looked at him enquiringly.

Sam was untying the latigos, the heavy leather straps that secured the cinches on the near side of the horse. He eased the saddle off the bay, carefully lifting the trailing cinches clear as he did so. Nothing spooked a young horse as much as the feel of something dragging across his back. 'It 'pears young Jordan was took by the Comanches when he was 'bout eight. He was with them nine or ten years, then he escaped. You know Comanches are the tops when it comes to workin' wi' horses, an' it seems young Jordan, an' his sidekick Larsen, picked up all their know-how.'

'Waal,' Mike removed the hackamore and stood back, 'looks like we're gonna have competition round here.'

The bay wheeled and trotted away.

'Anyways, right now we got a job to do.' Picking up his lariat he headed for the bunch of horses milling uncertainly in the holding corral.

CHAPTER 17

▼

It was dark in the pass, a darkness made all the more menacing by the occasional wavering light of a fitful moon. High on the rocky crags, a cougar screamed shrilly, like a lost soul in torment.

Red blew through his nostrils and tried to lengthen his stride. John Jordan held the big horse in and spoke softly. 'Easy, boy. Nothin' to worry about. That cat's a long way off.'

Beneath him he felt the giant gelding relax and drop back into the mile-eating canter that he could keep up for hours. The cougar screamed again, fainter this time, the sound in keeping with brooding menace of the pass.

Huntin' I reckon, movin' away now. John took in the loom of the cliffs on either side. This would be a bad place to get caught in. I can see why that station boss said it was best to travel it at night.

The clouds cleared momentarily and he swept the way ahead with a keen all-encompassing glance. Nothing, except the elongated shadows of the boulders on either side of the trail.

'Nother coupla miles I reckon, then you can drink your fill at Apache Springs. Mebbe we should look in at Fort Bowie, though I ain't overly keen. Reckon the less you have to do with the Army the better.

An hour later he picked up the light from the way station at the springs, and beyond that the squat bulk of the fort. There was a stir about the way station and he could see lanterns bobbing jerkily to and fro. Already the first flush of dawn was lightening the sky in the east. Faintly, on the morning breeze, he heard the shrill neigh of horses as the teams were changed. Red pricked up his ears and responded.

'Thanks, mister.' Hank Bristow, the stocky balding way station boss, squinted up at the tall man on the giant roan gelding. ' 'Preciate you tellin' us. Most trail herds barrel through here without as much as a fare thee well, so it sure is nice when somebody tells us what's happenin'. Anyways, plenty o' water an' feed, so a small herd like yours won't be no trouble.'

John indicated the square outline of Fort Bowie. 'What about the soldier boys? Reckon I should tell them we're comin' through?'

Bristow grimaced. 'Colonel Pettigrew ain't goin' to be happy whatever you do. We ain't had all that many trail herds through here in any case. Most folks like to keep their hair! Then the colonel, he figgers trail herds just stir up the Apaches an' make life hard for us folks that got to live here.'

'You feel that way yourself?'

A shrug of Bristow's heavy shoulders. 'Hell, it's a free country. Man's got a right to take his outfit anywhere. Nah, far as I'm concerned you're welcome to use the water an' feed when you come through.'

'Thanks.' John thought for a moment. 'This Colonel Pettigrew, what sort o' fella is he?'

Hank Bristow scowled. 'He's a real stiff-necked Yankee. Hates the South. From what I hear he feels he's been left here an' forgotten. Mebbe he has at that, but he sure is one mean cuss. Oh, something else, he likes horses, good horses. Reckon he'll be interested in that big roan o' yours.'

'Yeah? I'll bear that in mind. Adios an' thanks again. '

'You're welcome.' The station boss raised his hand in salute as John cantered away towards the fort.

Right nice young fella. Sure hope him an' his folks make out alright. Chancy business drivin' cattle through here.

'Trail herd you say?' Colonel Henry Curtis Pettigrew, a tall spare white-haired West Pointer, scowled as he stared at the young man sitting opposite. 'And a horse herd! Don't you people ever learn? That's just an open invitation to every Apache in the territory to come running!'

John Jordan bit his lip. 'Colonel, believe me, my folks gave this move considerable thought. You don't just pull up your stakes an' push a trail herd nigh on a thousand miles for nothin'. As I said, they were left this here ranch, the Flyin' W. It's down on the Border, near Dorando. Don't reckon you can blame them for wantin' to try their luck there.'

'Luck!' Colonel Pettigrew sneered. 'You'll need more than luck down there. From what I've heard, it's nothing but cactus, rattlesnakes, rustlers, Comancheros and Apaches. Nobody in their right mind would try to raise stock in that God-forsaken country. Horses ... ,' he went suddenly off at a tangent. 'What breed? Usual scrub stock I suppose?'

'Why no, Colonel.' John felt his temper beginning to build. 'We use a Cleveland stallion on Cleveland and Morgan mares. The foals make good ridin' stock an' good team horses as well. That way, we can try for the army an' stage contracts.'

'A Cleveland Morgan cross you say?' There was a friendlier note in Pettigrew's harsh voice. 'You could just be onto something there.'

'That's what Pa figgered. He reckoned that we'd get the frame o' the Cleveland an' the power o' the Morgan. Last couple o' years we've been supplyin' 'em to the Army at Fort Concho, an' Captain McMillan swears by them.'

'I know McMillan.' A faraway look appeared momentarily in Pettigrew's eyes. 'We were in the same class at West Point. Good man; never got the credit he deserved. Well, Mister Jordan,' he stood up and John rose hastily with him. 'I still think your family is making a mistake, but I admire their courage and I'll be interested to see the results of your horse-breeding.' He stared out of the window at Red pawing the ground impatiently by the hitching rail. 'That's a good-looking mount you have there. Is he your own breeding?'

'Red?' John came up beside him. 'No, m'brother Hardy bought him from a bunch o' Comancheros down in the Big Bend. Seems like they had roughed him up pretty bad, an' Hardy hates to see a horse ill-treated. Anyways, they turned him into a killer. He's killed one fella already, an' the only man he's got any time for is Hardy. Me he just tolerates, an' no more.'

Pettigrew turned abruptly from the window. 'Mr Jordan, if I seemed somewhat abrupt just now I apologise. As I said earlier this is a God-forsaken place, fit only for rattlesnakes and Indians. A man tends to forget the niceties of civilisation here. People like your brother and yourself, who have sympathy for a dumb animal, rate high in my book. Now,' he held out his hand, ' I'll wish you a safe journey. Watch out around Dragoon Springs. That's the next way station just under forty miles from here. The trail is mostly across open plain and the Apaches tend to keep it under surveillance from the hills. There's a young hothead, Little Elk, who's got together a small party of braves and he's been giving us a lot of trouble. According to my patrols, he's around there somewhere, so take care.'

The trail stretched across the plain into the distance. Alternately walking and cantering Red, John kept up a steady pace. He had a feeling that he was being watched, but there was nothing he could do about it. Time would tell.

He grinned as he mulled over his conversation with Pettigrew. Sure is a strange fella. Don't seem to care for folks, but he's got a real feelin' for horses. Red, old horse, he patted the big roan's neck, you might just have done me a good turn.

A movement at the base of one of the hills drew his attention, and he watched through narrowed eyes as a small group of horsemen issued from a draw and began to parallel his progress across the plain. Too far away to tell, but I reckon this could be Little Elk an' his boys. Waal, long as they don't try to close up we'll leave 'em alone. For the next half hour he watched his distant shadowers closely. Slowly, almost imperceptibly, they began to edge in towards him.

'Red,' John settled himself comfortably in the saddle, 'we got some serious runnin' to do.' He tapped the big horse with his heels and the roan lunged into his stride. A glance to his left showed that his pursuers had abandoned all pretence and were now riding hard to cut him off.

John gauged the distance carefully. Red was fit and hard from his weeks on the trail. The young rancher doubted if there was a pony in the pursuing band that could get near him. Still, there was no point in taking chances. Hauling the Winchester out of its saddle socket he lined up on the leading rider and triggered three quick shots.

'Damn!' John swore disgustedly. It was long range for a carbine, and he was shooting at a moving target from the back of a galloping horse, but even so, he had hoped that one of his shots would count.

Still, they had sheered off slightly. He shoved the Winchester back into the socket and settled down to outrun his pursuers.

Injuns right enough. Little Elk an' his boys I reckon. He looked again carefully. Nothin' to worry about, Red. Only one that might give you a run is the leader, that big paint horse.

A mile passed. John looked again and grunted with satisfaction. The gap was definitely widening. 'Red, old horse,' he patted the flying roan's neck, 'I reckon we got 'em beat.'

Dragoon Springs way station loomed ahead. The Apaches had seen it too and were swinging away to the south. 'Easy boy,' John reined Red in. 'It's all over, you beat them.' The big horse's all-out gallop dropped to a lope, then to a canter. Foam flecked his shoulders and he blew through his nostrils.

'Howdy, stranger.' Henry Glover, bow-legged grey-haired boss of Dragoon Springs way station, hosed a stream of tobacco juice from the corner of his mouth and squinted up at the tall rider on the big red horse. 'Seems to me you been pushin' your hawse some. Any trouble out there?'

'Injuns,' John said tersely, dismounting. 'Bunch o' them tried to cut me off but Red here outrun 'em.'

'Injuns you say,' Glover's voice sharpened. 'Any idea where they're headed?'

John shrugged. 'South, the last I saw. Five all told. One o' them was ridin' a big paint horse.'

'Mm.' Glover chewed reflectively, 'sure sounds like Little Elk an' his boys. He rides a paint stallion. Sets a heap o' store by that hawse. Hell!', he swore suddenly, 'the eastbound stage is due in another four hours. Sure hope them Apaches don't meet up with it first. Anyways,' he spat contemplatively, 'ain't nothin' I can do about it.'

'Now,' he looked at John expectantly, ' anythin' I can do for you Mister … ?'

'Jordan, John Jordan, headin' for the Flyin' W, south of Dorando. Like to rest m'horse for a few hours if it's alright with you?'

'Sure, turn him into the corral. Then come an' get some grub.'

'Ain't just as easy as that.' John swung down out of the saddle. 'He can be right mean with other horses. He's killed a man as well, so I don't want to take no chances.'

'Mm.' Henry Glover took a long look at the giant gelding. 'Tell you what; there's a little stable back o' the main building. It was added on during the war, but we don't use it now. Put him in there an' he'll be alright.'

'Thanks.' John led Red in the direction indicated.

Henry stared after them. Queer pair. Somethin' don't strike as just right. Still, he shrugged his shoulders, ain't no business o' mine. He spat accurately at an ant scurrying among the stones and turned away.

CHAPTER 18

▼

'So you want to stock up wi' supplies?' Jim Jordan looked shrewdly at his wife. 'That the only reason?'

Ma shrugged. 'Ain't sayin' I wouldn't mind a look at El Paso, an' it would be nice for Sara-Jane an' the gals. We've all been feelin' mighty low since Andy was killed.'

'Mm.' Her husband rasped the stubble on his jaw with a calloused hand. 'Mebbe it ain't such a bad idea at that. Grazin's right good round here, an' water's handy. We could rest the stock for a coupla days 'fore we strike north. Tell you what, I'll get Miguel to drive you in with the accommodation wagon. Ain't more'n four, five miles. Lance an' Rafe can tail along as well. Rest o' us'll hold the stock here.'

Ma frowned. 'Why're you so all-fired keen to send Lance?' she demanded. 'Shoulda thought you wanted him here. '

'Waal,' Jim Jordan paused for a moment. 'It's partly on account o' that deal we cut wi' Captain McMillan. Lance ain't had a real chance to get folks' views 'bout the Injun troubles out here. Mebbe this'll give'm the chance.' He frowned. 'Mind you, he didn't seem none too keen when I come up wi' the idea. Still an' all, he's goin'. Another thing, The Pas ain't the best town for wimmen to be on their own in, an' Lance knows the place. When me an' him had our last big bustup, he hung out there for a spell 'fore he joined the Army.'

'What about Rafe?'

'Young Rafe? Boy's got to grow up, an' I'd ruther he did it when there's somebody like Lance around to keep an eye on him.'

'You goin' to let Miguel take Buck an' Star?'

Her husband shook his head. 'That pair draw a lot o' attention. Some folks in The Pas might get the idea that there's quality horseflesh out here an' come callin'. So he can take Paint an' Dusty. Ain't nobody goin' to give them a second look.'

'You missin' them Clevelands?' Ma glanced at the small plump Mexican sitting beside her.

'Si senora.' Miguel Jerez eased Paint and Dusty onto the main El Paso trail. 'Buck and Star, they are the best. It has been an honour to handle them.'

'They're good alright.' Ma had a soft spot for Miguel. Not only did he handle the Clevelands like a master, but he could also keep Sarah and Mary amused for hours on end with his stories. Just goes to show, she mused, you cain't always judge things by the wrapper.

Looking back she could see Lance and young Rafe talking quietly together as they cantered along behind. That boy's done right well. Can see why Jim reckons he'll make a top hand some day.

Lance now; her eyes softened momentarily as she looked at her eldest son, he's been a real help. Dunno what was troublin' him back a ways, but he seems to be gettin' over it. Good to see him an' Pa hittin' it off so well. Pity he ain't never been keen on ranch work. Wonder if he'll stay in the Army when his time's up next year? Says he wouldn't mind sheriffin'. Absently she patted the long holdall beside her. Reckon he might do right well at it.

Below her, Sara-Jane smiled as she dealt with Sarah and Mary's questions. 'Yes, 'course I'll buy you some candy in town. No Sarah, Ma ain't cross with us. She's ridin' up top 'cause she wants to see where the general store is.'

Don't suppose the good Lord'll mind one little lie! I know Ma's up there 'cause she gets tired of your questions after a while. Me, I'm just glad I ain't drivin'!

Young Rafe glanced at Lance. 'Is El Paso as tough as folks say?' he queried.

The big sergeant frowned. 'Waal, it ain't exactly a Sunday school. You got to remember it's been here a long time. Useta be called Franklin. They changed the name just before the war. Then it's built smack on the Border. Right handy if the law is trailin' you. Been a long time since I was last here.'

Just got to hope none o' the old gang are still around. Wouldn't think so though. Not after all them years. Likely they're scattered to hell an' gone. He fingered his jaw. Anyways, I look a whole heap different wi' this beard.

'There,' Ma pointed ahead to a solid looking adobe building. Over the front a sign proclaimed 'General Store Proprietor A. Smith.' in imposing lettering. Miguel eased the wagon neatly into position and pulled up.

Lance and Rafe swung down and hitched their mounts to the rail. Crossing to the wagon the sergeant reached up for the canvas holdall and helped his mother alight.

'Thanks Lance.' Ma adjusted her hat and smoothed down her dress. 'Miguel, if you just wait here. Shouldn't be long'.

'Si Senora Jordan, as you wish.'

'What can I do for you ma'am?' Asa Smith wiped his hands on his apron, and surveyed the stocky, tough-looking woman with the holdall.

'Needin' supplies,' Ma said shortly. She laid a piece of paper on the scarred counter. 'Reckon you can fix us up?'

The tall lanky storekeeper delved into a vest pocket and produced a pair of half-moon glasses, which he donned before peering owlishly at the list. 'Mm. Why sure ma'am, we got everything you want, right here. Even got fresh vegetables. You got a wagon handy?'

'Sure, right outside. Boys'll carry the supplies out.'

Lance glanced at Rafe and rolled his eyes. The youngster struggled to suppress a grin.

Wide-eyed, the Johnson girls stared at the laden shelves. Mary plucked at Sara-Jane's sleeve.

'Sara-Jane.'

'Yes Mary?'

'Look at that striped candy! Isn't it nice?'

'Yes, would you like some?'

'Ooh, yes please!

'Lance,' Sara-Jane whispered. 'You got any money?'

'Sure.' Her brother delved into a pocket and produced a small moneybag. Undoing the draw strings he took out a silver dollar and passed it to her. 'That enough?'

'Yes thanks. Gals, let's go choose your candy.'

'That's the last, Miz Jordan.' Rafe passed a case of apples to Sara-Jane who stowed them in the wagon.

'Thanks son. Where's Lance?'

'Buyin' some Bull Durham an' talkin' to the storekeeper. Don't reckon he'll be long.'

Ma tapped her foot impatiently. 'Right, tell'm we're takin' the gals for a walk along the street. Miguel, you mind waitin' here? Shouldn't be all that long.'

'Si senora. I see a blacksmith's shop down the street. Dusty has a loose shoe. I will go there and get it tightened. Then I will come back here.'

Ma nodded. 'All set then, gals?'

'Ma.' Sara-Jane looked at her mother hesitantly. 'Just for once, couldn't you leave that holdall in the wagon. After all, we're in town. Ain't nothin' gonna happen to us here.'

There was a long silence, then her mother shrugged. 'Mebbe you're right at that. Guess I've just got so used to this here bag I feel lost without it. Here, Rafe,' she passed it to the youngster, 'stow it with the supplies in the wagon.'

'Thanks,' Lance picked up the sack of tobacco and his change. 'Quiet ain't it?' he added conversationally.

The storekeeper nodded gloomily. 'Trade's been poor lately. Injuns have been scarin' the hell out o' the outlyin' ranchers. Folks are either fortin' up on their ranches, or sellin' up an' movin' out.'

The sergeant frowned. 'Any idea what's stirrin' up the Injuns?'

'Waal,' Asa Smith rubbed his chin thoughtfully. 'Nobody's rightly sure. Some folks think the tribes are bandin' together to wipe out the whites. Then again, some reckon it's the Comancheros runnin' guns to them an' stirrin' up hell generally.'

'What d'you think yourself?'

'Me ... I reckon the Army are pushin' the tribes west an' south, an' we're gettin' squeezed in between.'

'Mm. You could be right. How about the ranchers? What's their views?'

'What d'you think? They just got one idea. The only good Injun's a dead Injun!'

Lance nodded. 'Yeah, I've heard that too often. Waal, thanks anyway.'

'Any time. Me, I got nothin' personal against Injuns, but then, if I was livin' fifty miles out o' town I might think different.'

'This is nice Ma.' Sara-Jane indicated the dresses in the shop window. 'Sure must be great to live in a place like this.'

'Depends what you want,' her mother said caustically. 'It ain't all candy an' frocks!' She indicated a saloon across the street. 'You want that on your doorstep all the time?'

'Went for a walk you say.' Lance scowled at Rafe. 'Which way?' he demanded.

Rafe pointed. 'Headed into town. Said they just wanted to look around.'

'Damn.' The big sergeant swore explosively. 'I sure am surprised at Ma. This ain't Greenhills, or Waco either come to that. This here's a Border town an' a rathole to boot.' Hurriedly he untied Buck. 'Grab your pony an' let's go find 'em.'

'Reckon we've gone far enough.' Ma cocked a wary eye at the tough-looking bunch on the opposite sidewalk. 'That four look like trouble. Watch it, they're crossin' over.'

'Howdy, miss.' The bearded leader stepped up in front of them and leered at Sara-Jane. 'Ain't seen you around before. Where you from?'

Sara-Jane paled and moved closer to her mother.

'Mister!' Ma's voice chilled like ice. 'You mind steppin' aside so me an' the gals can get past.' Mary-Lou you dang fool, why did you leave that holdall in the wagon?

'Ma'am,' The black-bearded man swept off his hat in an exaggerated bow. 'All we wants is the pleasure of this young lady's company for a spell.' His companions sniggered. Sara-Jane flinched as he reached out and laid a restraining hand on her arm.

'Get your hands off her an' step back!' The voice had the snap of authority about it. Folks passing ducked hurriedly into doorways. The four backed up slowly.

'Ma,' Lance spoke again, his voice tense with controlled rage, 'you an' the gals step into the street. I see Miguel headed this way.'

'Lance ... '

'Just do it, Ma!' His voice was cold and impersonal.

Ma and Sara-Jane hustled the wide-eyed girls across the street.

Miguel took in the situation at a glance. 'Get in senora, quickly. Your bag is on the seat.' They scrambled in hastily.

The four on the sidewalk shuffled uneasily.

'Now,' the cold authoritative voice spoke again. 'Get your hands in the air an' turn round.' Hands raised, the group turned slowly.

Twenty feet away, Lance and Rafe Allen sat their horses, guns in hand.

'That's just fine, fellas. Now, take your guns an' toss 'em in front of you. Be awful careful now.'

There was a momentary collective hesitation, then Ma spoke harshly from the wagon. 'Do like he says. I got two load o' buckshot for the first fella that makes a wrong move!'

Glancing sideways the four saw the twin muzzles resting on the half door of the wagon. Colt .44s and .45s thudded hastily into the dust.

'Rafe,' Lance's tone was softer now, 'light down an' pick up that hardware. Keep low. First fella that makes a wrong move stops lead.' Heart thumping, Rafe swung down off his pony and scooped up the discarded guns. This would be something to tell the folks back home!

'Now unload 'em an' pocket the rounds. I don't want nothin' lyin' about in the street where kids can pick 'em up.' The youngster went about his task quickly.

'Mister,' the youngest member of the quartet spoke hesitantly, ' we didn't mean no ... '

'Shut up!' Rage flared again in Lance's voice. 'I'd as soon kill you here as anywhere, so don't push your luck. Rafe boy, you all finished?'

'Yeah.' Rafe pocketed the last of the rounds.

'Right, run a saddle string through the trigger guards an' hang them on your horn.'

'Now gents,' he looked coldly at the four. 'We'll drop your guns off at the hardware store down the street. I'd suggest you mind your manners in future.'

'It ain't finished yet,' Ma's voice crackled from across the street. 'The four of you step across here.'

Cautiously the four edged across the street, the shotgun menacing them all the way.

'Right.' She scowled at them as they lined up beside the accommodation wagon. ' I want you to apologise to m'daughter. Let's hear you now.'

'I'll be damned 'fore ...' the bearded leader stopped abruptly as the shotgun swivelled to point directly at him.

'You'll be dead if you don't,' Ma said tersely. 'An' you wouldn't be the first man I killed. Likely you wouldn't be the last either,' she added darkly. 'Now, let's hear you!'

'Miss, we're right sorry …'

'Louder!' Ma gestured with the shotgun.

'We're right sorry. Didn't mean no harm.'

'That's better. On your way, an' I don't want to see you again, ever. Miguel!'

'Si senora?'

'Let's roll.'

Lance Jordan's mouth twitched as the accommodation wagon rumbled off down the street. He and Rafe fell in behind.

The black-bearded man's face twisted with rage. 'Nobody does that to me. That outfit's gonna find out it don't pay to tangle wi' Bart Saunders.'

They were clear of the town now; Lance leaned across and slapped his companion on the shoulder. 'Rafe, you did right well there. I can see why Pa hired you.'

The youngster flushed. 'Lance, I was scared!'

'Son,' the big sergeant's voice deepened, 'when the chips are down we're all scared, an' the man who says he ain't is a liar. Somethin' else. Stay away from Ma for a spell. She's mad clean through that she was caught without that sawn-off!'

CHAPTER 19

▼

The dripping cattle spread out across the bedground, tearing hungrily at the grass as they walked. Lance Jordan rolled a smoke as he sat watching them. His father ranged up alongside.

'Hey Pa. Grazin' looks pretty good here.'

His father nodded. 'Yeah. Now we got the Rio Grande behind us we'll rest up here tomorrow. No sense runnin' the stock into the ground.'

They lounged in silence, watching Ma and Sara-Jane preparing the evening meal while Ben and Miguel unhitched the teams and turned them loose. In the distance Jake, having finished setting the night riders, was now heading towards them.

'Jake sure gets through a power of work,' Lance observed. 'He couldn't work harder if it was his own.'

'It is,' Jim Jordan said shortly. 'When his old man was killed I said Jake would be part o' this family, an' I'm holdin' to that. If Ma or anybody else don't like it that's just too bad. Now hush up.'

Lance grinned as Jake reined in his pony and looked at them inquiringly.

'Howdy Jake. Suppose you want me on first shift? Man, you sure are one hard-drivin' foreman!'

Jake grinned in turn. He liked the big sergeant and he knew that Lance had no desire to come back to ranching. Not like Bull; the thought entered his mind unbidden. He'll allus want to run the show.

'Nah, got you down for the second trick.' He turned to Jim Jordan. 'You still plannin' to rest here?'

'Guess so. We'll let the stock drink all they want then we'll head upriver. Take care passin' round Messila. I don't want no complaints 'bout broken fences an' trampled crops. When we're opposite Dona Ana we'll water the stock one last time, then we'll head up through the pass an' make for Cooke's Spring. That's some fifty miles across the plain, so we'll have to dry camp one night. Still, reckon that shouldn't be too bad.'

Lance nodded absently, a faraway look in his eyes.

His father frowned. 'What's eatin' you?' he demanded. 'You still thinkin' 'bout that ruckus in El Paso?'

'Yeah, waal not exactly. Coupla times since we left El Paso I've seen riders watchin' us from this side o' the river. Reckon one o' them could have been that big black-bearded gent. I got a feelin' we might get trouble tonight.'

Jim Jordan looked at his eldest son closely. 'Why tonight specially?'

'Waal ... if somebody is plannin' to cut the herd they won't know we're restin' up tomorrow. Now, if we had been pullin' out tomorrow we'd be up through Pecacho Pass an' out onto the plain. That ain't no good for anybody wantin' to pick up some quick beef. They'll want to make their strike, cut out what they can, head south across the river an' sell anythin' they've got in Mexico. 'Nother thing, if they let us get beyond Messila 'fore they hit us then they got to get round all them Mex farms on the way back. Cain't go north. Nothin' but Injun trouble for them up there. Nah, it's south, an' if they're gonna do it, it's tonight. They'll swing wide an' come from the north though. Then if they stampede the herd they're runnin' the right way.'

His father rubbed his chin and looked at Jake. 'You got any ideas?'

Jake shook his head. 'Nah, reckon Lance is callin' the shots right. Thing is, where do we stop them? Cain't let them get near the stock or they might stampede 'em. Looks like we got to do it north o' here somewhere.'

Jim Jordan nodded. 'Looks like that way to me too. Right, I'll leave you two to work it out. Who you reckon you'll need with you?'

Jake Larsen thought for a moment. 'Ben, I think. Cain't afford to take any more away from the herd an' Ben's reliable. That leaves four riders to cover the herd an' the remuda. Miz Jordan, Sara-Jane an' Miguel will need to look after the wagons.'

The rancher laughed. 'Looks like you got it all worked out. Let's get some chuck then you can tell the others what you're plannin'. Ma's made a pan o' kidney stew an' I wouldn't like to see it wasted.' He swung his pony round and cantered towards the camp.

Lance looked at Jake. 'Seems like you an' me got elected to this one. You got any ideas?'

Jake scowled. 'Nary a one. Tell you what, let's eat first.'

'Jake,' Lance slapped him on the shoulder, 'that's the best idea I've heard in a long time, let's go.'

Laughing, they made their way towards the chuck wagon.

'Folks,' Lance glanced round the group at rear of the wagon. Only the two riders covering the herd, Mike Glenwood and Rafe, were missing. 'Jake an' me reckon rustlers will try to cut the herd tonight.' He went on to explain why they had come to that conclusion.

Ben Turner nodded thoughtfully. 'Makes sense an' I'll be happy to side you both. How are you plannin' to handle them?'

'Waal, we ain't got that figgered out yet,' Lance admitted. 'First of all we're plannin' to mosey up the north trail an' see if we can find a good place to jump them.'

'I got an idea.' Ben Turner had a faraway look in his eyes. 'Old uncle o' mine used it one time.' Quickly he explained.

There were grins all round and even Ma smiled approvingly. Jim Jordan laughed as he rose and rinsed his dishes in the wash basin. 'That's right smart thinkin' Ben. I'll go get a couple o' ropes right now. An' you'll need a mount. Take mine. Bob's already saddled, he stands when he's groundhitched and he don't spook easy. Ellie-May, head out to the herd an' tell Mike an' Rafe what the plan is. Then you can stay out there with them an' I'll be out as soon as I get the ropes for the boys.' He strode away in the direction of the big wagon.

Ellie-May put her foot in the stirrup and swung smoothly into the saddle. Carefully she checked and holstered the twin .44s. 'Leave some for me, you hear me!' Smiling coldly, she reined Goldie round and headed for the herd.

'Reckon this is as good a place as any.' Ben Turner pulled up and dismounted. Lance and Jake sat waiting. It was dark now. All around in the brush they could hear rustlings and in the distance coyotes howled mournfully.

Carefully the teamster stretched the rope tightly between trees on the side of trail. 'See anything?'

Lance peered into the blackness. 'Nah.'

'Alright, reckon they won't either. The rope'll snag them an' with luck pull them off. Then we grab 'em.'

'Mm. Still leaves us wi' them fellas to keep an' eye on though.'

Ben laughed. 'Said it wasn't perfect. You got a better idea?'

Jake sniffed the night air. Woodsmoke … !' Just might. They ain't that far away. Likely made an early camp, then they'll hit us maybe an' hour or so before dawn.'

'Alright.' There was a doubtful note in Lance's voice. 'What you plannin' to do?'

Jake dismounted and drew off his boots. Rummaging in a small bag hanging from his saddle horn he drew out a pair of moccasins and slipped them on.

'Reckon I'll run their horses off. If we've guessed right fellas like them ain't inclined to walk anywhere. So if we take their mounts that should hold them.' He handed his boots and hat to Ben Turner. 'I'll circle round an' come at them from the other side. If I can get close to their mounts I'll cut them loose.'

'Supposin' you cain't get near 'em?'

'Waal now, if that happens then I reckon I'll have to come back for you fellas.'

Lance thought for a moment. 'Horses can be awful edgy at night. If they start actin' up them fellas are liable to guess that somethin's out there.'

Jake laughed. 'Folks reckon that white mens' horses spook at Injuns and Injuns reckon their ponies spook at white men. Now me, I'm halfway! Don't reckon they'll know what to do. Anyways, I'm going to give it a try. You fellas wait here.'

'Don't like it,' Lance muttered sourly. 'Seems like you're takin' all the risks. Might be better if I came with you.'

'Listen,' Jake smiled to himself in the darkness. 'First thing, you didn't bring a pair o' moccasins. You start traipsin' around in the brush in them boots o' yours an' we sure will have trouble. Second, you might be a helluva good cavalry sergeant an' a fair to middlin' cowhand, but when it comes to stealin' horses you ain't no Comanche!'

'Now,' he handed his pony's reins to Ben Turner. 'You just hold on to Mouse here, till I get back.'

'Fair enough.' There was a pause then the teamster spoke again. 'How about the rope?'

'Good thinkin'. Tell you what. If you hear a Comanche yell, I've got away clear wi' their horses. Get the rope down fast. I'll barrel straight through an' you can just drop in behind me. You don't hear no yell then sit tight wi' the rope.'

He paused at the edge of the trees. 'And don't make no mistakes. I plan to stampede them horses this way. They'll be comin' fast an' I aim to be on one o' them.' There was the faintest movement and he was gone.

Silence, broken only by Ben Turner's quiet chuckle, then Lance spoke. 'Sure is feelin' his oats ain't he! Never heard him talk like that before. He's right though, we'd only get in his way.'

The bearded man picked up the coffee pot and poured himself a cup. He looked at his three companions seated round the fire and said something. There was a general shaking of heads. Shrugging his shoulders, he returned the pot to its place among the embers at the edge of the campfire.

Deep in the undergrowth, on the slight slope above the camp, Jake Larsen crawled forward cautiously. It had taken a long time to get into position, longer than he had intended. *Sure hope they ain't figgerin' to jump us early. Nah, most likely they won't hit us till just before mornin'.*

He moved cautiously towards the four horses tethered back in the trees. The slight night breeze blew from them towards him and he smiled with satisfaction. *Not much further.*

The breeze came again, mingled with the smell of horse sweat. He looked back towards the fire and the group sprawled at ease round it. From somewhere the bearded leader had dug out a bottle and it was passing from hand to hand.

Saloon rustlers! Jake sneered to himself. *Likely spend their time in The Pas. Betcha Ma an' Lance shook 'em up.* The nearest horse sensed his presence and blew softly through its nostrils. Like a shadow Jake flitted across the intervening distance, knife in hand. The horse blew again, then subsided as Jake stroked its neck.

Working quickly he cut through the hitching ropes holding each horse. They sensed something was amiss and started to move restlessly.

'Somethin's spookin' them horses.' Bart Saunders rose to his feet as he spoke.

'Nah.' One of his companions waved the bottle dismissively. 'There ain't nothin' out …'

Jake vaulted into the saddle and drove his mount forward. It cannoned into the others and the high-pitched Comanche warwhoop split the night. All four horses took off down the trail.

Behind him Jake heard scattered shots, then he was round a bend in the trail and away, the three loose horses racing ahead of him.

'Reckon they'll come after you?' They were well clear now and the loose horses had steadied to a canter. Ben Turner glanced sideways as he spoke.

'Nah. Figger they're saloon fighters. Outa their depth in brush country. 'Sides, that Comanche yell's gonna make them think the place is crawlin' wi' Injuns! My guess is they'll head back to Mesilla an' try to pick up mounts there.'

Jake paused for a moment. 'Still, reckon they'll be plenty mad. We've bested 'em twice. Might just be they'll try somethin'. How about I stay here an' keep watch for a spell?'

Lance grinned in the darkness. 'Yeah. An' if you got no objections I'll stay with you. Ben, you mind takin' them loose horses back an' tellin' Pa what's been happenin'?'

Ben Turner laughed. 'Fine by me. Don't reckon you'll have any trouble though. See you in the mornin'.'

The hoofbeats dwindled into the distance and they settled themselves to wait.

CHAPTER 20

'Rider comin' Boss.' Joe Masterson stuck his head through the stable door. 'Just fordin' the creek now.'

'Thanks.' Bull laid down the bridle he had been working on. *Lord I'm tired. Seems like we'll never get this place straightened out!* He eased his way through the doorway and fell into step beside the foreman.

'Anybody we know?'

Joe shook his head. 'Hard to say at this distance.' Together, they watched the mounted figure grow steadily larger.

'Tell you one thing, he ain't no youngster. That's a good mount he's ridin' though.'

'Yeah.' Bull looked more closely. 'Say, that's a quarter horse.'

'You're right.' Joe's gaze sharpened. 'Reckon I know him now. That's Jack Donovan o' the Diamond D. Wonder what he wants?'

Bull grinned. 'Might be he's come to thank us for gettin' his horses back.'

'Him!' Joe laughed. 'He's a cantankerous old cuss. Liable to bawl you out 'cause you let one go.'

      ✳   ✳   ✳   ✳

'Howdy.' Jack Donovan pulled the bay quarter horse to a halt and sat looking down at them. 'Lookin' for a fella called Jordan.'

'That's me.' Bull stepped forward. 'Guess you know Joe here. Light down. What can we do for you?'

'The name's Donovan, Jack Donovan o' the Diamond D. Depitty told me you got m'horses back. 'Preciate that. Right neighbourly.' He dismounted stiffly.

Joe Masterson blinked. The old buzzard, he thought wryly, remembering the old rancher's cantankerous behaviour at round-ups. He's after somethin'. Aloud he said, 'Boss, reckon I'll head down to the corral an' see how the boys are makin' out wi' that second bunch o' remounts.' He closed one eye as he turned away. Bull stared after him curiously.

'Waal now,' Jack Donovan leaned back in his chair and looked hard at Bull. 'Looks like you been right busy since you got here. Ain't seen that much stock up this end o' your range in years.'

Bull frowned. 'Seems that fella Sands had been workin' wi' Sanchez an' his bunch for a long time. Guess between them they'd have bled the Flyin' W white. Now we've combed the brush and pushed everything up here.'

'Mm.' Donovan shot a shrewd glance at the big man. 'That Sands was trouble. Beats me what Dave Wilson ever saw in him.'

'Can happen,' Bull said shortly. 'You got to remember his wife died about then. An' she'd been ill for quite a spell. Don't reckon he had all that much interest in the ranch at the time.'

'Yeah.' For a brief moment there was a faraway look in the old rancher's eyes. 'Know what you mean. Can be rough then. I hear your folks are headin' west wi' a herd?'

'That's right.' Well now, news travels fast around here. 'Durham bulls and first cross Longhorn cows. Be here in another week or so I reckon.'

'Durhams hey. Think they can last out here?'

Bull shrugged. 'Reckon so. Anyways, time'll tell. Plannin' to breed up our saddle stock as well. Folks are bringin' in a big old Cleveland stallion wi' a score o' Cleveland an' Morgan mares.'

'Morgans hey! Might just be interested. That quarter hoss o' mine got a lot o' Morgan blood in him.'

'Thought he had. Good lookin' bronc. Waal, once we get settled in you're welcome to look our stock over. Always ready to do a deal wi' a neighbour.'

'Boss!' Joe hailed from the porch.

'Yo.'

''Nother rider comin'. Just hittin' the creek now. Tall fella on a big red roan.'

'I'll be damned!' Bull rose quickly. 'Betcha that's m'brother John an' Big Red. Let's go see. Like you to meet John.'

'Yeah, it's them alright. Can tell that long stride o' Red's anywhere. Mean cuss; hates men. Bought him off some Comancheros down in the Big Bend. Somebody had roughed him up pretty bad. For a long spell I thought he'd turn outlaw an' I'd have to shoot him, but we got it together in the end. Only reason he tolerates John is 'cause m'brother's just about the best horse handler I've ever seen. An' everythin' he knows he learned from the Comanches.'

'How come?'

'It's a long story. Tell you about it some time. Watch out for Red. He can be right mean at times.'

John grinned as Red pricked his ears in recognition and jogged towards Bull.

The big horse blew through his nostrils and rubbed his head against his master's shoulder. Bull stroked the gelding's neck and grinned up at John. 'Howdy John boy. Good trip?'

'Seen better.' John swung down stiffly, relief visible on his face. 'Well praise be. Seems like I been worryin' 'bout nothin' after all.'

Bull looked at him in surprise. 'How come? Oh, 'fore I forget … this here's Jack Donovan. Owns the Diamond D. Neighbour o' ours. An' this is Joe Masterson, foreman. Joe tells me what to do.'

Joe grinned as they shook hands.

Bull indicated Clay Wallace who had joined them on the porch. 'Clay, you know already.'

John nodded.

'Alright, what's been worryin' you?'

'Red,' John said succinctly. 'He killed a man 'bout three weeks back.' Briefly he outlined the happenings at the spring. 'He's been actin' strange ever since. Moody, an' watchin' me all the time. Still, seems like he ain't forgot you, so maybe he'll be alright now.'

Bull nodded, his hand still on Red's neck. 'An' you don't know what set him off?'

John shook his head. 'Like I said, when I come to there was Red with blood all over his forelegs, an' this fella … Henry, stomped flat. Don't reckon there was a whole bone left in his body. Likely Red got too close an' Henry hit 'im. Red wouldn't take that.'

'Yeah.' There was a faraway look in Bull's eyes. 'You could be right. Nobody lays a hand on Red. Sometimes wonder why he puts up wi' me. Luck I guess.'

John shrugged. 'Hard to say. Anyways, he's your worry now. You got a horse for me? When I left the folks they were just headin' north from Horsehead Crossing. They're kinda tight on riders an' Pa reckons if you could spare two, three fellas to go back with me an' meet 'em it'd make things a whole lot easier.'

'Guess it would at that.' Bull paused, frowning thoughtfully. 'There's Jeff an' Chester, ex-cavalry sergeants. Just right for this kinda work. I'll speak to them. '

'I'll go as well.' Bull looked at Clay Wallace in surprise. 'Why not? The accounts are all straightened out. Things must be tight or your father wouldn't have asked. So, if you've no objections, I'll ride with John.'

Bull thought for a moment. 'Alright with me. Reckon four extra riders would make things a lot easier.'

Donovan grunted impatiently. 'Seems like you fellas got things to do. Reckon I'll be ridin'.'

Untying the quarter horse he paused for a moment and looked away. 'Some time when you're up on the north range ride across an' take a look at the Diamond D. Like to show you m'place.' He swung up into the saddle and lifted a hand in salute 'Nice meetin' you gents. Adios now.' Catlike, the pony was into its stride in a flash.

Joe Masterson whistled softly as they watched Donovan splash across the creek. 'Whoo-eeh, what's got into him?'

Bull glanced at him enquiringly. 'What's eatin' you ?'

'Boss,' Joe faced the big man squarely, 'They's two things you got to know 'bout Jack Donovan. First off, he don't thank nobody, ever. Second, he never invites folks to the Diamond D. That bein' so, what makes you so all-fired special?'

Bull shrugged. 'Just bein' neighbourly I guess.'

The foreman snorted derisively. 'You believe that, you'll believe anything. Nah ... he's got somethin' planned, an' you're in it. Anyways, I got work to do. You want to see Jeff an' Chester?'

'Yeah, they can meet John at the same time. Me. I'll go put Red in the stable. Keep him there at night till he settles in. John, you can have that big grey I been ridin'.'

'Waal, that's it fellas.' Bull looked at the two impassive faces in front of him. 'You've met m'brother here,' he indicated John talking quietly to Clay in the corner. 'An' you know Clay. How you feel about sidin' them on this trip?'

The two ex-sergeants looked at each other and grinned. Jeff spoke. 'Be a right nice change Ah reckon. Ain't been up near Apache Pass since we was ridin' with the old Tenth. Yeah, count me in.'

'That goes for me too.' Chester hitched his gunbelt. 'We rides for the brand, we fights for the brand.'

'Thanks.' Bull looked down at the table to hide his emotions. 'Don't know what sort o' outfit m'folks have managed to throw together but it cain't be much. Reckon the big outfits took all the hands early on in the spring.' The corners of his mouth twitched. 'You've met Ma so you know what to expect.'

Jeff and Chester laughed.

'You'll like m'old man. A mite easygoin' maybe, but he's your kind o' folks. Anyways, John's plannin' to leave some time in the mornin'. I'll see Joe an' tell him what's happenin'.'

'Sure thing.' Together they slipped quietly out of the room.

CHAPTER 21

▼

Jake looked across the bobbing dun coloured backs at Lance and frowned. Lord, I'm tired. Wonder how Lance feels? Must be a change from leadin' patrols down on the Border.

He twisted in his saddle and looked back. Behind him Mike Glenwood was hazing a determined cow back into the herd. The young half-breed shook his head sadly. Andy an' Mike weren't youngsters but now Mike looks real old.

Diagonally across from him Jim Jordan was working the swing position with his usual economical style. Thank the Lord for Pa. He watched the slight figure of Rafe Allen, the knotted bandanna pulled up over his mouth and nose, pushing busily in the dust of the drag … an' young Rafe. That boy's got the makin's.

In the distance he saw the flash of Goldie's flaxen mane and tail as Ellie-May swept around the remuda. She's as good as any man, he thought approvingly, workin' the remuda by herself through the day, then takin' her turn night herdin'. He grinned to himself. Wouldn't like to tell her that though. She reckons she's better!

He turned and looked ahead. No sign of the wagons. Must be makin' good time. That Ben Turner is quite a guy. Deftly, mind on other things, he eased a straying Durham bull back into the herd.

Ma Jordan peered out at a featureless landscape. Tough country; dry stretch too. 'Nother twenty miles to Stein's 'fore we strike water again. Hope the stock stand up to it. Ain't no use complainin' Mary-Lou, it was your idea. Her eyelids drooped and she nodded slightly.

'Are you alright Miz Jordan?' She came to with a start to find Sarah Johnson regarding her anxiously from the opposite seat.

'Yeah, I'm fine. Just feelin' tired, that's all.'

'Will it be long before we get to the ranch?'

'Be a week or so yet. You gettin' fed up wi' all this travellin'?'

'Well,' Sarah considered the question carefully, 'we like seeing everything, but it would be nice to be with Mister Bull again.'

Ma felt a lump in her throat. She swallowed. 'Yeah, guess we'd all like to see him again.'

Ellie-May brought Goldie across the rear of the remuda and turned to start another swing back. Hitching the bandanna higher across her face she wiped her brow with the back of her hand. Wish we was at the ranch. I could sleep for a week. She looked critically at the horses. The last twenty miles is goin' to be rough. Sure hope Pa an' Jake know what they're doin'.

'So Lance is with the herd?' Bull Jordan lounged comfortably in the big worn easy chair and looked narrowly at his younger brother. Supper was over and John was recounting the herd's progress to the Platte. 'Any reason why?'

John shook his head. 'All I know is Pa came in after his trip to Fort Concho an' said Lance was takin' a long furlough to help us out.'

'Mm.' Bull frowned. He turned to Clay Wallace relaxing on the big leather couch. 'You know anything 'bout this?' he queried abruptly.

'Can't say I do.' Clay looked at the big man closely. Something was troubling him. 'Last I saw of him he was leading a patrol down towards the Trinity. That was just when your folks sold the ranch.'

'Mm.' Bull was silent for a moment, then … 'Allus thought Lance had no time for cow work. Where does he fit in on the drive?' he demanded suddenly.

'Waal,' John paused in surprise, 'anywhere I guess. Point, swing, drag, night herdin'. You name it, he does it. Jake's the segundo an' Lance takes his orders from Jake like the rest o' the crew.'

Bull seemed satisfied. 'Jake's a good cowman, knows the score. He'll do alright.'

'Yeah.' There was a long silence, then John rose to his feet. 'Reckon I'll turn in. Looks like tomorrow'll be a busy day. 'Night, Clay.' He disappeared through the door.

Bull yawned widely. 'Reckon I'll do the same. Like to have a look at that north range tomorrow.'

Clay thought quickly. 'Mind if I say something?'

'Sure. What's on your mind?'

'You're wondering why Lance is with the herd?' He held up his hand as Bull opened his mouth. 'Let me finish. I've just remembered something. That day when your father clinched the sale of the Circle J to Dunc Paterson, Lance and I talked. I asked him if he was interested in the cattle business.'

Bull leaned forward and stared intently at the slim Easterner. 'An' what did he say?'

'He laughed and said no; the cavalry was in his blood now. Then he talked about all the work you had done to make the Circle J what it was, and how you deserved this chance. He reckons you'll be a cattle king some day. So you see,' he concluded, 'whatever is bringing him out here, it isn't the ranch. Hope that puts your mind at rest.'

The big rancher flushed. 'You don't think much of me do you?'

'You're wrong there. I owe you a great deal. Some day I'll tell you all about it. But you've got no worries as far as Lance is concerned.'

'Looks like old Lance knows me better than I know m'self!' Bull grinned shamefacedly. 'But he's right. I cain't help bein' like I am. This is my chance. I aim to make the Flyin' W a cattle empire. Anyway, thanks for settin' me straight. 'Night now.'

'Night.' Clay sat watching the dying embers of the fire. In spite of the warmth he shivered suddenly. Clay Wallace, he thought wryly, you were skating on mighty thin ice just now. Still, it was worth it.

Yawning widely, he stood up. Time to hit the hay I reckon. Tomorrow's another day.

Perched high on the corral fence, John felt the chill of the early morning air through his shirt.

'That him?' He pointed to the big steeldust grey in the centre of the bunched horses.

Bull nodded. He was aware that the Aldersons were watching closely.

Rope in hand, his brother climbed down into the corral. The bunched horses split and, just for a second, the grey hesitated. John threw, and the loop dropped neatly over the upraised head. Heels dug in, John held until the plunging horse slowed to a stop, then hand over hand he worked his way along the rope, talking softly all the while.

'Waal, he can rope,' Sam Alderson said grudgingly to his brother. 'I'll give'm that. But then, you'd expect that from a Texan.'

Mike nodded. 'Wait till he gets in the saddle. Kiowa likes to get the kinks out of his system first thing. Let's see how young Jordan handles that.'

Together they watched closely as John laid his hand on the big grey's neck, talking softly in the same sing-song voice. Kiowa surveyed him cautiously, ears pricked. Reaching inside his shirt, the young rancher stood for a moment still talking. The he brought his hand out and rubbed it gently across the grey's nose. The big horse whinneyed softly and nosed at John's shoulder.

Watching from the other side of the corral Bull grinned to himself. He had seen John do this several times and, although he had never queried the reason for it, figuring John would tell him in his own good time, he suspected that it had to do with the rider's body smell.

His brother stroked the grey's nose once more, then he turned, rope in hand and walked towards the corral fence, the big horse ambling quietly behind him.

The Aldersons looked at each other and grinned. 'Waal now, maybe he does know something about horses,' Mike said softly, as John tied Kiowa to the fence. 'Cain't say I've ever seen that trick before though.'

'Me neither,' Sam agreed. 'Let's see what he does next.'

John Jordan folded the wool saddle blanket and laid it on the grey's back, talking again in the same soothing murmur. He reached for his saddle hanging on the corral fence, and Mike Anderson's eyes widened.

'Hey, that's an old Spanish single rig. Ain't seen one o' them in years. Should'a thought he'd be a rimfire man.'

John eased the saddle onto Kiowa, taking care that the dangling cinch did not foul the horse's back. Reaching through he caught the trailing cinch and secured the latigo strap through the cinch ring. He drew the cinch tight and tested it to ensure that Kiowa hadn't been holding his breath. Then he tied the latigo off neatly and, picking up the bridle, slipped it over the horse's head. Holding the reins in one hand he eased gently into the saddle. The Aldersons watched closely.

Kiowa tensed for a second, then relaxed as John leaned forward and patted his neck. Quietly the young rider urged the big horse towards the corral gate. Bull swung it open and raised his hand as his brother rode through.

He closed it and turned to find the Aldersons coming towards him.

'Waal,' Bull grinned at them. 'You satisfied?' He saw them exchange looks and laughed. 'Reckon I'm blind or somethin'? You been sittin' up there wonderin' if he was as good as I said he was. You believe me now?'

They nodded together. 'Sure would like to know how he does it,' Sam said sheepishly. 'Kiowa allus bucks when you get on him first thing, yet he stood there as quiet as you please when your brother got up on him. How come?'

'You got to remember John grew up among the Comanches. You fellas do much Injun fightin'?'

The Aldersons looked at each other. 'Some,' Mike said slowly. 'Apaches mostly ... '

'Recall how they handled their ponies?' Bull cut in.

Mike shook his head. 'Nothin' special. Most o' the times I saw them they was comin' at us whoopin' an' hollerin'.'

Bull nodded. 'I useta think that. Then two, three times in the war I had to scout Injun villages for the cavalry. Watchin' them gettin' set to move in the mornin' I noticed they didn't have no trouble with their ponies. When an Injun got on his pony there wasn't no pitchin' or buckin'. Alright, I know our mounts are bigger an' they're grain fed, but I figgered that wasn't the full story. Tried askin' John an' his sidekick Jake Larsen, but they just laughed. Said you had to be a Comanche to know this trick. So now you know.'

CHAPTER 22

'Where d'you think the herd are now?' Clay Wallace glanced at his companion.

John thought for a moment. 'Reckon they'll be gettin' well along towards Stein's. 'Course that's tough country up there. Always the chance that they'll get jumped by Injuns. But … yeah, I reckon they'll be about there.'

'Think they'll run into trouble?'

'Waal, there's Injuns around, that's for sure. Accordin' to the cavalry, Cochise is havin' trouble holdin' his boys in.'

'What d'you make o' him?' Jeff gestured ahead to the tall young man on the big grey.

'Young John?' Chester shrugged. 'Seems an alright fella. Quiet though. Sure didn't say much last night.'

'Naw.' His companion laughed. 'But then the boss, he said enough for both o' them. That's one fella Ah wouldn't like to cross.'

Chester grinned. 'Yeah; still one thing's for sure, colour don't mean nothin' to him. Don't think he even notices we're black. Miz Jordan's the same. Now there is one tough lady. Wonder what the rest o' the family are like?'

'One thing at a time. We rides for the brand …'

'We fights for the brand! Ah've heard you before.'

Laughing together, they jogged on north.

October was drawing to a close and the days were shorter now. There was an autumn feel in the dry desert air. Rafe Allen turned a rumbling Durham bull back into the herd. Should have got me a brush jacket in El Paso. Still, once we make the ranch there'll be time for all that. Wish Pa could see me now. Ridin' swing on a trail herd!

He looked back at the lean figure of Jim Jordan, bandanna over his face, pushing the drag on. Sure was nice of Mister Jordan, offerin' to change places with me. Said he thought I deserved it. Nice folks the Jordans. 'Course, Miz Jordan is a mite fierce but she's alright. In the distance he saw the golden palomino swinging round the rear of the remuda. Even Ellie-Mae, she ain't so bad. An' she's coverin' the remuda on her own. Must be somethin' to own a pony like that Goldie. Still, I got nothin' to gripe about. Got me a job an' a string o' ponies to ride. Naw, things are just fine.

He's a good kid, Jim Jordan grinned to himself under the bandanna. Nothin's too much trouble for him. Lance too. Useta wonder if he would stick it, but there he is ridin' point with Jake an' doin' just fine. His mouth twisted wryly. Ain't sorry to see the back o' Stein's. Only good thing about it, we got the outfit watered an' rested. An' the next stretch to San Simon ain't that long. No sign o' Injuns so far, mebbe we'll be lucky. Sure hope so. He turned the big Cleveland across the rear of the herd on another swing.

'You are sure?' The speaker, a thickset Apache with an air of authority looked hard at the young warrior seated across from him. 'A small herd you say?'

'It is true.' The youngster met the keen gaze unwaveringly. 'Both cattle and horses. They will reach the water tonight. It is likely that they will camp there to water their stock.'

Black Knife, chief and leader of the twelve Apaches seated round the campfire nodded.

Red Buffalo, who considered himself a better leader than Black Knife, spoke. 'I say we should wait until they have gone through the pass and are in Little Elk's country. Then we will be stronger.'

There were several nods, and a few non-committal grunts, from the group round the fire. Red Buffalo permitted himself a slight smile which Black Knife noted. Some day, he thought sourly, that one will make trouble.

Aloud he said. 'The nearer we let the 'white eyes' get to the fort at Puerto del Dado Springs, the more difficult they will be to beat. I say we should attack them at the water.' He paused for effect. 'Then we can drive the horses and cattle north to the Gila river. There we will find Geronimo and we can trade with him and his tribe.'

There was general enthusiasm for this idea. Red Buffalo realised that he had lost out and quickly joined in. Fools, Black Knife thought to himself, are easily led. He rose to his feet. 'We will ride now. I want to plan our attack.'

'Ma ... you alright?'

Busily engaged in chopping vegetables for a stew, Ma Jordan turned to find Sara-Jane looking at her anxiously.

Ma shrugged as she scraped the contents of the board into the pot. 'Tired I guess,' she admitted reluctantly. 'Seems as though this drive'll never end. Sometimes I wonder if it's all worthwhile. Look at Andy, buried under a rock back there. Then there's Mike, mopin' around 'cause his buddy's dead. An' I started it all.'

'Ma ... !'

'Hush up Sara-Jane. Don't you go tellin' nobody what I just said. It'd take the heart out o' them. It's just between us, you hear.'

'Yes Ma.'

'Right then. Go check that batch o' biscuits in the oven. The boys'll be in from the herd right soon, so there ain't no time to waste.'

Jake Larsen frowned as he sat watching the last of the herd drink their fill at the river. He turned as Lance cantered up alongside.

The big sergeant grinned at him. 'Howdy Jake. You don't look none too chipper. What's eatin' you?'

'Got a feelin' somebody's trailin' us. Cain't be sure, just a feelin' I got. Thought I saw smoke a coupla days back. Could'a been mistaken.' He shrugged.

Lance looked at him closely. 'But you reckon you ain't?'

Jake nodded.

The lines on the big sergeant's face tightened. 'Guess I know what you mean. I've had the same feelin' myself, just before trouble hits. What d'you reckon? 'Paches?'

'Mm. Too far out for Comanches, less'n they're a bunch o' young bucks on the loose. Same goes for rustlers, they ain't goin' to risk their necks out here. Naw, got to be Apaches.'

Lance frowned. 'Spoken to Pa?'

Jake shook his head. 'Not yet. Kept hopin' Cougar would get back wi' two or three riders to help on the last stretch. Still a chance I suppose. Anyways, I'd better tell him now.'

Jim Jordan listened intently, frowning as he did so. 'Reckon you're right, Jake. Things have been a sight too peaceful lately. You feel the same, Lance?'

His eldest son nodded. 'Yeah, I'd go along wi' Jake. Somebody's out there an' I reckon it'll be Apaches.'

'That's agreed then. Question is, what we gonna do 'bout 'em? Jake?'

'Waal,' Jake paused to marshall his thoughts, 'we're here at the San Simon. Got water an' feed. Now I reckon they'll hit us just 'fore dawn. They got to come across open ground to get to the herd an' we can bunch up the remuda in front. Most o' the horses are gunbroke an' they're less likely to spook than the cattle. 'Course we don't know how many there are, but I reckon we can shake them up some when they make their play. Likely they'll swing off after the first pass, then it'll be a case o' outlastin' 'em.'

Jim Jordan nodded approvingly. 'Sounds right good sense to me. Anything you want to add, Lance?'

The big sergeant shook his head. 'Nothin'. Jake's said it all. We ain't got enough wagons to circle, so we might as well leave them where they are.'

His father nodded. 'Right. We'll wait till everybody's had their chuck then I'll tell 'em. Let's head back 'fore Ma gets tetchy!'

'So there you have it.' Jim Jordan gazed round the circle of serious faces limned by the flickering flames of the campfire. Apart from Jake and Lance taking the first night trick, and the Johnson girls, already in bed, everybody was there. 'It might not happen, but I don't believe in takin' chances. Come mornin' I want us all set.'

There was a chorus of agreement all round as they rose to their feet.

Sara-Jane shivered.

'You alright, gal?' Ma looked at her searchingly.

Her daughter bit her lip. 'Ma ... I'm scared!'

Ma scowled fiercely. 'Now you just listen to me Sara-Jane. When we had that run-in wi' the Andersons you did alright. No reason why you cain't do it again. That shotgun in the sleepin' wagon. Get it checked an' loaded. Ain't never met nobody who wasn't scared sometime. Thing is, you got to go on doin' whatever you're doin'. Now, go check that gun.'

CHAPTER 23

▼

Ben Turner delved into the old chest. Been a long time. Wonder what Pa would say if he saw me now? I swore when the war was over, I'd never fire a gun again an' I've stuck to that until now. Cain't let the Jordans down. His fingers touched oilcloth and he drew out the long carefully preserved rifle. Working by lantern light, he stripped off the wrappings. A sheen of oil gleamed on the barrel of the Sharps .50 buffalo gun. What would the folks say if they knew I served in the U.S. Sharpshooters during the war? Wonder how many good old Southern boys never saw home 'cause o' me an' Betsy here?

He shook his head and rummaged in the chest again until he found the box of cartridges. Extracting it carefully, he cut the seals. Should be alright, they're still in the original packin'. Man, I'd forgotten how big them cartridges were. Box o' a hundred … should be enough!

Laying the box down, he began to check the big rifle.

'I ain't doin' it Pa! I ain't hidin' in no wagon. The remuda's my job an' that's where I'm goin' to be!'

Jim Jordan looked at his furious elder daughter. 'You know it could get rough out there. Apaches don't fool around. They go for a quick kill. Think you can keep your nerve?'

'Pa, I faced Jack Anderson an' beat him. Mebbe I was lucky, but there ain't no Injun gettin' at that remuda while I'm around.'

'Alright!' Her father threw up his hands. 'Have it your way. Only ... for the Lord's sake stay outa trouble. Don't suppose you'd mind if Rafe sided you?'

'Rafe's alright.' A wintry smile showed briefly on Ellie-May's face. 'Him an' me got that remuda workin' real good. 'Course it ain't helped, him doin' that extra stint wi' the herd. Still, we'll manage.' She turned on her heel and strode away.

Lance drifted quietly round the herd. His mount whinneyed softly as Jake and his pony loomed out of the darkness.

'All quiet?'

'Yeah.' Jake's voice was tense. 'They're all bedded down. Your pa an' Mike'll be out soon. Sure wish we had more riders.'

'Mm' There was a pause. 'You still aimin' to cover the south side?'

'Yeah. We ain't got enough riders for every point so we got to gamble that they'll come from that stand o' timber to the south.'

'Horses comin'.' Lance's hand dropped to his gunbelt as they waited tensely.

Three mounted figures materialised out of the gloom. 'Jake? Lance?'

'Over here Pa.'

'Ben's with us. Got somethin' he wants to say. Reckon it's worth hearin'.'

'Right!' There was an incisiveness about Ben's voice that neither Jake nor Lance had heard before. 'This is it. 'Bout four hundred yards south o' here there's an' old buffalo wallow, two, three feet deep, an' some twenty feet across.

Now,' his voice sharpened, 'I'm a better than average shot. In the war I was a sharpshooter. Got me a 'Big Fifty' Sharps rifle. It'll kill at purty near a mile. Got field glasses as well. If Jake's right, an' I think he is, they'll come from that timber, 'bout threequarters o' a mile from the wallow. With luck I should shake them up. An' I got me a couple o' Dragoon Colts, in case things get kinda hot. Need you fellas to cover m'back though an' bring a pony out for me. My advice would be to light out when they're about halfway between the timber an' the wallow. That way we might just be able to turn 'em.'

'What if some o' them get through?' Lance interjected.

'Then it's up to Ellie-May an' Rafe. Shouldn't think there'll be many get through. Yeah ... I know it's rough on the kids, but if we let them into the herd an' the remuda we've lost everything. Anybody got a better idea?'

There was a long silence then Jim Jordan spoke.

'Alright fellas, let's do it.'

They were through the pass now and out into the open country. A fitful moon cast an intermittent light on the trail ahead.

John Jordan slowed Kiowa slightly and Clay Wallace's mount came up beside the big grey.

'Should make the San Simon wash by first light. If we don't find the herd bedded down there at the dam, then we can start worryin'. Only water for miles round.'

'What about Indians?'

'Accordin' to Colonel Pettigrew there's been a lot more Injun sightin's in the last few weeks. Tribes could be gettin' ready to start somethin'. The sooner we get to the folks the happier I'll be.'

'Mm.' Clay paused for a moment, then … 'Chester and Jeff are quiet.'

'Yeah, they're cavalry boys. They know you don't gab in Injun country 'less you have to.'

'Sorry.' Clay felt his face burning.

John chuckled drily. 'No harm done. Just somethin' to remember for the future.' They loped on steadily.

The eastern sky was beginning to lighten now. Bushes were coming into focus and minute by minute the light was strengthening. Black Knife looked along the line of mounted braves, waiting just inside the timber. His mouth tightened as he saw Red Buffalo moving out of the trees ahead of the line.

Peering over the edge of the buffalo wallow Ben Turner swept the edge of the timber with his fieldglasses. A faint movement caught his eyes. There! … again. The tiny dot resolved itself into a tall Indian on a pinto pony, looking directly towards him.

Ben lifted the big rifle and settled himself comfortably. It was all coming back. Slowly he sighted on the tiny distant figure.

Red Buffalo turned and looked directly towards Black Knife. He saw anger on the chief's face. Look at him skulking in the trees. The 'white eyes' are nothing. They do not know we are here.

Ben Turner squeezed the trigger gently.

Driven by 170 grains of black powder, the huge bullet smashed into Red Buffalo's ribcage and knocked him clean off the pinto's back, dead before he even hit the ground. The sullen boom of the big Sharps echoed across the bedground.

Black Knife slammed his heels into his pony and came out of the trees at the run. The fool, he raged as his braves fanned out on either side, now the 'white eyes' know we are here. The Sharps boomed again and beyond him a pony crumpled in midstride. Its rider vaulted clear and came up running.

'Let's go!' Lance Jordan spurred the big buckskin and the gelding flattened into an all-out gallop. His father and Jake fanned out on either side. Behind them Mike Glenwood raced for the wallow with Ben Turner's mount running beside him.

John Jordan topped the rise above the San Simon wash and took in the situation at a glance. 'Ride, we'll take them in their flank.' He urged his mount across the wash and the big grey went up the opposite bank like a cat, Clay, Jeff and Chester close behind.

Guns in hand, Ellie-May and Rafe waited tensely.

The shot that killed Black Knife's pony saved the herd. Just for a moment the Apaches hesitated, but it was enough.

John and the others swept in on their flank and unleashed a storm of lead. Three Apaches died in their first pass.

Beyond them Mike Glenwood sagged and fell sideways, the shaft of an arrow protruding from his chest.

Catching up one of the loose horses Black Knife signalled to the remainder of his band to pull out. Two young braves on the far right did not see it. Young Bull and Grey Wolf were on their first raid and nothing was going to stop them getting to the 'white eyes" horses.

'Here they come.' Ellie-May settled herself in the saddle as she and Rafe separated to cover the remuda.

Smoothly, Young Bull loosed the arrow he held ready. Rafe gasped as the barbs bit into his shoulder. The Colt dropped from his fingers, and he clutched one-handed at the saddlehorn.

The high Apache yell lifted on the morning breeze, as Young Bull, followed by Grey Wolf and Ellie-May swept past the first of the wagons.

Resting the sawn-off on the half door, Ma Jordan watched the three riders race towards her. Got to make sure o' the first fella an' hope Ellie-May can take the other one.

Sighting carefully, she triggered both barrels and watched impassively as Young Bull, and his pony, died in a hail of buckshot.

Got to stop him now. Ellie-May leaned along Goldie's neck and spoke sharply. The palomino lengthened his stride in a blur of movement and the gap closed suddenly. Grey Wolf looked back and snarled a curse at the golden horse overhauling him. The old Dragoon Colt, which he carried with such pride, boomed once and Ellie-May gasped as her hat was plucked from her head.

The .44 in her right hand cracked twice in quick succession. Grey Wolf sagged sideways and slid tiredly from the pony's back.

They were closing on the remuda now, and already some of the nearest horses were beginning to plunge and rear.

Desperately, Ellie-May grabbed for the trailing hackamore and held on. Goldie shouldered into Grey Wolf's mount and knocked it sideways. Hanging on grimly, the tall girl turned both ponies in a neat half circle and brought them to a plunging halt.

Shaking, she looked back at the remuda. They were settling down again, and big Dance was watching her placidly. It was over. She had done it!

CHAPTER 24

▼

'He's comin' round. Told you he wasn't dead.'

Grey Wolf stirred and groaned. His eyes flickered open and widened in sudden alarm.

'White eyes'! They were all round him. Attempting to rise, he realised that his feet were tied together and his hands lashed behind him. Exhausted, the young Apache sank back.

'Thought he was dead,' Ellie-May said soberly. 'Then I saw the bullet burn along the side o' his head an' the blood on his shoulder. Figgered my shootin' hadn't been all that bad, 'cause I only pumped off two rounds. 'Course, him blowin' m'hat off with that old Dragoon Colt didn't improve my aim none. Question is, what we gonna do with him?'

'Don't see nothin to argue about.' Shotgun in hand, Ma glared round the others. 'Out here it's kill or be killed. Him an' them others came bustin' in here lookin' for blood an' they got it. If we hadn't been ready we'd likely be lyin' where he is. An' he sure wouldn't be worryin' 'bout us. As it is, Mike Glenwood's dead, an' young Rafe's got an arrowhead in his shoulder that'll have to be cut out.'

She turned on her heel with a parting shot. 'Suit yourselves. Me, I got work to do. Ain't got time to argue 'bout an Injun who's lucky to be alive.'

There was a long silence as John, Ellie-May and their father, watched the small determined woman make her way to the accommodation wagon where Sara-Jane was attending to Rafe's wound.

Seated beside the chuck wagon, Miguel was keeping the Johnson girls occupied, teaching them how to plait a riata. Out beyond the remuda, guns at the ready, Jake and the others waited in a tense, strung out line.

Jim Jordan rubbed his chin. 'Well now, you heard Ma.' He looked at his son and daughter. 'Either of you got anything you want to say?'

Ellie-May shook her head. 'Seems to me there's been enough killin'. Once mebbe I'd have agreed with Ma, but not now. I say let him live.'

Her father frowned. 'I'd go along with you, 'cept for one thing. We cain't keep him prisoner, an' if we turn him loose he'll go back an' tell the others what he's seen.'

'Pa,' John hesitated for a moment, 'there may be another way. Let me try.'

He squatted down beside Grey Wolf and spoke in halting Apache, interspersed with sign language.

For a long moment the young brave was silent, then he threw a sharp question at John.

Slowly John unbuttoned his shirt and slid it off. The cougar claw marks on his shoulder showed up vividly, but Grey Wolf was more interested in the two deep scars on John's chest. He leaned forward and stared at them intently. Then, lifting his gaze he looked deeply into the young rancher's eyes and spoke again, a questioning note in his voice. John nodded and replied. Grey Wolf seemed satisfied and ready to talk. Jim Jordan watched closely as the two young men conversed. Once, his son said something and the Apache grinned. He made a short comment, and John laughed in turn as he answered. The conversation drew to a close and John rose to his feet.

'Waal,' his father looked at him quizzically. 'What was all that gabbin' about?'

His son grinned. 'Pa, this here's Grey Wolf, a young buck on his first raid. He was ridin' wi' Black Knife's boys. Seems like they're raidin' down from the Dragoons this way. They been trailin' you for two, three days.'

Jim Jordan nodded. 'Jake figgered that.'

'Right. Here's what I'd like you to do. Get Ma to dig the bullet out o' his shoulder an' fix'm up. Then we let him go. I've told him I want to meet Black Knife under a white flag. After that we wait an' see. But I'm bettin' that Black Knife'll be just curious enough to meet me.'

'Supposin' he does, what then?'

'I'll suggest a truce. We head out wi' the herd an' they go their way. If he don't agree then we got a fight on our hands. Right now it's a stand-off. What d'you say?'

His father thought for a moment. 'Alright, we'll do it your way. Ma ain't goin' to like it though.'

'Figgered as much. But it's either that or shoot our way out. An' we could lose a lot o stock doin' that.'

'You're right. Let's go see Ma.'

There was a strong smell of whiskey in the wagon. Ma straightened up as the side door opened. 'You've come at just the right time. I need you both to hold Rafe up 'fore I get this arrowhead out.'

Rafe Allen grinned through a haze of whiskey fumes and pain. 'Sure is nice to see you Boss. Miz Jordan, set up a drink for the boss!'

'He's drunk,' Ma said tersely, 'but there ain't no other way. Now Pa, John boy, hold'm tight. Sara-Jane, give'm that belt to bite on. I'm goin' to push this arrow right through.'

'You all set?' They nodded. Mopping her brow, she pushed hard on the projecting shaft. Rafe groaned deep in his throat and bit down on the leather. Ma increased the pressure. The groan rose to a bubbling scream as the point of the arrow showed darkly under the skin. Rafe screamed again, and was suddenly limp.

'Fainted,' said Ma shortly. 'The best way. Hold him still now an' I'll push it through.'

Carefully drawing out the wickedly barbed head and the section of shaft, she grunted with satisfaction as blood welled up cleanly in the wound.

'Seems alright to me. Get a pad on it Sara-Jane and bandage it up.' She looked critically at her white-faced daughter. 'How're you feelin' gal?'

Sara-Jane gritted her teeth manfully and fought the overwhelming desire to retch. 'I'm fine Ma.'

'You did right well there. Lotta gals would have been throwin' up at the sight o' all that blood.'

Her daughter smiled wanly. 'Maybe I'm gettin' better at it. Sure am gettin' enough practise.'

Ma straightened and looked hard at her husband and son. 'Alright, the pair o' you got somethin' on your minds. Let's hear it.'

Swiftly Jim Jordan outlined John's plan.

'No!' Ma exploded. 'I ain't doin' it. No way. I'd as soon dig lead out o' a rattlesnake as that murderin' heathen out there. He goes outa here, he carries that slug with'm an' that's final.'

'Mary-Lou ... '

'No Jim, m'mind's made up.'

'Ma!' There was a steely coldness in John Jordan's voice, which made both his parents pause and look at him. 'Ever since I come back from the Comanches you've been against me an' you've hated Jake. Don't know how come. Jake's old man died gettin' me back, an' Jake works harder round here than any o' the family.'

'I know I seem like an Injun to you but I cain't help that. Ten years o' your life is a long time an' you don't forget it easy. Pa gave Jake a place in the family an' I'm goin' to hold you to that. Sure, I want to be your son again, but I cain't do it alone. You got to meet me halfway. If you don't, then I'll be movin' on.

Right now though, we got a bunch o' Apaches out there in the timber spoilin' for a fight. We can slug it out wi' them an' a lot o' folks'll likely die. Mebbe the Johnson gals an' Sara-Jane'll be among them. Or we can try to work somethin' out. I ain't sayin' it's possible, but it's worth a try.

Now,' he turned away, 'I'll be around outside when you've made up your mind.' He climbed down out of the wagon and was gone. In the silence that followed Rafe Allen's breathing seemed unnaturally loud.

Sara-Jane bit her lip and looked at her parents. 'Ma … ' she began hesitantly.

Her father waved her to silence, then turned to his wife. 'Mary-Lou,' he said heavily, 'I've been tellin' you all along that this would happen some day, but you didn't pay me no heed. Now you got a choice. You can dig that lead outa that Apache, or you can lose a son. It's your choice. I'm sure sorry it's come to this, an' mebbe some of it's my fault. Anyways, I'm goin' out to see what's happenin'.'

Ma stood for a long time thinking deeply then, sighing, she climbed down from the wagon and made her way to where John was talking quietly to his father.

'John … ,' she began hesitantly, laying a hand on his shirt sleeve. Beneath the rough material she felt his muscles tense.

'Yeah Ma?'

'I been wrong for a long time son. Seems like I could never get rid o' the bitterness in m'mind.'

Her son nodded gravely. 'I know. Been watchin' it eatin' at you since I come back an' wishin' I could do somethin' about it. Sara-Jane told me what happened to your folks an' I guess you got a right to feel bitter. But why me an' Jake?'

'Don't suppose you'd understand, but every time I looked at either of you I saw m'folks lyin' there in the yard. Seems like I could even hear the fire cracklin'.

Anyway, that's how it seemed.' She paused for a moment. 'Will you give me one more chance?'

John smiled tightly. 'Yeah Ma. Reckon you're entitled to that. An' what about Grey Wolf?'

'The Apache? Yeah, I'll dig the lead outa him. Let's just hope he's worth it!'

Grey Wolf scowled as he watched Ma place a bucket of water on the ground beside him. He spoke suddenly to John as Ellie-May appeared carrying a towel, bandages and the long skinning knife. 'The old squaw, she hates me!'

'That is true,' John answered slowly, his tongue stumbling over the unaccustomed Apache phrases. 'Many years ago Indians killed her parents. She is bitter, but she will take the bullet from your shoulder.'

'What's he sayin'?' Ma demanded as she wiped the wound clean.

'Says you don't like him.'

'Cain't argue with that. Still, I gave m'word, an' he's only a youngster.'

'What did she say?'

'She says you are a great warrior who will be able to suffer pain.' John lied glibly.

'That is true. Apaches do not fear pain.' He looked closely at Ellie-May. 'This is the young brave who shot me?'

'Yes. He says he is proud to have fought you.'

'He rides well. Some day I will have a pony like his.'

'What did he say 'bout me?' Ellie-May demanded suspiciously.

Her brother's mouth twitched. 'Says Goldie's a great horse an' you're quite a warrior!'

'Didn't you tell him … ?' Ellie-May began furiously.

'Ellie-May, you mind hushin' up? I cain't tell him you're a squaw! It'd hurt his pride. Then he'd get all uppity an' sulk. Cain't risk that.'

'Right,' Ma cut in swiftly. 'Tell'm to set tight an' I'll get started. This is gonna hurt some,' she added warningly as she probed the wound. 'Does he want somethin' to bite on?'

John spoke swiftly to Grey Wolf. The young Apache muttered something, his jaw muscles tense.

'He says Apaches do not fear pain.'

Ma shrugged. 'It's his shoulder.' She bent to her task.

The muscles on Grey Wolf's neck corded, as he strove to cut off the scream that bubbled in his throat.

'There!' Ma held up the misshapen piece of lead. 'It was restin' against the bone. Just as well it come out. Could've cost him the arm. Now Ellie-May, clean that hole up an' get a pad on it. Reckon that should do it.'

CHAPTER 25

Grey Wolf sat stiffly on his mount, a neat bandage round his shoulder. He watched closely as Lance and Chester loaded the four dead Apaches onto the two Indian ponies the crew had picked up after the fight.

John stood beside him and spoke quietly. 'You will carry my words to Black Knife. I wish to meet him when the sun is high in the sky. Then I will ride out under a white flag to talk. If he does not come I will know it is war. I am a blood brother of the Comanche, Ten Bears.' He pointed to Jake. 'That one also. We understand your ways. Tell Black Knife this. Go now in peace.'

He stepped back. Lance passed the lead rope to Grey Wolf and the grim procession moved off.

'Think it'll work?' John turned to find his father looking at him quizzically.

He shrugged. 'Hard to tell. Don't know much 'bout Black Knife. Accordin' to any Comanches who did business wi' him he was alright. Just got to wait an' see.'

'This young 'white eyes',' Black Knife frowned, 'he understands our ways? He speaks our tongue?'

Grey Wolf nodded. 'That is true. When he was small he was taken by the Comanches. He lived with them for a long time. He is a blood brother of the Comanche, Ten Bears.'

'And you are sure of this?' Black Knife stared searchingly at the young brave. 'You have not been fooled by the 'white eyes'?'

The young brave drew himself up proudly. 'I speak the truth. The 'white eyes' showed me the Sun Dance scars on his chest. And he is not alone. There is another like him.'

'Ah.' The chief stood for a moment deep in thought. 'And he wishes to meet me?'

'Yes. He thinks that enough blood has been shed. The 'white eyes' wish to go in peace, but they will fight if they have to.'

Black Knife pondered. 'I will meet with him,' he announced finally.

There were rumblings from the depleted band. 'Fools!' He rounded on them. 'You saw what happened to Red Buffalo. He died when he thought he was safe. I do not fear the 'white eyes', but I respect their guns. This time I will talk.'

The big grey jigged nervously as John swung up into the saddle. His father handed him the long whip with the white linen square attached. 'Best Ma could do. An' Ben says he don't need the whip anyway.'

'Thanks Ma.' John raised the whip. Kiowa flattened his ears and rolled his eyes distrustfully.

Ma swallowed. 'You take care John. We got a lot o' time to make up.'

Her son nodded. 'I'll ride halfway an' then I'll wait. If anythin' goes wrong I'll be comin' fast. You fellas be ready.'

Kiowa cantered away in the direction of the trees. The Apaches watched the distant rider carefully. Black Knife turned to the surviving braves.

'He is alone and he carries a white flag. I will meet him. If there is treachery you know what to do.'

They eyed each other as the distance closed. Bigger than he looked in the fight, John thought. Looks like a chief though.

He is young, but tall and strong, Black Knife admitted grudgingly to himself. And his pony is good. We will see what he has to say. John halted Kiowa and waited quietly. Black Knife closed the distance between them and raised his hand. The young rancher acknowledged the signal. There was a long silence, then …

'You are the one who wishes to talk? I am told you speak Apache.'

John nodded. 'That is true, though sometimes I have to use sign language. You are the chief known as Black Knife? I have heard of you.'

'Yes, I am Black Knife. I am told you have the dance scars. Show me.'

Wordlessly John unbuttoned his shirt and bared his chest. Black Knife leaned forward and stared for a long time, then he nodded.

'It is true then. I did not think that a 'white eyes' would suffer the pain of the dance.'

John buttoned his shirt. 'The Kiowas who challenged me did not think so either. But I was a Comanche for ten years. I lived as a Comanche, I think like a Comanche and I can speak like a Comanche. Among the Comanches I was known as Yellow Panther.'

The chief looked at him closely. 'I understand. Why did you not stay with them?'

'I do not know.' John paused for a moment. 'Even now I am not sure. Maybe I wanted to be with my people again.'

'So,' Black Knife frowned, 'you wish to talk?'

'Yes.' John marshalled his thoughts. 'Blood has been shed. The fight was not of our seeking and we wish to go in peace.'

'That will not be easy. There are dead to avenge.'

'If you had not attacked there would be no dead. We too have a death but we do not seek revenge.'

There was a long silence, then Black Knife spoke again.

'It will not be easy. The young braves are angry. They wish to fight.'

John frowned. 'Some will die. The man with the long gun will take many scalps.'

'That is true.' Black Knife nodded gravely. 'But we must all die some day.'

John thought for a moment. 'What do they want?'

'They are young. When young braves see horses and cattle, they want them.'

'It is not possible for us to let them have horses, but in the matter of cattle, it might be that we could leave two or three steers.'

'Six.' Black Knife looked challengingly at John.

'Four, and that is final!'

'It is agreed. You may go in peace. '

'It is well. What if we meet again?'

'Then we fight. You 'white eyes' are many. The Apache will fight, but some day you will cover the land. Then the Apache will be gone.'

John shivered. It was true. There was an air of chilling finality about Black Knife's pronouncement. He raised his hand. 'We will move our stock soon.'

'It is well. Go in peace.'

John hesitated. 'There is one other thing. We have returned your dead. Now, we wish to bury our dead brother here. All we ask is that you leave him in peace.'

Black Knife paused. 'That will be done. You have not taken scalps. We will not trouble your dead.'

Jim Jordan looked across the tossing heads of the remuda and waved to his elder daughter. He grinned as she waved back. Sure pulled her weight on this trip. Seems to me she's as good as any man.

At least we got a full crew now. Looking ahead he picked out the tiny figures of Lance and Jake riding point, while further back Jeff and Chester covered the swing positions. Behind that again, bandanna pulled up over his mouth and nose, John was pushing hard at the drag. Now there's one surprisin' young fella. It don't matter what you throw at him, he seems able to handle it. Maybe we got somethin' to thank old Ten Bears for after all.

The wagons were moving up now to get ahead of the herd before Apache Pass. He nodded approvingly. Good thinkin' Jake. You'll ramrod a trail herd for somebody yet.

The Studebaker eased past, the six giant draft horses hauling it easily. Ben Turner raised his hand in salute. Jim waved back. That's quite a guy. Good brain, handy man in a tight corner an' a sharpshooter as well. Ain't never seen nobody handle a long Sharps like that. Sure hope he makes out wi' that freightin' business he intends startin'.

He watched the accommodation wagon edge into view next, the Clevelands prancing like coiled springs. Old Miguel's good, he's got them two hotheads eatin' outa his hand. Sara-Jane and the Johnson girls waved from the windows, and he saw Ma, bandage in hand, bent over one of the letdown cots containing a white-faced Rafe Allen. Damn, I sure hope that boy makes it!

Looking back, he saw the chuck wagon being driven by Clay Wallace and laughed quietly. Betcha Clay thought Ma would let Sara-Jane ride with him when he offered to drive that rig. He's a charmer alright an' Ma likes him, but she ain't nobody's fool. She thinks Sara-Jane's a mite young to be cuddlin' up wi' the likes o' Clay, an' chances are she's right. Only time'll tell. Deftly, he turned an inquisitive Morgan mare and headed up the side of the remuda.

CHAPTER 26

▼

The December morning was chilly and there was a cold wind blowing across the range. Big Red pranced gently, eager to be into his stride. Bull held him in and spoke softly. 'Take it easy boy, there ain't no need to get all het up. I know you're glad to see me, but just take it easy.' He eased the reins and the big horse settled into a long-striding lope, something he could keep up for hours.

Bull scanned the range. The cattle were looking well, even though the north end of the Flying W was carrying a lot more stock than normal since he'd combed the southern brush. Come spring we're gonna have a busy time brandin', he thought as he ran his eye over the number of 'in-calf' cows grazing contentedly. Have to be thinkin' 'bout a trail herd next year. In his mind's eye he saw a thousand head of prime Flying W beef heading north. 'Course we got to keep the army supplied with beef an' remounts, he reminded himself. That's ready money right to hand. Helps pay the wages. Something caught his eye and he looked sharply to his right. A Diamond D Longhorn bull was working his way south into Flyin' W range. Carefully he turned the sullen animal, talking quietly to Red all the while. Head down, the bull rumbled deep in its chest before reluctantly moving away north.

Curiosity stirred in Bull's mind. He remembered Jack Donovan's invitation and Joe Masterson's remarks. Why not? It might be interestin'. Anyway it won't do no harm. He headed Red in the direction taken by the bull.

✳   ✳   ✳   ✳

Ann Donovan was in the barn, bottle-feeding a foal whose mother had died, when the wolfhounds bayed thunderously from the yard. Setting the bottle down carefully, she peered through the doorway at the tall man on the giant red roan waiting quietly beyond the yard gate.

'Sara, Satan.' She didn't raise her voice but the ravening hounds subsided to a low rumbling as they slunk in behind her.

'Howdy miss,' Bull removed his hat carefully. 'Seems like you got a couple o' tigers there.'

'Sara and Satan?' Ann laughed. 'They're alright. Only thing is, they don't like strangers.'

Bull grinned. 'Sounds kinda like Red here. He can be right tetchy wi' strangers. Sorry miss, m'name's Jordan, Hardy Jordan, from the Flyin' W. Is Mister Donovan around?'

'Nice to meet you, Mister Jordan,' Ann twinkled. 'I'm Ann Donovan. Pa said he'd been over at the Flyin' W 'bout a week ago. He's out on the range right now, but I reckon he'll be back shortly. Why don't you step down and have a cup of coffee?'

'You sure it's alright?' He gestured dubiously towards the circling wolfhounds. 'Wouldn't want to lose an' arm or a leg!'

The tall girl laughed. 'They're my chaperones. Long as you don't make a wrong move everything'll be fine.'

Bull reddened. 'I sure don't mean … .'

'I know you don't. Was only teasin' you. Step down an' hitch your horse to the rail. Good looker isn't he?' She reached out to pat Red's neck and drew back hastily as the giant gelding snapped at her.

'Red!' Bull was shocked. 'Sure am sorry 'bout that, but he's like your dogs, he don't cotton to strangers.' He stepped down and tied the giant roan to the hitching rail.

'In fact,' he followed her into the house, 'he don't take to nobody but me.'

'How come?' Ann Donovan led the way into the big airy kitchen, and indicated the worn comfortable settee. The wolfhounds stalked in after him and sprawled at his feet.

'Waal,' Bull settled himself and put his hat down beside him, 'it's a long story.'

He outlined something of Red's history. How he had been sickened by the torture and abuse the horse had suffered, and how he had bought the giant gelding as a two year old from the Comancheros. Then his realisation that the horse would never be really safe with anyone else, though he had come to tolerate John, and finally how he had killed a man only a few weeks before.

Ann Donovan's eyes darkened. 'I hate to see a horse ill-treated,' she said angrily, handing a steaming cup to Bull. Cutting a wedge of pie, she flipped it onto a plate and placed it on the arm of the settee. 'Help yourself.'

'Thanks. Yeah, it bothers me some as well. Sometimes think it might be better if I let'm go to run wild, but he could do an' awful lot o' damage out there on the range.'

'Mm,' Ann sipped at her coffee. 'See what you mean.'

'Say!' The big rancher grinned appreciatively, 'this is real good pie. Old Tex now, he's a pretty fair cook, but he don't make pie like this.'

'Have another piece.' Ann rose and cut another wedge of pie which she levered onto his plate. 'When d'you reckon your folks'll get here?'

'Thanks. Another week or so I reckon. Mebbe you'd care to come over an' meet Ma an' m'sisters, Sara-Jane and Ellie-May?'

Ann Donovan nodded. 'Sure would make a nice change to have some female company round here.'

There was an awkward silence. Bull finished the last of his pie and, draining his coffee cup, stood up. The wolfhounds rose and regarded him suspiciously.

He picked up his hat. 'Look, I'd better be goin'. Thanks for the coffee an' pie. Tell your pa I'm sorry I missed him. Mebbe I could call again?'

Ann Donovan smiled. 'That would be nice.'

Outside, Bull untied Red and swung into the saddle. Anne opened the yard gate.

They looked at each other, the big man on the giant roan and the tall girl standing by the gate, her hair blowing in the breeze.

'Thanks.' Bull tipped his hat and Red sidled through the opening. 'Been right nice meetin' you. Adios now.'

'Bye.' Ann leaned on the gate and watched them jog down the hill. Ann Donovan, she smiled to herself, things are looking up round here.

'Red, old hoss,' Bull watched the gelding's ears twitch enquiringly. 'Take a good look at this here trail, 'cause you're liable to be travellin' it quite a bit!' He laughed softly to himself.

Prone on the ridge across the valley, Jack Donovan watched Bull leave. Recognising Red on his way in, he had purposely waited till the big man left.

A thin-lipped satisfied grin showed on his craggy features. Waal now, seems like things is movin' along just fine. He wriggled back from the ridge, before rising and making his way down to where he had hitched his pony.

'Course, he ruminated as he swung into the saddle, I ain't ready to cash m'chips just yet, but it sure feels good to have an ace in the hole. Chuckling to himself, he headed down off the ridge to circle round to the ranch.

Sara-Jane yawned tiredly and looked across at her mother. 'How much further?' she queried wearily.

Ma finished adjusting Rafe's bandages and glanced out of the window. 'Not far now. Soon be at the creek an' it ain't no distance after that.' She looked down at the whitefaced youngster in the cot. 'Now you take it easy, you hear. Don't want you startin' another fever.'

Rafe smiled wanly. 'Sorry to be so much trouble, Miz Jordan.'

'Shucks,' Ma scowled and looked away. 'You ain't been no trouble. Cain't afford to lose a good man.'

Sara-Jane bit her lip. She knew that at one stage Ma had almost despaired of Rafe's recovery. Even now it was going to be a slow process.

Behind them the herd and the remuda were shuffling along tiredly, heads down. Spaced out in their positions, the crew rode slumped in their saddles.

Ma thought for a moment of Andy and Mike in their lonely graves. Of Rafe lying there in the bunk and his slow recovery. You'd just better hope, Mary-Lou Jordan, that it's all been worth it.

The wagons splashed through the ford at the creek and up the rise to the ranch. Behind them the tired cattle spread out along the bottom land by the creek.

Joe Masterson came down the steps from the house and waved the wagons on towards the barn. Then he untied his mount and, swinging into the saddle, rode down to where Ellie-May and Pa were circling the remuda. A brief discussion and they turned the horse herd towards the open gate of the horse pasture.

Big Dance cantered through confidently and started to graze. The others followed. Joe shut the gate and secured it. Tiredly, Ellie-May and her father looked at each other. They had made it!

Bull opened the door of the accommodation wagon and picked up the two little girls. He hugged them for a long moment, then, grinning, he looked up at his mother.

'Welcome home, Ma!'

CHAPTER 27

▼

'A freightin' business hey?' Sheriff Dawson leaned forward in his chair and looked closely at the tall man sitting comfortably opposite. 'Waal, we sure could use one round here. Ain't nobody made a real go of it yet. Last fella tried it was Lige Jackson.' He shook his head.

'What happened?' Ben Turner looked at the thickset, grey-haired lawman curiously.

'Drink,' Dawson said tersely. 'Lige couldn't leave it alone. 'Course, he wasn't married. If he made any cash, he drank it. Wasn't long before he was messin' up deliveries. Then goods he was freightin' started gettin' lost; so he said. Anyway, it got so nobody would employ him. Next, he sold off his teams; they were only half-broken scrub stock anyway. Then finally the wagons. He had a couple. That was it. Last I heard he was a swamper in a saloon in Tucson.'

'Mm.' Ben thought for a moment. 'Did he have a yard or a barn?'

Dawson rubbed his chin. 'Funny you should mention that. He'd a right nice little setup just off Main Street. A stable wi' a feed store above it, an' a little corral at the back. Oh, and there's a lock-up store for the wagons and any goods passin' through. Used to belong to old Andy Easton. Lige won it off him in a poker game. Andy wasn't worth a damn when it come to playin' poker,' he added reminiscently.

'Think this fella Jackson would sell?'

The sheriff pulled his ear thoughtfully. 'Don't see why not. I happen to know it's up for sale. Lige has a lot o' debts to be settled, so he ain't goin' to be hard to deal with. There's an old lawyer, name o' Ivor Houston, handlin' Lige's affairs. Got a little office just across the street there. Go across an' see him. Tell him I sent you.' He grinned suddenly. 'Don't reckon Ivor is any more of a lawyer than you or me. He come out here about three years ago with a pile o' law books an' the next thing you know he's hung out his shingle. Ivor Houston, Attorney at Law.

'Course he don't do a lot o' business, but it's a livin'. One thing about old Ivor, he's a square shooter. Nobody gets shortchanged wi' him.'

'Thanks.'

Ben made to rise but Dawson waved him back into his chair.

'Set a spell. Got a coupla things I'd like to ask you. You mind?'

Ben shook his head, suddenly wary.

The sheriff saw the sudden caution and grinned. 'Ain't nothin' like that. Just want you to fill me in on a few things. I understand you come in wi' the Jordans. How come?'

Turner shrugged. 'Nothin' secret about it. I'd a little freightin' business in east Texas, wasn't goin' nowhere. The Jordans hired me to freight their stuff out here. I'd just lost my wife an' my boy, didn't much care what happened. Seemed like the best thing was to start again.'

Dawson shook his head sympathetically. 'Sorry I asked. Life can be awful rough at times. Mebbe a clean break is best.' He went off suddenly at a tangent. 'What kinda rig you got?'

Ben grinned. There was something likeable about the elderly lawman.

'Studebaker wagon. Ain't more than two years old; an' the team's Conestogas. Big fellas.'

'Conestogas hey?' There was a faraway look in Dawson's deep-set eyes. 'My old man was a teamster. He swore by them big horses. Ain't seen a Conestoga team in a coon's age. Reckoned they cost such a lot folks weren't breedin' them no more.'

Ben Turner nodded. 'Bought mine from a fella in West Virginia. He breeds 'em. Keeps a stallion and a few mares. Just likes to see 'em I guess.'

'Mm' Davis paused frowning, then suddenly ... 'Them Jordans, good folks you reckon?'

The tall teamster nodded. 'The best,' he said shortly, 'they'll do well out here. They're workers, every last one o' them. They've had a hard trip. Lost a couple o' good old boys, had a brush with Injuns up at San Simon an' a run-in with rustlers down near Messila.'

'Uh-huh.' The sheriff fiddled with a pencil on his desk. 'Heard tell them wimmenfolk o' theirs are right salty. They cleaned out the Anderson gang.'

'You'd better believe that. Miz Jordan, she don't scare none. An' that elder gal Ellie-May. Dresses like a man an' can handle a gun better than most men.

Rides a palomino that can run like the wind. Saw her an' Miz Jordan cut down a couple o' Apaches as neat as you please.'

'The younger gal now, Sara-Jane. She's a nice kid an' she's got sand. Trouble is she ain't tough like her sister or her mother, so life's goin' to be hard for her.'

Dawson nodded absently. 'What about the menfolk? Only one I know is that big fella, Bull.'

'Big, ain't he?' Ben Turner grinned. 'Hadn't met him 'fore I got here, but I sure know a lot about him. Reckon he's one tough hombre.'

'Yeah. He sure thinned out the Comancheros round here. Got so that Henry Wills, the undertaker down the street, was thinkin' o' takin' on extra help! What about the old man an' the other sons?'

'Jim Jordan's a good man. Good rancher too I reckon, an' he gets along well with most folks. Yeah, he'll do to ride the river with.'

'The other two sons? You couldn't get two more different fellas. Big Lance now, he's the eldest son. Sergeant in the cavalry down at Fort Concho. He's takin' a long furlough to help his folks move. Accordin' to what I heard down there he's a top sergeant. They reckon he could have gone a long way if he'd had a mind.'

Dawson's eyes narrowed. 'Think he might settle down here?'

'Lance?' Turner shook his head. 'Nah. Ranchin' don't interest him. Reckon he'll stay in the cavalry.'

'Mm. That's right interestin'. An' the other son? What's he like?'

'John?' Ben frowned. 'Now there's a strange fella, though it ain't rightly his fault. When he was eight the Comanches grabbed him, an' he was 'bout eighteen 'fore he managed to get away.'

The sheriff whistled incredulously. 'Whooeeh, ain't that something!' So what's he like?'

'He's a white Comanche. It's that simple. He thinks like a Comanche, he fights like a Comanche, an' he can talk pure Comanche. Somethin' else. He can get by in Apache if he has to, an' I've seen him do it. But it's goin' to be hard for him to settle into the family.'

'Only one that he's right at home with is Jake Larsen, a young Comanche half-breed who lives wi' the Jordans. Accordin' to Sara-Jane, Jake's old man was killed gettin' John away from the Comanches, an' Jim Jordan swore young Jake would have a home for life wi' them. Somethin' else. You ever need trackers, then you cain't do better than them two.'

'Uh-huh. I'll bear that in mind. Thanks for talkin' to me. '

Ben shrugged as he rose. 'Just one thing. The Jordans are my friends an' Ben Turner don't forget friends. 'Preciate it if you keep our talk to yourself.'

'What talk?' Dawson grinned. 'Adios now an' tell Ivor I sent you.'

CHAPTER 28

▼

Goldie loped easily along the north boundary of the Flying W. There was a cool breeze blowing from the north and Ellie-May pulled her windcheater more closely round her. Since arriving with the remuda, some three weeks ago, she had spent every spare moment riding round the vast ranch and gradually building up a mental picture of its rolling acres.

Now she was doing a chore she thoroughly enjoyed, line riding. All morning she had worked her way along the rugged northern slope, noting the condition of the stock, and watching for out of season calves. Competently, with a minimum of effort, she turned the occasional Diamond D animal back north, at the same time pushing the more numerous Flying W stock south.

The fact that she was further out from the home ranch than she had ever been before did not trouble her unduly. An instinctive loner, Ellie-May was happiest when she was out on the range with only Goldie for company. Pa said not to go too far, but Anders says the Flyin' W ain't had no trouble with the Apaches for quite a spell. Anyways, I ain't doin' no harm.

Now she suddenly felt hungry and thought of the bread and meat in her saddlebags. Leaning forward she stroked her mount's glossy neck. 'Alright Goldie, must be nigh on noon. Let's make for that spring we saw an' take a break. Reckon you've earned it.'

Turning the palomino, she cantered over the ridge and down towards the spring in the next valley.

Little Elk looked at the tracks. 'A 'white eyes', alone. We will have sport with this one.' He dug his heels into the stallion's sides and the pinto lunged forward, the other four riders close behind.

Finished, Ellie-May repacked everything and swung up into the saddle. Goldie danced sideways, ears pricked and nostrils flaring.

The five Apaches, Little Elk in the lead, swept over the ridge.

'Go Goldie!' Ellie-May screamed, and flattened herself along her mount's neck. The dancing palomino stretched into its stride and raced down the valley.

Behind, the Apaches settled down for a long chase. Little Elk's eyes narrowed. Swift Wind, his pinto stallion was noted for his speed, yet the distance between him and the flying palomino was not closing. If anything the gap was widening. This was a horse! He drummed his heels again and the pinto lengthened his stride.

Ellie-May darted a glance over her shoulder. She still had a good lead but Goldie would tire soon. He was a quarter horse with a phenomenal turn of speed, but he didn't stay.

Got to think o' somethin'. They raced up a long incline and down the other side. John says be different when you're fightin' Injuns. There! Swinging behind the giant boulder, she came out of the saddle like a cat, Winchester in hand, and hitched Goldie to the nearest bush. Flattening herself in the lee of the rock, she sighted carefully on the crest of the ridge, some four hundred yards away.

Any time now.

Swift Wind swept up over ridge. The Winchester cracked and the giant stallion collapsed in midstride, the bullet lodged in his brain. Little Elk threw himself clear and rolled behind a nearby rock. Ellie-May reloaded and waited tensely.

The remaining riders lunged over the crest, their ponies labouring.

Coolly, the blonde girl selected her target and fired. The leading Apache swayed, grabbed at his pony's mane and swung back out of sight beyond the ridge.

Cain't be picky. Working smoothly, Ellie-May slammed two shots into the mass of horses and Indians. A pony screamed and went down in a kicking heap, pinning its rider. It went on screaming for a long time. The remaining two braves swung their mounts back behind the shelter of the ridge. Reloading, Ellie-May gritted her teeth and waited tensely.

Nothing. Right! She came up smoothly and jammed the Winchester into the saddle boot. Mounting hurriedly, she urged the snorting palomino into his stride. As he flattened into a pounding run Ellie-May looked back. All she could see were the two dead ponies and the trapped Apache. John boy, you were right!

Little Elk rose from behind the rock and watched the flying palomino disappear into the timber. A cold, killing rage showed in his eyes as he looked at the dead pinto. Some day, he thought savagely, that 'white eyes' will pay and that pony will be mine.

Crossing to where the other dead pony lay, he bent and heaved. Muscles rippled across his back as he strained against the lifeless mass. Slowly, very slowly, it moved. The trapped Apache grunted an acknowledgement and dragged his leg free. He stood up, flexed it tentatively and nodded with satisfaction.

Two of the remaining Apaches appeared over the ridge. They glanced at the dead stallion and looked away hastily. Little Elk valued Swift Wind above anything. The 'white eyes' would pay for this.

Their leader scowled. 'Where is Lobo?'

'With the horses.' The elder of the two Apaches, a gaunt scar-faced brave, answered. 'He has a bullet in his chest.'

Little Elk bent and removed the hackamore from the dead stallion. Then he straightened and looked at the other three.

'There is a small ranch north of here. We will take horses from there.'

'It is not far from the town,' the oldest brave ventured uneasily.

'So?' Little Elk waved his hand contemptuously. 'We are the Apaches. The 'white eyes' fear us. We will make our raid at dawn. They will be asleep. Come,' he strode towards the tethered ponies. 'We will ride double.'

'You clinched the deal then?' Jim Jordan paused in the act of rolling a cigarette and cocked an interrogative eye at Ben Turner. 'Sure you done the right thing? Settin' up in business can be awful chancy.'

The teamster grinned. 'Never more sure. This is the place I been lookin' for. Goin' to put down some roots.'

He's changed, Jim thought. There's life about him now.

He struck a match and lit up. 'Wish you luck Ben, you know that. Anythin' we can do to help just ask.'

'Waal,' Ben hesitated for a moment. 'Been thinkin'. I need a roustabout. Somebody who's good wi' horses an' can drive if I get more business. You mind if I speak to old Miguel?'

'Say,' Jim Jordan's eyes narrowed thoughtfully, 'that's a right good idea. He's been helpin' that big Dane, Anders, in the forge, but there ain't much call for a teamster round here. Sure, you go right ahead.'

'Thanks,' Ben turned, then paused. 'You ever get round to haymakin', you might bear in mind that I'll be in the market for feed.' He strode away.

Jim Jordan blew a long streamer of smoke. Looks like we started something there.

CHAPTER 29

▼

Reining in on the creek bank, Sheriff Dawson sat for a long moment looking across the ford and up the long incline to the ranch buildings. The bawl of outraged cattle drifted down to him on the wind.

He twisted ponderously in the saddle and surveyed the cattle grazing the bottom land, on the other side of the creek. Durham Longhorn crosses, nice stock. An' there's a Durham bull. Looks like Ben Turner was right, them Jordan folks mean business.

Gently kneeing his mount, he splashed through the ford and up the slope towards the ranch. Got to hand it to Dave Wilson, he ruminated as he surveyed the solid adobe walled house, he sure set this place up right. Can remember when he had it built. Freighted timber out from Tucson, glass an' fireplaces from back east. Must have cost plenty. Wonder where in hell he got the money? Still, he was well-heeled when he got here, so it ain't none o' my business.

A youngster sitting in an old easy chair on the wide porch eyed him carefully as he approached. Sixteen, seventeen, mebbe. Looks right peaky. Blanket round him too. Reckon he's had a rough time.

'Howdy, son.' The sheriff swung down and hitched his horse to the rail. 'Scott Dawson, sheriff o' Dorando. Pleased to meet you. You don't look too chipper. How come?'

Rafe Allen grinned weakly. 'Howdy sheriff. Rafe Allen. Kinda off my feed I reckon. Took an Apache arrow in my shoulder up at San Simon. Still, Miz Jordan, she says I'm gettin' better now. Cain't come soon enough for me.'

Dawson nodded sympathetically. 'Know how you feel son. Hate to be laid up m'self.'

'Howdy, sheriff.' Bull Jordan stepped through the ranch house doorway. 'You here on business, or is this just a social call?'

'Both I reckon,' the sheriff scrubbed at his chin as he mounted the porch steps. 'You know old Cy Rogers?'

'Fella that owns the Cinch Buckle outfit up on our north line?'

Dawson nodded.

Bull shook his head. 'Only what the boys tell me. Been meanin' to visit him, but just ain't got round to it.'

'Mm. Waal, the Cinch Buckle's a two-bit outfit. Cy bought it when he quit ridin' shotgun for the stage, just after the war. Him an' his wife Helen, they raise some saddle stock an' a hundred or so beeves. Two old Mex vaqueros ride for him.'

'Anyway, coupla days ago they were checkin' stock an' they found sign that pointed to Injuns on a horse stealin' raid. Reckoned there were four, mebbe five Apaches an' they'd taken 'bout a dozen head. Cy an' his boys tracked them into the Dragoons an' lost them there. Then they backtracked them to your north line an' beyond. Found a coupla dead Injun ponies, one o' them a big pinto stallion. Whoever did it was a pretty fair shot an' they were shootin' from Flyin' W land.'

He looked hard at Bull. 'You know anythin' about it?'

Bull shook his head. 'Nary a thing. We've been busy brandin' the stock m'folks brought in. You know their brand was Circle J; waal, we're hairbrandin' 'em wi the Flyin' W. Let's go take a walk down to the corrals an' we can ask around.'

He checked suddenly and called through the open doorway. 'Ma, Ellie-May's been out ridin' most days. You got any notion where she's been?'

'All over I reckon.' Ma Jordan appeared in the doorway. 'Says she wants to get to know the ranch.' She glanced enquiringly at the sheriff.

'Ma, this here's Sheriff Dawson. Sheriff, this is m'mother. She's the new owner o' the Flyin' W.'

'Howdy ma'am. Sure heard a lot 'bout you.'

'Waal, howdy sheriff. Don't believe everything you hear!'

Dawson chuckled. 'I'll bear that in mind ma'am.'

Bull intervened. 'Sheriff says somebody had a run-in with a bunch o' Injuns on the north line 'bout three days ago.'

'Three days ago?' Ma's tone sharpened. 'Saw Ellie-May cleanin' her Winchester coupla nights back. Didn't pay no heed, she's always messin' with guns or harness.'

'Where is she now?'

'Helpin' Pa mend the horse pasture fence.'

'Right,' Bull said decisively, 'let's head up there now an' talk to her.'

The smell of burning hair came strongly to their nostrils as they strode past the branding chute, filled with bawling cattle. Sheriff Dawson raised his voice above the noise. 'Didn't want to say nothin' in front of your ma, but whoever did the shootin' winged one o' them Injuns pretty bad. Cy found where they'd put him down for a spell an' there was a lot o' blood.'

Jim Jordan paused with the posthole digger in his hands. 'Why Bull! You come to give us a hand?' He eyed the badge. 'Guess you must be Sheriff Dawson. Bull's told me a lot about you. Oh, this is m'daughter Ellie-May.'

Busy trimming a fence post, Ellie-May straightened up, axe in hand. 'Howdy,' she said warily.

Dawson nodded and tipped his hat.

'Ellie-May,' her brother said sharply, 'somebody had a run-in with a bunch o' Apaches up on the north line. You been up that way lately?'

The tall girl bit her lip and looked at the ground.

Jim Jordan's eyes narrowed and he stared hard at his daughter. 'You been keepin' somethin' from me Ellie-May? Come to think o' it you brung Goldie in all lathered up the other day. Reckon you'd better tell us what you been up to.'

'Wasn't my fault,' Ellie-May said defensively. 'When they come over that ridge whoopin' an' hollerin' I just lit out on Goldie. Now Goldie's nothin' but a quarter horse an' I knew he couldn't outlast 'em, 'specially that big pinto.

John, he told me once if you ever get chased by Injuns, do something they ain't gonna expect. Anyway, I let Goldie run till we got some distance, then I piled off beside this big rock an' waited for them as they came over the ridge. Just meant to shoot the horses, but I got a mite high with one shot an' winged the rider. They pulled back over the ridge an' I lit out for the ranch. Sure was a shame 'bout that pinto though. He was some horse.'

'For land sakes,' her father exploded. 'Why didn't you tell us?'

''Cause I knew you an' Ma would stop me ridin' on my own an' I like it.'

'You're darn tootin', we would ... '

'Alright!' Dawson cut in sharply. 'She did the right thing. Took a lot o' sand an' savvy to play her hand like she did with a bunch o' Apaches on her tail. They'll think twice 'fore they jump somebody round here again.'

'Just one thing ... ' he recounted the raid on the Cinch Buckle. 'There's an old Apache half-breed, name o' Blue Fox who hangs out in Dorando. Most folks call him Smokey Joe. He's married to an Apache squaw. She's related to Cochise an' she stays wi' the tribe, up there in the Dragoons. Joe, he visits her every once in a while. Reckon he tells Cochise what's happenin' down here, but then, he tells me what's happenin' up there in Cochise's camp, so we break even. 'Course,' he added reflectively, 'I slip him a little eatin' money every so often, mebbe that helps.

Joe tells me he's comin' down from the Dragoons an' he meets this bunch wi' Cy's horses. The leader was a buck called Little Elk. Now, this Little Elk, he's one mean hombre. He's killed a lot o' whites, chased stagecoaches an' burned a couple o' small ranches. 'Sides stealin' a lot o' stock at the same time.

Accordin' to Joe, Cochise has been threatenin' to run Little Elk out o' the Dragoons for some time, but he just never gets round to it.

Waal, Little Elk, he was as mad as a hornet. Seems like somebody shot his favourite pony out from under him. A big pinto stallion, could run forever accordin' to Joe. Little Elk, he wants revenge on the 'white eyes' that did it. Says he will know this 'white eyes' by the pony he rides, a palomino that can run like the wind.'

Ellie-May shivered.

'An' there's another thing. They were totin' a dead Apache. A buck by the name o' Lobo. Seems like the 'white eyes' got him as well.'

There was a long silence before Dawson spoke again. 'Miss Jordan, reckon you did the territory a service. Only thing is, I wouldn't be takin' no long rides on m'own for a fair spell.'

Ellie-May nodded shakily.

'She won't,' Jim Jordan said heavily. 'I'll see to that personal.'

Bull stood for a moment deep in thought. 'Reckon I'll go tell the boys to ride in pairs for a spell. You mind comin' with me Sheriff?'

'Sure,' Dawson tipped his hat. 'Been nice meetin' you folks.'

'Bull!'

'Yeah Pa?'

'Speak to John an' Jake 'bout this. They think like Injuns an' they might have some ideas.'

'Sure Pa.'

'Hear tell you got a brother in the cavalry?' Dawson ventured. 'Like a word with'm, if he's here.'

'Sure, that's him there. Big blond-haired fella usin' the brandin' iron. We're just hairbrandin'. Don't want to upset them in-calf cows too much. Come spring we'll brand 'em right. 'Sides,' he added as they reached the branding chute, 'they got the Circle J brand on 'em an' that's registered.'

'Lance,' he tapped his brother on the shoulder, 'Sheriff Dawson here would like a word with you. Gimme that iron an' I'll spell you.'

'Howdy,' Lance grinned as they shook hands. 'Ain't broke no laws I can think of. What can I do for you?'

'Waal now,' Dawson squinted at the tall sergeant, 'mebbe we can do somethin' for each other. How come a cavalryman's punchin' cows?'

Lance laughed. 'Ain't gonna ask how you know I'm a cavalryman. Anyway it ain't no secret. I took a long furlough to help m'folks move out here.'

'Mm,' the sheriff scratched his chin. 'Son, you ever thought o' leavin' the army?'

'Goin' back to cow work you mean?' Lance shook his head. 'That ain't for me. I quit it years ago.' He laughed. 'Wouldn't mind bein' a lawman, but I signed for four years an' I don't finish my stint until next year. 'Nother six months or so. So there ain't nuthin' I can do until then.'

'Alright, now it's my turn to talk. I'm sheriff o' Dorando. Been sheriff there for the last four years. Ever since the war in fact. Place was all to hell then. Had to start it from scratch again. Pay ain't bad an' I got a couple o' middlin' fair deputies that have been there nigh as long as m'self.'

'I don't see ... '

Dawson held up his hand. 'Hang in there son. I'm gettin' to it. 'Case you hadn't noticed I'm a mite long in the tooth to be tradin' shots wi' Apaches an' rustlers. M'deputies ain't no spring chickens either. Me, I'm aimin' to retire in a year's time. Don't reckon the other two'll be that far behind.'

He paused and looked hard at Lance. 'Now we're comin' to it. If you care to come back here when you finish your time an' sign on as m'deputy so you can get the feel o' the job, then it's yours when I retire. I can swing it.'

Amazement and disbelief flitted across Lance's face. 'Why me? What about your deputies?'

'Joe and Virgil? They've already told me they don't want the job. Then again, I reckon we're headin' for a heap o' trouble down this way. Apaches ain't gonna stand white folks pushin' in like they are an' that'll mean fightin'. There's a lot o' gunnies driftin' down from the north an' I can see rustlin' bein' a big problem. Plus you got the Comancheros wi' a foot in either camp. Nah, Dorando's gonna need a young sheriff.'

Lance took a deep breath. 'Yeah, alright, but why me?'

Dawson grinned. 'Son, I know somethin' about the Army. You don't get to be a top sergeant less'n you're somethin' special.' He looked challengingly at the tall sergeant. 'Now, you gonna tell me I'm wrong?'

Lance shook his head. 'Ain't sayin' you're wrong. Just surprised you chose me. Sure, I'm interested. Got that six months still to finish though. You prepared to wait until then?'

The stout sheriff nodded. 'That's only fair. Look in 'fore you head back an' let me know for sure. Just one thing more. Are you as fast as your brother when it comes to a draw?'

Lance laughed as he turned back to the dust of the corral. 'Whyn't you ask him?'

Dawson waited. He saw Lance slap his brother on the shoulder and jerk his thumb to where the sheriff was standing.

Bull handed over the glowing iron and walked towards him. 'Lance says you got somethin' to ask me?'

'Yeah.' Scott Dawson paused for a moment. 'Who's the fastest on the draw 'tween you?'

There was a long silence then Bull spoke. 'Ain't sure what you're drivin' at but I'll tell you this. I'm right glad it'll never happen!'

'That's what I thought. Thanks. Be seein' you.'

'Adios.' Bull wiped the sweat from his brow and watched the stocky figure bowlegging across the yard. Now what in hell was all that about? He shrugged and turned back to the corral.

CHAPTER 30

▼

'An' you've made your mind up?' Ma looked hard at Clay Wallace. 'What brung this on?'

Clay closed the account books and rose to his feet. 'Miz Jordan, I've been thinking about this for some time. Ever since I first came here in fact.'

'This territory's opening up. Settlers will flood in. Businesses will have to be run properly. That's where I come in. I'm an accountant and a property developer. Haven't seen one round here so I guess there's an opening. I'm planning to ride into Tucson this week and check out some premises. I owe you and Hardy a great deal.'

Ma frowned fiercely and shook her head.

'Oh it's true. Before I met you two I was just drifting; now I've got plans.'

He paused, embarrassed.

'Shucks, it weren't nothin'. Been real nice havin' you around.' She thought for a moment. 'Seein' you're goin' into business, don't suppose you'd mind takin' us on as clients?'

'Why, no.' Clay laughed awkwardly. 'In fact, I'd be honoured.' The young Easterner hesitated for a moment. 'There's something I've wanted to speak to you about. Only, I was hoping to get you and Mister Jordan together before I mentioned it.'

He swallowed nervously, and Ma stopped knitting. Her gaze sharpened. 'Alright, let's hear it if it's so all-fired important. I can allus tell Pa later.'

Why do I feel like a little boy caught raiding the cookie jar, Clay Wallace thought resentfully. He took a deep breath. 'I'd like your permission to court Sara-Jane!'

There was a long ominous silence, while Ma rolled up her knitting and stowed it carefully in the faded carpet bag. Finished, she leaned back in the worn armchair and directed a frosty stare at the ex-gambler.

'Well now, I figgered you and me had an agreement, and that you'd keep to it. Mebbe I was wrong?'

Clay flushed angrily. 'Miz Jordan, I gave you my word and I've kept it. However, since I met Sara-Jane I've become strongly attracted to her, and I think she feels the same way about me.'

Ma frowned. 'Seems to me you're takin' a lot for granted if you ain't said nothin' to her 'bout this. You sure it ain't just 'cause she's here, an' not back east like them high-toned gals you grew up with?'

The young man shook his head. 'I thought about that,' he admitted. 'But no ... Sara-Jane's a fine girl, and I'd like to court her, with your permission.'

'Mm,' Mary-Lou pursed her lips doubtfully. 'Seems to me you ain't thought this thing right through. Just supposin' she feels the same way 'bout you, an' me an' Jim agree to the marriage, what then? From what you say 'bout your folks, I don't see them takin' too kindly to a rancher's daughter marryin' into the family. Mind,' she lifted a hand to forestall Clay's protest, 'Sara-Jane's a good gal. She can cook an' run a house wi' the best, but she ain't got airs an' graces like your gals from back east. How're you gonna take it if your folks reckon she don't measure up?'

'It won't make any difference,' Clay Wallace said doggedly. 'If we love each other that'll be enough. Anyway, if I get the business going we'll be living in Tucson.'

Just for a second a spark of approval showed in Ma's wintry blue eyes. 'Waal, you got guts, I'll give you that. But supposin' the business don't take off. You cain't live in Tucson on nothin'. An' if you got any feelin's for your folks you'll want to keep in touch wi' them.'

She paused for a moment, deep in thought. Then ... 'alright, here's the deal. You move to Tucson and get your business goin'. I'll speak to Sara-Jane. If she feels the same as you then maybe I'll give things m'blessin'. But,' she added warningly, 'we're gonna take this real slow. From what you told me you're a fair piece older than her.'

Clay nodded. 'About nine years.'

'That bein' so, I want your word that things won't get outa hand. You follow me?'

'Yes, Miz Jordan. I give you my word on that.'

'Fair enough, we got a deal. Still want our business?'

Clay Wallace laughed, somewhat shakily. 'More than ever I guess.'

'So there you have it.' Doctor Kincaid threw the list onto the warden's desk and sat back with the air of a man who has done his best. 'TB. It's in those cells and I can't say I'm surprised. There's only five so far and they're just in the early stages, but I'm ninety per cent certain it's there. 'Course, I haven't told them. Just said it was a routine check.'

Warden Beale frowned. How did I ever end up in charge of such a hellhole, he wondered, not for the first time. It isn't as though I'm a drunk like Fisher, or a womaniser like La Roux, but they both got plum appointments back east, while I get stuck with this.

He looked at the list again. 'What do you recommend?'

Henry Kincaid yawned and mopped his brow. Typical buckpasser. No wonder they stuck him out here. 'Well, I've got to run some more checks to be absolutely certain. That means segregating them from the other prisoners.'

The warden frowned worriedly. 'It also means taking them out of the maximum security wing and they're all known killers.'

The little doctor shrugged. 'Your move I guess, but you know how touchy the governor is 'bout things like this. If it gets out of hand … '

'Damn it I know. Alright, we'll do it. Ask Roberts to come in. He'll moan that we haven't enough guards, but the hell with it!'

'Sure,' Kincaid closed the door.

'Yes I know, Roberts,' Beale looked up at the scowling guard chief, 'but there's no help for it.' He looked again at the list. 'Here are the names. Martinez, McQuade, Defarge and the Anderson brothers. See to it.'

CHAPTER 31

▼

'You sure 'bout this, Ma?' Jim Jordan frowned as he looked at his wife. 'Ain't more'n three weeks since Ellie-May had her run-in wi' them Apaches. Mebbe you should wait a spell yet.'

Ma shook her head stubbornly. 'Cain't wait no longer. We're low on supplies as it is. That party we had at Christmas used up a lot o' our stocks. Still, I don't grudge it none. Everybody's been workin' hard an' they deserved it. Anyway, nothin's happened so far.' She looked challengingly round the table. 'Anders can drive us. He's a good man to have along. Ain't all that far anyway. An' if we start holin' up every time somebody hollers Injuns, we ain't never goin' to get nothin' done.'

'Pa,' Ellie-May looked hesitantly at her father. 'I could ride along. Goldie's all fired up 'cause he ain't gettin' enough exercise, an' I sure would like to see how Ben an' Miguel are makin' out.'

'No!' Jim Jordan's reply was explosive. 'You ain't takin' no chances. That Apache ain't goin' to forget what you did in a long while. 'Sides, you ride into Dorando in them Levis, you'll have the whole town lookin' at you!'

Ellie-May looked daggers at her father. 'Just 'cause I had a run-in wi' them Apaches ain't no reason why I got to hide round the ranch forever. Anyways, I'll be wearin' my windbreaker, an' if I tuck my hair up under my hat ain't nobody gonna know I'm a gal.'

There was a long silence, then Lance laughed.

Jim Jordan scowled at his eldest son. 'You see somethin' funny 'bout this?'

'Pa, some years back you were sayin' Ellie-May was right to wear Levis, now you're sayin' she's wrong. You cain't have it both ways.'

'It's one thing to wear them round the ranch. Paradin' through Dorando in them is somethin' else!'

Lance shrugged and winked at Ellie-May.

Their father glowered round the table. 'Anybody else got anythin' to say?'

There was a discreet silence.

'Waal, mebbe I was a mite hasty, but you take care Ellie-May. Take young Rafe with you. He's itchin' to get back in the saddle. Now I reckon it's time we was all hittin' the sack. Come mornin' we got work waitin' for us.'

The Clevelands pawed the ground and champed at their bits, eager to be off. Jim Jordan grinned at Anders Lindstrom.

'All set, Anders?'

'Sure thing, Mister Jordan.' The big Dane's laugh boomed across the yard. 'This is some team. We make good time on this trip by golly!'

The rancher laughed. There was something infectious about Lindstrom's humour. Also, he loved horses.

'Just so you bring the rig back in one piece. Ma, Ellie-May, you take care, you hear me now. Rafe, have a good trip. Need you back in the crew.'

He stepped back and raised his hand. Anders slipped the brake and the team plunged forward. They swept out of the yard and down the slope to the ford.

Pa shivered in the cold morning air and turned to see John and Jake leading their saddled mounts across the yard to the water trough.

He made his way over to them. 'Fellas, where you headin' this mornin'?'

John glanced at him curiously. 'Joe wants us to check the west line. Says them Rockin' Chair cattle keep driftin' onto the Flyin' W. He reckons the Chair's overstocked an' they're driftin' this way lookin' for grazin'. Wants us to push them back. Why, somethin' botherin' you?'

'It's Ma. I ain't rightly happy 'bout this trip. Mebbe I'm gettin' edgy in m'old age. Think you could ride the high timber an' just keep an eye on things? Once they get within range o' Dorando you can swing off. I'll make it alright wi' Joe.'

'Sure Pa, me an' Jake'll cover.' John grinned, 'They won't know we're there. All set Jake?'

Jake nodded silently. Together they swung into their saddles and loped out of the yard.

Done all I can, Pa reflected, better go an' see Joe now.

'You sure this is gonna work?' Pony McQuade, a tall lanky Texan, looked dubiously at Diamond Jack Anderson. 'Seems chancy to me.'

''Course it's chancy you knothead!' Diamond Jack whispered furiously, 'But it's the only chance we got. An' keep your voice down. You want them guards outside to hear you? Defarge, get the cards out. Anybody comes in we're havin' a quiet game o' poker. Now listen up all o' you.'

Jules Defarge, a swarthy little Creole, dealt the worn cards and they settled down to listen.

Little Elk scowled as he stared down at the distant group of tiny figures on the trail below.

'Hai … more 'white eyes'. Soon they will be everywhere. And still Cochise waits. He listens too much to Taglito.'

Something caught his eye and he looked again. That flaxen mane and tail. It was the flying palomino!

Sudden rage surged through him and he urged his pony forward, signalling to the others as he did so. Strung out in single file, the four Apaches swept out of the timber and down the slope.

'Company,' Ma said tersely as she folded her knitting and delved into the long bag. 'Looks like Pa read it right. Pity I didn't listen. Close up you two,' she called sharply to Rafe and Ellie-May. 'No shootin' less'n we have to. Mebbe we can stand 'em off,' she added as she slammed two rounds into the shotgun and clicked it shut.

Lindstrom threw back his head and laughed. 'By golly Miz Jordan, you are one hell of a woman. Sure wish I'd met you 'fore you married Mister Jordan!'

'Watch your language Anders,' Ma said tartly, 'An' hold that team down to a walk. We ain't scared. Leastways,' she added, 'we ain't showin' it.'

High on the opposite ridge John sucked in his breath. 'This ain't good, Jake. Let's go.' They lunged out of the timber on the run.

Twenty yards from the buckboard, Little Elk pulled his pony round in a racing turn and halted. The others closed up behind him.

'Keep movin',' Ma said tightly, the shotgun rock steady in her hands. 'They ain't too sure o' the odds.'

The sound of drumming hooves came to their ears. 'Take a look Anders. Don't want to give this big fella the chance to jump us.'

'By golly, it's John and Jake!'

'Waal now, that evens things some. Seems I ain't the only one that likes to have an ace in the hole.'

The flying pinto pulled up alongside. 'Howdy Ma,' John grinned.

'Howdy John … Jake. You fellas mind droppin' back a mite? This scattergun spreads somethin' awful.'

John and Jake exchanged glances as they complied.

'You want me to talk to this bunch? Cain't do no harm.'

Ma mulled over his suggestion. 'Yeah, guess you're right. Don't want no shootin' less'n we have to. Find out what's eatin' him. Pull up Anders. If it's Little Elk we might as well settle this thing now. Ellie-May … Rafe, get set to back John's play.'

Rafe Allen watched as John hailed the Apaches in their guttural tongue. Sure wish I could do that. Wonder if he would teach me?

There was a brief silence, then a hesitant answer. John moved forward and waited.

A tall Apache urged his pony out of the group and confronted him. John gestured freely with his hands and spoke again.

There was an impassioned outburst from the Apache. John waited impassively until he had finished.

'This here's Little Elk alright. He says the young brave on the palomino killed his war pony Swift Wind. Says this pony was famous among the Apaches. Reckons we owe him many ponies. An' the young brave killed an Apache warrior. Says that has to be wiped out in blood.'

'Ask him why him an' his braves were chasin' me?' Ellie-May cut in.

John spoke again lengthily. Little Elk's tone was quieter when he replied. John Jordan listened intently before he turned to his mother.

'Reckons we got no right here. He says this is Apache land. '

Ma's face tightened. 'Tell him this here's Jordan land!'

There was a pause. Again John gestured and spoke at length. Then he turned and waved Jake forward.

A three-cornered discussion ensued. Finished, Jake edged his pony back beside Ellie-May and Rafe.

'Well?' Ma said testily.

Jake's mouth twitched. 'Says he wants to fight the young 'white eyes'. Says his honour is at stake. John's told him Ellie-May is a gal, but he don't believe it.'

'Ellie-May,' John called, 'Move out here.'

Slowly his sister edged Goldie forward. 'Now take your hat off.'

'Why?'

'So Little Elk can see you're a gal.'

Grudgingly Ellie-May complied. Little Elk stared at the short blonde curls. Then he turned and spoke again to John.

A heated discussion ensued.

'What's happenin' Jake?' Ma queried.

'Little Elk says he does not believe she is a gal. John is tryin' to convince him.'

The conversation seemed to reach an impasse. Suddenly John turned to Ellie-May. 'Take off your windbreaker.'

'What … ?'

'Do like I say.'

Reluctantly Ellie-May removed her leather jacket.

'Now, unbutton your shirt.'

'No!' Ellie-May shouted furiously, 'I ain't …

'Ellie-May!' Ma's voice cracked like a whip, 'Do like John says. I ain't startin' no Injun war just 'cause you want to go all girly now. Shoulda thought o' that when you started wearin' Levis an' guns. Now unbutton that shirt an' show'm!'

The tall blonde girl bit her lip and hesitated for a long moment, then slowly, very slowly, she undid the shirt buttons.

'Hold it open,' her brother said sardonically. 'This ain't no time to be choosy. Don't worry 'bout me. I ain't lookin'!'

Little Elk's eyes bulged and he leaned forward on his pony. Then, sullen rage showing on his face, he turned and spoke furiously to John.

Her brother nodded. 'Alright, button up, he's convinced. He says how was he to know that the white squaw dressed like a man?'

He switched to Apache. Little Elk replied volubly. Suddenly he made a dismissive gesture and wheeled his pony.

John drew a long breath and turned the pinto towards the wagon.

'What now?' Ma gestured with the shotgun to where the Apaches were talking amongst themselves.

Her son shrugged. 'Some good, some bad. There'll be no fight. We each ride away. But,' his face turned suddenly grave, 'you made a bad enemy there, Ellie-May. He feels put down 'cause a gal bested him.'

There was a sudden shout of laughter from the Apaches, then Little Elk pushed his pony through the group and headed up the slope. Whooping and shouting the others followed him. Just as they entered the timber one brave turned back and shouted something.

'Waal,' John Jordan looked quizzically at his sister, 'at least you got a name among the Apaches now. Ain't many 'white eyes' get that.'

'What did he say?' Ellie-May demanded suspiciously.

'He said goodbye Squaw-who-fights-like-a-man! This ain't goin' to do Little Elk's standin' in the tribe no good. Once the story gets out even the squaws'll rawhide him. Trouble is, that'll push him into doin' somethin' crazy just to get his standin' back.'

He shrugged. 'Can't be helped. Anyway, you're clear now Ma. Me an' Jake'll head off an' start shovin' them Rockin' Chair cattle back onto their own range. Just take care.'

'Thanks boys. Guess I should've listened to Pa.' Her eyes narrowed and she looked at them sharply. 'Suppose this was his idea?'

They grinned together and nodded.

'Just goes to show you should allus listen to good advice.' She broke the shotgun and extracted the two buckshot rounds. 'Right Anders, let's roll. We got supplies to pick up. Adios boys.'

The shotgun stowed away, Ma unrolled her knitting and settled herself comfortably.

Anders eased the team into their stride and glanced at the clicking needles. His shoulders shook as he tried to strangle the laugh which rose in his throat.

Ma scowled at him suspiciously 'You alright?'

'Sure Miz Jordan. Just choked on somethin' I guess.'

John and Jake watched the wagon disappear down the trail. They looked at each other, then Jake laughed. 'Your mother would scare Cochise!'

'Reckon she would at that. Sometimes I wonder if she has any fear?'

The young half-breed shrugged. 'Who knows? Anyway, we got cattle to move. Let's go.'

Laughing quietly together they headed for the west line.

CHAPTER 32

▼

'So they got clean away?' Warden Beale raised his head and looked bleakly at Chief Roberts.

The burly guard chief flushed angrily. 'If you remember Warden, I warned against … '

'Just answer my question dammit! They're no longer in the jail?'

'No sir, we've established that.'

'Hell, what a mess!' Beale rose agitatedly from behind his desk. 'Five killers and we let them get away.' Hands shaking, he lit a cigarette and inhaled deeply.

Roberts frowned as he watched the spare, balding warden. Easterner, he sneered to himself. Look at him shakin' so he can hardly hold that cigarette. Worryin' about his career I bet. What career? He never was worth a damn anyway! Betcha he's figurin' out how to make me carry the can for this.

The warden wheeled suddenly. 'You figured how they did it yet?'

'Well,' Roberts weighed his words carefully, 'accordin' to the survivin' guard who was with Doctor Kincaid; that's Aitcheson, they must have got a knife from somewhere. Seems Defarge knifed Aitcheson's sidekick McCall. That Creole is a bad man with a blade,' he added darkly. 'Then McQuade decked Aitcheson with a water bottle. He come to just in time to hear Kincaid arguin' with them.'

Beale swore furiously. 'Damn Kincaid, this mess is all his making. Should never have listened to him.'

'Didn't do him much good,' Roberts said caustically. 'When he refused to call the other two guards in, Defarge knifed him as well. Then they threatened Aitcheson that they'd do the same to him if he didn't play ball. So he did. Cain't say I blame him. Couple of dead bodies is awful convincin'. After that it was easy. Aitcheson called the other two guards in and they had a rifle stuck in their backs as soon as they walked through the door. Then they were tied up, gagged and dumped in the beds to look like the prisoners. 'Course by this time they had the guards' side arms and the rifles you instructed me to issue,' he added darkly.

Beale put a hand to his head. 'Don't remind me. How long a head start does Aitcheson reckon they've got?'

'Before we found him and his buddies you mean?'

The warden nodded.

''Bout an hour he reckons. 'Course,' Roberts added, 'by the time we'd checked that they weren't in here, as you ordered, I reckon they got another half hour.'

'Alright!' Beale raised his hands. 'I was wrong. It was just that I didn't want to look a fool. I'll be lucky if that's the worst that happens. Anyway, we notified the city marshall and the sheriff?'

'Yeah, we did. It was the marshall's boys that found them two stablehands in the livery stable down the street. They'd been stripped of their boots, Levis and shirts. Five horses and all their gear gone as well.'

'And nobody saw anything?'

Roberts shook his head. 'Nothing. Well, one old guy did think he remembered seein' five fellas headin' south, but that was all. No description or nothin'. I reckon they're halfway to the Border m'self.'

'Mm,' Beale stood for a moment deep in thought. 'Might be no bad thing if they made it to Mexico. Don't reckon they'd try to come back.' He waved a dismissive hand. 'All we can do right now is sit tight and hope.'

'At ease Norman.' Colonel Calhoun waved the ramrod straight captain into a chair. 'What's on your mind?'

McLean grinned and settled himself comfortably. 'Well sir, I'd like to take a patrol down the San Pedro valley. Then I'd swing west towards Dorando, and finally head north back to the camp. What with one thing and another we haven't covered that area for some time. Just recently there's been reports of hostiles there. More specifically Little Elk and his boys. It's reckoned from sign that the band numbers about a dozen, which likely means that some more hot-headed young bucks are tying in with him. Could cause us a lot of grief.'

The colonel nodded. 'Yes, you've got a point there. Alright, permission granted. How do you propose to handle it?'

'Sir, I reckon a fifteen man patrol will be enough. That includes the civilian scout. Plus a couple of pack mules to carry our supplies. We'll call in at the Jordan ranch on the way back. See how they're making out with that bunch of remounts.'

Calhoun's eyes twinkled and he looked shrewdly at the captain. 'This sudden interest in the remounts wouldn't have anything to do with the fact that Jordan's sisters will probably have arrived by now would it?'

McLean felt himself colouring. 'No sir,' he protested. 'It just seems a sensible thing to do when we're in the area. '

The colonel laughed. 'Relax Norman, I was only joshing you. It is a good idea. Go ahead. Then I can tell our lords and masters in Washington that we have the situation under control. Now, leave me to look at those returns in peace.'

Jim Jordan nodded gloomily. 'I think John and Jake are right. This Little Elk sounds like a bronco Apache to me, an' they're the worst kind. Most Injuns is reasonable, but Ellie-May shamed this fella an' he ain't goin' to forget it.'

He looked round the group. 'Anybody else think differently?'

From his seat on the grain bin Lance shook his head. 'Nah, reckon they called it right.'

'Joe? Bull?'

A shake of the head from Joe Masterson, leaning against the stall partition.

Beside him Bull frowned thoughtfully. 'Go along with it all the way. Thing is, what can we do? He can hold off an' pick his time.'

His father walked to the stable door and peered out. The sound of hammering clanged from the forge as Rafe Allen crossed the yard leading Dusty. The old horse balked for a second and then Rafe eased him through the forge doorway.

Down by the corral Sara-Jane and the Johnson girls were feeding the chickens, while beyond them in the horse pasture, John's Indian pinto and Big Red were gnawing quietly at each other's necks.

The rancher turned back grinning. 'Damned if I know how them two ornery critters get along together. That paint's the only hoss I've ever seen

Red take a shine to! Waal now, I called you in here 'cause I didn't want Ellie-May or Sara-Jane to hear us. What can we do 'bout Little Elk an' his boys?'

John raised his hand diffidently. 'Me an' Jake got an idea. There's four of us here pretty fair at trackin' an' night work. Lance, Bull, m'self an' Jake. Likely Joe is too but he's got enough to do ramroddin' this outfit. Now here's the plan. At night, one of us patrols round the ranch here. On foot an' wearin' moccasins. No rifle. Knife an' sidegun only.

If they come straight in an' make it a raid only, then the fella out there fires a warnin' shot. If they leave a horseholder an' come in on foot, which means they're lookin' for blood, we stampede their horses first, then fire the shot. That ought to hold 'em. Means tellin' everybody what we're plannin' though. Then they know what to expect.'

Lance whistled thoughtfully. 'Might just work. How long you gonna keep this up? Got to be thinkin' o' headin' back soon. Reckon I owe Captain McMillan that much.'

John glanced at Jake. 'We reckon 'bout a couple o' weeks. Them braves with Little Elk ain't goin' to wait all that long. They come down here lookin' for some easy pickin's. Scalps, horses an' beeves. If they don't get 'em they'll start driftin' away.'

Bull straightened up. 'Reckon you're callin' it right. What about big Dance an' the mares though? We been herdin' them down by the creek.'

His father frowned. 'Put them in the horse pasture an' move Red an' the pinto into the corral.'

'Alright,' Bull straightened up. 'I'll take the first trick tonight. Who's next?'

Jake nodded.

'John?'

'Yeah, sure.'

Lance grinned. 'Looks like I got no choice. Just leave some o' them 'Paches for me!'

CHAPTER 33

▼

The five riders plunged into the river. In the dark of the night Jack Anderson grinned wolfishly to himself. His horse lost its footing for a second and came up swimming strongly. Behind him there was a flurry of oaths as the other riders felt the pull of the current. Clint's mount panicked and he swore savagely as he lashed it.

'Shut your mouth,' his brother snarled viciously. 'You want all the rurales in Mexico waitin' for us on the other side. Let your mount take its time.'

The Mexican shore loomed ahead. As their horses scrambled up the bank, Diablo Martinez laughed exultantly. 'Amigos, we made it. We are home.'

'Shucks,' Pony McQuade's drawl cut the darkness. 'Might be home for you, but El Paso is my stampin' ground. I got a long way to go yet.'

'You take my advice,' Jack Anderson grated harshly, 'you'll keep ridin'. An' the further west the better. 'Less'n you've forgotten, we left two dead men back there in Austin. Californy's our best bet. Once we get to the goldfields ain't nobody gonna trace us.'

'Jack, my friend, you worry too much,' Jules Defarge chuckled quietly. 'What are two dead men among so many? But yes, I agree with you. The goldfields are our best bet.'

'Sure wish we could've gone to that ranch,' Clint Anderson muttered morosely. 'All I want is to get even with them Jordan wimmen. Seems to me we should've done that first.'

'Damn you!' His brother swore furiously. 'Ain't you got no sense at all. That's one o' the first places they'll look for us. Sure, I hate them Jordan wimmen as much as you an' some day I'm gonna get even. But right now we need a stake, change o' name an' a change o' looks. Beard mebbe and a moustache. Then, in a year or two we can drift back and even the score.'

'Bravo,' Defarge said drily. 'You hate well, Jack. I did not think you could. I say we all go to California.'

'Mebbe you're right.' Pony McQuade reined his mount round. 'Come to think of it, El Paso's still Texas. Yeah, count me in. How about you, Diablo?'

There was a long reflective silence, then Martinez spoke. 'It is true that this is my country, yet the rurales will come seeking me, for I am wanted here also. Amigos, I will ride with you. There are many of my countrymen in the goldfields.'

Diamond Jack let out his breath in a long soundless whistle. So much depended on Martinez if they were to cross Mexico without discovery. He grinned to himself in the darkness. 'Alright, Diablo, you call the shots.'

'Si amigo. First we will head for Palomas, a little town in Chihuahua. Then we will strike through the mountains to Janos. That way we will avoid the rurale patrols who stay close to the river.'

He wheeled his mount. 'Follow me. I have friends in the high country.'

The others swung in behind him.

Grey Wolf was worried. Something felt wrong. There was none of the underlying excitement that lifted most raiding parties. Instead, there seemed to be a dull acceptance of the inevitable. No, the omens for the twelve man band were not good.

Flexing his injured shoulder experimentally, he grunted with relief. There was a slight twinge, nothing more. The old 'white eyes' squaw had done a good job. That had been surprising. Gray Wolf remembered the naked hatred in her eyes as she dug out the bullet.

His thoughts moved on to the young 'white eyes' who spoke Apache and carried the dance scars. There was a strange one. Almost, he could have been one of us.

Glancing ahead at the broad back of their leader, Gray Wolf remembered Black Knife's look of amazement when he had thrown in his lot with Little Elk. The chief would be pondering why he had done it. What if Black Knife were to find out? His face burned at the thought. Little Elk wasn't the only brave to be bested by a squaw. He knew now who the young 'white eyes' on the flying golden pony had been.

What if the others found out? He had seen Little Elk's self control snap under the continual needling of the squaws. Cautiously Gray Wolf stole a glance over his shoulder at the big stolid brave riding behind him. Grass Bull grinned and pointed ahead, but then nothing ever troubled Grass Bull.

He brightened as he thought of the golden palomino. Maybe if the raid went well he would steal the flying pony and ride it back to Cochise's camp in triumph. That would be a feat to remember. Touching the spare hackamore he had tucked in his belt, the young Apache smiled to himself. Maybe things would go well after all.

John skirted the north end of the horse pasture and set out towards the crest of the ridge. The nights were milder now, and in any case, ten years as a Comanche had inured him to the vagaries of the weather. Now, stripped down to shirt, Levis and moccasins, he moved through the darkness like the great cat that he took his Indian name from. The weight of the gunbelt and the holstered .45 had annoyed him initially, but by the third circuit he had become used to it. It was necessary, as was the long Bowie knife riding in the scabbard on his left hip. He turned his head to listen and felt the familiar movement of the leather sheath between his shoulderblades. Reaching up, he touched the slim haft of the throwing knife. There was something comforting about its presence.

I'm gettin' leary he grinned to himself. This is the second week an' nothin's happened. Maybe Little Elk's give up. His instincts said differently. Little Elk was a wild one, a bronco Apache. He would not give up until he wiped out the slur on his manhood in blood.

Something moved up ahead. Every sense tingling he crouched and waited. Above him a grey form was quartering the hillside industriously. A stray eddy of wind brought the man's scent to the coyote and it scampered away towards the ridge. John rose grinning and resumed his patrol.

'You sure about this Jed?' Norman McLean looked sharply at Jed Morton, the civilian scout attached to his patrol. 'It's one thing to wipe out a couple of small ranches, but an outfit like the Flying W could be a tough proposition, even for a big raiding party.'

The tall lanky Missourian shifted his chaw from one cheek to the other and spat accurately into the glowing embers of the campfire. He liked the young captain and knew that McLean wouldn't have queried his information if he hadn't been worried. 'Waal now, Captain, I ain't rightly sure o' nuthin' out there.'

McLean grinned shamefacedly. 'Alright Jed, I'm sorry. It's just that something's bugging me and I don't know what it is.'

Morton looked at him sharply. 'So … seems I ain't the only one. I been feelin' that way ever since I run into old Smokey Joe. That's why I was late gettin' back. I hung on out there hopin' to pick up somethin' but …' He shook his head.

'No tracks?'

'Nothin'. 'Course, could be Joe was just hoorawin' me so that he could get some chewin' tobaccy, but I reckon not. He knew somethin'.'

'What was he doing out this way?'

'Didn't say and I didn't ask. M'self I reckon he trades wi' the Comancheros an' they got a meetin' place down here somewhere.'

McLean frowned moodily. 'I don't like it, I don't like it at all. Little Elk's never had more than four or five young bucks with him and he's raised enough hell in the past couple of years to tie down two companies of cavalry. Now you're saying he's got a dozen or more. That sounds bad to me.'

'Yeah, got to agree with you there. This business wi' the Jordan gal has made him real mad. Pity he ever found out that it was a woman that killed his pony. Accordin' to Joe, he's taken so much rawhidin' from the squaws that he ain't thinkin' straight no more.'

'Alright,' the captain came to a sudden decision. He turned to the burly sergeant, seated on the other side of the fire.

'Sergeant Peters!'

'Sir?'

'Have the boys ready to move at first light. We'll head straight for the Flyin' W. Now I suggest we get some sleep.'

There was the faintest hint of grey along the eastern horizon. The Apache ponies were down to walking pace now, their hooves shushing softly through the wet grass. Little Elk drew his mount to a halt and waited as the others closed round him.

'We will go down the slope. The 'white eyes' will be asleep. Try to get as close as you can. If we are seen then we will circle the ranch so that they will not be sure where we will attack. If need be we will fight on foot. Then those with the fire arrows will use them. I want all the 'white eyes' dead.'

High on the ridge John caught the faint sound of hooves on grass. Dropping flat he put his ear to the turf. Yes, there it was, fading down the slope. Hastily he rose to his feet and, stepping behind some scrub drew the big .45. Eyes closed to save his night vision he squeezed the trigger.

The crash of the shot high above the ranch unleashed a flurry of action.

Just for a second the raiding party halted irresolute, then Little Elk's voice lifted in a shrill Apache war cry as he raced for the ranch buildings, the others strung out behind him.

The defenders came awake with a start, reaching automatically for weapons laid ready to hand. For the past week they had been strung out through the square of buildings and they were prepared. Everywhere wooden shutters were hurriedly closed and battens dropped into place.

'Your Uncle Dave wasn't no slouch at Injun fightin',' Pa grunted as he peered into the darkness. 'Them loopholes is sited just right.'

'Yeah.' Pushing the shotgun through the opening Ma listened for the sound of galloping hooves. It came suddenly, swelling to a crescendo, and she loosed off both barrels as the attack swept past. 'Might as well let them know we're here,' she said tersely. 'Think John'll be alright?'

It was getting lighter now. The Apaches were fleeting dark shadows against the greyness. Jim Jordan snapped a quick shot and grunted with satisfaction as the pony went down. Its rider dropped into the grass and forted up behind it.

''Bout John? Yeah, I reckon so. Ain't much we can do about it anyway. If he's any sense he'll stay up on the ridge.'

A Winchester barked three times in quick succession from the next room.

'Sounds like Jake's busy.' Ma clicked the shotgun shut and peered out into the growing light. There was a bang and splinters flew from the wooden shutters. Ma ducked hastily. The attack swept out of sight round the corner. 'Wonder how Sara-Jane an' the kids are makin' out?'

Anders's big Henry rifle boomed sullenly from the blacksmith's shop. Rafe Allen shook his head, the noise was deafening in the small low-roofed building.

The Dane laughed as he spaced his shots among the attackers. 'Come on young Rafe. By golly we give those Injuns hell!' The youngster gritted his teeth and settled himself again at the loophole.

In the cook shack next door old Tex was pumping bullets wildly into the greyness. 'Damned if this ain't just like the time I was wi' Chisum.'

Chester grinned. 'You wasn't never wi' Chisum!' He peered out of the loophole and sighted carefully. The arrow took him high in the chest. Clutching at the shaft with both hands he staggered and fell.

It was getting light now. In the stable Bull wiped the sweat from his brow. 'You fellas alright?' There was a chorus of assent from the Aldersons.

Across in the bunkhouse Joe Masterson was asking the same question.

'Si amigo.' It was Manuel who answered. The attack swept round the corner close against the building. A .45 boomed at one of the openings. Jem Anson gasped and toppled sideways.

'Jem, you alright boy?' Jeff Short knelt and turned the motionless figure over. He rose slowly and shook his head. 'Jem's dead! They got him right between the eyes.'

The attack faded into the distance.

Captain McLean was cold, hungry and irritable. He'd also slept badly and that had not improved matters. He distrusted his own hunch, yet the feeling persisted. Still, another ten miles or so and they'd be at the ranch. Then he could laugh at his fears.

'Scout comin' back sir,' Peters reported, 'and he's in a hurry.'

Jed Morton reined in his mount. His normally saturnine features were alight with anticipation. 'Firin' up ahead. Sounds like a regular battle.'

McLean swore savagely. So I was right after all. He rose in his stirrups. 'Bugler, sound the charge. Forward yo!' The clear notes echoed in the still air as the patrol surged into a gallop.

John ran crouching along the lee of the horse pasture fence. Reckon they've pulled off for a spell but they'll be back.

He came to the rear of the corral and sank silently out of sight in the long grass.

'Well?' Mary-Lou and Jim Jordan looked at their eldest son. At the risk of being shot at from both sides Lance had made the rounds of all the buildings.

He shrugged. 'Bad enough. Jem Anson's dead an' Chester's hit bad. Took an arrow high up in his chest an' he's bleedin' some. Got'm bandaged up though an' I'll take his place wi' Tex.'

'We get any o' them?' Ma queried as she laid out shotgun shells on the table.

Lance shrugged. 'Doubt it. Remember, we was shootin' into the dark and they had muzzle flashes to work on. Be different now. Coupla dead ponies out there, but that's all. Wonder what they'll try next?'

'Fire arrows I reckon,' his father said, hurriedly loading more rounds into the Winchester. 'The house is 'dobe, but there's the rest o' the buildin's. If they can fire them, or the wagons, we got trouble.'

Ellie-May appeared in the doorway. 'Ma, Pa ... you alright?'

'Yeah sure. How about Sara-Jane an' the gals?'

Their elder daughter smiled tightly. 'They're fine, only don't go openin' that kitchen door in a hurry, else Sara-Jane's liable to blow your head off!'

Her brother laughed. 'Right, I'm on m'way. Reckon they'll be back soon.'

'No!' Little Elk shouted furiously. 'We will try again. This time we will use the fire arrows and we will triumph. All we have lost are two ponies and we will take the two that the 'white eyes' left in their corral. Grass Bull will lead while Grey Wolf and I do this.'

The attack swirled round the ranch once more. From his hiding place at the rear of the corral John watched tensely.

A fire arrow soared high and disappeared into the yard. Sure hope somebody's keepin' an eye on them wagons. Movement in the wash beyond the corral caught his eye, and his face tightened as he saw the two Apaches making a run towards the corral gate.

As they swung the gate open Red's ears went back and he bared his teeth.

Little Elk spoke sharply to Grey Wolf. 'Take the pinto. I remember this horse. He outran Swift Wind.'

He closed in on Red. The giant roan squealed and pawed the ground. Shouting threateningly the Apache struck at the big horse. In a flash Red spun and lashed out. The steelshod hooves caved in Little Elk's chest and he crumpled to the ground.

John shouted and raced forward, but he was too late. Red twisted like a cat, reared and came down stamping. The crippled Apache screamed once and was silent.

Struggling to get the hackamore onto the pinto, Grey Wolf turned quickly and reached for the old gun in his belt.

Smoothly, John's arm swept back and then forward. The long throwing knife flashed through the air and buried itself in the Apache's chest. Slowly, tiredly, he toppled forward and the gun dropped from his nerveless fingers.

Crossing to the prone figure, John bent and pulled out the long blade. He straightened up shaking his head. Guess you were always goin' to lose, Grey Wolf. The Apaches swept round the end of the bunkhouse and he drew the .45.

High on the ridge the clear notes of the bugle echoed in the morning air. The cavalry came sweeping down, a phalanx of galloping horseflesh and steel. Grass Bull darted a quick glance up the slope and wheeled his pony. With a chorus of shrill yells the raiding party raced for the ford, the cavalry close behind.

John walked slowly towards the yard. Jake met him at the gate. They grinned at each other. It was over.

CHAPTER 34

Midday. The riders came down the trail slowly, their horses shuffling tiredly in the dust. Everything about them spoke of men who had travelled long and hard. All five sprouted incipient beards and powdery dust lay thick on their clothing.

At the town outskirts they halted and spoke for a moment in low tones, before turning down a side street.

One of the somnolent figures sitting on the sidewalk rose and disappeared into a nearby alley. The sound of hoofbeats faded into the distance.

'Si patron.' The speaker was nervous. Looking into the patron's eyes always made him nervous. 'It is as I say. They are like men who have come many miles quickly. Gringos, at least some of them. The dust lies thick on their clothing and their horses move tiredly. Also, they are careful men, they do not ride boldly into town. Instead they turn off and ride down the street where Hernandez's cantina is. They may have stopped there. My eldest son is checking now.'

The cold black eyes narrowed. 'This son of yours. He knows how to watch without drawing attention to himself?'

'Si patron. I myself taught him. If they stay there he will let us know.'

'It is good.' The massive head nodded judiciously. 'You have done well, amigo. When your son returns send him to me.'

'Gracias patron. It is an honour to serve you.'

Domingo Sanchez raised a benevolent hand and watched with amused tolerance as the small peon scuttled from the room. These peasants, they are easily pleased. A few words of praise, a little money occasionally and they will lick your boots. He sat for a moment deep in thought.

A heavily built, powerful man in his late forties, Sanchez controlled the border town of Evalde and the surrounding territory. Something of a dandy, with a magnificent head of silver grey hair, his obsession to be treated as a hidalgo was known to all and sundry.

His father, old Roderigo Sanchez, had laid the foundations of the Comanchero empire which his son now operated.

Before that, trade with the Indians had been a chancy business, where the Comanchero traders took their lives in their hands every time they set up a meeting. Old Roderigo had changed that. In a series of treaties hammered out with Indian chiefs he had obtained guarantees of safe conduct and trading rights for the Comancheros. In return, he provided the tribes with trading outlets and far better deals than they had obtained previously. Behind the scenes he maintained contacts through which they could obtain arms and ammunition, at a price! He also ransomed selected captives, whom he turned over to the authorities for a handsome profit.

This was Roderigo's empire, control of which passed, on his death, to his son Domingo. With the end of the war however, Domingo realised that time was running out for the Comancheros. Now the Army was free to break the resistance of the tribes, and the need for his traders would disappear.

Before that happened he was determined that his business would have ceased to be associated with the tainted word Comanchero, and his descendants would take their place among the landed families of Sonora.

Frowning, he rose and, opening the door, called imperiously. A tall Mexican entered and made his way to the desk where he waited impassively.

'Tomas,' Sanchez eyed the tall major-domo. 'Find Senor Smith and bring him to me.'

Tomas bowed slightly.

'Also, when Pedro Rojas's son arrives send him in at once.'

The major-domo bowed again and withdrew closing the door softly behind him.

Domingo Sanchez smiled contentedly. Tomas was that rarity, a man whose loyalty was beyond question. In addition he was mute!

In his younger days he had fallen into the hands of Apaches, who had diverted themselves by cutting out his tongue, before eventually releasing him.

Sanchez had found him sweeping out a cantina in the little border town of Fronteras and had been quick to realise his possibilities. Over the years he had trained Tomas in all aspects of the business, and now he had a major-domo second to none, whose loyalty was unshakeable.

There was a knock.

'Enter.'

Tomas opened the door and stood aside.

The Comanchero pretended to study the papers in front of him, aware of the man standing by the desk. Let the gringo sweat, he thought sardonically. He will remember who is his master.

'You wanted to see me, Mister Sanchez?'

Sanchez looked up in well-simulated surprise. 'Ah, Senor Smith. Take a seat. There is a matter I would like to discuss with you. Leave us Tomas.' The major-domo bowed and withdrew.

Eyes suddenly wary John Smith seated himself uneasily.

John 'Panhandle' Smith, was something of an unknown quantity in Evalde. It was rumoured that he had once held a high position in a U.S. bank, before gambling activities and missing funds had caused him to flee south. Now he handled Sanchez's accounts and ran a reasonably straight poker game in the town's main saloon, owned of course by Sanchez. Neither man trusted the other, but the Comanchero held the whip hand and Smith knew it.

'Now … ' he broke off as there was another tap on the door.

'Enter.'

Tomas ushered a nervous Mexican youth into the room and closed the door behind him. Sanchez beckoned the youth forward. 'Ah, you are Pedro Rojas's son. You have news?'

'Si patron.' The boy licked his lips and darted a worried glance at Smith.

Sanchez waved a lordly hand. 'You may speak freely.'

'Patron,' he swallowed nervously, 'I have watched the strangers as my father told me too. Since they came into town they have remained at Hernandez's cantina. There they have eaten like men who have had little food for some time. Now they drink quietly amongst themselves. It seems they have come a long way and there is much talk of the goldfields among them.'

'Are they all gringos?'

'No patron, there is one of our blood. They listen to him, but Hernandez does not think he is the leader. Also, they do not seem to have much money. They ate cheaply and they are making their drinks last. Two of them wish to play cards, but Hernandez does not have such games in his cantina.'

Domingo Sanchez frowned thoughtfully. 'You have done well. Go back now to Hernandez. He is to tell them that they can have such games in my establishment, the Mexican Rose.'

'Si patron, I will tell him.' The youth bowed and left.

As the door closed Sanchez looked at Smith. 'Well, what do you think?'

The gambler frowned. 'Men on the run I'd say. Most likely just passin' through.'

'These are my thoughts also. But such men could be useful.'

Smith looked at him warily. 'What have you got in mind?'

Sanchez smiled thinly. 'All in good time. First we must wait to see if they take the bait. Then you will listen carefully to what they have to say.'

'Cards you say?' there was a faraway look in Diamond Jack's eyes. 'Sure would like to feel a deck in my hands again. How 'bout you, Pony?'

The lanky Texan grinned. 'Yeah, be just like home.'

'Jules?'

The stocky little Creole shook his head. 'The last time I play poker someone try to cheat. This make me very unhappy ... !'

Hernandez laughed. 'The game will be straight. Senor Sanchez will not have it any other way.'

Defarge shrugged. 'No card game is ever completely straight, but yes, I will go along.'

'Diablo, how about you?'

'Si, I will come.'

'Clint?'

Clint Anderson scowled. 'Don't feel so good. M'leg's achin' pretty bad. Reckon I'll just stay here.'

'You're comin' with us,' his brother snarled. 'Ain't leavin' you here to get drunk an' raise a ruckus. Finish your drink and we'll head round to the saloon.'

Hernandez walked to the bar and spoke to the barman. He in turn nodded to young Rojas who was stowing empty bottles in a crate.

Carrying the crate, the youth disappeared through the doorway leading to the storeroom. In the passage he put it down and vanished along the alley.

The five walked slowly down the street towards the saloon, Clint limping slightly on his buckshot-scarred legs.

'Gettin' low on cash,' Jack Anderson said quietly.

'Hadn't been for the roll we took off that livery boss we'd be in big trouble. So I suggest we play for small stakes till I see if I can spin it into somethin' better.'

The others nodded silently. They had all seen Diamond Jack's skill with cards.

'Right smart outfit,' Pony McQuade said as they pushed their way through the swing doors. 'Never thought I'd see somethin' like this below the line.'

Martinez laughed and veiled the anger which showed momentarily in his eyes. 'You think we are all ignorant peasants maybe?'

'Hey, Diablo!' McQuade protested. 'Didn't mean nothin' like that. Reckon it's a real fine place, that's all.'

'Pony my friend, there is no harm. Now we will get ourselves a drink.'

'Sure is quiet,' McQuade observed. 'Come to think of it, mebbe too quiet. Only that thin fella playin' solo at the card table an' the big man sittin' with him.' He turned back to the bar. 'How much?'

The barman shook his head. 'There is nothing to pay. The owner,' he indicated the big man at the card table, 'he say, on the house!'

'Does he now?' the five fanned out instinctively. 'Somethin' strange here.'

The barman grinned.' You are suspicious? He only wishes to talk to you. He say if you take your drinks and go across to the table, he will explain everything.'

Diamond Jack shrugged. 'Cain't see no harm in that. Let's go.'

'Howdy gents.' Panhandle Smith laid down the cards he had been shuffling and rose. 'This is Senor Domingo Sanchez who owns the joint. He's got a business proposition for you. When you're finished talkin' give me a shout an' we'll set up a game. Nice meetin' you.' He moved away to the bar.

'Senores,' Sanchez motioned them to sit. 'This will not take long. If you are not interested say so and I will leave you to your cards.'

There was silence and he waited until they were seated. 'Now, I do not wish to know your names. I do not suppose you would tell me anyway. No matter. I run a business. A good business. Trading. I trade with anyone, but especially Indians. I am a Comanchero!'

Around the table there was a sudden heightening of interest.

'You are surprised?' He smiled coldly. 'Do not be. Business is business. Until recently I had no trouble, my men came and went as they pleased across the Border. Now a man has come here who is making trouble for me, too much trouble. Many of my men have died because of him.'

He paused delicately. 'So if something was to happen to this man, let us say he was to die …', there were nods all round the table, 'I would pay well.'

'Senor Sanchez,' Defarge's eyes glittered coldly, 'what sort of money did you have in mind?'

The Comanchero leaned back in his chair and stared deliberately at Defarge. 'If this man was to die I would pay five thousand dollars to the person or persons responsible!'

The five exchanged glances. 'Waal now,' Pony McQuade was the first to speak. 'That there's real money. Cain't see you havin' no trouble hirin' somebody.'

Sanchez gestured expressively. 'The fates have not been kind. Also, he usually has some of his men with him.'

Diamond Jack leaned forward. 'Where does he hang out?'

'He has a large ranch, the Flying W, between here and Dorando. He and his family have only recently moved here from Texas.'

'What's his monicker?' McQuade asked idly.

'Eh ... oh you mean his name? Jordan.'

'Jordan!' The Andersons half rose from their seats, 'It cain't be!'

'You know this man?' Sanchez looked at them curiously.

'Maybe,' Diamond Jack said slowly. 'It was folks name o' Jordan that shot us up an',' he indicated Clint, 'crippled him some. Wonder if it's the same folks? They had a place in east Texas down near Greenhills.'

Sanchez shook his head. 'I know little about them, but can see you do not like this family.'

'Damn right we don't!' Clint said viciously. 'Them Jordan wimmen ain't human, blastin' away at folks wi' a shotgun. I'd give my right arm to get even.'

'Ah.' Sanchez held up his hand. 'Now I remember. This woman; she carries a shotgun!'

'It's her!' Clint Anderson's face contorted with fury. 'I ain't never forgotten that old bitch. Jack, this is our chance to get even.'

'Yeah,' Diamond Jack looked round the table. 'You fellas in?' The others nodded. 'Right, we'll do it.'

Domingo Sanchez smiled and signalled to the bartender. 'Senores, we have a deal.'

CHAPTER 35

▼

'You'll do like I say,' Ma said sharply as she lifted the tray from the bedside. 'I ain't nursed you this far to have you gettin' up too soon an' dyin' on me. 'Sides,' she added, pausing in the doorway, 'good hands ain't easy to come by an' I aim to get a lot more work outa you yet!'

'But ma'am,' Chester protested feebly, 'it ain't right me bein' here ... ain't fittin'.'

Ma scowled, tray in hand. 'Hush your fuss. Sure don't know where you get them ideas o' yours. You're the one allus says 'ride for the brand, fight for the brand!' Waal, the brand looks after its own. What's eatin' you? You scared your colour'll rub off on them sheets?' The door slammed and she was gone.

Chester grinned, then laughed outright. What a woman! She ain't happy less'n she's givin' somebody hell! One thing's for sure, colour don't mean nuthin' to her. He tried to raise himself in bed and sank back stifling a groan. Damn, that hurt. Sure glad Ah passed out when Miz Jordan was cuttin' out that arrowhead. Man, she is one handy lady with a knife.

He lay still and thought back over the intervening two weeks since the raid. Lucky the patrol arrived when it did. That Captain McLean, he's an alright guy. Said he wished he had a coupla sergeants like me an' Jeff to train the recruits. Reckoned the Apaches wouldn't trouble the ranch again seein' Little Elk was dead. He shivered. That Big Red is one dangerous horse.

Shame about Jem though. Still, the Jordans were fair with him an' he paid his dues. Accordin' to Jeff it was a right nice funeral. They even brought that young preacher out from Dorando to take the service. Now Jem's buried up there on the hill, an' Miz Jordan had Anders put a picket fence round the grave.

Faintly, he heard the enraged squeal of a horse at the corrals and the distant bawl of cattle down by the creek. Boys sure are busy right now, what with the remounts an' the beef contract. Wish Ah could swing a rope again, Ah ain't much good lyin' here, makin' work for Miz Jordan.

Joe Masterson touched a match to his cigarette and inhaled deeply. Expelling a long streamer of smoke he squinted at Bull. 'So you'll take the remounts up to the camp?'

Bull nodded. 'Yeah, gimme a couple o' the boys. That should be enough.'

'Alright, I'll set Jeff an' Manuel on this chore. Then I'll get the Aldersons to ride the west line. Them Rockin' Chair cattle is movin' across all the time. Reckon that outfit's overstocked. Anyways, Sam an' Mike deserve a break. They've been workin' hard gentlin' them remounts.'

Bull frowned. 'Yeah, though I'd like to see us gettin' another batch ready.'

'How 'bout John an' Jake?'

Bull shook his head. 'Pa wants to take a trip down into the brush in the south o' the ranch. Jake's been tellin' him about that mustang stallion in there. You know the one, that blue roan. Pa don't want him tanglin' wi' old Dance, so he'd like a shot at him 'fore he starts runnin' off any o' the mares. Thought Jake an' Rafe could ride wi' him. Good chance for young Rafe to learn about the brush country. Push any strays north at the same time. Don't want too many o' them calvin' down there if we can help it.'

'Yeah, seems fine to …' He broke off and listened intently as a horse clattered out of the yard.

'Lance,' Bull grunted. 'Said he was goin' to Tucson for a look around. Then he'd be callin' in at Dorando on the way back. Reckoned on bein' away three, four days. Seems he's got some business wi' Sheriff Dawson. Dunno what it is, he's bein' right close about it.'

Joe laughed. 'Waal, he's hardly likely to be on the run, him bein' in the cavalry an' all.'

The big rancher grinned. 'That's true.' He thought for a moment. ''Bout them remounts. What d'you say to John an' Ellie-May? Ellie-May's right handy wi' horses. Her an' Rafe worked the remuda on the drive.'

Joe frowned, then nodded. 'Fine. Anyways, Anders is here. He'll be repairin' that wagon that was burnt wi' the fire arrows. John can call on him if he needs muscle.'

'Don't let Ellie-May hear you sayin' that. She'll take it personal!'

'Alright.' Joe laughed. 'How's Chester?'

'He's comin' along fine. Ma says 'nother two, three days he'll be back on his feet. 'Course the two o' them are sparkin' just as much as ever, but it's all show.'

Chuckling quietly, they wandered out of the stable.

Jim Jordan sipped the scalding black coffee, and grinned across the small campfire at a serious-faced Rafe Allen sitting opposite. 'You make real good coffee, Rafe. 'Course Ma buys the right stuff, but wi' some fellas it wouldn't make no difference. They'd still spile it just the same.'

'Thanks Mister Jordan,' the youngster felt himself flushing and was grateful that the flickering flames masked his embarrassment. 'Sure appreciate bein' on this trip. '

'Yeah, waal … it's all learnin' son. Some day you might have your own spread an' you'll need to know the cow business.'

Rafe nodded gravely. That was something he liked about Mister Jordan. He treated you like you was a top hand, didn't put you down or nuthin'. Jake was alright but he didn't say much.

There was a long silence. He looked across the fire. 'Jake's awful quiet out there.'

Jim Jordan nodded and tossed his coffee grounds into the flames. 'Rafe, you got to remember Jake's half Comanche. Ten Bears's boys called him Runnin' Wolf, an' that's just what he is out there, a wolf. He's circlin' us now checkin' everything, then he'll come in.'

The night seemed to chill suddenly and Rafe shivered. 'Ain't seen nuthin' o' that roan stallion,' he ventured.

Jim Jordan shook his head. 'Likely long gone,' he said. 'Stud like that can cover an awful lot o' territory. Still, we've done right well wi' them strays. Reckon we should finish tomorrow, then we can head back.'

Jake materialised suddenly out of the darkness.

'Just sayin',' Jim squinted up at him, 'reckon we could be finished here by midday tomorrow. Then we can head back to the ranch.'

'Yeah.' Jake reached for the coffee pot. 'That seems 'bout right.'

'So you're takin' up m'offer?' Sheriff Dawson grinned. 'Best news I heard in a long time.'

Lance shrugged. 'Waal, it's somethin' I've always had a hankerin' for an' …' He broke off as Joe Ogilvy entered with a small sack. 'Picked up the mail,' the deputy grunted. 'Just came in.'

'Thanks Joe.' The sheriff slit the sack and dumped the contents on the desk.

'Dodgers,' he grumbled. 'Seems to me half the folks in the U.S. of A. are on the run, an' the other half's huntin' 'em. Let's see now … ', he riffled through the roll of 'Wanted' notices.

'Jules Defarge, wanted for murder and jail break. James 'Pony' McQuade, murder and jail break. Manoelito 'Diablo' Martinez, murder and jail break. John 'Diamond Jack' Anderson, murder and … say, ain't that the fella your ma an' your sisters put behind bars?'

'Lemme see that,' Lance rose from his chair. 'Hey, that's right. Diamond Jack Anderson. Say, he had a young brother … Clint I think his name was.' He grinned. 'Sara-Jane near shot the legs off him.'

'Mm.' Dawson was studying another poster. 'Clinton Anderson, murder and jail break.' He swore suddenly. 'Damn, where in hell have these dodgers been till now?'

'What's eatin' you?'

'There's a letter with this bunch,' Dawson's voice was suddenly serious. 'Listen to this. The five outlaws listed on the enclosed notices escaped from the state penitentiary in Austin, Texas, on January the third, 1870. Hell, that's six weeks ago! In making their escape they killed a guard and the prison doctor. It is thought that these men may have reached Mexico. They are armed and dangerous.' He looked up. 'You thinkin' what I'm thinkin'?'

Lance was already on his feet. 'I'm way ahead o' you. The Flyin' W ain't that far from the Border. If they was to find out that Ma an' the gals was out this way things could get real serious. Reckon I'll hightail it back to the ranch an' warn the folks. Adios now.' He vanished through the doorway at the run.

The trail wound through the chaparral and round clumps of saguaro cactus. Made originally by the wild black cattle, it had been adapted for use by the Comancheros. Here and there it broadened and at one of these points Pony McQuade moved up beside Martinez. He jerked his head in the direction of the silent figure up front. 'Tomas know his way round here?'

Diablo Martinez nodded. 'Si amigo. From what I have been told, he used to hunt all through this country until the Apaches caught him.'

'Thought Comancheros and Injuns were real close?'

'That is true. However, it seems there was some trouble over a woman. I do not know what happened, but the Apaches caught him and cut his tongue out.'

Pony scowled. 'Nice partners. Sure hope we don't meet up with them.'

Martinez grinned. 'Amigo, Apaches are clever fighters. They would think very carefully before they attacked us. We are a strong party. I sometimes think they would make good poker players. They always check the odds first.'

The bawl of driven cattle sounded ahead. Diamond Jack moved up beside Tomas.

''Case you all've forgotten,' he threw over his shoulder, 'if we run into anybody we're cowhands lookin' for a trail herd to sign on with. We heard that Jordan o' the Flyin' W is puttin' a herd together an' we're headin' that way to see him. That should be enough.' The bawling cattle were closer now.

'Damned ornery critter!' Jim Jordan wiped the sweat from his brow and eyed the wild-looking Longhorn cow as she pawed the ground. 'She near got a horn into Smoke there.'

The cow bellowed angrily and tossed her head. Jake eyed the very young calf tucked protectively in under its mother's flank. 'Tell you somethin'. Ain't no varmint gonna get that calf, that's for sure.'

Rafe Allen turned in his saddle. 'Riders comin'.'

'Howdy.' Diamond Jack drew his mount to a halt. The others spread out on either side.

Tough lookin' outfit, Jake thought, wouldn't want to buck them.

'Name's Anson, Dave Anson. Trail boss. Me an' the boys are just back from Californy. Took a herd through there for the Cabeza de Vaca outfit. Now we're lookin' for another to hook up with. Heard there's a ranch round here, the Flyin' W, that's puttin' a trail herd together. Fella name o' Jordan owns it.'

'Howdy.' Pa looked at them closely. Hard bunch. 'I'm Jordan, but …'

'You're Jordan hey,' Diamond Jack grinned as he glanced at the others. 'Ain't that somethin'! Boys, we're in luck.'

Jake tensed. Something was wrong. The Cabeza de Vaca did not hire gringos!

'Damn you!' Clint Anderson went for his gun, his face contorted with fury. Jake rowelled savagely with his left heel, and his pony squealed as it slammed sideways into Smoke.

Gunfire erupted. The cow bawled, a high strangled bellow, and charged.

Jake's mount drove Smoke sideways and Clint's bullet took Jake high in his chest. Desperately he tried to bring the big .45 up but a hail of lead plucked him from the saddle.

The charging cow crashed into Martinez's mount, the needle sharp horns slashing its side. The pony screamed and went down, trapping Diablo, as the raging cow trampled them underfoot. Jim Jordan, dying from three chest wounds, triggered one round in a purely reflex action. The bullet ripped into the brain of Clint's mount and it collapsed pinning its rider. A blinding light exploded in Rafe Allen's head and he pitched tiredly out of the saddle.

Diamond Jack slammed two quick shots into the berserk Longhorn. The wild-eyed cow lurched forward and fell across the two ponies.

'Gimme a hand,' Jack Anderson was out of his saddle in a flash. 'Clint's hurt bad.'

He tugged at his brother who screamed. 'M'leg! I think it's busted.'

Pony McQuade was already shaking out a loop. 'Got to get that cow off him.'

He dropped a loop neatly over the wide horns and took a turn round the saddle horn. Then he backed his mount and the dead cow slid clear. Defarge heaved desperately at Clint's mount and Jack dragged his screaming brother out from under the dead pony.

'What about Diablo?' Pony McQuade looked at Defarge who was on his knees beside Martinez. 'How bad is he?'

The Creole shook his head. 'His neck is broken. I think the cow stepped on him.'

McQuade freed his rope and cursed savagely. 'Hell, what a mess!' He rounded on Tomas. 'Waal, you satisfied we got your man? You heard him say he was Jordan.'

The major-domo ignored him and knelt beside the dead rancher. Carefully he began searching the body, examining every item closely. Suddenly he stopped and looked carefully at the small silver tobacco box. Then he rose and held it out to Diamond Jack. Stamped across the base were the words, J. JORDAN CIRCLE J.

'That's right. It's him. I remember seein' the Circle J brand on that team that hauled us into Fort Worth.'

Tomas nodded and pocketed the box.

'Right,' Pony McQuade looked at Diamond Jack. 'Let's get Clint onto one o' them dead fellas' ponies. Then we can get the hell outa here.'

Jack Anderson's temper flared and his hand dropped to his gun. 'Ain't nobody touchin' Clint till I say so.'

'Suit yourself.' Pony flicked a glance at Defarge, suddenly wary. 'But we got to get him to a doctor. Reckon the nearest one's Evalde. Either we splint the leg an' he rides out, or we make a travois an' take him out that way. '

Defarge nodded.'Pony is right my friend. We must do something quickly.

'Yeah, I know.' Jack Anderson was calmer now. 'Right, we'll make a travois. Catch up one o' them fellas mounts.'

Urged on by his rider, Buck splashed through the ford and swept up the slope towards the ranch. They clattered into the yard.

John appeared in the stable doorway. He looked at his brother curiously. 'You're in an all-fired hurry ain't you?'

'Bull around?' Lance demanded.

'Yeah, saw him in the forge with Anders as I come up from the corral. What ...'

'Right!' Dismounting, Lance ran towards the forge.

Anders and Bull looked up from the axle they were working on.

'Bull!' The urgency in his brother's voice startled the big rancher.

'Yeah?'

'Want to talk, now!'

Bull looked at Anders and shrugged his shoulders. He followed Lance out into the yard. John appeared from the stable and strode towards them.

'Trouble,' Lance said succinctly. Swiftly he outlined to his brothers what had happened.

Bull sucked in his breath. 'Damn, that's bad. You told Ma an' the gals yet?'

Lance shook his head. 'Nope, not yet. Wanted to hear what you fellas had to say. An' Pa. Where is Pa anyway?'

Bull and John exchanged glances. 'Pa ain't here,' Bull said slowly. 'He's down in the south brush right now!'

Lance's voice rose an octave. 'He's where?'

'That's right. Still, he's got Jake and Rafe with him.'

''Case you've forgotten,' Lance said caustically, 'there's five in that bunch an' they're all killers. When's Pa an' the boys due back?'

'Waal,' Bull said uncomfortably, 'they should have shown up by now. 'Course, mebbe they're still trailin' that stallion.'

'Mount up,' Lance said impatiently. 'Get your horses, both of you. We're ridin'.'

Bull stared at his elder brother. 'Ain't you kinda goin' off at half-cock?'

'Damn it, do like I say! Somethin's wrong, I can feel it. I'll go tell Ma to watch out.' He hurried towards the house.

Bull watched him go. 'Sure is jumpy ain't he?'

John shook his head. 'He's right. All day I've had this feelin'. I should have listened. Injuns know about these things.' He turned and ran towards the stable, Bull at his heels.

They were leading out Red and the pinto when Lance reappeared, Ma hurrying at his side.

Bull looked at his mother. 'Ma, I ain't right sure … '

'Hush up,' Ma said impatiently. 'Lance is right. We been gettin' careless. So what if we got it wrong? Your pa'll just laugh. 'Bout twenty miles from here to the Border. You got three, mebbe four hours o' daylight left. Get movin'. I'll go tell the gals. Then we're ready if anybody comes callin'.' She bustled away.

'Right,' Lance swung into his saddle and heeled Buck round. 'Bull, you know which way they headed?'

His brother nodded.

'Lead out then.'

They swept out of the yard and up the slope on the run.

CHAPTER 36

▼

Circling lazily the buzzards eyed the scene of death below. Eventually one, bolder than the others, swept in on silent wings and alighted cautiously. It waited, poised for flight, head cocked inquisitively. Satisfied, it stalked stiff-legged towards the dead cow. The others planed down swiftly and followed.

Jack Donovan watched narrowly as the birds dropped out of sight. Maybe the cougar had killed. 'Somethin' in trouble there, Satan.' The giant wolfhound looked up at him and whined eagerly.

Donovan frowned. He was beginning to think that the old tom cougar he had been trailing all morning had given him the slip. Waal, it wouldn't do any harm to take a look. 'Alright boy, let's go.'

The quarter horse wheeled obediently at the touch on the reins and took off at an effortless lope, the wolfhound running easily alongside.

Rafe Allen stirred uneasily and groaned. Faintly through the swirling mists that threatened to engulf him he heard noises. A dog barked close by and someone shouted a gruff command. He tried to sit up and gasped in agony as pain like a red-hot dagger lanced through his chest. An arm cradled him and he was eased upright. Something was held against his lips, he swallowed eagerly and choked, gasping for breath.

'Easy son.' Jack Donovan waited until the coughing subsided. 'You got a crease along the side of your head and,' he glanced at the blood on the youngster's shirt, 'by the looks o' things you got a slug in you somewhere as well. Let's see.'

Carefully unbuttoning the bloodstained shirt, Donovan sucked in his breath when he saw the blue-rimmed hole from which blood was leaking slowly.

Low down he explored gently; still in there. Cain't risk no more water. Got to get a bandage on that hole. Working one-handed, he removed his and Rafe's bandannas. Knotting them together he drew the knots tight with his teeth. 'Let's get this round you.' He eased the makeshift bandage into position.

'Got to get back ...' Rafe clutched at him desperately, 'got to tell Miz Jordan an' the others what happened.'

'Take it easy son. Lemme get this bandage tied.' He tightened the bandannas and the youngster gasped at the stabbing pain.

'No, no!' He struggled to rise. 'Got to get back an' tell them ... tell them I couldn't help it.'

'Sure you couldn't, son.' Easing off his vest Donovan rolled it up and slipped the bundle under Rafe's head. 'Rest easy now while I take a look at them other fellas.'

He rose and crossed to where Jim Jordan lay, face down, on the trampled grass. Turning the body over carefully, the old rancher's mouth tightened grimly at the sight of the bloodsoaked clothing. Gently unbuttoning the reddened shirt he eyed the three chest wounds and shook his head. Not a hope. He's all shot to hell. Looks like he took one in the heart. Guess he was dead 'fore he hit the ground. Well; he checked the big Colt; at least he got off one shot. Ain't right sure, but I reckon that's the Jordan boys' pa lyin' there. Seems to me there's a likeness.

Donovan moved on to Jake, sprawled on his back close by. Good-lookin' young fella. Got muscle too. Ain't seen 'im around here before. Guess he's one o' the riders the Jordans brung in. Unbuttoning the homespun shirt he checked again. 'Mhm.' He's taken four slugs. Likely they're all still in him. About to rise, he stopped suddenly and peered closely at the broad chest. There ... the faintest rise and fall. Hell! he's still breathin'. Who'd ha' thought it.

Rising, Jack Donovan surveyed the scene with a practised eye. Looks to me like them fellas got jumped by somebody, Comancheros maybe. He eyed the dead cow, and the calf, now bawling plaintively. Then that old Longhorn musta taken a hand. Likely them Flyin' W boys was tryin' to haze her out o' the brush, an' she was on the prod. She sure tore up that cayuse.

The two parallel traces heading south caught his eye. Well now; seems one o' them's hurt an' they took him outa here on a travois. Used one o' them Flyin' W ponies to haul it. Makin' for the Border I reckon. He looked speculatively at Martinez's twisted body, trapped under the dead pony. The unnatural angle of the head caught his eye and he nodded, satisfied. Don't need to waste no time on him; his neck's busted. Better figger out what I'm gonna do 'bout them two fellas that's still breathin'.

Damnation, what in hell am I gonna do. They're shot up bad. Reckon if I leave 'em out here like as not they'll be dead 'fore I git back wi' help. An' if I wait hopin' somebody'll come lookin', it could be too late.

For a long moment he considered the options, while Rafe moaned fitfully and the wolfhound nosed at his hand, whining uneasily. I'll stay. Them Jordans seem like smart folks. Reckon they'll come lookin' right soon.

A thought struck him and he crossed to the two remaining ponies standing patiently beside the dropped reins. Circling them he looked closely at the brands on their flanks. Hm, Flyin' W on one an' Circle J on the other. 'Waal now,' the Flying W mount, a deep-chested bay, pricked up its ears as he spoke. 'Reckon you can find your way back to the ranch? Anyways, we'll chance it.' Deftly hooking up the reins he slapped the bay hard on the flank and shouted. Startled, the pony headed away north and was soon out of sight.

Donovan looked at the sun. Ain't more'n a coupla hours daylight left, at most. Let's see if we can raise somebody. He crossed to his mount and, drawing the Sharps from its boot, pointed the big rifle at the sky. The boom of the shot echoed and re-echoed into the distance.

'You hear that?' Bull pulled Red to a halt, John and Lance piling up beside him. 'Where d'you reckon?'

'West!' Lance was already swinging Buck round. 'Let's ride.'

Bunched tightly, the brothers raced down the long slope and into the valley.

'Look!' John pointed to the riderless horse galloping across their front. His Indian pony stretched itself in an all-out burst of speed and closed on the bay. Reaching over, John grabbed the reins as the pinto turned neatly and halted the plunging runaway.

'Jake's pony,' he said grimly.

Lance nodded. 'Yeah, an' there's a bullet groove on the saddlehorn.'

'Come on!' Guns in hand they swept up and over the ridge.

Donovan rose quickly to his feet, empty hands prominently displayed. Big men, mean lookin' too. Reckon that's their pa lyin' there alright. The wolfhound growled menacingly. 'Easy now, Satan.'

Bull glanced at him wildly. 'What happened?' He dropped on his knees beside his father.

'Cain't tell you son. Saw the buzzards circlin' an' found them lyin' like this. The big young fella, he's just breathin' an' no more. An' the boy there, he's alive but shot up bad. Wants to talk to you … or your ma. Reckon they was jumped by the bunch that dead Mex was wi'. Comancheros or rustlers mebbe. They headed due south an' they're haulin' somebody on a travois.'

'Who's this?' Lance demanded.

Bull looked up. 'Jack Donovan. Neighbour. Owns the Diamond D … '

'He's right. Jake's barely breathin'.' Grim-faced, John rose from where he had been kneeling. 'An' his gun ain't been fired.'

'Pa's dead!' Bull climbed heavily to his feet. 'He got off one shot 'fore they gunned him down.'

'Lance!' Rafe tried to sit up. 'Got to tell you … got to tell … '

'Easy son,' Lance cradled the wounded youngster in his arms. 'Tell me.'

'We … we never had a chance. They said they was lookin' for a fella called Jordan an' …' He fell back exhausted.

'Right.' Lance laid the young rider down gently and stood up, his face set in grim lines. 'Mister,' he looked at the grizzled rancher, 'we're beholden to you. Right sorry I seemed kinda tetchy just now.'

Donovan shrugged, embarrassed. 'Didn't pay it no mind. Best I could do. Real sorry 'bout your pa though. An' them two young fellas; we got to get them to a doctor right quick. The boy there, Rafe you said, he don't weigh nothin'. One o' you could carry'm. But that Jake fella, we'll hafta go awful easy with him, he's real bad.'

'Yeah, you're right.' The big sergeant looked searchingly at his brothers. 'Reckon I could carry Rafe but … '

'Hold it!' There was a note of suppressed excitement in Donovan's voice. 'Got me an idea. 'Member seein' this done once, way back when I was wi' the Boundary Commission. Fella got stove up in the brush. Hawse fell on him or somethin'. Anyways, we had to bring'm out. Wagon couldn't get in. Didn't want to use a travois like them fellas here did. Couldn't tell how bad he was broke up inside, so we made a carryin' sling. That's how we'll take Jake out.'

Lance frowned. 'Never heard o' nothin' …'

'Lemme show you,' the old rancher broke in abruptly. 'Cut a coupla real straight saplin's from that stand o' young timber across there.' He gestured impatiently. 'Where them fellas got their poles. Need to be about fifteen feet long an' as thick as your arm. Oh, an' trimmed real neat. Don't want nuthin' gallin' them hawses. Move now!' He was uncoiling his lariat as he spoke. 'We ain't got time to waste jawin' here.'

Impelled by the driving lash of his harsh voice the brothers worked feverishly. Using their razor edged bowie knives, Bull and John cut and trimmed two suitable poles, while Lance and Donovan loaded Jim Jordan's body onto Smoke and roped it in position. 'Know what you're thinkin' son,' the old-timer growled. 'That's your pa there. The hell of it is we ain't got time to do things right. Got to get them wounded fellas back.'

Lance nodded. He couldn't trust himself to speak.

Bull and John returned with the poles. Donovan inspected them carefully and nodded with satisfaction. 'Yeah, they'll do. Lay them there, 'bout three feet apart, an' gimme them ropes.'

Five feet from the end of the poles the old rancher began to weave an intricate rope cradle using the two lariats. 'Like I said,' he grunted drawing the knots tight, 'Seen this done one time and allus kept it in mind. You fellas follow me?'

There were nods of comprehension from the three brothers.

'Right, we'll need hawses. One at the front an' one at the back. They'll hafta put up wi' a rope sling across their backs. Front hawse'll have it back o' the saddle. On the rear hawse it'll be in front o' the saddle. Don't reckon they'll like it much. You got any ideas?'

'Better leave Red out.' Bull decided. 'He don't take kindly to anythin' strange. Anyways, somebody's got to make a fast run to the ranch. Tell 'em what's happened, an' get the doc out from Dorando.'

Lance nodded. 'Go along wi' that. John, you reckon that pinto o' yours can handle the front end alright?'

'Sure. He's an Injun pony an' he's hauled a travois before now. He'll be fine.'

'Alright. I'll take the other end. Buck's a cavalry hoss. Things like stretchers don't bother him none.'

'Right.' Four feet from the rear of the improvised stretcher, Donovan knotted the end of the cradle securely and rose stiffly to his feet. 'There she is. Five feet o' bare pole at the front; six feet o' rope cradle in the middle. an' four more feet o' bare pole at the back.' He paused for a moment, thinking. 'Your pa an' the boys was carryin' bedrolls. Let's see how many blankets we can muster.'

They checked quickly. 'Two apiece,' Bull said, frowning. 'Four all told. Them fellas took Rafe's pony. What ...?'

'See them bare sections o' pole?' Donovan broke in impatiently. ' Tie the blankets round them. That'll make it easier for the hawses. Less chance o' rubbin' sores in their hides that way. I'll go get m'own roll.'

Finished, they watched the old-timer spread his bedroll over the rope cradle. He nodded, satisfied. 'Right, let's get Jake settled.'

Half an hour later they were ready. Lance eased into his saddle and nodded to Bull. Carefully his brother passed Rafe up to him. The big sergeant settled himself comfortably. Gonna be a long night.

'All set?' Bull looked up at him tensely.

'Yeah. Make that run now. Tell 'em we're comin' in, but slow.'

'On m'way' Bull was already in the saddle and swinging Red round to the north. The big gelding snorted and plunged forward. Horse and rider disappeared into the gathering dusk.

'What about him?' Donovan jerked a thumb in the direction of Martinez's body.

'Leave him, he ain't goin' nowhere.' Lance said tersely. 'Name's Martinez. He's a killer an' he's just broke outa jail. Ain't nobody gonna miss him. Let's get movin'.'

John Jordan twisted in the saddle and looked at the unconscious form on the improvised stretcher. Dear God, let this work. His gaze lifted to his grim-faced brother, Rafe cradled in his arms. Beyond him Donovan was climbing onto the quarter horse, Smoke's lead rope in his hand.

'All set?'

'Yo.'

Quietly the grim cavalcade moved off, the sling creaking slightly with the momentum. Behind them Donovan eased his pony into a walk; Smoke, with his tragic load, closed up beside him. Never knew you Jordan, but goin' by them boys o' yours I reckon you was an alright guy. Don't reckon they'll let this rest. That youngest one; John, he's primed to kill.

Satan whined uneasily and looked up at him. The smell of death was troubling the big dog. Donovan spoke quietly, and the wolfhound subsided, satisfied.

Bull Jordan never forgot that mad night ride. There was something unreal in Red's long machine-like stride; in his instinctive avoidance of obstacles as they materialised out of the darkness. Suddenly the ridge loomed ahead. They swept up over it and came thundering down the long slope leading to the ranch.

There were lanterns everywhere. Bull drew the big horse to a skidding halt by the house and dropped onto the porch running.

Ma and Joe Masterson met him at the door, a tense Ellie-May peering over their shoulders. He saw by their faces that they feared the worst.

'Jake's pony come in a while back,' the foreman said tensely. 'There was a bullet groove on the saddlehorn.'

Bull nodded, suddenly unsure. 'Ma ... it's Pa. He's ...'

The lines on Mary-Lou's face deepened. 'He's dead, ain't he?' she asked huskily.

'Yeah. Lance and John are bringin' him in, along wi' Jake an' Rafe. Jake's real bad. Don't know if he'll make it. Donovan's wi' them. Joe,' he looked directly at the red-haired foreman, 'get Manuel to ride into Dorando an' tell the doc we need'm here, right quick. Have Jeff go with'm. An' have somebody watchin' the yard gate. I ain't takin' no more chances.'

Masterson nodded and ran for the bunkhouse.

'Was it the Andersons you reckon?' Ma's voice was harsh but she had herself under control.

'Yeah. There was a dead fella lyin' near Pa an' the boys.' He described the scene briefly. 'Lance says his name's Martinez. He broke jail with them. We left him there.'

Ma nodded grimly. 'Best way. That's all them kind are good for, buzzard bait.' Her mood changed suddenly. 'How bad are the boys?'

'Well …' Bull paused, thinking. 'Rafe's got a gut wound, an' the slug's still in there. Ain't good, he comes an' goes all the time. But he wants to talk to you.'

'Mm; an' Jake?'

Her son grimaced. 'Real bad. He's unconscious. Got four bullets in him. Dunno how he's still alive. They're carryin' him in a sling.' He described Donovan's innovation. 'Don't know if he'll make it.'

The sudden racing beat of hooves made him turn quickly. Manuel and Jeff swept through the pool of light and were gone. Joe materialised out of the darkness. 'Told 'em to pick up Doc Sims an' hightail it back here. Anything else you got in mind?'

Bull frowned. 'Yeah, tell the boys to keep their Winchesters handy. You never know, them Anderson fellas might decide to come callin'. Oh, an' tell 'em to come up here when Lance an' John get back. We'll need help to carry the boys in.'

CHAPTER 37

▼

It was after midnight before the grim cavalcade finally crested the ridge and saw the lights of the ranch below. By now the pinto and Buck had adapted to their unfamiliar role and picked their way carefully down the long slope.

A silent Joe Masterson, lantern in hand, opened the gate, and escorted them across the yard to the waiting group on the porch. Anders Lindstrom took Rafe from a tired Lance and carried him indoors.

'In here!' Her face like stone, Ma opened a bedroom door. 'Put him on the bed ... gently now.'

She was turning to leave when Rafe stretched out a hand. 'Miz Jordan, got to tell you ... got to ... ,' his voice tailed off.

'Boys!' Ma called sharply. 'In here. You too, Joe. Sooner he talks, the sooner he'll rest.' Her sons and the red-haired foreman filed in.

'Rest of you bring in Pa an' Jake. Lay Pa out decent in the front room. Take Jake into that room at the end o' the passage. The one him an' John share. Anders,' she looked up at the big Dane, 'you see to it.'

'By golly yes Miz Jordan. Come boys.' Chester, Tex, and the Aldersons nodded wordlessly.

Mary-Lou turned to her daughters. Ellie-May looked white and drawn, while Sara-Jane was weeping unashamedly.

'Sara-Jane, go along an' see them gals don't wake up. Ellie-May, get some hot water an' a cloth. Cut the shirt off Jake and clean 'im up. Get Anders to help you. Now son,' she settled herself by the bedside, 'you just tell me what happened.'

Slowly, haltingly, they pieced the story together. 'An' then Jake,' Rafe's voice was weakening now. 'He … he musta guessed. When the boss said he was Jordan, the … the young fella drew. Jake, he jumped his horse into Mister Jordan's. He took the bullets ma'am.' His voice rose again, pride in it. 'He was shot up awful bad an' he just fell outa the saddle. But he took the bullets meant for Mister Jordan.'

There was silence for a long moment. They waited, hardly daring to breathe. Then the wavering voice came again. 'Mister Jordan, he got off one shot 'fore they gunned him down. Then the old cow … '

'Yeah,' Ma leaned closer. 'What about the cow?'

'Old outlaw Longhorn. Leastways, that's what the boss said she was. Mebbe the noise set … set her off. Charged right into them fellas … Miz Jordan, I never got m'gun out. I'm … I'm right sorry.'

'Son,' Ma's voice was rough, 'you did alright. Ain't nobody coulda done better.'

'Gee, thanks ma'am … then … then I got hit. Don't remember nothin' more till I heard a dog barkin' … ' He fell silent.

Ma looked at the others enquiringly.

'Donovan's wolfhound,' Bull said shortly.

The boy on the bed stirred and cried out. 'Ma … you'll be alright. I'm comin' back Ma … I'm …' His voice died away and he was silent. Mary-Lou Jordan leaned forward and listened intently. Then she closed the staring eyes and stood up.

'He's dead!' she announced with heavy finality. 'Reckon it was only 'cause he wanted to talk that he kept goin'.'

The muffled thunder of racing hooves grew on the night air. There was a flurry of activity outside. Wheels rattled into the yard and pulled up at the porch. A door banged. There was a sudden exchange in raised tones, then the sound of rapidly approaching footsteps. Ellie-May appeared in the doorway, young Doc Sims behind her.

Mary-Lou shook her head. 'Rafe's gone,' she said huskily. 'Take the doc along to Jake, I'll be right behind you.'

The small indomitable woman looked at her three silent sons. 'Reckon you ought to sit with Pa for a spell.' Overcome with emotion, she swallowed, then went on, 'Ma allus said it helped just to sit beside them an' think o' the good times. I'll be along later, but first I got to go help the doc.' Mary-Lou paused in the doorway. 'Reckon that's the way your pa would have wanted it.'

Her footsteps echoed down the passage. They heard the bedroom door open and close. John made as though to follow, but Lance shook his head.

'Leave her be, John boy. This is something Ma's got to do. Right now she's hurtin' real bad. Joe, you mind seein' to things for a spell.' He looked at his grim-faced brothers. 'Reckon we'll go sit with Pa.'

'Got it!' There was a triumphant note in Doc Sim's voice as he held up the forceps, with the misshapen lead slug clasped firmly in the long jaws. 'Went in at an angle. It was lodged against the ribcage at the back. Just missed the lung. That's the last one.' He looked across Jake's unconscious form at a grey and drawn Mary-Lou. 'Swab this incision, then I'll stitch him up.' A sudden engaging smile transformed his somewhat angular features. 'Got to thank you, ma'am. Don't know where you learned your nursing, but you're good.'

'Picked it up as I went along.' Ma said tiredly. 'Out here things happen suddenlike, an' you cain't never be sure there'll be a doctor around.'

Kevin Sims nodded understandingly. 'Guess that figures. Miss Jordan;' he turned to a white-faced Ellie-May, 'Bring that lamp closer. There, that's fine.'

Ma watched the needle flickering in the lamplight as the dark-haired doctor stitched quickly. Finished, he straightened up and grunted with relief. 'Well, so far, so good.' His brow creased in a frown. 'Still unconscious though. Wish I could figure that out. Shock maybe. Watch him for fever. If he starts to burn up try an' keep him cool. He's a strong young fella. Might be he'll make it but ...' he shook his head dubiously.

Something of her old fire flared briefly in Ma's cold blue eyes. 'I ain't givin' up on him yet!' she snapped.

Doc Sims grinned. 'Never doubted it, ma'am.' He washed and dried his hands carefully, deep in thought.

The door opened quietly and Joe Masterson peered in. 'Doc, we got the buggy in the barn an' your horse has been rubbed down and grained.' He turned to Ma. 'Sara-Jane says to tell you she's got coffee an' grub waitin' for the doc in the kitchen.'

Kevin Sims shrugged into his coat and picked up his bag. 'Now that's an offer I can't refuse. Got to be gettin' back soon though. Young Miz Oatman out at Red Buttes, she's expectin' her first tomorrow. She's small, and I don't reckon it'll be an easy birth. Anyway,' he patted Mary-Lou's shoulder, 'you know the score. Keep him quiet and watch out for fever. I'll look in again in a day or so.'

'Anything else?' Ma looked at him intently.

The doctor paused in the doorway. 'You could try prayer.' He disappeared down the passage behind Joe.

Mary-Lou sighed as she turned to her white-faced elder daughter. 'You mind sittin' wi' Jake while I go talk to the boys? Then I'll get John to spell you.'

Ellie-May smiled wanly. 'Sure, Ma ... reckon it's the least I can do.'

'We're agreed then?' Lance glanced at his brothers. 'Day after the funeral we'll light out.'

Bull nodded. 'Only beef I got, trail's gettin' colder all the time.'

'No matter.' There was a tamped-down ferocity in John's cold tones. 'I'll find them, even if I have to trail them to Hell!'

Lance flinched at the raw hatred in his young brother's voice. *John's gone Injun. I was allus scared o' this. Them fellas are dead an' they don't know it.*

He looked up as his mother entered the room. John rose quickly, a question in his eyes.

Ma nodded. 'He's alive, an' the doc got all the bullets. Still unconscious though. John boy, you mind settin' with'm for a spell. Tell Ellie-May to get some sleep. There's got to be one of us there all the time. Fetch me if you see any change.'

John nodded wordlessly and slipped silently through the door.

'How's he takin' it?' Ma looked from one to the other.

Lance shook his head. 'Bad. He's wound up like a fiddle string. Reckon he won't rest till he hunts them fellas down.'

'Dear God, what a mess.' Mary-Lou sank into the worn armchair. 'What did I ever want to come here for anyway?'

'Ma!' Bull was on his feet. 'You ain't bein' fair to yourself,' he protested. 'Anybody's to blame it's me.' Grief and regret were etched on the big man's face. 'If I hadn't gunned down them Comancheros, likely Pa an' Rafe would still be alive.'

'You reckon?' Lance looked up at him.

His brother shrugged. 'It figgers. You heard Rafe. They was lookin' for a fella called Jordan. Reckon them killers threw in wi' the Comanchero boss man, Domingo Sanchez. Pa an' the rest of you just moved here. Only Jordan he'd call to mind would be me. Yeah, it figgers alright.'

'Mm.' The big sergeant frowned doubtfully. 'Mebbe so. Still, we ain't gonna get nowhere blamin' ourselves. Pa wouldn't have wanted that anyway. Seems to me we should be makin' plans. Bull, you got a ranch to run. Me, I'll see about the funeral. Let's get started.'

'Lance is right.' Ma was pale but determined. 'It's what your pa would have wanted.' She paused, then went on, her voice charged with emotion.

'Leave us alone for a spell. We had a good life together an' I'd just like to say my goodbyes.'

The door closed quietly behind them.

For a long moment Mary-Lou stood looking at her husband's body, then ... 'Jim,I know you were never all that set on comin' here, but you came 'cause I wanted it. Now you're dead an' I reckon I'm to blame. Mebbe Hannah was right; mebbe you shoulda been stronger an' not let me have my own way all the time.' She paused, the tears trickling down her cheeks. 'Mebbe I could have been a better wife, but we had some good times an' I just hope you'll forgive me.'

Taking a deep breath she spoke again. 'I don't deny I was against Jake all them years.' She sobbed suddenly. 'I couldn't help it Jim. Seems like it was there in my mind, that hatred I got for Injuns, eatin' at me all the time. You allus said that boy was family, and you were right. When the chips were down he proved it. Forgive me Jim, 'cause if he dies as well it'll haunt me for the rest o' my days!'

Sitting there beside her dead husband, Mary-Lou Jordan wept bitterly. The sound of Doc Sim's buggy fading into the distance seemed like a requiem for her thoughts.

CHAPTER 38

▼

The handful of sunbaked clay thudded on the coffin lid. In the stillness, broken only by Sara-Jane's uncontrolled sobbing, the sound seemed unnaturally loud.

From his position at the head of the grave, Lance Jordan looked down at his father's last resting place. Well Pa, don't reckon you ever thought you'd end up here when we used to have our fights at the Circle J. Sure glad we made it up in the end. Pity I didn't tell you my plans. Sheriff o' Dorando. You'd have liked that. Thanks for getting' me outa that shootin' scrape. For a second Jud Moore's face leered at him again across the lamp-lit room. Reckon I shouldn't have done it, an' likely I'll have to answer for it some day, but Jud was a killer an' got what was comin' to him.

Reverend James, the young circuit preacher, whispered meaningfully and stepped back. Lance came out of his reverie with a start and moved away from the graveside. The others followed. Out of the corner of his eye he saw the crew pick up shovels and begin to fill in the graves.

That'll be Joe. He's good at that sort o' thing. He eyed Ann Donovan talking to Ma, who had been standing off to one side flanked by Sara-Jane and Ellie-May. His mind wandered again. First time in a coon's age I seen Ellie-May in a dress. Her face is set just like Ma's. It ain't like that wi' Sara-Jane. She was close to Pa an' she's takin' it bad.

That Donovan gal now, she's somethin'. Seen the way her an' Bull looked at each other. Never thought Bull would get hooked, never had no time for wimmen. Me? … well, some day I suppose.

He saw John talking quietly to Ben Turner who had taken a cord at the graveside. Good man Ben. Him an' Pa hit it off real well. Doin' alright with his freightin' business. John now, he's somethin' else. Seems to have turned Injun in the last couple o' days. He shivered suddenly. If Jake dies …

The big sergeant swallowed hard as he thought of the young half-breed lying unconscious in the ranch-house below. Wonder if I could've taken four bullets meant for somebody else like he did? Jake boy, you're one helluva guy. You sure proved it to Ma. All them years she's hated Injuns, now she's hellbent on keepin' you alive! Don't reckon she's had more'n three-four hours sleep since we brung you in. She's got big Anders sittin' wi' you right now, an' I reckon as soon as the folks have paid their respects and gone, she'll be back in that chair herself.

'Lance,' he turned to find Clay Wallace at his elbow. As usual the Easterner was immaculate.

'Yeah?'

'I'd like a word with you.' Lance nodded and they moved away from the others.

Clay turned and faced the tall sergeant. 'It's John. He's taking Jake's shooting hard.'

Lance shrugged. 'Cain't expect nothin' else. He's closer to Jake than any of us. They useta gab away to each other in Comanche when they thought nobody was listenin'. An' Ma not takin' to Jake made them even closer. Still, mebbe once we track them fellas down he'll lighten up some.'

'But surely,' Clay stared at him, 'Sheriff Dawson will deal with them? According to Bull he came through here yesterday with a posse.'

'That's right,' Lance watched his brother handing Ann Donovan into the Diamond D buckboard. 'But this ain't the East. That bunch o' snakes'll be in Mexico now an' Dawson cain't go no further than the Border. So it's up to us three.'

He eyed Norman McLean, resplendent in dress uniform, talking to Sara-Jane, who was smiling tremulously. 'Seems like Captain McLean's havin' more luck wi' Sara-Jane than the rest of us.'

'Yes.' Clay frowned. 'But then Norman was always quite a hand with the ladies.'

Lance looked at him closely. 'Thought he was your buddy?' he demanded.

'He is,' Clay said hastily. 'It's just …'

'You don't want him round Sara-Jane,' the sergeant cut in shrewdly. 'Wouldn't let it worry you. Happen to know she thinks a lot of you. So does Ma, come to that. Now,' he raised a hand to Ben Turner, 'I'd best be goin'. Ma's movin' an' she'll want me at the house to talk to folks. Be seein' you.'

'Six?' Lance stared up at Sheriff Dawson. 'You sure 'bout that? Accordin' to them dodgers there was only five, an' one o' them's lyin' dead out there.'

Dawson frowned. 'That's right. Fella name o' Diablo Martinez. There's a thousand dollars reward for him, dead or alive. Reckon it's yours. Anyway, there were five horses headin' south an' one of them was haulin' a travois. Looks like one o' them fellas is hurt bad. Waal, we trailed 'em down to the Border an' that was it. Ain't got no jurisdiction across there!'

'Think they'll be around?' Bull tightened the cinch and warded off Red's attempt to bite.

'Might be.' The sheriff looked at him sombrely. One thing's certain, I sure as hell wouldn't if I thought this bunch was on my trail. 'With one o' them injured they could be holed up in Evalde, on the Mex side.' He looked hard at the three brothers. 'You fellas ain't plannin' to start no war down there?'

Lance shook his head. 'This here's personal. Anyway, Manuel's ridin' with us. He wanted to, an' it seems a right sensible idea.'

Dawson nodded. 'That's smart thinkin'. We'll be headin' back now. Take care boys. Adios.'

He raised his hand and the posse cantered out of the yard and splashed across the creek. The brothers watched them go.

Manuel came out of the stable leading Buck. This had been Lance's idea. He'd argued that the vaquero could hardly ride into a town looking for information, if his horse carried a Flying W brand.

In his place Lance had the big grey, Kiowa. He checked his cinches and turned to see John tying a long rifle into his saddle boot.

'New gun?' The big sergeant nodded towards the weapon.

'Yeah.' There was a cold finality in John's voice. 'Ben Turner's Sharps. He loaned it to me. Said to use it on this trip.'

Lance frowned. He's like somethin' waitin' to explode! Aloud he said 'Let's go see Ma.'

Their mother was standing on the porch waiting for them. She looks old, Lance thought. The years are catchin' up with her.

'You boys all set?' Ma queried tautly.

Lance nodded. 'Yeah. Don't know when we'll be back.' he said awkwardly.

'Son,' Ma's voice was like ice, 'time don't matter. Just come back when it's finished. An' take care, all of you. '

'Adios Ma.' They turned away.

'John!' Surprised, her youngest son swung round and looked at her.

His mother came down the steps and laid a hand hesitantly on his arm. 'Son, I sat with Pa the other night. Talked some an' did a lot o' thinkin'. Mebbe he'll forgive me for bein' the way I was. I surely hope so.'

John nodded gravely. 'I know Ma. I heard you talkin' an' cryin'.' He bent his head and his lips brushed her cheek. 'Don't worry. Everything'll work out. Adios now.'

Ma watched him stride across the yard to where his brothers waited. She touched her cheek gently. Glory be, he ain't never done that since he come back from the Injuns. Jake boy, hang in there. Mebbe the three of us can make it yet.

She lifted her hand and waved as her sons rode out of the yard and headed south.

Pedro Rojas polished industriously at the already shining bar top. Cautiously he stole a quick glance at the three gringos sitting at the table nearest to the bar. Bad hombres, he decided. I have seen some hard men in here, Senor Sanchez does not employ weaklings, but these ... he shivered.

'How's Clint makin' out?' Pony McQuade leaned back in his chair and looked quizzically at Jack Anderson.

''Bout the same,' Diamond Jack grunted moodily, his fingers riffling the playing cards automatically. 'Fever's gone but that young Mex doctor reckons it'll be another week until he can get up. Dunno how long it'll be 'fore he can sit a horse.'

Jules and Pony exchanged glances. 'Amigo,' Defarge watched the long fingers shuffle, cut and shuffle again. 'Me and Pony, we have been thinking, maybe we should ride on. As you say, it will be some time before your brother is ready to travel and we are no nearer the goldfields.'

The gambler frowned heavily. 'Don't see why you're in such an all-fired hurry. We got money, livin's cheap, an' the U.S. law cain't touch us. Hell, we got it made. Accordin' to that Mex that Sanchez had lookin' out on the Arizona side, the posse came down from Dorando, had a look round an' went back. Nah, I reckon we're safe here long as we stay quiet.'

'That's just it Jack,' Pony McQuade complained. 'It's too quiet. This ain't the good old U.S.of A. Me, I like a little excitement. Good, rip roarin' poker game. Not this penny ante stuff we been playin'. Down here it's all siesta an' tequila.'

Diamond Jack glanced at Defarge. 'How about you Jules?'

The Creole looked at him carefully. 'Me and Pony, we go back a long way, … but yes, I too crave a little excitement.'

'Waal,' Jack Anderson moved restlessly in his chair, 'I ain't sayin' I wouldn't mind settin' in on a big game again.'

He frowned, then came to a sudden decision. 'Tell you what. If you fellas hang on until Clint is ready to ride, then I'll ease up some. Startin' tomorrow night we'll slip across the line an' have some fun on the north side. Now,' he held out the pack, 'you ready to play?'

His companions nodded and settled themselves comfortably in their chairs. It would be a long session.

'Evalde, U.S. and Mex.' Prone on the ridge Lance peered through the field-glasses at the two towns sprawled in the heat distorted distance. 'Right handy little rathole. You got trouble south o' the line, you head north. Trouble this side, you move south. Not more'n eight, nine miles between 'em. Couldn't be neater.'

'Si.' Manuel nodded. 'It is perfect.'

'Right, let's talk this over with Bull and John.' They slid back off the ridge and, rising, walked downhill to where Bull and John sat patiently waiting.

'Well?' Bull looked at his elder brother.

Lance shrugged. 'Like Dawson said. Two towns close together an' the Border in between. It's the neatest little setup you ever saw.'

Bull frowned. 'How are we gonna play it?'

'Manuel figgers it'd be best if he went in on his own an' had a look around. He reckons if they're still there they'll be holed up on the Mexican side.'

'Si.' Ortega grinned, showing a flash of white teeth. 'I will come in from the west. I am an honest vaquero and I am looking for work. The Californios stole my cattle and my woman and I hate them. I will check both towns. It will take some time.'

'We have plenty of time,' John said coldly as he dismounted. 'We will wait.'

Bull nodded. 'Sure appreciate your help Manuel. We'll be here when you get back.'

'Gracias. It is an honour to ride with the sons of Senora Jordan.'

They watched the stocky Mexican ride away. 'Thinks a lot o' Ma, don't he?' Lance observed.

'Yeah.' Bull unbuckled Red's cinch and hauled the saddle off. 'He was there when Ma scared the hell outa Dave Sands, that foreman I was tellin' you about. All the crew think a lot o' Ma. Let's rub them mounts down. This could be a long wait.'

Madre de Dios, Manuel crossed himself. They are hard men, but that John, he is a killer. I see it in his eyes.

'Caballo,' he patted Buck's neck, 'I am glad we are on the same side!'

✳   ✳   ✳   ✳

'So,' Domingo Sanchez looked keenly at Rojas. 'The gringos, they crossed the line last night?'

'Si patron,' the small Mexican twisted his hat in his hands and bobbed his head nervously. 'I watched them as you tell me to do. They ride into Evalde on the American side and they go to a saloon. There they settle down to drink and play cards. I leave my eldest son to watch, he is a good boy. He says it is morning before they come back. I came as soon as I could.'

The big man waved his hand. 'You have done well. And your son. There will be a place for him in the organisation one day. You may go now.'

'Gracias patron.' The little man bowed and hurried out.

'So Tomas,' Sanchez looked at the tall major-domo, 'our gringo friends are restless are they?' He pondered for a moment, then shrugged.

'If they are caught, what does it matter? Their work for us is done and they have been paid. They mean nothing to me now.' He waved a dismissive hand. 'Forget them. Pay Rojas and his son. They have done well.'

CHAPTER 39

▼

'Ma!' Sara-Jane's excited voice echoed down the long passage to the big warm kitchen. Mary-Lou, dozing in the big worn armchair by the stove, woke with a start, her tired brain attempting to adjust to the sudden summons. Still only half-awake she stumbled down the dark passage to the dimly lit room beyond.

'Hurry Ma,' Sara-Jane's eyes looked enormous in her pale face. 'He's tryin' to talk!'

Breathing heavily her mother surveyed Jake's motionless figure. 'What happened?' she queried tensely, bending over the bed.

Sara-Jane paused for a moment, collecting her scattered thoughts. 'I was just sittin' there, quiet like, when I heard this noise. I listened real close then. It was Jake's voice but I couldn't make out what he was sayin'. Then it come again. That's when I yelled for you.'

'Hm.' Ma frowned doubtfully. 'Quiet enough now anyway.' She rested a work-roughened hand on Jake's forehead. 'He's hot though. Burnin' up. Remember what Doc Sims said? I reckon he's got a fever.'

The man in the bed stirred suddenly. There was a low mutter, rising in a crescendo until it culminated in a hoarse shout. Mary-Lou Jordan froze. 'That's Injun talk,' she said shortly. 'He's got a fever alright.' She thought for a moment, then came to an abrupt decision. 'Go rouse out Joe. Tell'm we need Anders here.' She nodded towards the bed. 'Once the fever gets a real grip, we'll never hold Jake in there. Oh, an' get Ellie-May as well. Tell her we're gonna need cold water. Lots o' it. We got to keep him cool. Hurry now.'

As her startled daughter disappeared through the door Ma leant over the bed. 'Right, Jake boy. If you could take them slugs meant for Jim, then I reckon a smidgeon of Injun talk ain't goin' to hurt me none!'

The early morning was cold and clear. Lance inhaled deeply, the scent of sagebrush strong in his nostrils. He focussed the glasses on the moving dot. Somebody headin' this way. Takin' their time too. Yeah, he grinned to himself. Thought as much, it's Manuel.

The stocky vaquero swung down from the big buckskin, his eyes sparkling. Wordlessly, John handed him a cup of coffee.

'Gracias, Senor John.' He took a long swig at the black liquid. 'We are, how you say, in luck. First I check the north town and it seems there is nothing. Then a peon who works as a swamper in the Last Chance saloon, he tells me that two nights ago three gringos came in together, from south of the Border. He does not know them; they are strangers. Last night they come again. I tell him I hate gringos. They take my cattle and my woman. I would kill all gringos if I could. He laugh and say these are malo hombres, bad men. They work for Domingo Sanchez, the Comanchero leader. I sneer … poof … what are their names, these so-called malo hombres. He say one is called Pony-'

'Pony McQuade!' Lance cut in excitedly.

'Si, Senor Lance. He heard the tall man with the …' he gestured expressively 'how you say … stitched … ?'

'Embroidery? … embroidered vest?'

'Ah, that is it!'

'Diamond Jack Anderson,' Bull growled deep in his throat. 'Ellie-May told me 'bout that vest. He must've got another one.'

'The third man?'

Manuel shook his head. 'I do not know. My friend say he could be Mexican.'

'Defarge,' Lance said slowly. 'Jules Defarge. He's Creole an' some o' them could pass as Mexicans. 'Course,' he added, 'it could be this sixth fella but I doubt it. No sign o' Diamond Jack's brother?' he queried sharply.

Manuel shook his head. 'Senores, I am sorry …'

Bull put a hand on his arm. 'Manuel, you did right well. We're beholden to you. We sure as hell couldn't have got this information ourselves.'

His brothers nodded.

'These gringos,' Lance grinned, 'what do they do when they come north?'

Manuel shrugged. 'They drink, play cards, visit the bordellos ... the usual things that gringos do!'

Lance frowned. 'Wonder what happened to Clint Anderson?'

'Senores!' Manuel struck his head dramatically, 'Almost I forget. My friend, he hear the one called Pony ask the tall man when his brother will be able to travel.'

'That's it!' Lance said excitedly. 'Betcha young Anderson's been shot an' he's laid up where they're hangin' out.'

'Makes it tricky,' Bull grumbled, 'them split up like this. An' we ain't found that sixth man yet.'

John spoke suddenly. 'Manuel, you got any idea where they're stayin' south o' the Border?'

'I regret no, Senor John. When I learn of these men I return at once to let you know.'

'No, no Manuel.' John raised his hand. 'What you did was right.' He looked at his brothers. 'Mebbe we can play it this way.' Slowly he outlined his plan.

Bull rubbed his chin. 'Might just work.'

Lance nodded. 'It's the best chance we got o' bringin' them back. We start anything in a saloon an' some guy havin' a quiet drink an' mindin' his own business is liable to get hit. Naw, I reckon this is best.'

'Right,' John said crisply, 'if they ride north tonight we'll take them.' His eyes glittered coldly.

Manuel looked hesitantly at the brothers. 'Senores, it would be an honour to side you.'

'Amigo.' He looked at John Jordan in surprise. 'There ain't nobody I'd like more, but this is family. These men killed Pa and young Rafe. Mebbe Jake too, for all we know. As the Comanches say, such an insult must be wiped out in blood.'

'I understand.' Manuel nodded gravely, 'and I will play my part. The Flying W is my home,' he added simply.

Bull held out his hand. 'An' as long as we run cattle there, you got a home,' he said gruffly.

The stocky vaquero turned away to mask his emotions and swung up onto the big horse. He looked at the brothers for a long moment, then raised his hand in salute and cantered away through the trees.

*   *   *   *

'Hold him Anders!' Ma panted, as they grappled with a struggling, sweat-soaked Jake who was attempting to climb out of the bed. 'Don't let him get away.'

'By golly Miz Jordan, that is not so easy.' Muscles rippled in the giant Dane's powerful arms as he strove to pin the raving youngster down. 'It is as if he has the strength of ten men.'

The incoherent shouting died away and an exhausted Jake slumped back on the pillows, staring vacantly into the distance.

'Alright.' Mary-Lou brushed her damp hair back from her brow. 'Seems as though he's settled again. Let's get cleaned up while we got the chance.'

On her knees mopping up spilt water, Sara-Jane looked up worriedly at her mother. 'Sure wish Doc Sims would show up. Jake scares me the way he's goin' on.'

Ma scowled as she and Anders exchanged the twisted soaking sheets for fresh ones. 'Joe sent Jeff in to fetch him. Likely he'll be here as soon as he can. Anyways, don't see what more he can do. Fever's got to burn itself out. Hold him up Anders while I change them pillows. There, that's better.' She collapsed into the nearest chair. 'The pair o' you get some rest while you can.'

Her elder daughter peered into the room.

'Ellie-May, go fix us some grub an' a pot o' coffee. Looks like bein' another long night.'

The man slumped against the warm adobe wall waited quietly, his sombrero tipped over his eyes to guard against the probing rays of the late afternoon sun. He spat into the dust and licked his dry lips, eyes flickering cautiously under the broad hat brim.

Across the street Buck's head drooped and he stood in the relaxed hipshot stance that horses affect when they know they may be tied to that particular hitching rail for a long time.

Manuel Ortega cursed to himself. Madre de Dios! This was not the steamy heat of the brasada. This was a dry pulsating heat, which seemed to radiate from the very buildings themselves.

He tensed as the three men came quickly through the scarred cantina doors. Two laughed noisily together and the third snarled at them savagely. They untied their horses and, mounting, loped away down the dusty street.

The hoofbeats died away in the distance, but still he waited patiently, eyes probing the shadowy doorways, ears alert for any unusual sound. Eventually, satisfied that all was well, he rose and crossed the street to the run-down cantina.

Entering, he made his way up to the counter. A jerk of the head drew Herrero Hernandez aside. 'The gringos who are staying here? I have a message for them from the patron.'

The stout cantina owner looked at him suspiciously. 'Who are you? I have not seen you before.'

'Fool! The patron does not tell you all his plans. I live on the American side and I have a message about this Jordan the gringos kill. There is some doubt … '

'How can this be? Tomas was with them and Tomas is never wrong.'

'I do not know. The patron says only that I am to give this message to the tall one, no other.'

'Well,' Hernandez thought for a moment, 'they have not been gone long. There is of course the young one with the broken leg. He lies upstairs.'

'No, no,' Manuel gestured impatiently. 'He is of little importance. It is the tall one I must speak with. I, Emilio Salvada will follow them.' He paused for a moment. 'You will tell no one of this, you understand.'

Hernandez nodded. 'It is forgotten already.'

CHAPTER 40

▼

'Jack, you got to ease up some,' Pony McQuade said angrily. 'Me an' Jules, we know Clint's givin' you a bad time but it ain't our fault. Quit needlin' us.'

Diamond Jack bit back a retort. These were two dangerous men, and besides, he could not afford to antagonise them. Too much depended on them sticking together.

He swallowed. 'Guess you're right. It's just that he never lets up. I swear if he wasn't my brother I'd have split with him a long time ago.'

Defarge nodded. 'It is true. I was one of many. Often we fought, yet there was a bond. But for tonight amigo forget your troubles. We will enjoy ourselves. Your luck has been good. Maybe it will hold.'

The gambler grinned. 'Let's hope you're right Jules.'

They loped on north towards the Border.

The shadows were beginning to lengthen now. Lance Jordan glanced at the sun slanting down to the western hills. 'Be dark in a coupla hours I reckon,' he said quietly. 'Hope they come tonight. One good thing, the sun's behind us.'

He looked at his brothers. 'Reckon we're doin' this the hard way. We could bushwhack them an' nobody'd ever know.'

'We'd know,' Bull grunted. "Sides, I want to see their faces when you tell them who we are.'

John held up his hand. 'Horses comin' from the south.'

'Damned if I know how you do it John,' Lance said admiringly. 'Alright, let's move. Spread yourselves, one each side o' me. If it's them, we're ready.'

'Up ahead!' Pony McQuade's voice sharpened. 'Comin' this way, three fellas spread across the trail.' His gunfighter's sense stirred. 'Could be trouble.'

The distance closed rapidly.

Right,' Lance said quietly to his brothers, 'that's close enough.' Twenty feet away the others halted also.

'Howdy,' Diamond Jack squinted into the setting sun. 'You fellas lookin' for somebody?'

'Trail hands.' Lance looked at him carefully. 'We're gettin' a trail herd together an' we heard you were interested.'

The gambler scowled and shook his head. 'You got it wrong mister … who the hell are you anyway?'

'Us?' Lance took a deep breath and relaxed. 'We're the Jordans!'

'Jord … !'

Shocked surprise made the fractional difference as both groups went for their weapons.

Lance Jordan's hands blurred and he blasted Diamond Jack out of the saddle, the gambler's guns, still unfired, dropping from his grasp. To his right Bull and Pony McQuade drew almost as one. Bull grunted at the sudden pain in his arm, but Pony was leaning forward hard hit. Desperately, the tall outlaw tried to bring his guns up; coldly Bull shot again and McQuade toppled off his mount to lie sprawling in the dust. Defarge went for his knife in one flowing continuous movement. He, Jules Defarge, was the best. He was still thinking that when sudden agonizing pain lanced through his body. Hands scrabbling desperately at the haft of the slim throwing knife protruding from his chest, the little Creole fell tiredly from his saddle as blackness descended.

Far down the trail Manuel heard the shots and spurred Buck into a gallop.

The echoes died away into the distance and the brothers looked at each other in silence.

Bull was the first to speak. 'Hell, that was close!' Gingerly he explored the raw furrow across his upper arm and heaved a sigh of relief. 'Just a flesh wound.' Grinning, he looked at his brother. 'Often wondered how good you were. Now I know, remind me never to tangle with you!'

Lance laughed. 'That ain't likely.' He turned in the saddle. 'How about you, John?'

'Nothing,' his brother said shortly. Dismounting, he retrieved his knife from Defarge's body and returned it to its sheath. Straightening up he listened intently for a moment. 'Rider coming from the south.'

Bull and Lance thumbed fresh rounds into their guns. 'Likely it's Manuel,' Lance grunted, 'but we ain't takin' no chances.'

'Madre de Dios!' Manuel pulled Buck to a halt. He dismounted and crossed himself. 'I am glad I work for you and not against you!'

Bull laughed. 'Yeah, alright Manuel. Help me tie my bandanna on this graze, then we'll load them fellas onto their horses an' get the hell outa here.'

'Senores!' The vaquero looked at them excitedly, 'I have found where the other gringo is and I also know the name of the sixth man!' He explained swiftly.

'So Sanchez was behind this mess?' Bull shook his head regretfully. 'Should've guessed as much. Still, reckon we'd best leave it right now. We want to be well clear wi' them bodies come daylight.'

'No!' There was a harshness in John's voice that made the others look at him in surprise. 'I'll deal with them if Manuel will side me?'

The Mexican nodded gravely. 'I will be proud to ride with you, Senor John.'

Bull pondered for a moment then shrugged. 'Alright, we'll head north with them bodies. Just make sure you come back, you hear me.'

'I hear you.' John smiled coldly as he slipped off his boots and donned the moccasins he always carried. Handing the boots to Lance, he swung up onto the pinto.

For a long moment he looked at his brothers. Finally he spoke. 'Tell Ma I'll be back.' He turned the pinto and headed south followed by Manuel.

Lance paused in the act of roping Defarges body into the saddle. 'Reckon he'll ever be the same again?'

'John?' Bull frowned. 'Dunno. If Jake lives, mebbe. If he dies … .'. He shrugged. 'Anyway, we'll just have to hope. Let's get movin'.'

CHAPTER 41

▼

Doc Sims straightened up and frowned. 'You say these quiet spells have been getting longer?' he queried sharply.

Ma shrugged tiredly. 'Ain't rightly sure, but I reckon so. Thing is, he still don't make any sense. Nuthin' but Injun talk. An' when he ain't shoutin' and ravin' he just lies there lookin' right through you.'

'Strange.' The tall rawboned doctor ran a hand through his unruly hair. 'Sounds as though his brain just shuts down between those times when he's raving. Is there nothing that would interest him?'

Mary-Lou reddened. 'If my youngest boy was here I reckon it would be different,' she said slowly. 'They was awful close. Don't know when John'll be back though.'

'Mm.' Sims closed his bag with a snap. 'Well, you've kept him alive, and his wounds are healing. Never thought we'd get him this far. That's a miracle in itself. Now you've got to give his mind something to bite on.' He paused, thinking deeply.

Sara-Jane appeared in the doorway and handed him a steaming cup.

'Thanks.' He sipped the hot coffee, a faraway look in his eyes. 'Try reading to him,' he said abruptly. 'Remember a case like this back east once. Patient was a newspaper editor. Wasn't getting nowhere until somebody read the front page to him. Maybe Jake's the same. If you haven't got anything to read, then talk. Anything to get him interested and … '

'Ma!' Sara-Jane broke in excitedly. 'What about the Bible? You remember how he was always there when you read it on Sundays. An' how he used to talk about it with Pa and John after you'd finished.'

'Glory be!' Sudden hope flared in Mary-Lou's voice. 'You're right, Sara-Jane. Go fetch me the Bible. It's by m'bed. Let's get started.'

The lanky doctor drained his cup and handed it back. 'Thanks again, Sara-Jane. Got to be movin' on.' He paused for a moment, bag in hand. 'You win this one Miz Jordan, we'll split the credit three ways. You, me, and the good Lord!' He chuckled dryly and disappeared down the passage.

A cool night breeze ruffled the tattered curtains. Clint Anderson stirred in his sleep and muttered uneasily. The shadowy figure sitting at the bedside leaned forward and shook him gently. Clint came awake slowly.

'Jack, what … ?'

The point of the knife pricked his throat and he gasped.

'Who are … ?'

'Quiet!' The pressure increased and he lapsed into silence.

'That is better.' The pressure was relaxed and Clint gasped audibly.

'I am Cougar Jordan.' He felt Clint start and continued gently, 'you helped kill Pa and Rafe. Mebbe Jake too, for all I know. Now it is your turn!'

'No … !'

The long Bowie knife drove down, then up in the classic ripping knife-fighters stroke. John threw himself on Clint and clamped a hand over the dying man's mouth. There was a last convulsive effort, then everything was still.

John rose and stood for a long moment looking down at the bed. Then he stooped once more over the body.

Quietly he slipped through the open window, the way he had entered, and closed it behind him. Cautiously he made his way over the roof and dropped lightly to the ground.

At the end of the alley Manuel waited with Buck and the pinto. He watched silently as John hastily stowed something in his saddlebag, something which made the pinto shy nervously. His rider spoke soothingly and swung into the saddle.

'It is done?'

John Jordan nodded. 'Where is Sanchez?'

'He will be at the house.'

'Alone?'

'I do not know. Certainly Tomas will be there. There may be others though I would not have thought so. The town has belonged to Sanchez for years. He has had no need of guards, until now!' They walked their horses down the dark street.

Domingo Sanchez studied the papers in front of him and nodded contentedly. Business was good. Now, with the removal of the troublemaker Jordan, he would be able to start operations again in that area. He picked up the silver tobacco box and smiled as he looked at the inscription. This action he had taken, it would teach the gringos not to meddle in his affairs.

Tomas took a last look round the kitchen. It was likely the patron would be some time yet. When he came to Evalde on business he usually worked late. The house servants had already gone to their quarters. No matter, the tall major-domo settled himself comfortably and thought of the future. Some day soon, he would leave here and go south to the hacienda where the patron's family lived. Then life would be good.

A faint scratching at the rear door caught his ear. It came again, and then the sound of something whining. A stray dog most likely.

Picking up a stick he opened the door quickly. A dark figure rose from the ground almost at his feet and the deadly knife ripped upwards in the killing thrust. He pitched forward and, catching his lifeless body, John lowered it gently to the floor.

Quietly he padded down the long passage. A sliver of light under a door caught his eye and he knocked gently.

'Enter!' It was a commanding voice, a voice accustomed to being obeyed.

The young rancher opened the door and stepped into the room.

'Ah Tomas.' Sanchez looked up. His eyes bulged. 'You are not ... ' His hand darted towards the open drawer.

The long throwing knife flashed in the lamplight and buried itself in his throat.

Horror showed in the burly Comanchero's eyes and he plucked futilely at the protruding hilt before falling forward across the desk.

His face an expressionless mask John Jordan crossed to the body and, propping it up in the chair, withdrew the knife. A pity, he thought, he'll never know who it was. A moment's hesitation, then he stooped over the dead Comanchero, knife in hand.

Quickly he made his way back down the passage to the kitchen. Once more the knife flickered over Tomas's body, then he closed the door quietly behind him and melted into the darkness.

Manuel watched in silence as John opened the saddlebag and added something to the contents. 'It is done?' he ventured.

The young rancher nodded. 'It is done, Manuel. We can go home now.' Side by side they loped northwards through the night.

Ma pursed her lips and frowned. 'Wish you'd made him come back with you,' she said grimly. 'That boy's still grievin' 'bout Pa. An' he don't know that Jake's still alive.' Even though I ain't sure how he'll end up, she thought tiredly.

'Don't reckon you understand, Ma.' Bull was tired, reaction was setting in. 'John's wound up like a spring an' he ain't goin' to listen to nobody till this thing's over. Me, I'm just glad he ain't on my trail.' He removed the saddle blanket from Red and picked up a brush.

Ma thought for a moment. 'You say Lance took them bodies right on into Dorando to Sheriff Dawson? Surprised you bothered totin' them in. Sure, there's the reward money, but I wouldn't want to touch it an' I thought you boys would feel the same.' She paused and looked searchingly at Bull. 'Mebbe I was wrong?'

Her son swept the brush down Red's glossy flank and turned to look at his mother. 'Ma, don't you credit us with any feelin's? This is Lance's idea an' I think it's a damn good one. He wants that reward money to take back to Rafe's folks. Accordin' to the boy they had a little place near Austin. They're a big family, an' from what Rafe let slip life was kinda hard. Lance figgers that four thousand dollars might just put them on their feet. He's plannin' to deliver it when he goes back.'

Ma Jordan flushed. 'Seems like I been wrong too often lately. Should've known Lance would think o' somethin' like that.'

Sheriff Dawson studied the three corpses closely. 'Waal, like you say, them three are Defarge, McQuade, an' Diamond Jack Anderson alright. Then we got Martinez planted in Boot Hill. Say, what happened to Anderson's brother, Clint?'

Lance Jordan paused, a faraway look in his eyes. 'Don't reckon you'll be seein' Clint Anderson again,' he said quietly, 'but that's a personal matter. Kinda pity in a way, 'cause all the reward money's goin' to young Rafe's folks back in Texas. How long before you can pay out?'

Scott Dawson frowned. 'Week at most, I reckon. You headin' straight back after you pick it up?'

'Yeah, I'll head south to Austin an' see Rafe's folks. Then I'll swing north to the fort an' tell Captain McMillan m'plans. Reckon he ain't goin' to be none too pleased, but it can't be helped.'

Dawson rose and held out his hand. 'We got a deal then?'

Lance grinned as they shook. 'Yeah, we got a deal.'

CHAPTER 42

▼

The two riders paused on the slope above the ranch and gazed down at the neat buildings basking in the sun.

John broke the silence. 'Reckon this feels like home now, Manuel.'

The stocky vaquero nodded gravely. 'Si Senor John, I know what you mean. Sometimes there has to be pain before happiness. This is a good place.'

'Yeah, just wish Pa an' Rafe were here.'

'Si, but as my church says, some day we meet again.'

'Mm … Manuel, just one thing,' his hand rested lightly on the saddlebag. 'What I did back there, I will never do again.'

'Si, I understand. It was a matter of family honour. In my country we know of these things. Amigo, you have my word, it is forgotten.'

John nudged the tired pinto with his knee and they rode quietly downhill towards the ranch.

'It's them alright.' Lance lowered the glasses. 'Don't seem nothin' wrong wi' either o' them. Wonder how they made out?'

'Guess we'll know soon enough,' Bull growled. He unbarred the yard gate and swung it wide. 'Me I'm just glad they're back.'

✶   ✶   ✶   ✶

'Well?' Bull looked up searchingly at his younger brother. 'What happened?'

'It's done. Tell me about Jake.'

Lance took a deep breath. 'Still alive,' he said carefully. 'Ma's with'm right now.'

The coldness disappeared from John's eyes. He swung down from the pinto and, delving into a saddlebag, drew out a bundle, which he passed to Bull. Then he turned away and led his mount towards the stable.

'What … ?' Lance stared at the bloodstained bundle.

'Senores.' Manuel paused, Buck nuzzling at his arm. 'It is best you do not ask. All those I spoke of; they are dead. The matter is finished. Let it rest.' He turned away, the buckskin ambling tiredly behind him.

Carefully, Bull Jordan opened the bundle. The brothers stared in shocked amazement at the three raw and bloody scalps.

Hastily Bull rewrapped them and looked hard at Lance. The big sergeant shook his head. 'Hell, I knew there was a lot o' Injun left in John, but I never thought he'd go this far! Seems I was wrong.'

'Yeah, seems you were.' Bull stood with the bundle in his hand, thinking. He watched John come out of the stable and stride towards the house. 'Look, we got to get rid o' them scalps 'fore Ma finds out. Get a spade an' meet me back o' the barn.'

*   *   *   *

John Jordan paused on the porch and took a deep breath. This time, he thought, we've got to make it work. Silently, still in his moccasins, he stepped through the open doorway.

Sara-Jane looked up in surprise as he entered the kitchen. 'John!' She eyed him anxiously. 'You alright?'

Her brother smiled gently. 'I'm fine. How's Jake?'

His sister bit her lip. 'John, I don't rightly know. He's actin' awful strange. Ma's sittin's with'm. Guess she ain't had more than four, five hours sleep in the past week. Doc Sims reckons she's pulled him through the fever, but … ,' she broke down suddenly, in tears.

John put his arm round her. 'I'll go see him. Mebbe it'll help.'

He could hear Ma speaking as he approached the room. Something in the cadence of her voice made him pause uncertainly in the doorway.

'Jake, listen to me,' John stared in fascination. Ma was pleading with the unconscious figure in the bed. 'Jake, you got to make it. Jim was right an' I was wrong. He said you was family.'

Tentatively, she reached out and picked up one of the young half-breed's limp hands.

'Jake!' A steely note of desperation crept into her voice. 'Damn you, Jake Larsen, don't you go givin' up on me now! Could be I got a few good years left yet, an' I aim to set things straight 'tween you an' me. Reckon you got to give me that chance.'

There was the slightest movement from the bed and Ma leaned forward, listening intently.

'I hear you.' It was the faintest whisper,' … looks like I ain't got much choice!'

Tears streamed down Mary-Lou's face. 'Glory be. You're back with us, Jake. Reckon the good Lord heard m'prayers!'

'Ma. '

She turned. John stood framed in the doorway.

'Son, you alright?'

He nodded tiredly. 'Yeah, I'm fine. Ma, I heard you an' Jake. The three of us are goin' to make it.'

His mother ran to him. John held her close, while tough Mary-Lou Jordan wept unashamedly on her son's shoulder.

Joe Masterson and Manuel leaned on the horse pasture fence and watched Dance and the breeding mares grazing peacefully.

'So you ain't gonna tell me?' the foreman said in exasperation. 'Even though we've been pardners all them years.'

'Joe!' Manuel threw up his hands, 'I cannot. I gave my word. All I can tell you is that those who killed Senor Jordan and Rafe, they are dead. And Domingo Sanchez, he too is dead.'

'Sanchez, eh!' Joe let out a long whistle. 'So he was behind … ?'

'Please,' Manuel gestured dismissively, 'Do not ask any more. I only tell you this because we are amigos.' He rolled a cigarette slowly. 'And please, never speak of this again.'

Side by side they leaned on the fence and smoked quietly in the gathering dusk.

The youngster hoeing the vegetable patch straightened his back and wiped the sweat from his brow. Although worn, his Levis and shirt were clean and neatly patched. He paused and watched carefully as the tall rider manoeuvered the buckskin through the gate and closed it behind him.

He could be Rafe, Lance Jordan thought, when he was twelve or thirteen mebbe. He was suddenly aware that the boy was waiting for him to speak.

'Son, I'm lookin' for the Allen place. This it?'

'Yeah mister, sure is. You want to talk to m'pa? He's in the barn but I can get him. I'm Jody Allen.'

Lance smiled. He's got right good manners, just like Rafe.

'Thanks Jody, I'd be obliged. M'name's Jordan, Lance Jordan.'

Jody Allen paused. 'M'brother Rafe rides for a fella name o' Jordan. You him?'

Lance shook his head slowly. 'That was my pa.'

The man who appeared from the barn had the careworn look of someone scraping a living and not much more, from a small homestead.

Lance swung down and held out his hand. 'Mister Allen? I'm Jordan, Lance Jordan.'

'Vance Allen, Mister Jordan. Nice to meet you. Rafe wrote a coupla times, told us about your folks. Cavalryman ain't you?'

The big sergeant shrugged. 'Yeah; not for much longer though.'

A woman's voice called from the house. 'Who is it Vance?'

'It's a Mister Jordan, Martha. You know, them folks that Rafe rides for.'

'Ask him to come in then.' There was the sound of a chair being pushed back.

Vance Allen grinned awkwardly. 'Say, I'm sure sorry 'bout forgettin' my manners. Martha'll give me hell after you've gone. She sets a lot o' store by manners.'

'Yeah,' Lance nodded sombrely as he followed the homesteader into the house. 'I guessed as much.'

The woman who motioned him to a chair was still pretty, but it was a worn prettiness. Years of hard work and childbearing had taken their toll.

Now she bustled about preparing coffee while telling the four younger children to go and play in the yard.

'Jody,' Lance looked hard at Vance Allen, 'wonder if you'd mind takin' old Buck there down to that water trough at the barn. Don't let him drink too much an' walk him for a spell. Sure would appreciate it.'

The boy glanced at his father who nodded. He rose and hurried out importantly.

The Allens looked at each other. 'It's Rafe ain't it?' Vance said heavily. 'Something's happened?'

Lance nodded. Suddenly he wished he had never undertaken this trip. 'Yeah, it's Rafe … he's dead!'

Quietly, he told them how it happened. How Rafe had hung on to tell them all he could, and how the youngster had died then, his self-imposed task completed.

When he had finished he sat for a long moment listening to Martha Allen sobbing quietly.

Vance Allen spoke. 'He was a good boy.'

Lance nodded. 'He was the best.' Reaching into his vest pocket he pulled out a bulky envelope which he pushed across the table. 'He would have wanted you to have this. 'Course, it don't mean much compared with him but ... ' He paused and fell silent.

The homesteader opened the envelope and sat for a long moment staring at the money, then he lifted his gaze and looked hard at Lance. 'Why?'

Lance shrugged. 'It's the reward money for them killers. It was a personal thing with me an' m'brothers. We don't want no part of it. Can tell you somethin' else too. Rafe an' Pa is buried side by side an' there'll be headstones on their graves. Ma's seein' to that an' she'd take it right kindly if you'd let me have all his details. When he was born, his age an' his full name.'

'Rafe Anderson Allen,' Martha Allen said quietly. 'Fourth April, 1853. He was just comin' up for seventeen. Mister Jordan, you tell your mother that we're right proud that Rafe is buried beside your pa. Now,' she rose from the table, 'I reckon we could all do with a cup of coffee.'

CHAPTER 43

▼

Clay Wallace eyed Ellie-May cautiously. He always felt uneasy around Sara-Jane's sister. There was a hardness about the tall blonde girl that grated on him. 'Where is everybody?' he queried.

Ellie-May pointed with the hammer she was holding. 'Ma's gone up to the graves. She's lookin' at them headstones you got her,' she said abruptly.

A shouted curse, followed by a frantic squawking, made them both turn quickly. A panic-stricken Rhode Island Red shot out of the cookshack door, pursued by an irate Tex Morton brandishing a meat cleaver.

'Dang chickens. Allus in here thievin'. One o' them days I'll fix you good!' Muttering angrily, the feisty old cook disappeared indoors.

Ellie-May smiled briefly. 'Well, now you know where Tex is.' A hammer stuttered on iron in the forge. 'That's Bull and Anders. They're workin' on a set o' shoes for Red.'

'John an' the Aldersons are breakin' remounts round at the corrals. Jake's sittin' on the fence watchin' them.'

'How is he making out?' Clay asked quietly.

'Pretty good.' Her tone was friendlier now. 'Doc Sims reckons he'll be ready to straddle a horse next week. Oh, and Joe's got the rest o' the crew gettin' another herd o' beef together for the Army.'

Clay Wallace grinned. 'So that leaves you mending the stable door,' he said recklessly.

The blonde girl scowled. 'You got eyes ain't you?' she demanded caustically. 'Anyways, somebody's got to do it.' She glanced diparagingly at his neat dark suit. 'We can't all ride around duded up!'

Clay felt his temper beginning to rise. 'I think I'll go see Sara-Jane,' he said tightly.

Ellie-May picked up a nail and banged it home with quite unnecessary force. 'You might as well,' she said tartly. 'You ain't doin' no good hangin' around here!'

The Easterner gritted his teeth. Keep your temper he warned himself. Some day, if you're lucky, she could be your sister-in-law!

Better try again. 'How come the Flying W has a stable anyway? Most ranches round here stick with corrals.'

'Accordin' to Anders, this was Dave Wilson's idea.' The friendly note was back in her voice again. 'He come from up north originally. It's colder there and they like to stable their mounts. Reckon he just couldn't change.'

'Thanks for the information.' Clay kneed his livery stable mount into motion and made his way across the dusty yard to the house. The smell of baking wafted through the open window, and hitching his horse to the rail, he sniffed appreciatively.

A flushed Sara-Jane straightened up from the stove. 'Howdy Clay, what brings you out here?

You actually, he thought wryly. 'I came to see if your mother was happy with that stonemason's work.'

The dark-haired girl smiled. 'Yeah, she was talkin' 'bout him only the other night. Sayin' how she would have to get him back soon as Lance sent on all the details about Rafe.' She tipped a measure of flour onto the baking board. 'How about a cup of coffee and some fresh biscuits?'

A sudden recklessness swept Clay Wallace. 'I'd rather have a kiss!' he said abruptly.

'Clay!' Sara-Jane's eyes looked enormous in her pale face. She stared at him nervously. 'What if Ma … ?'

'Your mother's up there on the hill. Anyway,' he swept her into his arms, 'I think we've waited long enough, don't you?'

Sara-Jane hugged him fiercely. 'Ohh … yes!' Time seemed to stand still as they kissed; a long lingering kiss that went on and on.

'Sara-Jane, come and see!' Sarah and Mary Johnston stood framed in the doorway. 'We've found a nest … oh!'

There was a long pause while Sara-Jane and Clay separated hurriedly and tried to pretend nothing had happened. Then Sarah spoke again with all the crushing superiority of her nine years. 'There see, I told you they'd get married some day!'

'Clay,' Ma Jordan turned and looked at Sara-Jane and Clay Wallace, 'You did a right nice job and I'm beholden to you.'

For once the slim Easterner looked embarrassed and lost for words. 'Miz Jordan,' he said eventually, 'it was the least I could do.'

'Waal,' Ma said gruffly, 'I'm grateful. You must have spent a lot o' time gettin' them headstones out here, an' arrangin' for that stonemason fella to come out from Tucson. '

She paused looking into the distance before speaking again. 'Reckon you two will get together whatever I say, so I'll just tell you now it's fine by me.' A wintry smile lifted the corners of her mouth. 'Guess if it was me though Clay, I'd clean the flour off the back o' my suit 'fore I went anywhere!'

She waved aside a blushing Sara-Jane's embrace, and her murmured 'Thanks, Ma.'

'Now you just leave me here for a spell. Want to take another look at them headstones.'

Wonder how that pairing'll work out, she mused watching them make their way downhill. Still, might be they'll surprise me.

Slowly Ma turned for a last look at the three headstones. 'Jim,' she said quietly, 'I done the best I could. Just hope you're pleased.' Gently Mary-Lou Jordan closed and latched the gate in the picket fence, before making her way downhill.

The setting sun glinted on the nearest headstone and lit up the gilt letters.

JAMES JORDAN
Born 4th January 1817
Killed 16th February 1870
Age 53 years
He Was A Good Man

If you have enjoyed 'Jordan Land', look out for 'Jordan Law'. The beginning of its first chapter follows.

Jordan Law

CHAPTER I

Sheriff Dawson should have died at half past three that hot August afternoon. His watch (an American Horolodge, in a gun metal hunting case) testified to that. So did the .45 calibre bullet lodged deep in the intricate mechanism of the timepiece.

For a fleeting second Scott Dawson felt as though he had been slammed squarely under the heart by a kicking mule. His hands clawed feebly at the saddle horn, the burly sheriff toppled tiredly out of the saddle, unconscious before he hit the ground. The reverberating echoes of the shot rebounded from the towering rock walls and died away in the distance. Slowly the wisp of powder smoke dissolved in the still air above the canyon rim. There was a momentary silence, then the sound of rapidly receding hoofbeats.

On the trail far below, the bay gelding fidgeted uneasily and sidestepped delicately round the dropped reins. It turned its head, ears pricked inquiringly, and surveyed the recumbent form sprawled in the dust.

*　　*　　*　　*

A mile west, in a narrow arroyo opening off Diablo Canyon, Pete Iverson dropped his shovel at the sound of the shot. Reaching instinctively for his rifle, leaning handily against a convenient boulder, he waited tensely.

Silence, deep and menacing, closed round him. The small grey burro grazing close by paused and gazed at him intently. 'Somebody huntin' mebbe, Jinny?' The burro's ears twitched at the sound of the bearded propsector's voice, then it dropped its head and began grazing again.

Pete shrugged and relaxed slightly. Still, he reflected, that shot could bring any Apaches within earshot runnin'. Best to move out, for a spell anyway.

Working quickly, he lashed the shovel to the burro's pack then, lead rope in one hand and rifle in the other, he started down the arroyo, Jinny following docilely behind. At the mouth of the arroyo they turned and headed east down the canyon.